The Remarkable Retirement of Edna Fisher

E.M. ANDERSON

Cover design by Elizabeth Jeannel

ISBN 978-1-956037-22-7 (hardcover)

ISBN 978-1-956037-21-0 (paperback)

ISBN 978-1-956037-18-0 (eBook)

First Edition

First Edition: April 2023

This eBook edition first published in 2023

Published by Hansen House

www.hansenhousebooks.com

AUTHOR'S NOTE

You're probably here because this book sounds funny. An 83-year-old Chosen One? Laugh city! And, I mean, you're kind of right. *Remarkable Retirement* is a warm and funny book about an old woman going on a fantastical adventure, found family, and dragons who, okay sure, might occasionally set a city on fire, but *more importantly* think they're lapdogs.

That said, this book isn't farcical. While it's often humorous, the story involves loss, grief, and unresolved trauma. Some of the characters have anxiety or PTSD and suffer from panic attacks, nightmares, and flashbacks on the page. Some scenes involve physical violence, fire, injury, blood, and death. Additionally, while physical abuse does not occur on the page, it is discussed frequently throughout the story.

If any of these topics might be triggering for you, you may want to proceed with caution. If you need to set the book aside, read it later, or not read it at all, please do so: Edna would want you to take care of yourself, and I want that, too. If you do choose to pick the book back up someday, I hope it proves a comfort read despite the tough topics.

to grandpa

CHAPTER ONE

Golden Years Senior Care Center was a strictly nonmagical nursing home. Other homes had enchanted board games and classes on spellwork; Golden Years didn't have so much as an enchanted bedpan. The activities director made up for this by planning day trips, macramé classes, and other equally magicless events to enhance the seniors' social lives.

Today's offering was bingo. As they did every Thursday, the seniors crowded around cafeteria tables in the lounge as an orderly called numbers for them. Half of them had fallen asleep. The other half played with an air of unpleasant necessity—except for the front table, who generally showed more enthusiasm for the home's activities than warranted.

Edna Fisher hadn't planned to live out her days in a place like this, but it had been the most affordable option close to the cemetery. If she'd wanted a magical home, she would have had to move to Pittsburgh. Goodness knows how often she could have visited if she were living in Pittsburgh.

She should have been on her way to the cemetery now, but the activities director, Jeanine, had roped Benjamin into helping with the game; he was Edna's ride. She was stuck here until bingo was over.

Jeanine stopped by their table for the third time that morning to give Edna a sugary smile. Benjamin was helping Edna's roommate fill in her bingo card, but Edna's card was blank. She'd been knitting a scarf and reading the funnies in the paper instead of playing bingo, as she did every Thursday when Jeanine dragged her from her room "for your own mental health, Mrs. Fisher."

Now, Jeanine leaned over the table to examine Edna's card. Her smile sharpened.

"We've called a lot of these numbers."

Edna replied with her own sweet smile. "Have you now? I hadn't noticed."

"If you'd been paying attention, you could've won something by now."

Edna counted her stitches. "Would that be the gardening tool kit I can't use because I don't have a garden, or the bath bombs I can't use because my room doesn't have a bathtub?"

Jeanine sighed. "The prizes aren't the point."

"Thank goodness for that. They're not very good prizes."

Benjamin, sitting beside Edna, nudged her under the table with his foot. She nudged him back.

Jeanine didn't notice. She pinched the bridge of her nose and recovered her smile. "You know, Mrs. Fisher, I'm not trying to bore you. Seniors need consistent socialization. You may not think so now, but at your age it's important to..."

Edna surreptitiously turned down her hearing aid as Jeanine droned on. Jeanine liked to wax poetic about the value of cultivating a social life at Golden Years. It might have meant more if anything about bingo day resembled social life and if Edna weren't subjected to the exact same lecture every week.

Benjamin elbowed Edna. Jeanine had finished her lecture and moved on to harass another resident. Edna turned her hearing aids back up.

"It'd be easier to humor her," Benjamin said. "I know you don't like bingo, but it wouldn't kill you to get in on the action."

Edna snorted, losing count of her stitches. "Bingo isn't action, young man. Tell me when they get a blackjack table in here."

Benjamin marked off another box on Marguerite's card. He was in his early thirties, bespectacled and broad-shouldered, with deep brown skin. His eyes were the same deep brown, big doe eyes that made Edna want to take care of him. But it usually went the other way around: he was an orderly, though not for much longer. He'd given his notice a week ago, planning to apply for a doctorate program at a university in California.

Edna was proud of him. She'd never gone to college, and here was Benjamin, already with a master's degree in theoretical magic and magical anthropology, off to get his MgD.

But he was the only person who made the home bearable, and he'd be clear across the country. Somewhere prone to more frequent and worse dragon attacks than the East Coast.

She tried not to think about that.

"I could be wrong," Benjamin said, "but I don't think people would like it if we let their parents gamble."

"You can gamble at bingo."

"We can't go until it's over. Try to enjoy yourself."

"I am enjoying myself," Edna said stoutly. "I'm enjoying annoying Jeanine."

Benjamin sighed. Edna finished with the funny pages and turned to the news. She hummed tunelessly to herself, worked on her scarf, and skimmed the newspaper until a headline partway down the page caught her eye.

HUNDREDS REPORTED DEAD OR MISSING AFTER ATTACK ON SAN IGNACIO.

Odd phrases leapt out at her.

Base destroyed...civilians dead...first responders still searching the rubble...a flight of dragons...thought to be the work of Redway...

The front table cheered. A scrawny old bat named Mrs. Macready demurely claimed her prize, a car freshener she couldn't use because she no longer owned a car.

Edna's eyes fell on a single sentence toward the end of the article.

Although the Assembly of Knights-General hasn't yet released a final count, dead Knights are thought to number in the dozens.

In a small, grainy photograph, a young Knight with a squire's epaulets carried a body over his shoulder. His face was strained, his shoulders bowed. He looked a little like Edna's son had at that age—

Edna shoved the paper aside.

She busied herself with her knitting. The next time Jeanine approached, Edna gave her such a steely smile that she passed by without comment, except to tell Benjamin he was helping her roommate wrong.

The scarf was coming along nicely. Lost in row after row of stitches, Edna forgot the article, the photograph, and her impending trip to the cemetery. She added several more inches to her scarf before realizing Benjamin was saying her name over and over.

Edna tore her attention from the scarf. "What is it, dear?"

Benjamin pointed at something. Or rather someone.

The someone was clearly a wizard. He wore the purple robes of the Council of Wizards and had a lengthy beard, a staff, and flashing eyes. No one would pressure *him* to move into a nursing home.

Around the room, the seniors perked up. A nonagenarian asleep at the next table jerked awake.

"It's a wizard," her neighbor shouted into her ear. "No, dear, a *wizard.*"

The room buzzed with whispered speculations about the wizard's presence in a nursing home, and a nonmagical one at that.

The wizard spoke in thunderous tones, as wizards are wont to do.

"I have come for Edna Fisher."

Surely, she had misheard. He hadn't said *her* name.

Before Edna could respond, Jeanine was on the move.

"Excuse me," she called. "You can't pop in here like that. All visitors must sign in at the front desk."

The wizard deflated. Jeanine had that effect on people.

"But," he said, "I'm a wizard."

Jeanine looked down her nose at him like a stern librarian. "Our rules don't say 'all visitors must sign in unless they're wizards.' You can go to the front desk and sign in like you're supposed to, or I can have you escorted out."

The wizard reddened. "I've come on a matter of great importance."

"So important you've forgotten your manners, I see. Which will it be?"

His bushy eyebrows dipped low over his eyes as if he'd never seen the likes of Jeanine before—which he hadn't. In over nine hundred years, no one had ever greeted him with "go sign in at the front desk."

He vanished with a small pop.

Benjamin blinked. Beside him, Marguerite employed herself filling in random squares on her bingo card. Edna gazed at her knitting needles, hoping they might come to life to confirm she'd indeed heard what she thought she'd heard.

Jeanine clapped her hands for attention, pulled a number, and read it out with a dramatic flourish.

"B6!"

The seniors returned, with a sigh, to bingo.

CHAPTER TWO

Shortly after his disappearance, to the seniors' relief, the wizard traipsed back into the lounge with a sticker reading HELLO MY NAME IS METHODIUS THE JUST stuck to his robes.

He glanced at Jeanine. "...Edna Fisher?"

Edna's knitting needles remained unhelpfully silent. "That would be me."

She stuffed her knitting in her handbag and collected her cane. She stumped into the lobby with Methodius the Just, visitor, in tow, muttering under his breath.

"In all my centuries—never expected—the disrespect—I ask you—"

The receptionist, listening to a true crime podcast, glared at the wizard and turned up her computer's volume.

With a groan, Edna sank into the faded loveseat by the desk. Her hip ached thanks to a botched hip replacement years ago. Her knees, too, although that was just your standard old age.

"Sorry about that," she said. "Jeanine's mad about rules and regulations."

Methodius stopped muttering to himself. "So it would seem."

The wizard smoothed his beard, rearranged his robes, and fussed over the exact placement of his staff at his side. Edna waited, wondering whether the staff was a magical aid or a mobility aid like her cane—or both. But she stopped wondering, as he went on fidgeting with his beard and robes and staff, and pulled her knitting back out of her handbag.

He stopped fidgeting. "What are you doing?"

"Knitting."

The receptionist's podcast played an ad for a true crime-show streaming service.

Methodius frowned. His face seemed most comfortable with that expression. "I'm a wizard."

"Yes, so you mentioned. It's nothing personal. I like to keep my hands busy."

His brows scrunched together.

"What's this about?" Edna asked. "I'm not a witch. I don't have a first-born son to offer you. And if you need virgin's blood for some sort of spell, well, I'm afraid I haven't been able to provide that in a very, very long time. What could you possibly want with me?"

He considered her from beneath those bushy eyebrows. Her own eyebrows had all but disappeared in her old age; she colored them in every morning so she didn't look permanently surprised. But that was a perk of being an enchanter. He might be nine hundred years old, with white hair and wrinkles, but he probably didn't have arthritis, diabetes, or a botched hip replacement—and he still had eyebrows.

"Have you heard of a sorcerer called Redway?" he asked.

Edna paused in her knitting, remembering the photograph in the newspaper. "He's been all over the news. Something about dragon attacks."

Methodius tugged at his beard. "Dragons have been attacking Knights."

"Dragons are always attacking Knights."

The American Knights had spent more than two centuries slaying dragons or driving them into the Amazon basin—often simply called

Dominion—but it took a lot of men and weapons and work to keep them there. Men and weapons and work cost money, especially since the Assembly of Knights-General had to pay the Brazilian government for the authority to keep bases within Brazil's borders armed and manned. Edna could remember when the government cut funding to the Knights during the Cold War to sink it into the arms race against Russia instead. Historic numbers of dragons had winged up into Central and North America in search of more territory as their population grew. Edna's son and his elementary school classmates had practiced hiding under their desks from atomic bombs and dragons, neither of which could be withstood by a silly little piece of wood.

Methodius frowned. "Dragons are not 'always attacking Knights.' A dragon, alone, might attack a city. That city might happen to have a base. But they're dumb beasts. They don't amass into whole flights to wreak havoc. They can't target Knights. But that's what this sorcerer is doing with them. Redway."

Understanding flashed through Edna's brain.

"I imagine," she said, trying not to sound too excited, "the Council will be naming someone to stop him any day now."

Methodius pursed his lips. "It's already done."

The news media must not have caught wind of *that* yet. The Council of Wizards hadn't named a Chosen One in almost eighty years.

Edna hesitated.

"I don't mean to sound...it's not that I think I..." The idea was preposterous. "Will I be mentoring them?"

The wizard looked sourer than ever. "It's you."

"Oh—" Her breath hitched. This could be her ticket out of the home. "Really? It is? I'll be mentoring a Chosen One?"

Methodius pinched the bridge of his nose. "No. You *are* the Chosen One."

This pronouncement should have excited her, but she merely blinked at him. She could have been the poster child for elderly white women: pasty, wrinkly, with an old-lady perm and old-lady glasses on a chain, and a blue housedress that hadn't been in fashion since the 1960s, and a faded floral handbag that had never been in fashion at all.

Besides, old people weren't Chosen Ones. Old people were mentors.

Never mind that all she could teach someone was knitting.

She didn't know how to respond to this momentous news, so she asked the obvious question. "Aren't teenagers traditional?"

The wizard snorted. "Traditional, yes. But one of my colleagues did the naming, and his methods are, shall we say, unorthodox. You'd think good old-fashioned prophecy would be as good for him as for the rest of us, but no, *science* has to be involved in some way. Algorithms and equations and the Internet, if you can believe it..."

He devolved into muttering about the offending colleague. Edna tried not to worry that, evidently, the Internet rather than an oracle had foretold her destiny. Then again, in her experience, most fortune-tellers were frauds anyway.

She resumed knitting. In the process, the white noise in her brain formed into coherent thought. She was the Chosen One. She was leaving the nursing home, with its Thursday bingo games and its stark, white rooms and its rules and activities and Jeanine. She was going on an adventure.

If it went well, she was going to save Knights like the squire whose young face had been so strained in the paper—Knights like her son.

"Where should I start?" she asked.

Methodius raised his eyebrows. "Aren't you going to reject the offer?"

Edna laughed. "Good heavens, what for?"

"Well," he said, "it's traditional..."

"It's traditional for the Council of Wizards to name a teenager, but here we are."

The wizard cleared his throat. "Right. Yes."

He thunked his staff on the floor. The lights in the lobby went out. The computer screen illuminated the receptionist's glare, but her glare faded: a magical blue halo glowed around Methodius. The receptionist leaned forward with begrudging interest, muting her podcast.

The wizard ignored her. With another thunk of his staff, an image appeared in midair: a sword with a glittering, jeweled hilt.

Edna knew nothing about swords, but it was beautiful. "Is that for me?"

"The Sword of Destiny," Methodius intoned. "Yes."

"All right," Edna said, and she held out her hand.

The blue glow fizzled. Methodius raised an eyebrow. "What?"

"What, indeed. The sword. Give it here."

She looked him up and down. He didn't appear to be hiding a sword on his person, but with wizards you never can tell.

He sighed, more loudly and dramatically than was strictly necessary. "I don't *have* it. You have to *get* it. It's—"

"If you say 'it's tradition' one more time—"

Methodius glared.

"To prove you're worthy of your offices. Pay attention." He closed his eyes. The blue glow shivered, then stabilized, mysterious and impressive once more. "So. Yes. The Sword of Destiny."

He cracked an eye open, expecting another interruption, but Edna was mulling over the fact that she'd have to collect a weapon he ought to have brought her and probably could have.

"You will find it in the keeping of a man named Theobald Smith." Methodius's voice deepened as the conversation continued more like he'd expected. Chosen Ones were supposed to listen to their destiny in awe and silence, not interrupt. "Give him my token, and he will give you the sword. You will find Theobald Smith in..."

Edna leaned forward, hoping her pre-quest quest would take her somewhere interesting. Atlantis. The Bermuda Triangle. France.

"...Michigan."

Well, that was disappointing.

But it had to be more exciting than the nursing home.

Evidently, the receptionist disagreed; she rolled her eyes, unmuted her podcast, and got back to work.

"When you have the sword in your possession," the wizard continued, "you will travel to Dominion, find Redway, and end his reign of terror."

He made it sound so simple.

The blue glow faded, as did the image of the sword.

"So that's easy enough," Edna said.

Methodius worked a heavy silver ring off his finger. A round, blood-red stone glinted dully in its setting.

"Give this to Theobald." He hesitated before dropping it into her hand. "And for the love of Merlin, don't lose it."

His eyes lingered on the ring until she stowed it in her handbag, wrapped in a lace handkerchief. She'd never bought a handkerchief in her life, but somehow, she could always find one when she needed it.

"Thank you," she said, but Methodius was fidgeting with the sleeves of his robe.

"Well," he said in lofty tones, "if you don't have any questions..."

"Questions?" She had the ring, her destiny, a Fateful Object to retrieve. The excitement flurrying through her whirled away any questions she might've had. "No, I don't think so."

"Good."

Methodius peeled off his name badge. Edna watched him without seeing. She was leaving Golden Years. Heading off on a trip—well, all right, a *quest,* if you wanted to be technical about it—a journey, an *adventure* the likes of which she'd only imagined.

Admittedly, her first stop was Michigan, two states away and with more roadwork than magic. A change of scenery nonetheless. She couldn't remember the last time she'd left the home for so much as one of Jeanine's day trips.

"By the way—" The name badge stuck to Methodius's fingers. "I should mention. You have three days to retrieve the sword."

Edna chuckled, her mind on her journey. "Is it going somewhere?"

Methodius shredded the badge between his fingers.

"To prove your worth, you must retrieve your destined weapon within the allotted time, or the Council will deem you unworthy and name a new Chosen One."

Her heart skipped a beat. "Surely they can't do that?"

Methodius scowled. "They, which is to say *we*, certainly can, and certainly will if we must. Do you think this is a vacation? You can't go meandering about like you're out for a stroll. Redway means to destroy the Knights! Do you understand what that means? Do you know what it was like when dragons roamed the land unchecked?"

"But it's my destined weapon. You said so. You can't destine it to someone else."

"It's the Chosen One's destined weapon," Methodius snapped. "If you can't retrieve it in time, you're clearly not the true Chosen One, and frankly, given how you were chosen and by whom, I'm not convinced you are!"

Edna almost snapped back, but an angry wizard is nothing to sneeze at. This wasn't going at all how the biographies and memoirs had always made it sound.

Methodius tapped his cane. The remains of his name badge vanished.

He tugged at his beard, red-faced. "If you'll excuse me, I have an important meeting to get to."

He vanished in a swish of his robes. The receptionist's podcast ended.

It occurred to Edna that she hadn't asked where in Michigan Theobald Smith lived.

CHAPTER THREE

The seniors had quit bingo. Jeanine hurried from table to table, encouraging her residents to mark their cards as the assigned orderly steadfastly called number after number. But bingo paled in comparison to what a wizard could possibly want with one of them.

"She must be a witch," Mrs. Macready said.

Her neighbors had flocked to her side the moment the wizard had stridden into the hallway with Edna Fisher. Mabel Macready was the self-appointed president of Golden Years, but the other residents scoffed at her pronouncement. Surely a witch wouldn't retire to a nonmagical home, if indeed she moved into a home at all.

"Shows what you know," Mrs. Macready sniffed. "Spend centuries doing magic and retire to a place with more magic? I think not. A witch would want a break. But now that wizard's come for her help."

"I don't think it has anything to do with magic." Mr. Benson leaned forward, waggling his eyebrows. "I'll bet he's here on personal business."

Mrs. Macready snorted. "Don't be silly."

"She was a heartbreaker back in the day, I'd guarantee it. Look at her."

The whole table turned toward the door, but neither Edna Fisher nor the wizard was visible through the glass.

"I don't think so," Mrs. Macready said.

"I30," Jeanine snapped, so close it made them jump. They hadn't noticed her coming back around to their table. "If you insist on not playing, we'll put everything away until next Thursday!"

To her consternation, none of the seniors objected.

"I still say he's a long-lost boyfriend," Mr. Benson said. Mrs. Macready smacked his shoulder with her bingo card.

Jeanine ground her teeth. "Cooper!" she barked.

Benjamin snapped to attention. He'd been sitting with Marguerite, dutifully helping her mark her card though the rest of the room had quit the game.

Jeanine gestured irritably at the abandoned cards. "Pick these up."

Benjamin almost asked if he could take Edna to the cemetery afterwards, but he thought better of it. Asking Jeanine questions when she was in a mood was a bad idea. She'd probably give him busy work to keep him at the home until it was too late to take Edna anywhere. She'd been doing that a lot since he'd given his notice, even when she wasn't in a mood.

Instead, he gave Marguerite a napkin to draw on while he collected bingo cards. He put the cards in their bin, put the bin away, and handed Marguerite off to the orderly who had been calling numbers so she could be escorted back to her room. Before she left, she stuffed the napkin into his hand.

He smiled at her. "Thanks, M. I'll add it to my collection."

She smiled back, clinging to the other orderly's arm as they shuffled out of the cafeteria.

Benjamin smoothed the napkin: it was flowered with poppies. He folded it carefully and stuck it in his wallet. Marguerite needed help playing bingo and finding her way to and from her room. She confused her children with cousins, siblings, and long-dead friends when they came to visit—but she hadn't forgotten how to draw. After eight years at

Golden Years, Benjamin had a bedside drawer full of her napkins. He was glad to finally get the hell out of here, but Marguerite and her napkins were one of the few things he'd miss about the place.

He poked his head into the lobby. The wizard had gone. The receptionist was listening to '90s pop music and mumbling along to it as she worked.

Edna was sitting on the floral loveseat nearby, gazing absently at the front door. She was the other thing Benjamin would miss. But they still had a week left together, so he dismissed the thought.

"Edna? They're finished up in there, so if you want to get going—" He stepped into the lobby, closing the cafeteria door softly behind him. "Are you alright?"

She was whiter than usual. Her knitting was in her lap, but her fingers were tangled in the yarn, unmoving.

"Edna?"

She giggled. Benjamin frowned but caught himself, smoothing his expression into one of professional concern. Jeanine didn't like orderlies to frown at residents, even if out of concern.

He crouched in front of Edna and touched her knees. "Is everything okay?"

"I'm the Chosen One."

"...What?"

"It's true," the receptionist said in a bored voice. "That wizard wouldn't shut up about it. I missed half my podcast."

Benjamin frowned again, waiting for someone to shout "APRIL FOOL'S" even though it was mid-July. Edna did like to prank the orderlies, though she never pranked him. Just yesterday, she'd put her dentures in her pocket and watched the two new hires tear her room apart when she insisted she couldn't find her teeth. Benjamin had found them at it, sighed at Edna, and told them he'd take over the search if they'd bring Mrs. Macready her medication. The moment the door had closed behind them, Edna put her dentures back in.

It had been a worse prank than usual, but her pranks were always worse at this time of year. Not that anyone else noticed. But they didn't know what July was to her.

Benjamin hesitated. "What about the cemetery?"

The cemetery.

Edna's brain had been buzzing with confused images of swords and dragons and wizards and Knights and grand adventures, but now it quieted. Today was her son's birthday. In a cemetery ten minutes away, a headstone was carved with his name and two dates much too close together.

She twisted her hands in her lap. "What about the cemetery?"

Benjamin's lips moved soundlessly for a moment before he said, "It's the eleventh."

"I know what day it is."

"You always go to the—"

"I know."

"Edna..."

She stopped twisting her hands. "I'm fine, dear."

"You're not—"

"I'm fine," she snapped, then took a breath. "Sorry."

Benjamin stared at her. She busied herself with her knitting. The receptionist mumbled along to a Backstreet Boys song.

"So," Benjamin said. "This is real. You're really the Chosen One."

"So it would seem."

He plopped onto the loveseat. Edna could hear the gears turning in his head as he tried to work out how to say what he wanted without it coming out cruel. She decided in advance not to hold it against him.

"Look," he said, "you're, well, you're..."

"Old?"

He nodded. "Yeah. I mean, you know. There's your diabetes, and your arthritis, and your cane, and your medication, I mean, you're not the picture of health, you can barely walk—"

"I can walk," Edna said. "It just takes me a little longer to get where I'm going."

"—there's a reason you're in a home—"

"Only because my niblings insisted," Edna said.

"—and being the Chosen One, you know, it means a lot of travel and a lot of physical activity, and, well, don't take this the wrong way—"

"Too late," Edna said.

"—but I'm not sure you're up to it."

"I'm eighty-three, not dead."

"I know." He squeezed her hand. "I didn't mean it that way. I'm worried about you, okay?"

"Worried, I'm sure."

The fact of his leaving hung between them. She wished she hadn't said it.

"That wasn't fair," she said. "I'm so proud you're getting your doctorate."

"At least someone is."

She didn't ask what he meant, and Benjamin didn't explain. He didn't like talking about his family. They didn't understand his fascination with magic. Or his sexuality. Or, well, most things about him.

Benjamin bit his lip, looking at Edna's white hair, her wire-framed glasses on their chain, her withered hands tangled in her yarn.

"Is it Redway?" he asked quietly. "The dragon attacks? I've heard about him, Edna. He's got, like, a whole flight of dragons. No one knows how he controls them, but they say he uses magic, and if that's true, do you know how much magic it would take to control *one* dragon?"

"A lot, I imagine," Edna said, but he continued as though she hadn't spoken.

"Dragons are seriously powerful magical creatures—look at them, for god's sakes. They shouldn't be able to fly. Their wings would have to be, like, stupidly bigger than they are, or else they'd have to flap a lot faster, and their bones would have to be lighter"—he spoke faster and faster—"and most spells won't work in areas dragons have inhabited for a long time, like their magic is so powerful it cancels things out. Like, you could probably do small charms or a short-range spell, but if you wanted to do anything powerful or long-range and a bunch of dragons were living nearby—"

Edna patted his arm. "Yes, dear. A lot of magic. I understand."

Worry shone in his eyes. "Do you understand? Because you don't know how to use magic. And they're sending you after a sorcerer. With dragons."

Edna leaned into him. "I'll have a sword."

He stared at her.

"I'm sure it's a very powerful sword," she said.

"Do you know how to use a sword?"

"Not exactly."

"Edna—"

Edna balled up her knitting, stuffing it into her handbag.

"I'm tired of sitting around a nursing home, feeling useless and being treated like a child by people young enough to be my grandchildren. I don't mean you, dear," she added, as Benjamin tried to interrupt. "But there's Jeanine always bothering me about her durned activities, as if it matters whether I knit instead of playing bingo, and you've seen how the other orderlies talk to us."

She didn't mention that he was the only one who would take her to the cemetery. She didn't want to think about the cemetery.

"That's the stupidest thing I've ever heard," Benjamin snapped.

Edna gaped at him. He rarely used that tone, and even more rarely with residents. "What?"

"You." He snorted. It might've been funny if he hadn't been so angry. "Are you kidding? You don't *have* the sword, you don't know how to *use* the sword, you don't know any magic, you have to fight a *sorcerer* with *dragons*—but it's okay because you're leaving the nursing home? Is this seriously what's happening? You're willing to put yourself in danger for a reason to leave the stupid nursing home?"

The receptionist turned her computer's volume up again. Edna twisted the straps of her handbag.

Benjamin sighed. "That can't be all it is."

"Of course that's not all it is," Edna said, thinking of her son and the young Knight in the newspaper. "You don't like it here either."

"It's not that bad."

"Benjamin."

He picked at his nails. "Yeah, okay. I mean...I like my residents."

He paused. "Some of my residents."

Another pause. "Okay, mostly you and Marguerite."

He didn't even mention the rest of the staff. The newbies weren't bad—he was usually their go-to guy, because the other old hands met their questions with impatience—but the good ones never stayed long. The older staff he'd liked had retired or gone on to better things, one at a time, until he was the only one left.

"Okay," he said. "Okay, no, I don't like it here either. But that's no reason to run off into danger alone."

"It's not as if I have anyone to go with me."

You have me, Benjamin almost said, but he caught himself. Edna had been at Golden Years for six of his eight years, and she was his favorite resident. But she was a *resident.* Not his grandma, no matter how much she acted it.

Then again, he'd been planning to leave the home anyway—for exactly this sort of experience, though he hadn't told anyone and had no guarantee he'd get one.

Now one had dropped right into his lap. One that would let him stick around definitely-not-his-grandma longer than popping off to California by himself, if she'd agree to take him along.

He scuffed his shoes on the floor tiles. "What about me?"

"What was that, dear?"

He cleared his throat. "I said," without looking at her, "you have me."

She smiled at him. She used to hope he'd fall in love with one of her grand-nieces and join the family. Every time one of them had visited during her first year at the home, she'd tried to set something up.

Then he'd realized what she was up to and told her he was gay. There went her dream. The youngest of her nephews was old enough to be his father, and the grand-nephews were children.

"What about your doctorate?" she asked.

He fiddled with the hem of his t-shirt.

Edna nudged him with her elbow. "What about it?"

His hem was bunched up. "The thing is, I haven't been accepted yet."

"But you want to be ready when they send your acceptance letter, don't you?"

Benjamin polished his glasses on his t-shirt so he wouldn't have to look at her. His fingers shook. Admitting this shouldn't have made him anxious, but his anxiety disorder never cared whether or not something *should* make him anxious.

"I'm not sure they will accept me. I don't have any field experience with magic, like, at all."

"So?"

"So the head of the program said it doesn't make me look competitive. That's why I was going to California. There are a lot of opportunities for internships in magical fields out there."

If the head of the program had been there, Edna would've walloped them with her handbag.

"Anyway," Benjamin said, replacing his glasses, "there's no guarantee I'll get an internship—"

"Of course you will."

He shook his head. "No, look. I've got my degrees, but I don't know how interested people are going to be in someone whose whole background is in theoretical magic if a *theoretical magic program* doesn't want someone with no practical experience. None of the homes I've worked at have been magical. I have literally no field experience. None.

A doctorate in theoretical magic has been my dream since I switched majors from nursing in undergrad, and now it turns out I've screwed myself out of it by being *too* theoretical."

Edna squeezed his arm. He cleared his throat again, embarrassed.

"Sorry." His voice shook, but he fought it under control. "The point is...what could be better field experience than helping the Chosen One fulfill her destiny?"

"Are you sure?"

His voice steadied. "If you'll write me a good reference letter afterwards."

Edna bumped him with her shoulder. "Like you said, it'll be dangerous."

"Yeah. No. I know. It's fine. I'm fine." He took a deep breath, focusing less on the danger and more on all he might learn. "A quest could be good for me. You know. Like maybe I could meet some different people."

"You'll probably meet some dragons."

"Don't remind me. No, I mean, like, I don't know, maybe a fae or an elf or something." His eyes lit up. "That would be cool, right? Getting to know more about an ancient magical culture? We mostly focused on witches and cults and stuff in my master's program, it was all magical human cultures."

At his words, fresh excitement bubbled up inside Edna. She'd hardly been outside the home in the last six years, let alone to far-off places rife with magic. She recaptured the feeling she'd had when Methodius first appeared, when the day shone with possibility.

"Yeah. Yeah, it'll be great," Benjamin said, as though he'd convinced himself the danger would be nothing compared to the potential learning experience and admission to his intended doctoral program. "So where are we going first?"

"Er," Edna said.

CHAPTER FOUR

They didn't leave for hours. First, Edna had to check out of the home. It should have been simple; she'd looked into state law and the home's policies before moving in, just in case.

But Jeanine entered the lobby right as the receptionist thrust the necessary paperwork across the desk. Jeanine hated losing residents.

An argument ensued, which turned into a shouting match, which made Benjamin panic when he returned from re-giving his notice, effective immediately. Rather, it made him panic more. He was already in the grips of a small panic attack over resigning immediately when he was supposed to have worked another week.

Edna hadn't yet told Benjamin they were on a deadline, but he was shaking and hyperventilating and trying to act like he wasn't doing either, so it seemed best not to mention the time constraints.

Then, while the other seniors were at lunch, they had to pack her things: denture cream, a blanket she'd knitted for a competition (she'd lost, but it was a nice blanket), a photo of her son, another of his father, her prescriptions, anything they thought she'd want for the trip.

Edna called her oldest nephew about getting the rest into storage. Normally she loved talking to him for hours; he lived in Manhattan and couldn't visit often, but he called every week. This time she said, "Well, I should get going..." fifteen times before managing to get him off the phone.

By then, lunch was over, as was the afternoon's activity (a guided painting class that might have been fun if Jeanine weren't breathing down everyone's necks, making sure they were using only the directed colors). Marguerite returned on the arm of an orderly, with a painting in one hand whose colors were surely not representative of the instructor's directions.

The orderly settled her in bed and turned on *I Love Lucy*, and Edna paused in her packing. Marguerite smiled at her and turned to the TV, humming the theme. Watching *I Love Lucy* together was their afternoon ritual. Marguerite remembered little and said less, but she always knew when it was time for Lucy. She and Edna had a good time for one hour every afternoon, laughing at reruns together. It was one of the few things Edna liked about the home.

But Edna had work to do. And overall, she hated it here. Marguerite seemed happy enough. She had children and grandchildren and great-grandchildren in the area, at least a few of whom visited each week, which was a good deal more than Edna had. Marguerite would be fine. Jeanine notwithstanding.

Edna finally clambered into Benjamin's van, out in the staff parking lot, at four in the afternoon. You wouldn't have expected him to have such a vehicle. You'd have expected this van to belong to a stranger offering kids candy: it was white, rusting, with no side windows farther back than the front seats.

The van rattled and squealed as Benjamin steered toward the interstate. He was so cautious a driver that if Edna had been in the car behind him instead of in the van with him, she would've expected to see a little old man driving.

She picked at her yarn. "Do you think she'll be all right?"

"Who, Marguerite? Sure, they all like Marguerite. She doesn't prank the orderlies."

An unwilling smile crossed Edna's face. "I'm serious."

Benjamin drummed the steering wheel. "Look, Edna, I already had this crisis. Weeks ago, before I put in my original notice."

"You did?"

"Yeah–you didn't think I was going to quit without thinking about my residents, did you? I worried about Marguerite, I worried about you..."

Her smile became less unwilling. "You know you don't have to worry about me."

"Yeah, that was my conclusion."

She chuckled. He flashed her a smile.

"No, but I mean it," he said. "I thought really hard about what would happen to you both if I left. And honestly, I was more worried about you. I know you always act like you're fine," he added, as she opened her mouth to object, "but Jeanine hates you, in case you hadn't noticed."

"You don't say."

Benjamin snorted. "Yeah, I know. And like, Marguerite has family, you know? I don't mean to visit, I mean she's got, like, advocates in case anything were to happen. With you I thought...she doesn't have anyone. If I go, she doesn't have anyone."

"I have my niblings," Edna said indignantly, though she'd thought the exact same thing when he'd told her he was leaving.

"Yeah, but they're all over the place, right? Like, they're not *here*." He hesitated. "I'm actually really glad to be going with you. Like. Just so you know."

Edna smiled at him, patting his arm across the center console. "I'm glad, too."

They drove to northwestern Ohio that night. Benjamin spent most of the drive mouthing along to songs on the radio and pretending he'd been doing no such thing whenever Edna noticed. Her nephew had called back to tell her he'd found a reasonably priced pocket dimension in which to store the things she'd left behind.

So far, everything had gone smoothly. They hadn't run out of money or food, the van hadn't broken down, and they hadn't gotten lost once. They even found a hotel near the interstate and got a room on the ground floor so Edna wouldn't have to climb stairs.

She sighed, sitting on one of the beds with a glass of water and her medication.

"It's not what I'd imagined." She gazed at her pill organizer. "I thought it would be more exciting."

Benjamin unpacked his toothbrush and toothpaste. "I'm sure it'll be too exciting before it's over. I bet the second we see dragons, you'll beg me to take you back to the nursing home."

"I certainly won't." Thinking of Golden Years made the mundane trip better. "Now, Benjamin, I've been thinking, there must be an easy way to find this Theobald Smith."

"Oh, yeah?" he said in a toothpastey voice.

It was a grand idea, a simple idea, an obvious idea.

She wasn't sure he'd like it.

"I was thinking...you did study magic, after all, so I thought maybe you could...divine him."

Benjamin gaped at her, his mouth foamy with paste. He turned to the sink and spit. "No way."

"It was just a thought. If you'd rather drive all over Michigan—"

"Edna," Benjamin said, wiping his mouth, "I studied theoretical magic. It's not even like *magic*-magic, my concentration was magical anthropology, which is a totally different beast. I've literally never done a spell in my life, which means it would probably blow up in my face if I tried one now, not to mention the fact that divining magic is tricky and a little unethical and really nosy and you have to have the proper licensure if you want to practice serious divining magic, so if your goal was to have me burn down the hotel and get arrested for practicing divination without a license—"

"All right, all right. No need to get grouchy. It was just an idea."

Benjamin rinsed his toothbrush, dropped into bed, and pulled out his phone. "I bet I can find this guy on Google." He snorted to himself. "And you wanted to use divination."

Edna often forgot about Google. In her defense, magic had been around a lot longer than the Internet. Her niblings frequently told her she ought to get social media to see pictures of their children and grandchildren, but she hadn't.

"Got him," Benjamin said. "At least, I think I do. There are seven different Theobald Smiths in Michigan, so I'm not entirely sure it's this one, but..."

He showed Edna a staff photo of an assistant professor in the Department of Magical Archaeology at the University of Detroit. Aside from the obvious profession, he *looked* like he'd have the Sword of Destiny. His face was sad and square, his beard and hair peppery, his spectacles wire-rimmed, and the effect was one of intelligence, respectability, and wisdom.

Edna studied him. "You'd think wizards would be smart enough not to put an important magical artifact in the hands of someone with an uncommon name who works in a field known for dealing with magical artifacts. Anyone could find him."

Benjamin yawned. "I'm sure no one's looking. It's not exactly a well-known object."

CHAPTER FIVE

Four thousand miles away, a storm raged in the highlands of Dominion. Rain veiled the jungle below, already black in the night. Thunder drowned out the bellowing of Amazonian River dragons.

Rain soaked through Kiernan's locs, seeped into the collar of his jacket, and trickled down his back. He settled Basil in for the night and trudged up the mountainside, hoping Red was around. Thunder and lightning never stopped Redway from flying out when he meant to.

As luck would have it, he hadn't set out yet. Kiernan had always been particularly lucky, even for an elf. Luck was his people's primary magic, and he had been born with more than his fair share.

He found Red in the mouth of the cave toward the top of the mountain. Red had already mounted Copernicus, their biggest dragon, already donned his jacket and pulled his flight mask down over his eyes. Clouds roiled in the sky. Lightning struck farther down the mountainside. Rain beat against the rocks.

Kiernan pushed his damp locs back from his face. "Red!"

Red dismounted. "What news?"

"It's the Sword of Destiny."

Red pushed his flight mask up, revealing blue eyes that were unfairly piercing. Humans weren't supposed to have such eyes.

"Are you sure?"

"It's been moved," Kiernan said. "The other Fated Objects are still in place. It has to be the sword."

"Do you know where it is?"

"Yeah."

Red's eyes narrowed. "Have they named a Chosen One?"

"They haven't announced it yet, but if the sword's been moved it has to be soon."

Red ran a hand over Copernicus's scaly side absently. "Sooner than expected. We'll have to move fast."

"You want me to—"

"Yes. Find the Chosen One and bring them to me."

Kiernan resisted the urge to roll his eyes. He scratched his forehead instead.

"Okay," he said, "first of all, it's not going to be easy to figure out who it is. The sword's going to be sold at an auction in a couple days. I guess there's a festival going on. Which means there are going to be tons of strangers pouring into town. Which means no one's going to stand out. Which means it's going to be impossible to figure out who the Chosen One is until they nab the sword."

He didn't mention his luck. It might help, but the others didn't know about luck magic, and Kiernan preferred not to tell them. If they knew about it, no doubt they'd want him to use it constantly. But luck magic was finicky; overuse wore it down. It was bound to give out at the worst possible moment.

Red sighed. "What's second of all?"

"Second of all," Kiernan said, "what's this bring-them-to-me bullshit? It'd be easier if I killed them."

"Well, well. Someone's eager for blood." Red's eyes slid past him. "No, Kiernan. I need to know who they are. How much they know. If they have an army ready and waiting."

Kiernan let out a breath. "Red—"

"We need to know what we're up against."

The urge to eye-roll grew stronger. Everyone knew the history of Chosen Ones and the ones they were destined to defeat. What did Red plan to do once he got his hands on the Chosen One? Monologue until they inevitably killed him?

Kiernan pinched the bridge of his nose. "Listen. I go up there. I find them, I kill them, I'm back before you know it."

"The council would name a replacement. We can stall them if we take the Chosen One alive."

"Red—"

"I said no."

Red's voice simmered with anger. His fists clenched; magic sparked from his fingers. Kiernan raised an eyebrow.

Red breathed deeply. The sparks died away.

"I'm not going to kill them until I have to."

"Red. Come on."

Copernicus stamped a taloned foot. Red stroked his side. His blue eyes glinted, reflecting a flash of lightning outside.

"If I talk to them—"

Kiernan snorted. Red glared at him, but this time there weren't any sparks, so the elf forged ahead.

"Talking to the Chosen One never works, Red. Never. You know what happens when guys like us try to talk to the Chosen One?"

Red's eyes crackled red with magic, but Kiernan was getting angry now, too. This was stupid.

"They end up dead. Every. Single. Time."

"Kiernan—"

"Killing them's the safest bet. I'm in, I'm out, I take the sword for good measure—"

"Kiernan—"

"We can destroy it—I've heard there are ways to deal with Fateful Objects. When the Council of Wizards *does* name another Chosen

One, they'll have to find a new weapon. By the time they find us, it'll be too late. And you won't be dead."

"Enough!"

Steam burst from Red's nostrils as if he were a dragon. Kiernan backed away before he could stop himself, but he steadied himself against Copernicus. Red's anger didn't often alarm him, but when it did, he preferred to pretend it hadn't. Too many of the others were scared by every outburst.

Copernicus roared fire at the ceiling to show Red how it was done.

Red gritted his teeth. "You'll do as I say. Bring me the Chosen One, alive."

"Red—"

Red snapped his flight mask back over his eyes and hoisted himself onto Copernicus's back. The dragon roared. He was ready to fly, storm or no storm.

Red patted his neck, the magic in his eyes flickering out. "Don't wait up."

Copernicus lumbered from the cave, stretched his wings, and took off. Kiernan watched them spiral into the sky until the rain swallowed them up.

He headed farther up the mountain, toward the keep. It was the tallest peak for miles, less a mountain than a finger of rock stabbing into the sky. Over time, Red had carved rooms and hallways into it by magic.

Kiernan pressed the palm of his right hand to the rock wall. The outline of a door shimmered into being. He stepped inside, wringing out his locs and drying himself with a charm. He didn't do many spells; he relied mostly on his luck and weapons. With so many dragons around, you could only do so much magic anyway. But he liked knowing simple spells of convenience.

He passed through the mess hall, cavernous and empty, and the kitchen, crowded with bodies. Too many people lived in the keep to eat in here together. But when the weather kept them inside, half the mountain turned up, warm and dense and noisy. They clustered around the rough wooden table and squished together by the woodstove, growing noisier as Kiernan's friends called greetings to him. He waved back vaguely and headed down the stairs at the back of the room, continuing through the lower hall until he reached his dormitory.

Those who needed them could get single rooms, but Kiernan had grown up crowding into hammocks with his cousins and siblings. He found it easier to sleep if other people were breathing and snoring nearby. Another thing he'd never told anyone.

His bed was in the back corner. He opened his bedside drawer and removed the false bottom, considering. He had an assortment of daggers. A sword he rarely used except in training sessions. A blow gun given to him by a friend from one of the tribes living at a lower elevation, more for hunting than assassination.

And hanging on the wall over his bed, his father's bow. It was cool and smooth with decades of use, except for the triangle carved into its belly, which matched the one inked into his wrist to signify his nation and rank.

The bow was almost the last relic he had of his people. His father's bow, his grandfather's lessons and high cheekbones, his mother's wisdom and deep brown skin, the faded triangle on his wrist. His bow and his body were all he had left.

He slipped one of the daggers into his boot, another into his belt, stowed extra arrowheads and fletching in his jacket pockets, and slung the bow over his shoulder. He preferred to strike quick and get out clean.

An arrow would be enough to take care of the Chosen One. It didn't matter what Redway said. Kiernan hadn't followed him this far to watch his plans fail.

CHAPTER SIX

By ten the next morning, Edna and Benjamin were in Detroit. Cars choked the freeway, honking as they careered around each other. Flying carpets, Detroit's other major industry, choked the skylanes a few yards above.

Benjamin tried to change lanes, cursing under his breath. He clenched the steering wheel and sucked in his cheeks.

"Oh, look," Edna said, hoping to take his mind off the traffic. "Construction trolls."

"So?" Another car merged into their lane, too close to their bumper. Benjamin honked. "Trolls are like the least magical magical creatures."

"Maybe so, but they're good at building skyscrapers."

They slipped into the right lane. Benjamin muttered curses under his breath as they pulled off I-75. Edna had been working on her scarf again, but she stuffed it into her handbag as they pulled into a university parking lot. Cracked pavement and potholes riddled the lot, but trolls were filling in a pothole in the far corner, while dryads planted flowers along the sides of the nearest building. A clock tower rose above the other buildings, gleaming in the sunlight.

Benjamin helped Edna out of the van, glancing around like he expected to be mugged. Detroit may have had a reputation, but the campus looked nice. And dryads almost never portended danger.

They found the Department of Magical Archaeology on a campus map near their parking space and started toward it.

"Are you going to be all right?" Benjamin asked. "It's halfway across campus."

"I'll be fine, dear."

Edna's hip had grown stiff during the long car ride and ached with every step, but the university was small. Halfway across campus wasn't far.

The Magical Archaeology building had a face of clean, smooth, white stone and flowerbeds that wouldn't have been out of place at a botanical garden.

Unfortunately, it also had a dozen stairs.

"Can you make it?" Benjamin asked.

"Of course," Edna said, and she stumped up the steps to prove it.

Benjamin slowed to her pace. "We should find you a chair."

"I'm fine."

"There's going to be a lot more walking than this before we're done."

They stopped at the top of the stairs so Edna could breathe a minute, stretching her leg and rubbing her hip. "Do you have my painkillers?"

"Of course." Benjamin poked through his messenger bag for her NSAIDs and a bottle of water. "Here."

The door opened on a lobby scattered with tables and chairs for study, all empty. Birdsong and the rumble of traffic drifted through the cracked windows.

Benjamin consulted a bulletin board hanging on the wall beside the door. "Staff offices are up a floor."

Edna grimaced.

"I'm sure there's an elevator somewhere," Benjamin said.

There was indeed, and Edna gave profound if mute thanks for it as they rode up to the second floor. Her cane helped, but sometimes it wasn't enough; maybe she did need something to make getting around easier. A walker, maybe, or a wheelchair. Or maybe a magical aid, like a one-seater flying carpet. She chuckled to herself, imagining Benjamin's expression should she go zipping around in midair.

The elevator doors slid open. Tinny polka music played faintly off to their left.

"Someone must be home," Edna said.

The upper hallway was squished with offices. Jewel cases containing magical artifacts in various states of shabbiness lined the walls, making the hallway narrower but far more interesting. Edna devoured the sight of cursed necklaces, good luck charms, cracked cauldrons used for potion-making centuries ago. She dawdled, reading the placard beside a jeweled knife used to assassinate the first Chancellor of the Council of Wizards.

Benjamin lingered with her. He stood so close to the case, as he tried to examine a two-century-old agate pendant, that his breath fogged the glass. *"Awesome."*

What a display! Small trinkets, mostly, almost nothing of supreme historical importance, but magical trinkets nonetheless. Edna's last museum had been a farm museum with no magical farming implements whatsoever. Jeanine had planned it as a field trip more than a year ago.

Good heavens, Edna thought. Had it really been so long since she'd left the home?

The polka music drifted from an office so small and cramped it might've been a repurposed closet. Takeout containers, books and papers, milk crates stuffed with unidentifiable junk, and magical objects lay about on every surface, obscuring the desk and chairs. A narrow bookcase and filing cabinet crammed into the corners. Photographs, maps, and diagrams papered every inch of wall space.

A plump man in a sweater vest rifled through the bottom drawer of the filing cabinet.

Edna stepped into the room. "Professor Smith?"

He straightened, whacking his head on a low-hanging light fixture. His face was exactly the wise, square-jawed face from his staff photo, but the piles of magical junk scattered about gave Edna pause. She hoped the sword was somewhere more secure.

"Please have a seat," the professor said in a dignified voice, rubbing his head.

Benjamin unburied the chairs in front of the desk so he and Edna could sit. A crystal ball sat on the desk in front of them, but Edna wasn't tempted to touch it. She knew what it would feel like. Ice-cold and smooth, dead without a seer to call it to life. She'd felt a live one once, more than a year after her son's death. The crystal ball had warmed to her touch and glowed with golden fog, but nothing else happened. The seer hadn't even had the decency to pretend Percival's spirit was with them. If you were going to be a fraud, Edna thought, you might at least comfort people.

Professor Smith switched off his radio, grimaced at his own chair's clutter as if clearing it was too much work, and remained standing.

"Now then." He gave an out-of-place fatherly smile: he looked half Edna's age and not old enough to be Benjamin's father. "How can I help you?"

Edna dug Methodius's ring out of her handbag.

The professor rubbed his glasses on his vest. "Oooooh. That's a wizard's ring if I ever saw one."

Edna adjusted her glasses. "Well, yes."

"May I?"

He plucked the ring from her palm without awaiting response. She pursed her lips but said nothing.

Professor Smith examined the stone and band with a magnifying glass that distended his eye until he looked like some strange Australian bug.

"Bloodstone, I'd surmise, but I'm not as up on my gemstones as I should be. Beautiful condition. It's been cleaned regularly, I take it?"

He raised an eyebrow inquiringly, but Edna was lost.

"I don't know."

"Where on earth did you get it? Not that bloodstone rings are particularly rare, but to see a wizard's ring in this condition, without it actually in possession of the wizard—"

Edna's grip tightened on her handbag. This wasn't going how she'd pictured it.

Nothing for it but to take the plunge.

"It is in the possession of a wizard, or it was until he gave it to me. Methodius the Just?"

She hoped he'd say, "Oh, of course it's Methodius's ring, how could I not have recognized it? Here's your sword. Good luck to you, now."

What he actually said was, "Methodius? Doesn't ring a bell, and more's the pity. Famous wizards' rings are worth so much more—although, of course, I'm not in this field for the money." He tittered. "Not much money to be had in magical archaeology unless you make a habit of selling to collectors. Naturally, an academic is above such pursuits."

"Naturally," Edna said. "Professor Smith, we've come to you about the Sword of Destiny."

He tapped the magnifying glass against his vest. "So you're not interested in selling?"

"No," Benjamin said. "And we'll take that ring back now."

The professor dropped the ring into Edna's palm with a sigh and shifted junk off his chair. Edna stowed the ring in her handbag. They should have used divination, no matter the risks.

"Now." The professor folded his hands on his desk in a way meant to give him an air of academic gravitas. "What's this about a sword?"

"We were hoping you had it," Edna said.

"I do have several lesser swords in my collection. What did you say it was called?"

"The Sword of Destiny," Benjamin said.

Professor Smith frowned, sticking one end of his glasses in his mouth. "What on earth do you want with the Sword of Destiny? Unless—"

He rammed his glasses back on, looking at Benjamin with interest. "Unless you're the Chosen One? Teenagers are a more traditional choice, but—wands and cauldrons, the Chosen One, right here in my office, how positively thrilling! You simply must let me interview you for a book. The royalties alone—"

"I'm not the Chosen One," Benjamin said.

The professor deflated. "You're not?"

"I'm not."

He turned to Edna hopefully. "Then it's you?"

"I'm afraid not," she said.

It seemed safer not to tell anyone. In the biographies, the trouble always started once people knew who the Chosen One was. Regardless, Edna thought, she wouldn't have told *him*.

"But—" Professor Smith slumped in his chair. "It's a common property of magical swords that only a person who is worthy can wield one."

Methodius certainly didn't think Edna worthy.

She forced a laugh. "Oh, we're not planning to wield it. The Council of Wizards wants it back, that's all."

The professor nodded to himself. "Of course, of course. They're naming a Chosen One soon, I imagine? This business with that sorcerer—"

"Couldn't tell you," Edna said breezily. "I'm an ordinary old lady, after all, not even a witch. I did want to be one when I was a little girl, but life happens, you know. I'm sorry to have disappointed you, but it really is important that I collect the sword as soon as possible. So if you have any idea where it is..."

"None whatsoever." The professor flipped through a book at random. "Which is the point, I suppose. The Council tries to get its hands on as many Fateful Objects as possible and hide them until they're needed. It makes magical archaeology exceedingly difficult in the field, I can tell you."

A disappointment but not a surprise. One of the six other Theobald Smiths would have the sword. It was a matter of figuring out which one, as quickly as possible: their second day on the road, and they were no closer to finding the sword.

Professor Smith abandoned his book as Edna and Benjamin picked their way back toward the hall. "What made you think I had the sword, anyway?"

They paused between piles of junk.

"Oh, you know," Edna said. "You're such a well-respected name in the field. We thought if anyone knew where it was..."

The professor blinked at her. "I didn't realize I had achieved such renown."

Edna wasn't sure how to respond, but it didn't matter: he was too engrossed in his own fame to pay her any mind. "It is true, that paper I did last year on the evolution of cauldron thickness through the centuries caused quite a stir in the department..."

The next Theobald Smith lived in Ann Arbor, in a drafty old Victorian that had been grand—once. The beams were rotting, the lumber in the ceiling coming loose. The floorboards objected to every step.

Benjamin flinched as knocked on the door. "I hope we're not here long."

A lawnmower coughed across the grass next door. A car door slammed. The porch creaked.

Benjamin raised his fist to knock again when a rickety man, maybe a decade older than Edna, opened the door. He propped himself up on a walker, peering at them through owlish lenses too big for his face.

His voice creaked like the porch. "Can I help you folks?"

"Theobald Smith?" Edna said.

"Yes'm."

She produced the ring. "You wouldn't happen to recognize this, would you?"

The old man shoved his glasses up his nose to study the ring as well as his rheumy eyes permitted. "No, ma'am, I can't say I do. Did someone lose it?"

"Yes." Edna hid the ring away again. "Yes, someone lost it."

"We'll be going now," Benjamin said, relieved not to enter the decrepit house. "Sorry to have bothered you."

"Wait, now." The old man shuffled onto the porch after them. "You don't really have to be going so soon, do you? At least let me get you folks something to drink."

"Actually—" Benjamin began, but Edna recognized the hopeful gleam in Theobald Smith's eyes.

"A drink would be wonderful," she said.

They sipped lemonade for three hours with this Theobald Smith who knew next to nothing about magic but talked on and on about his son, who never visited, and his daughter, who was long dead in service of the Knights like Edna's son. They could have left sooner, but she and Benjamin knew from their time at Golden Years that elderly people whose families never visited sometimes needed a good talk.

Then there was his house. The creaking didn't stop at the porch. Rats, or possibly a poltergeist, skittered inside the walls. Benjamin jumped at every sound. He interrupted the old man's story of the day his daughter was born to ask if their host had a hammer lying around. After that, hammering and the occasional curse interrupted the old man's tales as Benjamin fixed up some of the loose boards on the porch.

"If anyone needs a nursing home, it's him," he said as they drove away. The old man stood on the newly sort-of-fixed-up porch and waved them off before limping back inside.

The Theobald Smith after that was worse. He turned out to be what Edna called a gun nut and what Benjamin, who had grown up on a farm in upstate New York, more kindly referred to as an enthusiast.

They weren't on their way to meet the fourth Theobald Smith until late the next morning. Only seven Theobald Smiths in Michigan, and they'd been through half. Perhaps their Theobald had moved away or died, or perhaps the Internet simply didn't know about him.

"This is a nice change of pace," Benjamin said as they headed toward the fourth Theobald, into a town called Marine City. Its main road boasted a library, a bank, an apothecary, and more pizza parlors than you'd think could stay open in a small town.

They followed the curve of the road until a river spread before them, glittering in the sunlight. People were everywhere, and so were vehicles: cars parked fender-to-bumper along the curb, broomsticks and bicycles chained to racks, flying horses grazing in small riverfront parks, and magic carpets stacked haphazardly in the carpet shelving at the nearest intersection.

The street running along the river had been roped off. An SUV pulled out of a parallel space on the street they were on, so they parked and clambered out of the van.

Benjamin consulted the fourth Theobald Smith's address on his phone. "It's a bit of a walk, if you think you can make it? If the road weren't closed—"

"I'll be fine."

Benjamin hitched his messenger bag over his shoulder, looking around like he was already enjoying the heat and sunshine. Edna was too preoccupied with her failure thus far to enjoy anything. Methodius's three days loomed larger with every passing hour. She still hadn't told Benjamin. She'd been waiting for the right time, but it had never come.

Now she didn't want to tell him at all. Today was her last chance.

"Earth to Edna," Benjamin said. "Come on, let's go."

Beachgoers in bathing suits crowded the small beach at the near end of the street; freshwater mermaids stretched out in the sand to sunbathe. The rest of the street was a confusion of tents, carnival rides, neon-shirted volunteers, goblins singing out their wares, a libations tent for over-twenty-ones, the blare of radios in every shop competing with live music from a local band of sirens...

"Maritime Magic Festival," Benjamin read, from a bright yellow sign hanging on the side of a tent. "Live music, fortune-telling, games, rides, libations magical and nonmagical, classic stagecoach show."

Edna grabbed his arm, more interested in the flyer taped beneath the yellow sign.

"Look at this."

AUCTION, the flyer declared. MAGICAL ITEMS FOR EVERY INTEREST! SCHOLAR, COLLECTOR, WITCH/WIZARD, HOLIDAY GIFTS. TODAY ONLY, 5P.M.

Benjamin scanned the flyer and shrugged. "Yeah, so?"

"The picture!"

Beneath the word "auction," above "magical items for every interest," was a photograph of a sword with a jeweled hilt.

"Is that—?"

"The Sword of Destiny," Edna said.

CHAPTER SEVEN

No one was home at Theobald Smith's white two-story at the other end of South Water Street, so Edna and Benjamin backtracked to the stone church that the flyer had named as the site of the auction. It had stained-glass windows and heavy wooden doors.

And stairs. Stairs so steep and wide there seemed to be more of them than there actually were. The mere sight of them tired Edna.

Volunteers in neon t-shirts and nuns whose sweatshirts defied the July heat streamed up and down the stairs, carrying magical artifacts into the church. A young priest directed them from the top.

On the bottom step, a pink-faced blond in a neon blue shirt did the same, clipboard in hand. The words *Maritime Magic Festival* were splashed across the front of his shirt.

He smiled at Edna and Benjamin as they approached. "Here for the auction? We'll be in the gym, but the doors don't open for another twenty minutes."

"Oh, no, we're here to help," Edna said. "Someone at the libations tent said you could use more hands, but I see you're full-up—"

The man's eyebrows knit together in confusion.

"Can't remember his name." Edna tapped the side of her head. "Mind like a sieve. I can't keep a thing in my noggin anymore! Might've been..." She tried to think of a name reasonably common in a small Midwestern town. "Jim, or..."

The man's expression cleared. He scratched the back of his neck the way you do instead of giving a resigned sigh. "Oh, sure, Jim. I told him we were set, but..."

"He said to ask for Theobald Smith," Edna said boldly, taking full advantage of her age to talk over him. Behind her, Benjamin reverberated with panic.

The man's brow furrowed again. "Sure, Theo's my husband. He's here, but I don't see why—"

"Why what?" a deep voice said.

Its owner was a powerfully built man with dark brown skin. He had the same peppery beard as the first Theobald and a face even sadder and squarer, but his frown made it clear that carting magical artifacts up the church steps wasn't his preferred way to spend an afternoon. He held a travel mug of coffee. He kissed the blond man's cheek, glowering over his mug at Edna and Benjamin.

The blond man slipped an arm around his waist.

"I guess, uh," he said, with a quizzical look at Edna, "I guess Jim sent these people over to lend a hand and said they should talk to you?"

Theobald raised an eyebrow. "You're in charge."

The man shrugged, but a teenaged volunteer carrying several crystal balls stole his attention. He hurried in her direction. "One at a time, how many times do I have to tell you—?"

Theobald sipped his coffee, observing Edna over the rim of his mug. "Should I know who you are?"

"Probably not, dear." Edna fumbled with her handbag. "But I hope to goodness you recognize this."

She held out the wizard's ring. The bloodstone glinted.

Theobald Smith's jaw tensed. His fingers tightened on his mug.

Edna grasped the ring tight; they were getting somewhere at last. Benjamin wrapped his arms around his abdomen, considerably less optimistic.

"You're not the Chosen One," Theobald said. "You can't be."

Edna sighed. "Well, I am, although I admit I can't see how this will help me. I don't know the first thing about swords."

"The first thing is, don't hold the sharp end."

He said it in a serious tone, his face as mistrustful as ever.

"It's a Fateful Object," he said, frowning. "The Sword of Destiny. It's not an ordinary sword. It has powers of its own. Protects you from attack spells, breaks through protective spells, things like that."

That was something. "What else does it do?"

Theobald shrugged.

"He didn't tell me. Tho." He fidgeted with his wedding ring. Glanced at his husband, who looked ready to bop the reckless volunteer on the head with his clipboard. His tone softened. "Methodius."

Oh, Edna thought, *oh.* Hard to imagine Methodius–any wizard on the Council–with a significant other. Council members were married to their work. It wasn't a rule, officially, but the Council only admitted the wizards who were most serious about their study of magic, even to the neglect of personal relationships. In practice, the Council was like a magical order of monks.

"Can we have the sword?" Edna asked.

"No," Theobald said.

"But you have it, don't you?"

His eyes wandered up the church steps. "Not anymore."

The ring dug into Edna's palm. "So, it *is* at auction."

Theobald didn't answer. The blond man finished admonishing the volunteer, sent her on her way with a single crystal ball in hand and a scowl on her face, and headed their way, shaking his head.

"It wasn't your sword," Edna said. "How could you auction it off when you promised the wizards you'd keep it safe?"

Theobald stopped with the mug halfway to his lips.

"I was promised things too," he said through gritted teeth. "I don't owe anyone anything."

The blond man had been consulting his clipboard, but at these words his head snapped up. His eyes bored into his husband. Theobald lost his grip on the mug. It bounced hard on the concrete, popped its lid, and sent grayish liquid spraying across the pavement. Volunteers leapt aside, squealing as they protected their precious artifacts.

Theobald left his mug where it had landed. "Harvey—"

"It's been *thirty years,* Theo. I thought you were past this." The blond man shoved his clipboard into the hands of another volunteer, said, "Left the stove on, be right back," and walked off.

Theobald's chest heaved. He jammed his hands into his pockets and strode after his husband.

"Wait," Edna cried. "What about the sword?"

Theobald sped up, didn't answer. Benjamin picked the mug up like he thought it might bite him.

"That went well," he said weakly. Edna handed him an embroidered cotton handkerchief. He wiped the mug off and handed it to the volunteer with the clipboard, who looked bemused at being handed something that wasn't a magical artifact. "What now?"

Edna started up the steps. "Now we talk to the man in charge."

The stream of volunteers had thickened. Cars and flying stagecoaches lined the curb, doors open, laden with magical items for the auction.

A volunteer rammed into Edna on her way up the stairs. Edna staggered. A thick stack of spell books tumbled to the ground.

"Watch it!" Benjamin said in alarm, reaching for Edna.

A flash of long, dark curls, copper skin, a rumpled neon shirt, a scowl. The teenager who had been carrying too many crystal balls.

"Watch it yourself." She flicked her hair out of her face, piled the spell books in her arms, and raced up the steps.

Benjamin gaped after her.

"Hey—" he called, but Edna put a hand on his arm. They had business to attend to.

The priest standing on the top step had noticed, however, and jogged down to them.

"Are you all right?" He put a solicitous hand on Edna's elbow. "I'm so sorry about that. I can go after her if you—"

"No, no, that's quite all right," Edna said. "Actually, Father, I was on my way to talk to you."

The priest smiled at them. Benjamin returned his smile with something more like a grimace.

"Anything for one of my parishioners," the priest said. Edna hoped he meant it. Even if she wasn't one of his parishioners, technically speaking. "Why don't we talk inside? It's cooler."

It wasn't. If anything, it was warmer, as are most nineteenth-century churches with no air-conditioning. But the doors were propped open for the volunteers, and a breeze drifted in. Fans spun lazily on a ceiling painted with stars and portraits of the Twelve Apostles. The building was large and airy, much nicer than the last church Edna had been to. Golden Years bused the seniors to service on Sundays, if they wanted to go, but the minister there was the old-fashioned type, all hellfire and brimstone. His church was narrow and dark, which Edna imagined he had orchestrated somehow, to better illustrate what hell would be like when they inevitably went there. She hadn't gone back.

She slid into the back-most row of pews. The priest stood behind her. Benjamin started to genuflect, changed his mind, and ended up in an awkward half-crouch. He slunk into the row on the opposite side of the aisle and rested his head against the back of the pew in front of him.

Edna hooked her feet under the kneelers like she had when she was a child. "Thank you, Father."

The priest rested his hand on the back of the pew.

"What's on your mind?" he asked. "I have to head over to Nautical Mile for the antique stagecoach show in a few minutes but—"

She hadn't decided exactly what to tell him or how, but her mouth decided for her. "It's the Sword of Destiny."

In the pew across the aisle, Benjamin shifted in his seat. He mumbled something akin to "dammit, Edna," although it was probably more like "darn it, Edna," because Benjamin was superstitious about saying things like "damn" in church, even if it was a Catholic church.

"What about it?" the priest asked. "I'm afraid I'm not very knowledgeable. Theobald didn't really—"

"Mr. Smith is the problem, I'm afraid."

She tried to sound calm, but this was it. The moment she would claim her destined weapon. The moment she would come into her own as the Chosen One.

The moment she would wipe that sneer off Methodius's face and secure her freedom from the nursing home.

"You see," she said, "the sword isn't actually his."

The priest's smile took on a quizzical quality. "Whose is it?"

"The Council of Wizards." A forgotten something niggled at the back of her mind. "They gave it to him for safekeeping. He was supposed to wait until they named a Chosen One and hand it off to them. But he donated it to your auction instead."

The priest's smile disappeared. "What Chosen One?"

The Church has never liked Chosen Ones. They view Jesus as *the* Chosen One—God's, that is—and find it infuriating that a group of perfectly ordinary wizards has the audacity to name their own saviors of the world in times of crisis.

Oh, well.

"Me, actually," Edna said. "You've heard of Redway, I suppose?"

His grip tightened on the back of her pew.

"I need the sword to stop him. So if you would be so kind—"

With a renewed, strained smile, he asked "You have proof, of course. That the sword belongs to you and not Theobald?"

Proof. That was what she'd forgotten.

"It doesn't exactly belong to me," she said. "It's...destined for me. It belongs to the Council of Wizards, I suppose, if Fateful Objects can be said to belong to anyone. Oh!"

Methodius's ring. She pulled it back out of her handbag and held it out, but the priest looked at it blankly.

"Am I supposed to know what this is?"

Edna's face slackened. "It's, it's, it's the ring of the wizard who gave the sword to Theobald for safekeeping. It's proof."

"Hardly," the priest said. "There are several rings just like it going to auction. How do I know whose it is?"

Edna stowed the ring away again, crestfallen. "But I told you—"

"Right. You told me. What proof is that? I don't know who you are. I don't know whose ring that is. And I can't see how it would matter if I did. What does a wizard's ring have to do with the sword?"

"If you call Mr. Smith back here and ask him—"

"I'm sorry," the priest said, not sounding sorry at all, "but I'm afraid I'm running late."

"Father, please—"

"Good day to you."

"But—"

The priest hurried from the church. Edna watched him go with her brow furrowed.

She wasn't an expert on the history of Chosen Ones, but there are a few key things everyone knows. One of them is that the universe is supposed to align in a series of helpful coincidences to make things easier for the Chosen One so they, in turn, can do their duty.

So far, the universe wasn't keeping up its end of the bargain.

At the front of the church, tables lined the altar rail, end-to-end, piled with magical artifacts Edna couldn't make out from here. Among them was the Sword of Destiny, but she couldn't jump up and retrieve it with all these people around.

Benjamin crossed the aisle and plopped down beside her.

"It's okay," he said, sounding like it was no such thing. "It'll be okay. It'll be fine."

"I know," said Edna, not knowing that at all.

"We'll come up with something."

"I know, dear."

"We have plenty of time."

"I—oh," Edna said. "Actually..."

Benjamin tugged at the strap of his messenger bag.

"We have plenty of time, right? That wizard didn't..." He sucked in a breath. "He didn't give you a deadline or something? We're not on a time crunch here? You would've told me if we were on a deadline?"

The question marks increased in intensity at the end of each sentence.

"I'm afraid," Edna said, "if we don't have the sword by the end of the day, they'll send me back to the home."

"They wouldn't."

"They would." She peered at her handbag. "He doesn't think I should be the Chosen One. Methodius. I'm not traditional enough."

Benjamin put a hand on her shoulder.

Edna smiled at him. "Oh, I'm fine. As if I care what that old codfish thinks. It's like you said: it'll be fine."

But she could only see one course of action now. She edged out of the pew.

Benjamin followed. "What do we do now?"

Edna didn't answer. They were still in the church; it felt like bad luck to say. And the volunteers might hear.

"Edna?"

He jogged past her and walked down the stairs backwards, peering at her. Edna reached for him, afraid he was going to trip and crack his head on the pavement.

He dodged her. "Hey, look, I'm not trying to be pushy, but you said it's gotta be today. What are we going to do?"

He wasn't going to like it.

"Steal the Sword of Destiny," Edna said.

CHAPTER EIGHT

Church bells rang. Volunteers streamed out of the church and down the stairs. Festival crowds strolled past, heading for the community center beside the church. Benjamin and Edna joined them. The auction was starting soon.

Benjamin fidgeted with the strap of his messenger bag, looking suspicious indeed. Edna walloped him with her handbag.

"Stop it," she whispered. "They're going to think we're up to something."

His eyes darted around the crowd, his voice cracking. "We *are* up to something."

"Hush."

The girl who had slammed into Edna stood in the community center doorway with her arms folded, wearing a denim backpack and the bored expression perfected by generations of teenagers. She wore a different t-shirt now, black with the logo of a popular musical on the front.

Edna caught her eye. The girl scowled. Edna gave her the same smile she'd given Jeanine during bingo. The girl rolled her eyes and looked away.

Edna watched her as they approached. The girl drummed her fingers on her arms, adjusted the straps of her backpack, twisted her curly hair into a ponytail and tightened it compulsively. Unclasped and reclasped her necklace. Slipped a tube of lip gloss out of her pocket and applied it, though she already had a full face of makeup.

Perhaps she was waiting for someone. Perhaps the someone was running late. Perhaps that was why she was so antsy.

Or perhaps there was a different reason.

The crowd carried them through the door, into a cool, dimly lit hallway. Edna sidled away from Benjamin, craning her neck to keep an eye on the girl.

He noticed at once. "Where are you going?"

"Nature calls. I'll catch up to you."

He eyed her.

"What?" she asked. "I need the ladies' room. You can come with me if you don't believe me."

"No thanks."

"Well, then."

She waited until he had taken his suspicions down the hall. Then she shuffled back toward the door. Not too close; she didn't want the girl to see her.

To her left were a ramp and a door leading into the church; to her right were bathrooms and a drinking fountain. She slipped into the ladies' room, listening to the crowd's burbling as they headed toward the gym.

The girl was still lounging in the doorway, piling her ponytail on top of her head and letting it cascade down her back again, over and over.

When the last voices died away, she hitched her backpack higher on her shoulders and turned inside.

Edna pulled the bathroom door almost closed and peered through the gap.

The girl trudged up the ramp across the hall to try the handle of the door into the church. It was locked, as you'd expect if a collection of valuable magical artifacts was on the other side.

She bent close to the handle. With a soft click, the door opened. The girl slipped inside.

Edna charged out of the bathroom and barreled up the ramp. The handle gave under her fingers.

Her heart pounded.

"Easy there, old gal," she whispered to herself. "No sense exciting yourself right back into the nursing home."

She opened the door.

Perhaps her intrusion would have been noticed immediately if the girl, one Clementine Rodriguez, hadn't been so staggered by the magical objects littering the tables by the altar rail: opal necklaces, bloodstone rings, figures carved from onyx and quartz, heavy spell books with weathered binding, self-drying coats and gloves of invisibility, daggers with glittering handles and blades inscribed with runes...

"Jesus," Clem muttered. "What I couldn't do with half this shit."

But she wasn't here for half this shit. She was here for one particular piece of shit, so she scanned the tables for the particular piece of shit she was looking for.

Unbeknownst to either of them, it was the same piece of shit Edna was looking for. The Sword of Destiny.

Clem spotted the sword the same moment Edna spotted her, bending over the end of the farthest table. Blue and red light from the stained-glass windows danced in Clem's curls, weaving watery patterns on her jeans and skin. Her necklace glimmered in the winking light. She set her backpack on the floor, lifted a cracked leather scabbard from the table, and pulled the sword free.

Edna's breath caught. The colored light fell on the blade and glittered in the jewel-encrusted hilt. The Sword of Destiny was beautiful.

And huge. A broadsword nearly half as long as Edna was tall, with that hilt so lovely but impractical. She'd be lucky to lift the thing, let alone swing it.

Not that it mattered. First, she had to get it away from Clem—who was equally transfixed but much more capable of running someone through.

Clem set the scabbard on the table, gripping the hilt of the sword with both hands. It was a good sword, silly decorative hilt aside. Good balance. Nice and sharp, unsurprisingly, because it's a property of magical swords in general to neither rust nor dull.

Clem was more interested in its other properties. Like its ability to slice through defensive spells. Sure, you could use any old sword on a sorcerer, if you had one. But any old sword wouldn't break through the barriers he cast to shield himself, now, would it?

Her stomach clenched as she thought of the sorcerer in question. Redway. With his daggerlike blue eyes and his nonchalant stance as he stood beside a *dragon* with his hand on its fucking side like it was no bigger than a mastiff. Clem closed her eyes briefly, sucking in a long breath, *one two three four five,* until the memory of Redway vanished. She focused on the sword in her hands. Its heft. Its hilt.

She whirled it slowly around above her head. Behind her, Edna watched, mesmerized. She'd attended a tournament once when her son was a little boy, but she'd never seen someone handle a sword this way. Knights approached swordplay like they'd confused it with football, bashing into each other as hard as they could.

Clem slid the sword back into its scabbard. Beyond her, past the other end of the communion rail, another door led outside. Edna would have to block it if she wanted to prevent the girl from running off.

Then she realized Clem could easily escape through the door to the community center or the main doors at the back of the church. Either way, this teenager, who probably did not have arthritis or a gammy hip, was going to have an escape route and a sword.

In which case Edna might as well reveal herself.

"Wonderful," she said, of the girl's swordplay.

Clem jumped, swinging the sword around at her.

"My goodness," Edna said. "I certainly would be frightened if you'd remembered to remove the scabbard."

Clem eyed her but didn't lower the sword. But she didn't remove the scabbard, either, and the cracked leather ruined the effect.

"It's a beautiful sword." Edna wasn't sure how long she could keep the girl here by talking, but she was going to find out. "Not that I know anything about swords. Knitting needles are my weapon of choice. They're much easier to hide in a handbag. What's your name?"

Clem's eyes gleamed in the light of the stained-glass windows. She mumbled her name—not loudly enough for Edna, who took the opportunity to step closer.

"You'll have to speak up, dear. My ears aren't what they used to be."

To her surprise, the girl repeated herself as if used to speaking to people who were hard of hearing. Louder and clearer, rather than slower. Edna frequently had to tell people she was half deaf, not confused.

"Clem. Clementine Rodriguez. Clem." The girl picked at the scabbard. "Why were you watching me?"

"You're a good swordsman. Swordsperson, I should say."

Clem made a face at her. "No, why did you follow me? What do you want from me?"

"My, aren't we suspicious!" Edna chuckled. "What on earth makes you think I was following you? I came to admire this remarkable church. It's lovely, isn't it?"

She gestured at the masonry and white marble, the painted ceiling, the colorful light dancing over the pews, the massive organ gleaming up in the choir loft over the heavy main doors. Clem's eyes flickered out at the church. Edna took another few steps before the girl's eyes trained back on her.

"I guess."

"I'm surprised they left it unlocked with so many valuable items inside," Edna continued. "Anyone could waltz in here and steal something!"

Clem flushed, hugging the sword to her chest. "I wasn't stealing it."

"I didn't say you were. But I know perfectly well that door was locked before you got in here. Now it's unlocked, and you're standing here with possibly the most valuable item in the whole building. So tell me, young lady, what exactly do you want with the Sword of Destiny?"

Clem glanced over her shoulder. Edna hoped she wouldn't bolt for the outside door.

"I need it," Clem said.

"And why is that?"

Clem's eyes darkened. "I'm the Chosen One."

It took Edna thirty seconds to recover, thirty seconds in which she ran through every bad name she could think of and applied them all to Methodius. The old codfish! This was his doing. Just because he didn't like the idea of her being the Chosen One, just because she was older than he would've liked—well, she was a good nine hundred years younger than him, the insufferable dolt, and within spitting distance of the sword with hours to spare. Oh, what she wouldn't say to him if he were here now—

The girl's eyes flickered over Edna, guilty and defiant.

Would Methodius really do such a thing? Wizards were bureaucrats, everyone knew that. And since Methodius had banged on and on about tradition, surely he wouldn't go against the council's decisions, even if he disagreed with them.

Edna polished her glasses on her sleeve. "You're not the Chosen One."

"How do you know?" Clem demanded.

"Oh, dear." Edna smiled at her. The girl fiddled with her necklace, a pendant reading *rise up*. "If someone says, 'you're not the Chosen One,' you don't ask how they know. You stick to your story and insist you are. Not that it will do you any good. I know for a fact you're not the Chosen One."

"You can't. There's no way you could know for sure."

"Oh, but there is." Edna drew herself up to her full height, shorter than Clem by half an inch. "You see, I'm the Chosen One."

The girl sneered. "I know that's a lie. What are you, like ninety?"

"Eighty-three, actually."

"Whatever, Grandma. You don't actually expect me to believe the Council of Wizards chose an old lady to save the world?"

"It's no less ridiculous than expecting a fifteen-year-old to save the world," Edna said stoutly.

"Sixteen." Clem strapped the Sword of Destiny to her hip. Edna moved closer to the outside door. "Everyone knows the Council always chooses a teenager. You can't stop Redway, that's for certain."

"I'll certainly try," Edna said cheerfully. "How much do you know about him?"

"More than you, I'm betting."

The door to the community center opened again. Clem froze, but Edna took a few steps closer to the outside door behind her.

Benjamin poked his head inside like he thought he might get in trouble just for that.

He frowned at Edna. "You said you needed the bathroom."

"Well, I lied."

Benjamin slipped into the church, casting an anxious glance behind him. Clem's eyes darkened again. She had one hand on the hilt of the sword. She may have been young and skinny and not very tall—especially compared to Benjamin—but her expression and the placement of her hand stopped him where he was.

"Hi...?"

"Clem," Edna supplied, scuttling toward the outside door.

Clem whipped around at her. Benjamin put his hands up as though expecting the girl to arrest him.

"Take it easy. We don't want to fight a kid."

Edna blinked. Sparks danced at Clem's fingertips and faded away. Or Edna thought they did. Maybe it was a trick of the light.

"I'm not a kid," Clem spat. "I'm sixteen."

"Saying it twice doesn't make it sound any older, dear," Edna said.

Sparks again, flaring and dying.

Edna gained the door.

Clem drew the sword and pointed it at her. "Get away from there."

Edna's heart pounded, but she smiled. "Not until you give me the sword."

Clem let out an ugly laugh. "You can't tell me what to do."

"What's the good of being old if I can't boss people around?"

Benjamin sighed.

"Where are your parents?" he asked Clem, advancing again.

Clem's jaw clenched. "None of your business."

"But—"

"I said"—Clem's nostrils flared, and no mistake this time, sparks danced from her fingers and up her arms—"none of your business."

Something about her anger and the sword and her desperation made Edna's heart clench. Maybe the girl's parents were dead.

"Clementine," she said quietly, "if there's anyone we can call for you—"

Apparently, the same thought hadn't occurred to Benjamin, or maybe he was more concerned about the weapon in Clem's hand. He tackled her, grappling for the sword. Clem yelped and wrestled it away from him.

With a noise like an angry cat, she thrust him back.

Edna shrank against the door, frightened of the girl's sudden strength. Ancient but unpleasant memories flooded through her.

Sparks leapt up and down the length of Clem's body, faster and brighter than ever. Clem gasped for breath, gripping the sword tightly in both hands, shuddering. Sparks gathered like a lightning storm around her.

"No—"

She seemed more panicked than angry now. Edna chanced a step forward, but the sparks tightened around Clem, rushed up toward the ceiling in a flashing, golden pillar.

They exploded with a flash that hurt Edna's eyes, showering over the altar, the tables of magical objects, the pews.

They erupted into flames.

The flames flickered on the floor uncertainly. Then, with a roar, they raced up the backs of the pews, the walls, the altar rail.

Benjamin scrambled to his feet. The flames danced and howled in delight, jewel-bright. Smoke roiled up to the ceiling, obscuring the faces of the apostles. Clem fell to her knees, dropping the Sword of Destiny.

"No—I didn't mean to—"

Edna hurried toward her, yanking a blue satin handkerchief out of her handbag. The fire raced up to the choir loft to eat the organ.

Edna touched Clem's shoulder and handed her the handkerchief. "Come on. Put this over your nose."

"What?"

Benjamin sprinted toward them, already coughing. Edna's head fuzzed.

"The handkerchief, dear," she said. "Put it over your nose and let's get out of here. Quickly, now."

Clem's eyes glazed over.

"I didn't mean to." Her breath was short, from the smoke or panic or both. "I tried to stop, I didn't mean to—"

Benjamin coughed and hacked and spit milky purple phlegm on the floor, which might have worried him if he hadn't already been panicking about something more important. Plenty of time to feel sacrilegious later.

"Edna," he said in a high-pitched voice, "we have to get out of here."

"I'm not leaving her here."

The pipe organ groaned like a prehistoric monster trapped in a tar pit. The choir loft collapsed, crashing to the floor with a metallic screech in front of the main doors. Fire leapt through the rafters, devoured the paintings of the apostles, rained down onto the pews.

Clem reached for the Sword of Destiny as if it could help. Alas: it was a magical sword, not a magical fire extinguisher.

"Come on." Edna tugged her arm. Flames roared around the door to the community center. "Come on, now, let's go."

Benjamin's eyes were the size of saucers. "Oh my god, we don't have time for this!"

He slung Clem over his shoulder. Edna expected her to object, but she gave a strangled sob and clung to him like a frightened child.

Edna snatched up the Sword of Destiny and shouldered Clem's backpack as best she could. She shuffled in the direction of the last remaining door, past the end of the communion rail.

"Where are we going?" Benjamin's voice climbed still higher. "The doors are blocked, where are we—?"

"There's another door over here."

Hopefully over there. The smoke rolled thick through the church, and she could no longer see the door.

Probably best not to say so.

With Benjamin and the catatonic girl close behind, she shuffled onward—right into a wall.

"Why are we stopping?"

Pick a direction, Edna told herself. Fifty-fifty chance of getting it right.

"Edna?"

"This way," she said cheerfully. "It's this way, come on."

The heat blurred her vision. Smoke stung her eyes and choked her. She groped behind her for Benjamin and grabbed hold of his shirt. It felt like they would never reach the door.

Must be nearly there, she told herself, not much farther now, almost...

There it was! She grabbed the knob but let it go with a cry, her palm red and smarting from the heat. She plunged her other hand into her handbag and found another handkerchief.

Heat radiated through the handkerchief, but she could touch the doorknob without burning herself. She tugged on it. The door didn't open. Was it locked? No, the knob had turned. Maybe if she pushed—

Behind her, Benjamin gabbled at her to hurry, his voice several octaves higher than normal. She wanted to tell him he could do it, if he thought he could pull open a heavy door with a girl slung over one shoulder like roadkill and smoke in his eyes and nose and lungs.

She groped for the knob once more, turned it, and wrenched the door open. Smoke billowed out. Sunlight spilled into the church. Edna stumbled back, squinting.

"Go!" Benjamin screamed.

They staggered into grass already curling in the heat.

With a roaring, sucking sound, another prehistoric groan, the roof of the church caved in. Sirens blared. Benjamin hitched Clem higher up his shoulder, grabbed Edna's hand, and dragged her down the sidewalk.

They'd made it several blocks when a muffled voice spoke into Benjamin's shoulder.

"Put me down. I can walk."

Benjamin set Clem down without stopping. "You better walk fast."

Clem yanked her backpack away from Edna. "I'll take that."

Edna wished she'd left it in the church to burn. "You're welcome."

"Shut up and let's go." Benjamin's voice had returned to its normal register. He grabbed them both by the wrists, hauling them down the sidewalk. "We can't stay here. We're running away from the scene of a crime with a Fateful Object we stole from a building on fire. If anyone sees us with that stupid thing—"

Clem yanked her hand from his. "I could transfigure it. Turn it into something smaller."

Benjamin grimaced. "Yeah, thanks, I think we've seen what your magic can do."

Clem blanched. She fiddled with her necklace.

"Benjamin," Edna said.

"She set a church on fire. This is why you don't mess with magic."

Edna couldn't argue that, but she staggered to a halt and held out the sword.

Clem took it. Her eyes wandered down the street like she was considering running off with it. Instead, she ran a hand over the blade, muttering under her breath.

The sword glowed softly gold and vanished. A thick silver ring set with several small gemstones gleamed in her palm.

"See?" She held the ring out to Edna. "I can do magic, sort of."

"Great," Benjamin said. "Now let's go."

Edna tugged the ring onto her pinky. It was too small, but she wasn't about to say so. "Thank you."

Clem blushed.

Sirens wailed from one end of town to the other. Festival-goers screamed and either fled or ran toward the church to help. Benjamin jogged down side streets with his hands tight on Clem and Edna's wrists, dodging passersby until they reached the van. He threw open the front door and stuffed Edna inside. Clem scrambled in back.

Benjamin slammed the door shut, sprinted around to the driver's seat, threw the van into gear, and pulled out. The van jolted over a pothole. Something ka-clunked-ka-clunked-ka-clunked.

With a despairing sigh, the van died.

"Oh no," Benjamin said.

CHAPTER NINE

"What's the hold-up?" Clem asked.

"This stupid thing is older than dirt." Benjamin revved the engine. The van whined. "Oh no, oh no, oh no, oh no—"

"Shut up," Clem said, "and hold on."

"Hold—?"

Clem spat out a word. The van gave a metallic pop. Benjamin's foot was still on the gas when the van's whining gave way to a triumphant roar. It shot off down the street. Benjamin yelped. Edna's handbag slid off her lap.

Benjamin tried to wrestle the van under control. "What did you do?"

"I don't know! It was supposed to help it run; it wasn't supposed to—"

Whatever magic she'd attempted had decided running was no fun. Too pedestrian, in a manner of speaking. The van's wheels left the pavement. Edna dug her fingernails into the arms of her seat.

"Uh, Clem?" Benjamin's voice shook. "I think you overdid it."

The van zoomed up, up, up. Michigan receded into a patchwork of greens, yellows, grays, squared off and sliced up by rivers and roads.

"Benjamin, dear," Edna said, sinking back against her seat, "you might want to take your foot off the gas."

His hands tightened on the steering wheel. "I'm scared to."

Clem unbuckled and crawled out of her seat. "Give me a minute. I'm sure I can fix it."

She didn't have a minute. The van whined.

"Oh *no*," Benjamin said again.

The engine revved half-heartedly as he pressed the gas pedal to the floor. The van slowed, stopped climbing, and leveled out. Wobbled.

In slow motion, it turned earthward and dropped out of the sky.

"Clementine," Edna said. "Clementine, if you're going to do something, maybe you could do it now?"

Benjamin closed his eyes, like they wouldn't hit the ground if he couldn't see it.

"Clementine?"

Clem swallowed. She squeezed her eyes shut, muttering a long string of words under her breath. Her fingers found Edna's wrist.

They hurtled toward the cornfield below. A scream like a tea kettle boiling spilled from Benjamin, his fingers clamped to the wheel so tight it would've taken a crowbar to pry them loose. Clem muttered on, her eyes scrunched closed. Edna's thoughts rattled around her brain, rolling from one side to the other like cargo in a storm-tossed ship. Things like, *oh, dear, I always hoped I would go in peace* and *I certainly hope it doesn't hurt* and *I did so want to finish that scarf* and *I really should have visited the cemetery.*

Clem's fingers tightened on Edna's wrist, glowing gold. The golden glow traced up her forearm, up her upper arm, up her chest and neck and face. Edna's chest buzzed.

The van slowed—Benjamin had not let up his shrieking-kettle noise—Edna's stomach lurched, jumped, plummeted, and sloshed—she extracted a white linen handkerchief from her handbag and held it to her mouth, certain she was going to vomit—

They landed, without the decimating crumple and metallic screech she'd expected. The van bounced, as if they'd landed on a moon-bounce, then stilled.

Clem released Edna's wrist and crumpled to the floor.

"Clem?" Edna's voice quavered. "Clementine?"

The shrieking-kettle noise cut off. Benjamin turned his head without letting go of the steering wheel. "I think she's unconscious. Are you okay?"

Edna cackled hysterically. "We're alive. Oh, my. Oh, goodness. Oh. I thought—"

Benjamin laughed too, more hysterically. "Me too."

He threw open his door and retched into the corn.

Edna struggled with her seatbelt, which refused to relinquish its protection. Perhaps it thought the van would try to kill them again. She freed herself and shook Clem's shoulder, but the girl was out cold.

Benjamin scrambled out of the van and wrenched Edna's door open. He dragged her from her seat, firing question after question at her about how she felt. Giving her a medical exam calmed him; the panicked expression in his eyes faded into the concerned, clinical, no-nonsense look he wore whenever faced with potential medical trouble.

He examined Edna up and down until he was satisfied with her condition.

"Thank god." His voice steadied, though it was still higher than usual. "That could've been so much worse."

They stood in the knee-high corn to survey the damage. Although Clem had slowed its descent, the van was a wreck: dents in the sides, a crack across the windshield, rusted parts scattered in the grass. The tires sagged. The passenger's side mirror was askew.

"That's not going to get us far," Edna said. "We'll have to get something new."

Benjamin kicked the rear tire. "We can't afford something new. We could barely afford gas for this piece of junk."

Inside the van, Clem stirred. She pulled herself into a sit, grabbing her head. Her hand glowed faintly. The golden light throbbed and pulsed, sank into her skin, and vanished.

"What happened?"

Benjamin's eyebrows contracted. "You crashed my van, that's what happened."

"You saved us," Edna said.

Clem gazed up at her. "I did?"

"Yes, dear. Are you all right? Can you stand?"

"Yeah." Clem's legs wobbled, but she got out of the van, blinking in the sunlight. "I don't know how—"

She staggered.

Benjamin steadied her. "Let me take a look at you."

He hovered over her, examining her eyes and feeling her pulse.

She tried to push him away. "You don't understand. I couldn't have done it."

"You said you could fix it."

"Okay, yeah, what was I supposed to say? Sorry, everyone, we're going to die. My bad."

"Fair point," Benjamin said, now feeling the top of her head for bumps.

"Cut it out." Clem batted his hand away. "That magic should've been beyond me. I would've needed help from someone."

"You couldn't have had any," Edna said. "We don't have magic."

Clem gave up and let Benjamin examine her in peace. "Maybe you haven't studied it, but everyone has magic. Even if they don't use it."

It took several more minutes and many more questions before Benjamin was confident she didn't have a concussion.

"A minor case of magical exhaustion," he said to Edna. "That's why she passed out, not the actual crash. She used more magic than she's used to. Good thing she's young, or it would've taken a lot longer for her to bounce back."

"I'd have thought—" Edna said, but stopped because it seemed best not to say anything more about the fire.

Clem stared at the ground. "What, that setting a church on fire would take more magic than this?"

"Well..."

"That was different." Her voice was so soft that Edna almost didn't hear her. "I was angry."

Every response that came to mind might hurt Clem's feelings, so Edna said nothing. Flushed and staring at the ground, Clem looked young indeed. Despite everything, Edna found herself wanting to take care of her.

Clem cleared her throat.

"So," she said. "So, uh, is there anyone we could call?"

Edna sighed. "Yes, but I don't have his number."

Clem pulled a cell phone from her pocket.

"I don't have his number," Edna repeated.

"You don't need it," Clem mumbled. "It's magically enhanced. I didn't do it," she added quickly as Benjamin raised an eyebrow at her. "Abuela made some modifications for me. She doesn't really get smartphones, but she loves playing around with tech and she's seriously good at magic..."

Edna took the proffered phone, but she didn't really get smartphones, either. Her younger sister had been much better with technology.

Clem shook her head, took the phone back, poked at it, and gave it to Edna again. "There's a function like a magic mirror? As long as you know who you're trying to reach, you don't need a number."

Edna was at least as inexperienced with magic mirrors as she was with smartphones, although if given a choice she would've preferred the mirror.

The screen shone the royal blue of an evening sky. Edna put it to her ear.

Clem rolled her eyes. "Not like that. Just look into it. Unless you want to give them a close-up of your ear canal."

Edna lowered the phone. "Well...I'd like to speak to Methodius the Just. Please. If you could..."

Her reflection broke and swirled. The screen settled on the image of what might have been a ceiling.

A bad-tempered Methodius came into view.

"I know you have the sword," he said before she could speak. "There's no need to gloat. I was wrong. Well done and so forth. Are you calling from a magic mirror? Where on earth did you get one?"

"That's not why I'm calling," Edna said, noting his utter lack of enthusiasm. "Although I could very well say something about how difficult it was to get the sword. What on earth did you do to poor Theobald Smith?"

Methodius blanched.

"Oh," he mumbled. "You, er, you know about that, do you?"

"Yeah, we do," Benjamin said, "and, like, respectfully, what the fuck? Did you ghost him thirty years ago, or what?"

The mirror showed the ceiling again as Methodius took their call out of the room. It settled back on his face a moment later. He'd gone from white to red and was tugging on his beard.

"Did he take the ring back?" he asked anxiously.

Benjamin glowered at him. "Should he have?"

"It's his. He gave it to me, I mean. I thought when he saw it, he might..."

Benjamin opened his mouth, but Methodius looked so pitiful that Edna said hastily, "I have it right here. I'll send it to you as soon as I can."

"Did he seem...is he..." Methodius tugged at his beard so hard it seemed in danger of coming out. "...doing all right?"

"He's married," Benjamin said bluntly, "and he'd probably be better if he never thought about you again."

The wizard stopped tugging his beard. He was silent for a long moment, the color ebbing from his face.

"You must understand," he said miserably, "I didn't want to leave. But the Council called me back. I didn't think I'd be gone so long, but..." He devolved into mumbles unintelligible except for something about "disciplinary action." He cleared his throat. "The Council didn't think I was taking my responsibilities seriously."

"Never mind about that now," Edna said, as Benjamin opened his mouth again, possibly to argue about their respective definitions of responsibilities and to whom. "I have the sword, at any rate, but I have a burned-down church and a tagalong and a crashed van, too. I dare say I've exceeded your expectations."

The wizard paled. "You burned down a church?"

"Not me personally. That was Clementine."

He frowned, tugging at his beard again. "Not Clementine Rodriguez?"

"You know her?" Edna said in surprise.

"She was the front-runner," he said. "The perfect candidate for Chosen One. Sixteen, athletic, handy with a sword, out for vengeance..."

Edna's eyes turned toward Clem.

"We were sure our chancellor would name her," Methodius said. "So sure, we'd started betting on who her mentor was going to be. But the day came, and he was out with the flu, and it fell to Philostratus to name someone..."

He remembered who he was talking to.

"Not that I don't think you'll do perfectly fine," he concluded.

Edna sighed. She turned the mirror so he could see the wreckage.

"I don't suppose there's anything you can do about this?"

"Pigs of Circe! That wasn't the Rodriguez girl, too?"

"Never mind that. Can you help us? We haven't got money for a new one."

The wizard's brow furrowed.

"Perhaps it's best she wasn't named after all. If it came out that the Chosen One we named had burned down a church..." He cleared his throat. "What do you expect me to do about it?"

"Surely you can do something?" Edna said impatiently. "I've got the sword. I've proven my worth. But I'm not going to get far without a vehicle."

"I'm not a mechanic."

"You're not very helpful."

"You're not very good at being the Chosen One."

"Well, you're—"

They bickered for some time. By that point, Benjamin was on the phone with his insurance company, trying to see if they'd pay a claim for an accidental flight and the subsequent crash without raising his rates. Clem huddled in the van's doorway with her backpack in her lap.

"All right!" Methodius snapped at last. "I think I know someone who can help. Amir Ansari. He's a carpet-enchanter and a dear friend of mine. He might be willing to put something together for you."

Edna's annoyance vanished. A flying carpet? That was more like it.

"I'd be much obliged," she said.

CHAPTER TEN

She wasn't obliged for long. Amir Ansari's carpet shop was in Detroit, and while Methodius promised to call ahead so the carpet-enchanter would expect them, they had to find their own ride there.

"What do you mean, we have to find a ride?" Edna asked. "You're magic. Can't you poof us there?"

The wizard sighed. "I certainly can't. Surely you know better than that."

Edna did not know better than that. Magic was magic and ought to provide a, well, magical solution to everything. She'd never understood why it didn't.

He hung up before she could ask any more.

Clem mumbled something at her.

"What was that, dear?"

"I said," Clem's face was rather pink, "I could put an extension spell on your purse, if you want."

Her voice suggested she expected Edna to turn the offer down.

"You could carry more," she said. "Take some of this stuff with you."

Edna snuck a glance at Benjamin, who was prying open the glove box to get at his registration and insurance information.

"I would appreciate it," she said.

Clem turned pinker. "Even though I crashed the van?"

"It could've been a lot worse," Edna said. "And you did turn the sword into a ring for me."

For the first time, she wondered if Clem could undo it once they needed the sword to be a sword, but she didn't ask.

Clem nodded, took Edna's handbag, and ran her hand along the bottom of it. It didn't feel any different when she handed it back, but as Clem started handing her things from the van, Edna found she could fit everything inside: clothing, toiletries, even her knitted blanket—all without making it any heavier, which was everything Edna could have wished for.

They picked their way out of the corn. Benjamin searched for a cab company or rideshare, cursing under his breath; the nearest of either was more than half an hour away and too expensive.

Edna's hip and knees ached worse than ever. Clem stood beside her, hugging herself.

Edna coughed a rattling cough. "Clem, dear—does anyone know where you are?"

Clem didn't answer.

"I'm guessing that's a no," Benjamin said. Clem stuck her tongue out at him. "Okay, that's definitely a no."

"Shut up."

"Clem?" Edna said gently. "You should call, don't you think? Won't someone be worried?"

She turned it into a question, but it wasn't, really. She worried constantly when Percival was in the Knights, worried every time he went more than a week without calling. She always pretended, when he finally did call, that she hadn't been worried at all. She'd plaster a smile on her face so he'd hear it through the phone. He'd grown up dreaming of being a Knight; she hadn't wanted to ruin it for him.

If Clem were her child and ran off this way, she'd have a heart attack.

Maybe Clem's parents were gone. Edna hadn't forgotten how her jaw had clenched back in the church. Surely the girl had *someone*.

"They have other things to worry about," Clem said quietly.

Whoever "they" were, Edna was sure they couldn't be worrying about anything right now more than Clem's whereabouts.

"You're not coming with us," Benjamin said. "You might as well go home."

Clem scowled. "I'm not going anywhere without the Sword of Destiny."

"You can't use it. Everyone knows the Chosen One is the only one who–"

"Can she use it? It's a sword, not denture cream."

Benjamin didn't have anything to say to that, and frankly, neither did Edna.

An idea cut through the questions rattling around her head.

"Could you teach me?" she asked.

Clem fiddled with her necklace. "I almost killed you."

"Not on purpose."

"Are you kidding me?" Benjamin muttered, but Edna pretended she hadn't heard.

"I saw you with the sword. You know how to use it, don't you?"

"Yeah, but–"

"Edna," Benjamin said. "You can't be serious. She can't come with us. We have to send her home."

Clem glared at him. "I'm not going home."

"You have to."

"Says who?"

"Says us."

Edna sighed. She was going to have to put up with a lot of arguing from here on out if she stuck to her offer.

"How do you propose to send her home if she won't tell us where home is?"

Benjamin opened his mouth to argue, but then his expression brightened. "Hey—a car."

A battered old Ford slowed as Benjamin stepped into the road, waving. A peeling logo splashed on the passenger's side read: FRUIT SO GOOD, IT'S ALMOST MAGICAL! Rust ate at the doors and undercarriage. Tattered black plastic flapped over one of the back windows. Piles of wooden crates teetered in the bed.

The truck slowed to a crawl as it neared, its driver regarding them with suspicion. "You folks lost?"

"Not exactly," Benjamin said. "We're, uh, we're..."

He looked at Edna helplessly. At the sight of an old lady leaning on a cane in the middle of the road, the driver rescinded his question. "Hop on in."

They were gone by the time Kiernan Abbott found the van's wreckage. It didn't matter. He might've missed them in Marine City, but now he knew who the Chosen One was.

He dialed Red's number from the roadside.

"I hope you aren't calling to tell me you've killed them."

"That's a hell of a way to answer the phone," Kiernan said. "I found her."

Red's voice was triumphant. "The Chosen One?"

"No, Morgan le Fay. Yes, the Chosen One. A teenage girl stole the Sword of Destiny from the auction. She's got a couple people with her. An old woman who's probably her mentor and this young guy who's...I don't know what he's for."

"So, you're on your way?"

"Er," Kiernan said, staring back at the cornfield, which was sadly lacking in Chosen Ones. "Not exactly."

"So, you haven't found her."

"I found her," Kiernan said. "I just...don't know her exact location this minute."

Silence. Kiernan scowled.

"Do you have any leads?" Red asked.

Kiernan surveyed the field: the broken cornstalks where the van had crash-landed, the scattered detritus of rusted metal and shredded rubber.

"A couple," he said. "She needs a new ride."

"Where are you going to start?"

"Detroit," Kiernan said.

CHAPTER ELEVEN

Edna and Clem were squished into the backseat of the pickup with Clem's backpack. Benjamin had won their chauffeur's favor by asking about the slogan on the side of the truck. Their driver was a farmer, they learned, and he and Benjamin spent the whole ride jawing about the intersection of agricultural sciences and magic, magical irrigation systems, and other things that confused Edna and bored Clem.

"So you're saying you actually create small rainstorms over each field to water the crops?"

"Not me, no, never did go to college, and that's tricky magic, let me tell you. My youngest, he's just about finished with his MgD. We have to pay tempestarii to water the fields now, but when he's done with school—"

There were only two brief reprieves: when Edna gave the driver the address of their destination, and when Benjamin, after twenty minutes of nonstop questions, realized how much he'd been talking and stammered, "Sorry, that was a lot, I shouldn't have—"

It happened often, Edna had noticed in the past six years. Benjamin's excitement about magic would crack and shatter, like he was certain he was annoying people. She didn't know who had done that to him—his parents, or an ex-boyfriend, or an ex-friend, or many people throughout his life. Someone, at some point, had told him he was too much, had shut him up, and now he did it to himself, even when whoever he was talking to didn't seem to mind.

But the farmer, not used to anyone taking such an interest in his work, said, "No, no, no bother, honest. You were asking about crop rotation, now, well—" and Benjamin relaxed and renewed his questions.

Clouds scudded across the sky as they passed out of farmland. The Detroit skyline rose before them, but Edna couldn't tell if they were anywhere near the university where they'd found the first Theobald Smith. The concrete barriers of the freeway and the rundown buildings on either side all looked the same. Traffic crowded the roads and the skylanes above.

Clem bumped her toes against Benjamin's seat. "Are we there yet?"

"Is the car still moving?" he said. "Then no, we're not there yet." He turned back to the farmer. "Okay, so when you're breeding magic *into* plants—"

They left the freeway behind. The carpet-enchanter's shop was around the corner from Eastern Market. The pickup truck slowed, as did Benjamin's flow of questions, as the farmer navigated the market crowds. Flying carpets and flying horses touched down in the grass outside the market sheds. Pedestrians and cyclists wove through the street traffic as tardy vendors rushed to set up tents outside the already-crowded sheds.

The pickup trundled onward and turned down a side street.

If not for the sign over the doorway, they wouldn't have noticed the shop at all. Its door faded into the dusty brick façade, which vanished against the abandoned storefronts on either side.

The sign was old too, the wood worn and weathered, but someone had freshly painted it. Inky-black script curled over and under the glossy image of a rug: Arabic above and Urdu below. Painted at the bottom of the sign, in English, were the words *Amir Ansari, Carpet-Enchanter.*

"Good luck to you, now," the farmer said as they clambered out of his truck.

The clouds had slowed and thickened, casting a gray pallor over the city.

"Are you sure you have the right address?" Benjamin asked, in a voice you might use in an empty theater.

Edna surveyed the sign. "Amir Ansari, that's what Methodius said."

"No way," he whispered.

A bell over the doorway tinkled as they entered. A tall young woman in trousers, a sweater, and a hijab was trying to convince coffee rings to come out of the yellowed Formica counter by the door. She smiled at them, stashing her washcloth behind the counter.

"Can I help you?"

"Er..."

Edna wasn't sure what Methodius had said—whether he'd given her name, told them to expect the Chosen One. Whether she should mention him. Whether he'd spoken directly to his friend or to this young woman.

Clem pushed past her and leaned on the counter. "We're expected."

The woman raised her eyebrows but turned to an ancient computer monitor in the corner and clicked around. Edna batted Clem's elbows off the counter.

The woman sighed, smacking the computer. "There we go. Do you have an appointment?"

Clem opened her mouth, but Edna elbowed her into silence. Benjamin pulled the girl back from the counter. He polished his glasses on his t-shirt so he could see better, wearing a reverent expression like a tourist at Stonehenge. Edna wasn't sure why. The space was cluttered and dimly lit.

"Not precisely," she said. "That is, I'm not entirely sure. That is, Methodius the Just called ahead?"

The woman turned away from the computer gratefully. "Oh, that. Edna Fisher?"

"Yes, dear, that's me."

The woman shook hands with her. "My name is Akida. My uncle is resting, but I'll tell him you're here."

"That's all right," Edna said. "We can wait."

Clem huffed. Akida didn't hear her. She picked her way across the cluttered shop and disappeared through a door at the back.

"We can wait," Clem mimicked. "Are you the Chosen One or not? We need a carpet ASAP."

"Hush. I'm sure he needs his rest. And if he's going to make us a carpet, we're not going to be pushy about it, are we?"

Clem put her elbows back on the counter.

"Are we?" Edna said, eyeing her over the top of her glasses.

Clem clacked her teeth together, studying the shop. "I guess not."

It was more a workshop than a storefront. Aside from the counter, with coffee stains aging it like tree rings, and the threadbare carpet hanging in the display case behind it, the room didn't seem meant for customers. Beyond the counter was a worn worktable cluttered with parchment and scraps of carpet, fountain pens and ink and glue, spare yarn and staples and scissors and needles. Rickety shelves buried every inch of wall. Bottles and jars glinted beneath the worktable and on the shelves, where they were stacked three deep. In the gloom, Edna couldn't tell what was in them.

"I can't believe we're here," Benjamin said in a hushed voice.

"What do you mean?" Edna asked.

"Amir Ansari? The carpet-enchanter?"

Edna readjusted her grip on her cane. Clem shrugged.

Benjamin gaped at them.

"For real? He's a world-famous carpet-enchanter. Which, okay, doesn't mean much outside of carpet-enchanting circles, but still. He's, like, the standard by which all other carpet-enchanters on earth are measured and *we are in his shop.* He revolutionized carpet-enchanting in the 1970s or something. I can't believe we're going to meet him. This is. Oh my god. I can't believe you guys don't know who he is."

Edna smiled at him. "Not all of us have master's degrees in magical anthropology."

Clem slapped her hands on the counter. "Some of us have more important things to worry about."

"Hush."

Akida returned with an old man in tow and resumed her post at the stained counter.

"My uncle," she said.

Her uncle's appearance gave the impression of suddenly lighting the shop. He had long white hair, a neatly trimmed beard, and bushy white eyebrows, and he wore a sky-blue salwar kameez embroidered in gold. His smile was perhaps less white than his hair but no less bright. Edna liked him immediately.

"Welcome, friends of Methodius!" He came toward them with arms outstretched and clasped Benjamin's hands. "I am Amir Ansari."

Benjamin pumped his hands up and down. "It's an honor to meet you, sir."

Amir laughed and turned to Clem. He patted her on the head as if she were a small child. Edna expected her to object, but she didn't. Her eyebrows contracted.

The carpet-enchanter bowed to Edna. "You must be Mrs. Fisher! Methodius tells me you are the Chosen One."

Edna tried not to feel pleased at the expression on his face. "Edna, please. And yes, I am."

"To think! At our time of life. You must have strong magic."

Clem snorted. Benjamin stared at the carpet-enchanter with a star-struck expression.

"I don't really have any magic to speak of, actually."

"Of course not," Amir said, waving it aside. "They chose you for your prowess with the sword."

"Oh, no. No, I never had the chance to learn swordplay."

"Your experience with dragons?"

"I'm afraid not."

The carpet-enchanter looked at the others as if hoping someone would let him in on the joke.

"I have knitting needles," Edna offered.

Amir was perplexed. "And very fearsome I'm sure they are."

She grinned.

He smiled back, a little bemusedly. "Of course, I am honored to serve the Chosen One. I have the perfect carpet for you."

"Thank you." Edna hesitated, not sure how much Methodius had told him about their situation. "We don't have much money, but—"

He held up a hand. "Please. It is my pleasure. Methodius once did me a great favor. I would do anything to repay him."

Methodius wasn't the one getting the carpet, but if he was happy with this arrangement, Edna was happy, too.

Amir turned to his niece. "I don't know when you are leaving, but—"

"Mira's ballet lesson doesn't end for another hour, and Hassan said he would pick her up today. I can stay until closing."

"Ah, Akida, what would I do without you?"

"This is why you should have had children, uncle," Akida said, but he merely chuckled.

Amir led them through the shop. Edna placed her cane carefully, certain she would slip on one of the floor's many jars and break her hip. An embarrassing end for the Chosen One.

Naturally, the door opened onto stairs. Switchback stairs, steep and narrow, with steps that weren't up to code but had been perfectly legal when the shop was built. Clem took the downward stairs two at a time, disappearing through another door at the bottom.

Edna took them one at a time, with her hand on the railing.

At the bottom was a gallery, well-lit, with rugs in various stages of completion stretched over wooden frames. More rugs hung front to back on racks along the walls. In the center stood a shining table with several chairs around it and a binder of colors and designs on top. Overall, much more impressive than the messy, dimly lit shop above.

Amir smiled at Edna like he knew what she was thinking.

"People like to see evidence of my spellwork," he said. "No one who sees my workshop thinks, what an untidy man he is! They think, he must be very busy, and a hard worker, too, and they wonder what I keep in my jars."

"What do you keep in your jars?" Benjamin asked with interest.

Amir tapped the side of his nose. "Enchanter's secret."

Edna wrestled the ring that was the Sword of Destiny off her finger, set it on the table, and eased into one of the chairs. The ring had dug into her skin, leaving an angry red ring around her pinky. Maybe she should ask Clem to resize the ring. But she couldn't bring herself to disappoint the shy pride Clem had shown at getting this particular magic right.

She could always keep it in her handbag instead of wearing it. It could keep Methodius's ring company until she sent it back to him.

Benjamin leaned on the back of her chair, itching to examine the nearest carpet up close. Clem hooked her thumbs through the straps of her backpack.

Amir wheeled one of the wooden frames forward. Stretched across it was a deep blue rug, thick and plush, with coppery designs swirling across it and a golden border.

"It is some of my finest work. I've been working on it for months."

"Perfect," Clem said. "Let's go."

"Clementine," Edna said.

"It doesn't fly yet," Amir said. "Carpets are not winged horses that come into existence ready to take to the skies. I have to enchant it still."

Clem rocked back and forth on her heels. "What about that carpet in the case upstairs? The red one."

Amir shook his head. "Local flights only. For such a long journey, a carpet needs special modifications."

Clem scowled. "We need to get a move-on. They killed dozens in San Ignacio."

"Dozens dead," Edna said vaguely, remembering the article in the newspaper that last morning at the nursing home.

"Yeah. Southeastern California. If we don't beat Redway to the next site, they'll do it again."

Questions spiraled through Edna's head, questions about how fast Redway moved, where he was heading next.

A word broke through her thoughts. "They?"

Clem's eyebrows knit together. "Yeah? He's not on his own—you know that, right? Like it's not just him and a zillion dragons. He's got, I don't know, soldiers or something who ride out with him. You don't know anything about him, do you?"

Edna didn't. She tried and failed to remember what Methodius had told her, what she'd heard about Redway in the news. He was a sorcerer; he had tamed dragons, somehow, and used them to attack Knights.

The Knights were all she could think of. Knights on television, marching and running and shouting and retrieving weapons so they could stave off the flight overhead. Squires panicking as they faced their first dragons, more dragons than they'd ever expected to see in one place at one time. That young Knight in the newspaper, carrying a dead comrade over his shoulder.

Knights like her son.

She should have realized she wasn't up against Redway alone, but she hadn't. It worried her. She'd barely managed to get the Sword of Destiny with no one but Clem in her way.

"I told you, you don't mess with magic," Benjamin was saying. Edna suppressed her panic. "Cutting corners on powerful enchantments always ends badly. If it takes three days, it takes three days."

"We can't wait three days," Clem snapped. "Redway is on the move now."

Amir stroked his beard. "I cannot possibly get it done in less time."

"Then what good are you?"

Her voice rang out in the small space. Amir's face crumpled.

"Clementine—" Edna said.

Clem rounded on her long enough to say, "It's Clem," and turned her attention back to the carpet-enchanter.

Benjamin scowled at her. "If you're so stoked, why don't you run along after him now?"

"Benjamin," Edna said, but he cut her off.

"No, I really want to know. We don't need a snotty teenager to babysit. Get going."

Clem put her hands on her hips. "Give me the sword, and I will."

"Not a chance."

"Stop it, both of you." Edna rose stiffly. "Mr. Ansari has offered us one of his best carpets—for free, no less—and your thanks is to squabble like children."

Clem's eyes bored into Benjamin. "I'm not squabbling. I'm trying to make sure we get to Redway before he kills more Knights. I thought you wanted that too."

Edna wrung her hands. Redway had been around for several years, but in the past year, especially the past few months, the attacks had grown more frequent. Knights dead, cities aflame, families fleeing the Southwest. The attack on San Ignacio the other night. She thought of the cemetery and a headstone thirty years old.

"Of course I do."

Clem's nostrils flared.

Edna bit her lip and asked Amir in apologetic tones, "You're sure you couldn't finish it any faster?"

He shook his head. "I wish it were so. The enchantments are old and complex. If I cut corners, you will find yourself in need of another ride within days, even hours."

Clem hitched her backpack higher up her shoulders and glared at them. "Then I guess I'll have to find my own way there."

She snatched the ring off the table and ran.

Benjamin sprinted after her, but she had vanished by the time he reached the street. He turned back inside and shouted from the top of the stairs, “She got away!”

“With your ring?” Amir asked.

“With the Sword of Destiny,” Edna said.

A trail of broken jars tracked Clem’s path through the shop. Akida had a broom in her hands but didn’t use it, shock frozen on her face. Amir came up the stairs behind Edna and stopped dead.

“Is it a girl or an elephant who has run through my shop?” he said in bewildered tones.

“I’m so sorry,” Edna blurted as she hurried past. “I’m so sorry, I’ll find her and–”

And...she wasn’t sure what. She followed Benjamin out onto the street.

“Which way did she go?”

“I don’t know. She got across the street and this truck went by and she was gone.”

Delivery trucks rumbled down the road. Pedestrians strolled in and out of Eastern Market. Overhead, the clouds had darkened into thick storm clouds.

“You stay here and help Amir and Akida clean up,” Edna said. “I’ll search the market. If I don’t find her...”

“We’re screwed.”

“Don’t be a negative Nellie.”

Edna started off, but Benjamin stopped her.

“Take my phone. I don’t want you getting lost. If you don’t find her–be back here in an hour?”

Edna nodded, slipped his phone into her handbag, and plunged into the crowds.

CHAPTER TWELVE

Edna couldn't be sure Clem had entered Eastern Market. But surely a teenage girl with a mission, a temper, and a thwarted desire to be the Chosen One would run somewhere she could find a vehicle ready to go. The market was the nearest place that fit the bill.

Eastern Market was one of the largest magical trading hubs in North America and the strangest grab-bag of magical and nonmagical products Edna had ever seen. Vendors sang out to passersby, advertising produce, halal meat, carpet repair, magically enlarged purses and wallets, potions ingredients, cauldrons, dragon's-tooth jewelry, protective amulets, homemade soaps and lotions, wand-cleaning kits, skeins of yeti's wool. Hard-faced dwarves offering metal items and repair rubbed shoulders with human metalsmiths. Farmers tried to outsell goblins and gardener gnomes. A trio of mermaids in a claw-foot bathtub on wheels sang to the fiddling of a human folk group.

The darkening clouds had done nothing to deter the crowds, who wandered the market sheds without concern. Some vendors pulled down the garage doors that sided the sheds, normally left open during market hours so vendors could park right outside their stalls, but that was the only sign anyone had noticed the coming rain.

The crowds drifted along like molasses. Vendors accosted Edna every few yards. In any other circumstances, she would've been extremely interested.

"Need to update?" A man with a dozen expensive handbags gestured at his table. "Stylish, modern, and with a built-in pocket dimension for that extra storage!"

"iPhones! Magically enhanced, guaranteed never to lose a signal–"

"They're not real iPhones."

"Are too!"

"You're not allowed to enhance iPhones–"

Edna shoved past. A sea of people flooded her.

"Clementine!" she shouted, but the crowd's babble absorbed her voice. She should have sent Benjamin. He was taller, had those broad shoulders that could forge a path through a crowd, and he could move faster.

She dismissed the thought. Clem rubbed him the wrong way, and the feeling was mutual. Clem wasn't her biggest fan, either, but at least she and Clem (probably) wouldn't pick a fight with each other at first sight.

A voice, a whisper in her head.

This way.

Edna drifted toward a booth. The voice approved. Clem was there; she had to be. Edna sensed it. She knew how silly this was, but Clem had said everyone had magic.

Maybe this was Edna's magic. This quiet whisper, this tug at her heart.

The tug grew more urgent as the crowds buffeted Edna past a table of CDs, mouth organs, and lutes. She fought her way toward it.

A trio of buxom women with blue-tinted skin stood behind the table, smiling as Edna panicked over to them. She wasn't sure why she was panicking—she didn't often panic—but her lungs seized and her forehead shone with perspiration. Her hip throbbed.

The women looked like they had recently crawled out of the ocean, blue-lipped. Dark hair rippled down their backs.

"There is no greater magic than music," one of them said.

Edna nodded, examining their wares. Why, she couldn't have said. She had little money, no musical talent, and no interest in buying a CD.

Clem, she thought to herself. She had to find Clem. She had to...she had to...

She had to make a purchase. Bad things would happen if she didn't. She'd never find Clem if she didn't buy something from these women. Her heart twanged like a badly tuned banjo.

"Looking for something in particular?" the second woman asked sweetly.

Clem, Edna insisted to herself, but the woman's voice eased her panic. This woman would help her. Everything would be all right once Edna bought something.

"I don't know," she said. "I—I don't know."

The third woman smiled quietly. "I'm sure we can find something to suit your needs."

I don't need any of this, Edna wanted to say, but now she couldn't remember the girl's name, and what she heard herself saying instead was, "Oh, thank you. *Thank you.*"

"Mrs. Fisher!"

Edna's need to shop vanished as suddenly as it had come. The women's smiles sharpened. Edna pushed away from their table, dizzy, and stumped away as fast as she could.

Amir hovered outside the market shed on the frayed red carpet from the display case in his shop. Edna pushed through the crowd to the grass outside. The wind picked up, stinging her face with an unseasonable chill, but she breathed it in. The cold cleared her dizziness.

Amir lowered the carpet so she could step aboard.

"I thought this might be easier for you," he said. "Benjamin says too much walking gives you difficulty."

He would say that, Edna thought, but her knees were stiff and her hip still throbbing. And she wasn't about to complain about riding a flying carpet. She wobbled, plopping down on her backside with a groan. The carpet rose into the air.

"Do you know where she might be?" Amir asked.

Edna shook her head. "I don't know the first thing about the market. But if there are magical vehicles for sale somewhere..."

Amir steered toward the largest market shed, which twinkled with warm yellow light in the gathering darkness.

"I'm sorry about your shop," Edna said.

Amir stroked his beard. "Benjamin and Akida cleaned it admirably."

Unsure what to say, Edna patted his arm. He stiffened imperceptibly.

"Oh—" She put her hands in her lap. She hadn't meant anything by it; it was what she did when she didn't know what to say. "I'm so sorry."

The corners of his beard lifted into a small smile, but Edna was embarrassed at the imposition. All the impositions. Bringing someone into his shop who had yelled at him and made such a mess, when he'd been so gracious.

The carpet ducked into the largest market shed, which was, if possible, noisier than the others. Livestock and conveyances magical and nonmagical bleated and roared and whinnied and coughed and puttered.

The carpet slowed, winding its way around airborne buyers testing vehicles. In a corral by the entrance, an aerquestrian spread the wings of a winged horse so a client could examine its pinfeathers. A flying stagecoach whipped past at top speed, with a buyer in the driver's seat and the white-faced salesman trying not to puke beside them. Amir's carpet zipped out of the way. Edna searched the crowd below for Clem.

Outside, it grew darker and windier. More vendors rolled down the garage doors on the sides of the shed to protect their wares.

Deep in the recesses of Edna's handbag, Benjamin's cell phone rang. She rooted around for it with one hand. The call rang out.

Amir watched her. "We'll find her."

"Mmmm," Edna said, but she was focused on the crowd. "Can you take us closer?"

"Only so far. There are rules about where one can fly in the market."

He lowered the carpet as much as possible. Edna kept her eyes peeled.

"There!"

She'd caught sight of the familiar long, curly hair and an equally familiar backpack crouched low beside a carpet-vendor's table. Carpets were stacked less than a foot away. The vendor was busy with customers.

Edna clasped her hands together. "Oh, hurry, hurry."

Amir took her as close as he could, but the crowds made landing impossible. Edna sucked in a breath, sticking her legs over the side of the carpet.

"What are you doing?" Amir asked. "Mrs. Fisher—"

She slid from the carpet, staggering on the ground, which was closer than she'd thought. Her knees screamed in protest.

Clem's eyes were on the carpet-vendor. Her fingers curled around the edge of the topmost carpet in the stack.

"Clementine," Edna whispered. The girl jumped. "Come on, dear. Let's talk about this."

Clem eyed her. Her fingers slowly uncurled. With relief, Edna beckoned her toward Amir.

"Hey!" The vendor had seen them. "What are you doing?"

Clem yanked the carpet off the stack, leapt aboard, and zoomed away.

The carpet-vendor chased after her. "Thief! Thief! Someone stop her!"

"Snickerdoodles," Edna said. "Amir!"

He pulled up beside her, lowered the carpet with difficulty so she could board, and took off again. The carpet-vendor's cry rippled along until everyone knew someone had stolen a carpet. Customers leapt onto tables, standing on tiptoe as Clem flew past with her dark hair streaming behind her. Vendors either joined them or tried to shoo them away.

"Get your feet off–"

"Watch out, those are seven-league boots!"

"Don't let her get away!"

Clem flew higher to avoid the grasping hands, but it trapped her inside, racing along the ceiling, too high to duck out through the sides of the shed. Throughout the building, vendors with stalls still open to outside pulled down the garage doors behind them so she couldn't escape.

Unbeknownst to any of them, Kiernan Abbott was crouched by one of those doors, with his bow trained on Clem, swearing under his breath as he waited for a clean shot.

He had half a mind to take the best shot he saw, clean or not. But he didn't relish the manhunt that would follow if a random bystander fell down dead with an arrow in their gullet.

"She's getting away!" the carpet-vendor screamed.

Police officers converged on the vendor's stall. One of them glared. "Why are you running after her, you idiot?"

He hopped on a carpet, raced to the nearest exit, and blocked Clem's escape. She veered away.

"Secure the area!" the officer shouted. "The rest of you, grab carpets and go after her!"

"My carpets," the carpet-vendor moaned, but the police commandeered them all. The aerquestrian circled outside with her winged horses in case Clem escaped. Clem zoomed back and forth like a moth at a windowpane.

Amir hovered over the carpet-vendor's stall, pursing his lips. He made a few uncertain attempts to fly out into the shed's center, but the air was thick with pursuit. They could only zip back and forth along one wall.

"What are you doing?" Edna cried. "Let's go after her."

He shook his head. "What would you have me do? There are too many people."

Clem flashed by, her hair whipping her face. A swarm of police officers zipped after her, closing in.

Edna's heart clenched. She bumped Amir aside.

"Move over and tell me how to drive this thing!"

"Mrs. Fisher—" Amir said in alarm, but too late.

Edna gripped the front edge of the carpet, looking for an opening, any opening, any way to get to Clem and—what? Pull her aboard so they could fly off together? Distract the police? A thousand half-baked ideas tumbled through her brain.

With Edna in uncertain control, the carpet jerked to a halt. It zipped forward again, twisted left, right. Then it barreled toward the pursuit, but Edna didn't stop, or rather couldn't. Clem was shuttling toward the exit, but the aerquestrian and her horses were waiting outside—

Clem's carpet stopped. The police officers rocketed past her, through the exit and out. The flying horses whinnied; the aerquestrian shouted in triumph; the police yelled in confusion.

Clem's carpet plummeted from the air.

"Clementine!" Edna cried.

Clem's carpet hit the ground, skidding into a collection of old-fashioned pickle barrels standing sentry by a still-open garage door. The crowd scattered. Several people shouted, "Where'd she go?" Confusion reigned as everyone headed for the barrels in a manner that suggested they thought someone else was about to crash down on their heads. Thunder rumbled outside.

Edna forgot about controlling the carpet, which hovered above the chaos until Amir took over. His chest heaved, but he sounded calmer now that he was driving again.

"We'll find her." He nudged his glasses up the bridge of his nose with a knuckle. "She can't be far now."

He flew them out the main entrance and around to the other side of the barrels. A police officer was yelling at the aerquestrian, but most of the officers sprawled in the entryway with glazed eyes. Their carpets had crashed to the ground moments after Clem's.

Amir clicked his tongue. "That's what you get for subpar carpet-enchanting."

The carpet-vendor made his way outside. The officer who had been yelling at the aerquestrian shouted at the vendor instead, bellowing about price-gouging, false advertising, and flouted carpet regulations.

Clem's carpet, crumpled and exhausted, had been found and thrown onto a nearby table. There was no sign of Clem.

Benjamin's cell phone rang again.

"Can you take us higher?" The carpet rose, circling the area. Edna blushed. "I'm sorry. I don't know what I was thinking. I shouldn't have tried to take over."

"Your granddaughter must be very important to you," Amir said gently.

Her blush deepened. "She isn't actually my..."

He didn't question her, for which she was grateful. She couldn't explain why she needed to take care of Clem, except that the girl was sixteen and traveling alone. Except for her tone when she'd said, "See? I can do magic" after disguising the sword.

Lightning flashed. The sky broke open, drowning out the shouts from the market. Barely visible in the silvery sheen of rain, a figure hurried away from the market.

"Is that her?"

Rain smeared Edna's glasses and soaked her clothes, the carpet, and Amir, but the carpet-enchanter headed toward the figure. It disappeared in the drizzle.

Amir urged the carpet faster, zipping up and over a street as a semi rumbled past, its headlights blinding. The carpet slowed as the buildings on the other side of the road loomed out of the rain. Raindrops pinged off their awnings. Water gurgled into a storm drain.

Edna stepped off the carpet with Amir. Water flooded her shoe.

"Clem?" The rain drowned her out. She tried again, louder. "Clementine?"

Someone was lounging against the building. But up close, even through her rain-spattered glasses, Edna could tell it wasn't Clem. Too tall, too broad, with deep brown skin and long locs.

Edna patted her hands on her wet dress. "Oh, I'm sorry."

"It's all right." He had a calm baritone. "Thought I'd wait out the rain, but it seemed best to wait outside the market, what with the disturbance. Come dry off."

Amir frowned. At least, Edna thought he did. His face was a smear.

"I do not understand," he said.

The figure beckoned them closer. "See for yourself."

Amir stiffened. Edna resisted the urge to grasp his hand reassuringly. Behind them, the carpet lowered to the ground, ready for a quick getaway.

The stranger sighed. "If you'd rather be wet..."

They stepped closer. Without any flash, bang, or weird glow to let you know anything magical had happened, they were suddenly dry. Amir relaxed.

"You see?" The stranger swept his locs out of his face and tied them back. The triangular tattoo on his wrist meant he was an elf, but Edna couldn't have said what nation. "A simple charm."

Amir bowed. "Forgive me. I should have realized. I'm afraid I am a little on edge, with the disturbance, as you say."

The elf turned unsettling brown eyes on Edna. Elves' eyes always seemed to see more than you could ever hope to see, things you might not want anyone else to see. Like their owners could read your thoughts—although elves always insisted this wasn't the case.

Edna would say the same thing if she could read people's thoughts, though.

"We're looking for our granddaughter," she said. "She ran off after dinner, upset over nothing. You know how teenagers are—"

Amir tried to look like it wasn't news to him that he and Edna had a mutual granddaughter. Kiernan—for that, of course, was who it was—tried to look like he believed it, when he already knew the old woman was the girl's mentor.

Admittedly, she didn't look much like a mentor. Kiernan would have expected an enchanter to mentor the Chosen One. Or a once-hale, now-withered warrior. Someone who could teach her to wield a Fateful Object. But the old woman looked like, well, an old woman. Someone's grandma. Someone whose idea of a good time was playing bingo on Thursday mornings and cooking too much food for the grandchildren.

"Why don't I help you find her?" He thrust out a hand. "Kiernan Abbott."

Edna shook his hand. "Edna Fisher."

Amir took the proffered hand hesitantly, introducing himself in a delicate voice.

"Not Amir Ansari the famous carpet-enchanter?" Kiernan asked as they set off into the rainy night together. Now, whatever charm had dried them off acted as an umbrella. Raindrops bounced off an invisible barrier overhead.

"I don't know about famous." Amir peered at him with sharp curiosity. "You are familiar with my work?"

Kiernan thought of his grandfather, the flying carpet he'd commissioned almost thirty years ago. He'd invited the carpet-enchanter to their home outside Bahir Dar to dine with him in celebration of the carpet's completion. "Not personally."

Amir's carpet drifted after them, bumping into Edna and Amir's ankles like a nervous puppy. By now, the night had quieted. The police had stopped yelling at the carpet-vendor and aerquestrian and moved into the market shed's shelter.

Benjamin's cell phone rang and rang.

"Shouldn't you get that?" Kiernan asked after a while, because asking distracted him from the carpet-enchanter. When he looked into the wizened face, he was five years old, sitting on the old man's knee as his grandfather questioned Amir about his work.

Edna fumbled in her handbag and tried to figure out how to answer the phone. The darned thing didn't have any buttons.

"Try swiping," Kiernan said helpfully.

"Swiping?"

The phone rang out but started up again immediately. Edna stopped walking to peer at the screen. No buttons, none. Just a green icon saying *answer* and a red icon saying *ignore* and a screen smudged with fingerprints. She frowned at it.

Her thumb brushed across the screen. Benjamin's voice was in her ear without her having any idea how it had happened.

"—should call someone if they don't—Edna? Edna! Is that you? Are you there?"

"Yes, dear, I'm fine."

"Where have you been? You were supposed to be back an hour ago. I tried to find you, but I can't see my own feet in this downpour—"

"I'm still looking."

He sighed, a crackle of static in her ear. "If it weren't for the sword, I'd say forget it, but I guess... You're sure you're okay? I can come find you if—"

She spent several minutes convincing him she was fine. As she babbled on, Kiernan started to wish he'd followed them to the girl rather than introducing himself. He could've waited until she was alone, killed her, and slipped away again. Perhaps he should've left it to his luck.

But his people had sayings about luck and what happened if you pushed it. His mother's voice rang in his head, warning him not to rely on luck when he didn't need to. And he didn't need to if the girl's companions led him straight to her.

Even if it meant listening to an old woman ramble into a phone.

At last, Edna hung up. They'd been walking as she talked, ending up back by the market. Nearby were an abandoned storefront and an alleyway half-hidden by trash cans.

In the alleyway, something rustled.

Edna stopped in her tracks. "Did you hear that?"

Amir shook his head, but Kiernan's eyes brightened. "Yeah. Over there."

More rustling. An angry whinny.

Edna stepped up to the trash cans. "Clem?"

An expletive. Someone sobbing. Edna picked her way around the trash cans.

A winged horse stood in the alleyway. It shook its mane, snorting. Clem huddled against the brick wall beside it, curled around her backpack and crying. Edna could only make out a few words in the midst of the crying, mostly "stupid" and "horse."

The horse glared as Edna neared.

"Oh, dear," she said, reaching out to pat it. "Hello. Nice horse..."

The horse snapped at her. She withdrew her hand.

"I can handle him," Kiernan said. "I didn't realize she'd run off on a flying horse."

"She didn't," Edna said.

Slowly, stiffly—carefully, and in the hopes the others would be able to get her up again—she sat beside the girl. Mud seeped into the seat of her house dress. Outside the circle of Kiernan's charm, she was soaked again.

"Clem?"

The rain plastered Clem's hair to her back. Her face shone wetly. She wiped her nose on her sleeve, crying harder.

Edna put an arm around her and rocked her like she'd rocked her son a long, long time ago. Clem thrust her fist at Edna. The ring that was the Sword of Destiny glinted in her hand.

"Take it," Clem said shakily. "Just leave me here. I can't do anything right."

"That's not true. You saved us when the van crashed."

"It's my fault the van crashed. I couldn't've stopped it without the extra magic."

Edna gave the girl a squeeze.

"Well, I'm certainly not leaving you here in the rain with the police and who knows who else looking for you."

Clem wiped her nose on her arm. "I'm sorry I ran away."

Edna kept her voice light, like she was within distance of some rare, shy creature that would run off if she spoke too loudly.

"You don't have to apologize to me. But I expect you to apologize to Mr. Ansari for upsetting his workshop."

Several feet away, Kiernan stroked the horse's neck and murmured in its ear until it calmed, looking ready to eat out of his hand. Amir stood closer, with the air of one who is trying not to eavesdrop but can hardly help it if people are going to talk about sensitive things within earshot.

"Why did you run off?" Edna asked. "I know you're disappointed about the delay, but—"

Clem curled back around the backpack, her wet hair hiding her face.

Edna touched her shoulder. "Clementine?"

The girl pushed her hair behind her ears. She wiped her eyes on her arm, streaking her mascara and eyeliner.

"Redway killed my sister," she said.

CHAPTER THIRTEEN

Outside, the rain pattered on. Inside, Amir's apartment was cozy. Kiernan dried them off magically before they entered, but that didn't stop Benjamin from dragging them inside, a pile of blankets already in his hands.

Clem batted him away with a terse, "I'm fine," even though she wasn't, and stalked into the living room. She sat before the blackened fireplace with her knees drawn up to her chin.

Amir and Edna didn't escape so easily. Benjamin threw blankets around their shoulders, his eyes wide and concerned. "Where have you *been,* why didn't you answer the *phone,* I was getting so *worried,* you could've caught your *death,* you're too old to be—"

The sight of Kiernan brought him up short.

"Who are you?" he asked.

Things were going shockingly well for Kiernan so far. Amir had invited him to come upstairs out of the rain with them. Edna was too worried about Clem to worry about him, and Clem, since mentioning her sister, was mostly trying to pretend the rest of them didn't exist.

Amir's niece was the only one who had viewed Kiernan with suspicion so far, but her suspicion wasn't particularly directed at him. Akida clearly thought her uncle was nuts for inviting them in after the damage Clem had done. She'd bidden him goodbye with a faint frown when her husband and two little girls picked her up.

For a moment, Kiernan thought Benjamin would be the one to finally object to his presence. Then Benjamin's eyes flickered over him, his expression familiar, and Kiernan stopped worrying. He didn't understand the big deal about his looks, but he knew people found him attractive.

The others had tried to explain it to him, once. Something about his cheekbones. And his eyes, or eyelashes. And his height and his muscles and how he dressed—in plain t-shirts and black jeans and black jackets and black boots, which made him look, according to them, cool and mysterious.

He still didn't get it.

But if it helped him stick with the group until he could get the girl alone and kill her, so be it.

So he introduced himself, with a smile intended to disarm Benjamin. It worked far too easily. Benjamin stared at his outstretched hand until he remembered shaking hands was a thing, fumbled through his own introduction, and rounded on the old folks before he could further embarrass himself.

Clucking over them, Benjamin soon forgot his awkwardness. He hustled them into Amir's living room, covering them with still more blankets.

The living room, like the rest of the apartment, was cramped and worn but meticulously tidy. The armchairs now occupied by Edna and Amir crowded either end of a coffee table with a cracked top. A loveseat sagged between them. A prayer rug was rolled up in the corner by the fireplace poker.

Amir and Edna snuggled into their blankets. The charm had dried them, but the bone-deep chill from the drenching rain remained. Benjamin sat on the sagging loveseat beside Kiernan, sneaking glances at the elf's mouth and cheekbones and muscular arms and looking away again whenever Kiernan caught him. Water boiled in the kitchen for tea. Fire crackled in the grate.

Clem watched the dancing flames. The others had questions, but she didn't like thinking about it. She'd been there that day. Barely twelve, visiting Marisol for her birthday after begging her parents for six solid months to let her go.

She tried to say something that wouldn't dig into her own head too much.

"She was a lot older than me."

There. That didn't matter. That didn't make her ache, not if she didn't think about it.

If she did, she remembered she was the oldest now.

"She was a Knight?"

Edna was knitting again. Clem tried not to take it personally. Knitting was Edna's natural state of existence.

Clem nodded. "She always wanted to be a Knight. She told me all these stories about great Knights and battles they'd been in and dragons they'd slain and how they saved everyone and gathered up the dragon's hoard afterward and got rich." She ran a hand through her damp hair. "I wanted to be just like her."

Marisol's laugh sounded in her head. Clem braided her hair in silence. The laugh morphed into a voice, Marisol's, quoting her favorite movie as she crept up on Clem with fingers raised.

My name is Inigo Montoya. You killed my father. Prepare to die.

And Marisol jumped on her and tickled her to death.

Clem squeezed her eyes shut against the memory.

In the kitchen, the kettle whistled. Amir hobbled off to make tea, but Benjamin leapt up from the loveseat, said, "I got it," and disappeared into the kitchen before Amir had taken two steps from his armchair. The carpet-enchanter sank back into his blankets gratefully.

"She must have been like my son." Fond pride crept into Edna's voice. "Eager to get right to the front lines in the fight against dragons."

Clem picked at her jeans. "Your son was a Knight?"

"Oh, goodness, some thirty years ago."

Benjamin returned with a tea tray in his hands and set it on the coffee table. Clem turned a hand back and forth in front of the fire. The flames waved back and forth with it. Her sister's voice fuzzed in her head like a YouTube video somewhere with spotty Internet access.

The six-fingered man!

Get me an orange, chamaca?

"Clementine?"

Marisol's voice melted into Edna's.

Clem's hands clenched into fists. "I was there when she—when it happened."

The silence in the apartment deepened, broken only by the popping and crackling of the flames as they danced and flickered. Clem hugged her knees to her chest.

She was remembering.

She was twelve, and she was out in the city. She'd wanted to watch the squires train, to see what Marisol was learning, but they wouldn't let her. She tried, once. Marisol's friend Lena had shown her a broken window in the gym, a tree next to it. The drill sergeant caught Clem in the tree, peering through the window, and yelled at her. Said he didn't want her distracting his troops.

So many places inside the compound were off-limits—it was so boring. Nothing what Clem had thought it would be like, when she spent so much time begging her parents to let her visit.

She spent a lot of time outside the gates. Sometimes, Marisol gave her errands to run; squires didn't get much free time.

Get me an orange, chamaca?

"Clementine? Are you all right?"

Clem hugged her knees tighter.

"I thought," she mumbled, "if I found some oranges for her, they'd see how grown-up I was and let me watch the squires train. Or maybe they'd tell me I was just the kind of person they were looking for and let me sign up right away."

Hardly any oranges were for sale in the market. When she found some, they were small and shriveled. Some were white with gunk. A bell rang to release the Knights from morning training, but Clem stayed at the orange cart, haggling with its owner, who was as small and shriveled as her wares.

Clem picked out the smallest, least-shriveled, least-gunky oranges.

The bell sounded again.

It didn't ring this time. It gonged deeply, throbbing in her ears. Too early for the lunch bell. The wrong sound, too.

The market broke into panic. The orange-seller shooed Clem away, closing her cart. Clem tried to give her money, but she wouldn't take it.

Please, Clem said, *I just want some oranges, my sister wants oranges,* but the woman told her to go to hell.

By the time Clem made it back to the compound, the whole place roared with flames. The dormitories. The mess hall. The gym. Fire devoured the tree she'd climbed; the heat had shattered the unbroken windows. People screamed in the upper floors of the dormitories. They leapt from the windows, desperate to escape buildings whose doors were barred by flames and smoke. The sky was black with dragons.

In front of Amir's fireplace, Clem buried her head in her knees with a low sob. Dragons swam before her eyes, a whole flight of them. The fire flickered on her knees, glaring as big and bright as that other fire four years ago.

Couch springs creaked. Someone sat cross-legged beside her, putting an arm around her. Benjamin. It would've shocked her if she'd been capable of shock right now; she was pretty sure he didn't like her. Most adults didn't. She had a "problem with authority figures," according to her teachers.

To be fair, Clem wasn't sure she liked him, either. He was bossy and overly cautious. Clem didn't like bossy people—her *problem with authority figures* again—and she didn't like people who hesitated instead of acting.

Right now, that didn't matter. She focused hard on his arm around her. His solidity and warmth at her side. She squeezed her eyes tight and then forced them open.

The dragons were gone. The fire was a small, cheerful fire in a blackened grate.

She exhaled shakily. A fat silver tear rolled down her cheek, gleaming in the firelight. She dashed it away, but another followed, and another, and another.

"Sorry," she said in a muffled voice.

Edna gripped her teacup tightly. Bad enough, thinking Clem's parents were dead. Learning it was her sister was somehow worse. Maybe because Edna knew exactly how Clem's parents must have felt, losing a child.

"Clem—"

Clem wiped her eyes. "Don't."

Edna gulped down half her tea. It had gone cold.

"If you don't want to talk about it—" Benjamin started.

"Don't," Clem repeated, but she let him keep sitting with her, begrudgingly grateful he hadn't left her side when she snapped at him. Her arms tightened on her knees. "I found her outside the gym."

The gym was still burning. What was left of it. A dragon stood nearby. Clem grabbed a stick and ran at it, too terrified for her sister to be scared of the beast. She just wanted Marisol. She even didn't know what she meant to do. It was a dragon. She was a twelve-year-old with a stick.

She saw him bending over something on the ground. Redway. She didn't know who he was, then. But this man *must* have been involved in the attack, because he stood beside the dragon like it didn't bother him. Like it was his pet.

He was dressed in leather, with a leather flight mask covering the upper half of his face, revealing only his eyes: a bright, paralyzing blue.

Marisol was sprawled on the ground in front of him.

Clem screamed. He turned those blue eyes on her—

"What did he do then?" Edna whispered.

Clem put her head in her hands, exhausted. She felt older than Edna.

"He left."

"He left?"

Benjamin shifted at Clem's side.

"We heard Knights shouting nearby, I think they heard me scream, and he swung himself onto the dragon's back and flew off."

In the movies, when someone dies, there's a moment when a person who loves them runs to their side. Last words are exchanged, of love, of forgiveness. A plea not to die.

This was not like that.

Marisol was dead by the time Clem reached her.

"Oh, Clem—" Edna said, but the girl cut her off with a ferocious, *"Don't."*

Edna clutched her tea but said nothing more.

Clem shrugged off Benjamin's arm. "I'm going to bed."

"Good night," Edna called softly. The girl waved vaguely in response.

Amir hurried after her to make the spare room comfortable. She and Edna would share that bed, and Benjamin would sleep on the couch. They'd offered to find a hotel, though they didn't know how they'd either get to one or pay for it, but Amir insisted they stay until he completed their carpet.

Benjamin sighed, leaning back on his elbows. Edna settled deeper into her armchair with a groan.

Kiernan turned his gaze from the fire for the first time in hours.

"You must be uncomfortable," he said to Edna. "Surely you'd prefer to retire for the night?"

Edna closed her eyes. "Standing up will be much more uncomfortable. Being old does that to a body, not that I suppose you'd know anything about it. You could be five hundred years old and I'd be none the wiser."

He huffed a laugh. "I'm thirty-two."

She cracked an eye. Strange, thinking of an elf as such a young, ordinary, human age. Then again, it wasn't as if they sprang into being from nowhere, already five hundred years old.

Amir bustled into the living room with extra bedclothes.

"Have you anywhere to stay for the night?" he asked Kiernan.

"'Fraid not. I came into town for a seminar on dragons and thought I'd end my day at the market before heading out again, but with the uproar and the rain—"

Benjamin twisted around. "A seminar on dragons?"

Kiernan laughed softly. "Draconology's not a large field, I grant you, nor a popular one, for obvious reasons. And difficult, obviously, because few people can get close to a dragon without being eaten or burnt up, and forays into Dominion are—"

"Suicidal," Edna said.

"Not always. I've taken several trips, gotten pretty far in. Barring its inhabitants, I probably have more experience traveling through Dominion than almost anyone in the world."

Edna and Benjamin glanced at each other. Someone familiar with Dominion would come in handy if they could convince him to guide them there.

"You're welcome to stay," Amir said, "if you do not mind the living room floor."

"Much obliged," Kiernan said.

Benjamin helped Edna down the hall. They stopped outside the spare room. A sliver of light from the fire flickered across Clem's face. She'd already fallen asleep. With her makeup washed away, she looked younger than ever.

"Where'd you pick up an elf?" Benjamin asked absently.

Edna swayed and clamped down on his arm. "He helped us find Clem. Good thing, too. She'd stolen a flying horse. Or tried to."

Benjamin rubbed his forehead. "She's a mess. But with a story like that, I guess I don't blame her."

Edna didn't say anything.

"Are you all right?"

She smiled despite herself. His expression was medical, analytical, ready to examine her on the spot if he thought she had the slightest physical ailment.

"You worry too much. I'm fine."

"Hmmm."

She whapped him with her handbag, not as hard as she normally would have. He grinned.

"Do you think he'd take us to Dominion?" Edna said.

Benjamin's grin faded.

"I don't know how we could explain why we want to go. Not without telling him you're the—" He mouthed the words *Chosen One*. "If he's really got the experience he says he does, I mean, he's probably working on mapping it out. The Knights would pay through the nose for something like that. I can't see someone guiding us for free when they have that kind of opportunity."

Kiernan had settled on the floor by the fire and lay on his back with his hands linked behind his head.

"We'll think of something," Edna said.

But she didn't think of Kiernan as she lay tucked in bed beside Clem, listening to the girl's soft snoring. She didn't even think of Redway.

She thought of her son.

She thought of Marisol Rodriguez.

She thought of cities on fire and the squire in the newspaper and how he'd looked so strained, his shoulders bowed under the weight of another Knight's body.

She lay awake for hours. The others had long since fallen asleep.

Then, in the still, dark night, floorboards creaked.

Edna sat up.

It was probably nothing. So many people were in the apartment right now.

"Hello?" she called in a cracked whisper.

Clem turned over without waking up, no longer snoring.

Edna grabbed her cane and crept out of the bedroom.

CHAPTER FOURTEEN

Rain pounded the windows. Edna stole through the apartment with one hand on the wall. The floorboards chilled her feet; her slippers had gone into storage with her other things.

Benjamin was snoring on the couch. She considered waking him, not that she knew what she'd say. He'd ask what was wrong, and she'd have to tell him she'd heard floorboards creaking. In a hundred-year-old building. With an apartment full of people.

His foot dangled over the arm of the couch. A street lamp outside flickered dimly on his sock.

Another floorboard creaked.

Edna tested the boards beneath her feet. Nothing.

In the dark maw of the kitchen, something thumped to the floor.

Benjamin shifted without waking. In the kitchen, a voice spat out a low, guttural word, unfamiliar but unmistakably an oath.

Edna shuffled toward it, gripping her cane. She told herself she didn't have anything to worry about. Herself didn't listen.

"Amir?"

Silence.

Edna felt around for a switch. Light flooded the room.

A figure bent over one of the kitchen chairs.

"Good heavens, Kiernan!" Edna massaged her chest. "You scared the living daylights out of me."

She laughed weakly. Her heart pounded like a jackhammer.

He hooked his fingers through the straps of Clem's backpack. It had been sitting on a chair since they'd returned from the market but was now on the floor.

"I had hoped my clumsiness didn't wake anyone." He set the backpack back on the chair. "I couldn't find the light."

Edna sat, heart still hammering. She felt sick.

Kiernan sat across from her. "Are you all right?"

The sickening sensation ebbed away. She took several deep breaths. Her heartbeat calmed.

"Just peachy. You gave me quite a scare."

"I didn't mean to."

"I know, dear."

Kiernan's brows contracted like he expected her to expire right there in the kitchen. She chuckled at his expression, but it made her feel sick again, so she stopped.

"Can I get you anything?" he asked.

"A glass of water, please."

Kiernan searched the cabinets for a glass. It occurred to Edna that Clem's story had obliterated her lie that she and Amir had been out searching for their granddaughter. If Clem were their granddaughter, it implied that they were, ahem, acquainted in a certain way, in which case she probably would have gone to bed with Amir instead of in the spare room, and she also would have known which cabinet contained the drinkware.

Kiernan filled a glass with water, set it before her, and resumed his seat. He was wearing the clothes in which they'd found him, the black denim jacket and black jeans and even his boots.

"What are you doing up?" Edna asked.

His lips quirked. "Couldn't sleep. I spend a lot of time outdoors in my studies. It's difficult getting used to sleeping inside again."

His studies. Draconology, of all things.

What were the odds, Edna wondered, of running into someone else with his kind of knowledge?

"What's it like, Dominion?" she blurted.

The corner of his mouth turned up. "Jungle, mostly. Highlands. Some mountains."

"What else?"

"Rains a lot."

"What *else?*"

He straightened the cuffs of his jacket. "Planning a trip, are you?"

She sipped her water. "Of course not."

She wasn't sure how to ask him to guide them through Dominion. It would take more lies, and she was garbage at lying. But she couldn't tell him she was the Chosen One.

She had no idea he was wishing he could offer to guide them through Dominion, but he had to pretend he didn't know they wanted to go. He couldn't offer until they asked.

Benjamin wandered in, yawning.

"What are you two doing up so late?"

"Oh, you know me." Edna smiled at him. "Always scheming something."

"Perhaps I'd better get back to bed," Kiernan said. "It seems I'm on course to wake the whole household."

Edna wrenched her thoughts away from Dominion.

"Nonsense. I'm sure Benjamin would be interested in hearing about your studies, if you don't mind."

"Not at all."

Kiernan pulled out the chair beside him. Benjamin sat, feeling somewhat sheepish next to someone looking cool and mysterious in that black denim, and wide awake to boot. Benjamin's feet were bare, and he wore sweatpants and the kind of ratty t-shirt he'd sleep in for years before finally throwing it out. Not how he would've preferred to be seen by a guy with Kiernan's cheekbones and locs and muscles. Benjamin, while tall and broad-shouldered, was a little bit dad-bod and a little bit too aware of it for his own comfort, especially dressed as he was now.

But his interest in all things magical—even dragons—quickly overtook his awkwardness. He peppered Kiernan with questions, leaning toward him without realizing he was doing it.

"What's the closest you've ever gotten to a dragon?"

"A mountain dragon?"

"Yeah, I thought that's the main focus of—wait—"

Benjamin may have been fascinated, but Edna was busy thinking about Kiernan's studies. How much he knew about dragons. How much he knew about Dominion.

"How many different kinds of dragons have you actually seen? How many different kinds of dragons do you *study?*"

"Mountain dragons are my primary focus."

Benjamin flinched, suddenly too aware, as usual, of his own excitement.

"Sorry," he stammered, "I don't mean to ask so many questions—"

The corner of Kiernan's mouth turned up. "It's all right. I'll tell you anything you want to know. You were asking about different types of dragons?"

They needed him. Shame he wouldn't know the location of Redway's evil lair, but an experienced draconologist was nothing to snit your nose at.

At Kiernan's encouragement, Benjamin's eyes shone, and his enthusiasm for the topic redoubled.

"Well, yeah, because there are, like, four major subgroups, right?" He scooched his chair closer to Kiernan's, counting off on his fingers. "Mountain, aquatic, grasslands, and I forget the last one—"

Kiernan laughed softly. "Arboreal. Pretty much all the smaller species."

"Right—"

Edna downed half her water.

"—and that's the newest subgroup, right? I saw an article about a new species discovered in Sri Lanka, I think, it's only six inches long or something—"

Edna steepled her fingers. "If we wanted to go to Dominion—"

Benjamin blinked like he'd forgotten she was there. Kiernan smiled crookedly.

"If we wanted to go," she repeated, "could you take us?"

Benjamin's eyes widened. He glanced at Kiernan, his brow furrowing.

Then he realized how close he'd gotten to Kiernan's chair and jerked away.

But jerking away might look suspicious, given the change of topic, so he scooched closer again, so quickly his chair threatened to tip over. It scraped horribly on the floor as he righted it. Kiernan huffed a laugh, steadying Benjamin's chair with a hand.

"I can't see why you'd want to," he said to Edna, as Benjamin made frantic facial expressions at her beside him, "but I could, if I thought you had a good reason. I wouldn't endanger an old woman's life for nothing."

Edna's fingers tapped on her glass. If only she had more time—as if she could've come up with a good lie regardless. Her lies so far wouldn't have stood up to the puff of air the optometrist used to test for glaucoma.

She frowned at Benjamin. He looked so suspicious, eyeballing her that way. She wasn't born yesterday. She wasn't planning to tell a stranger she was the Chosen One.

Kiernan glanced at Benjamin's twitching face. "Are you all right?"

Benjamin stopped making faces. "It's a tic I get sometimes."

"I'm only asking," Edna said.

Kiernan drummed his fingers on the table. "So this has nothing to do with your granddaughter's dead sister?"

Benjamin made a mouse-like noise but passed it off as a sneeze.

Kiernan's mouth twisted into a smile. "Come on. You didn't really think I bought that? For one thing, if—what's her name?"

Benjamin trained his gaze on the tabletop.

"Clem," Edna said.

"If Clem were your granddaughter, you'd already know her sister was dead, and why and how. I suppose Mr. Ansari isn't your husband, either?"

"Afraid not," Edna said absently. She'd had an idea. "I never was married."

Benjamin fussed with the hem of his t-shirt. "I never knew that."

"Oh, everyone always assumes. I stopped correcting them long ago."

Edna folded her hands, meeting Kiernan's gaze with difficulty. Those durned elf eyes burned right into you. Maybe he could read her mind.

Maybe this was a bad idea.

"It's true," she said. "Amir isn't my husband. He's working on a carpet for us, one that can get us to Dominion. And Clem isn't my granddaughter."

Benjamin kicked her under the table. She nudged him back with a toe. He didn't need to worry. She wasn't stupid.

Perhaps, if they hadn't been so preoccupied with each other, one of them might have noticed the gleam in Kiernan's eyes.

Clem would be angry, but it was her lie anyway.

"She's the Chosen One," Edna said.

Benjamin relaxed. Marginally.

"Is that a good enough reason for you?" Edna asked.

Kiernan leaned back in his chair. "I'd say so. When do we head out?"

Edna crept back to the spare room a quarter of an hour later. Kiernan had been planning to return to the Amazon soon to further his studies; he was happy to guide them as far as he could. He might have seen through Edna's other lies with ease, spur-of-the-moment fabrications she hadn't realized were so flimsy until later, but he seemed to really believe Clem was the Chosen One.

It did make a lot more sense.

Maybe Clem would be in danger if people thought she was the Chosen One. But after all, it had been Clem's lie first. It was Clem's lie first.

The quilt was bunched around Clem's feet. Edna smoothed it and tucked her in.

The girl stirred. "Abuela?"

"I'm afraid not, dear. It's just me."

Clem sat up, rubbing her eyes. "What time is it?"

Edna closed the door. "I haven't the foggiest, but never mind that now."

She told Clem about their deal with Kiernan. A half burnt-out street lamp lit the room dimly.

Clem's curls hung mussed around her face, hiding her expression. "Why exactly does he think I'm the Chosen One?"

"We told him you were."

Clem said nothing. Edna sighed.

"Oh, all right. I told him. But we couldn't tell him the truth, could we? I don't know about you, but I can't think of another reason anyone would want to go to Dominion."

"Draconology."

"Yes," Edna said, "and I'm sure he'd believe you and I were draconologists."

"Benjamin's the draconologist."

"And he's taking his grandmother and little sister on a pleasant sightseeing trip to Dominion because it's fun for the whole family?"

Clem considered this. "I guess not."

"Besides," Edna said, "you told *me* you were the Chosen One."

Bedsprings creaked as Clem shifted. The rain beat the windows with renewed vigor. The streetlamp's light wavered.

"We don't know anything about him."

"We know he has experience traveling through Dominion. Isn't that enough?"

Thunder cracked like cannon fire. Clem lay back under the covers.

"I thought I would be the Chosen One." She curled onto her side to face Edna. "I guess they picked you because of your son."

Edna flushed. "Oh—no—no, he died almost thirty years ago. I really don't know why they chose me."

Clem turned onto her back, contemplating the ceiling. Edna slipped in gingerly beside her. Thunder rumbled, nearby but not overhead this time. The rain lightened from a gale to a squall.

Clem's phone pinged.

She jerked upright and grabbed it. "We don't need him."

"Why not? Have you got a tour guide hidden in that backpack of yours?"

"No."

"Well, then."

Lightning flashed, but the rain lightened more definitely.

Clem held up her phone. "Because we don't need to go to Dominion."

CHAPTER FIFTEEN

"What do you mean, we're not going to Dominion?" Benjamin asked sleepily the next morning.

He was seated at the kitchen table with Clem, Edna, and Kiernan. Clem hadn't been sure about including Kiernan. They didn't need him. They weren't going to Dominion.

But Edna pointed out that he was tall, strong, and probably handy with the bow and quiver leaning against the mantel, all of which was sure to be useful somewhere down the line. What if they ended up in Dominion after all? It was a million to one they'd run into someone else with his experience.

Clem was too tired to raise further objections. So there he was, sitting beside Benjamin, more awake than the rest of them despite Edna's suspicion that he hadn't slept.

The rain had stopped, but the bright, damp sheen outside reflected light into the room. Amir had set breakfast to making itself and headed downstairs to work on their carpet. Eggs scrambled themselves on the stove. A bowl of figs glided from the counter to the table.

Clem glowered. Purple crescents ringed her eyes. "Why the hell would we go to Dominion, where there are plenty of dragons to roast us alive and Redway is on his home turf, when we could take him by surprise somewhere else?"

Turkey bacon laid itself into a pan with a sizzle. When this was over, Edna thought, she needed to learn to cook like that.

"She has a point," she said, counting her stitches. "And trekking through Dominion is bound to be hard on an old lady's knees."

Kiernan raised an eyebrow. "I thought that's why you needed a flying carpet."

"We'll still need that." Clem reached for the coffee pot, but it lifted itself off the table and poured her a cup. She scowled at it. "Cut it out. I can pour my own coffee."

A spoon dipped itself into the sugar bowl and hovered beside Clem's mug, but she shoved it away.

Benjamin gave a long, shuddering yawn but ducked as plates zipped out of a cabinet to set themselves on the table. The pans drifted off the stove, depositing eggs and turkey bacon onto the plates.

Kiernan reached for a fig. "I'm not sure how you plan to find Redway without going to Dominion."

Clem unzipped her backpack. She may have objected to his presence, but she liked pretending to be the Chosen One: she got to be in charge for a change. "Look."

She produced a leather journal crammed with loose pages, charts, and photographs. The binding was cracked, the pages torn, the corners scuffed. The papers inside were in worse shape still.

Clem opened the journal carefully. "I've been tracking dragon attacks since Marisol died."

She set aside maps, news clippings, and photographs of shadowy figures and distant dragons, all covered in cramped handwriting.

"Most of them aren't far from Dominion. A single dragon or maybe a pair, like in the old stories. Mountain dragons are supposed to be really territorial. But this attack wasn't some random dragon, it was a whole flight of them. And people. And there have been more like it since, a lot more." She examined a page. "Okay, a lot more when you consider this is pretty much unheard of in the history of ever."

She extracted a square of paper folded over and over on itself.

"How have you been tracking dragon attacks?" Kiernan asked.

Clem raised an eyebrow with supreme disdain. "Newspapers. Internet. The same way everyone else does."

He nodded to himself. Edna started another row of stitches.

"Anyway," Clem said primly, turning back to her paper, "for a long time I was really frustrated, because the attacks seemed completely random, except that most of them were on places heavily populated with Knights, which, like, duh. Although if he really wanted to fuck the Knights up, he'd go after the AKG."

Kiernan shifted in his chair, but Edna looked at Clem blankly.

Clem sighed. "The Assembly of Knights-General?"

"Oh, that," Edna said, intelligently.

"They make all major decisions for the entire organization. If he took them out, the Knights would be scrambling to find new leadership, and I guarantee the infighting would make them easier to pick off. So that's what I would do," Clem said, as if considering what she would do if she were a sorcerer destroying cities and people was no big deal. "But last year..."

"He started heading northwest," Benjamin said, sounding more awake.

"Yeah."

Clem smoothed out the paper, which now took up half the table. It was a map from inside the Amazon basin northward all the way to Canada. Pinholes dotted it from top to bottom, clustered heavily in the American Southwest. Ink starred the sites of major attacks. Clem's cramped, rounded handwriting recorded numbers dead and injured.

But only a thin line drawn in Sharpie made it seem like Redway was heading northwest instead of attacking at random.

"Whoa." Benjamin leaned in for a better look. "You did all this?"

"Duh," Clem said.

"What's northwest?" Edna asked, feeling like the Chosen One should know a lot more than she did.

Clem shrugged. "A lot of stuff. Major training camps. Plenty of Fateful Objects he might want for some reason."

"But which one is he heading for?"

"No clue."

Clem's plate shuffled closer to her. She pushed it away from the precious map.

"You really should eat, dear."

"I'm not hungry."

Kiernan started in on his eggs, though they'd grown cold. "I'm not sure I see what your plan is. If you don't know where Redway is headed or what he's planning—"

Clem flipped through her journal, to a page marked with a frayed ribbon. A dozen thumbnails of women were taped inside.

"I don't need to know," she said, "because she's going to tell me."

Each portrait was an ID photo, head-on, unsmiling, but each showed a different woman. Blonde, brunette, red-headed, even a gray-haired old woman who glowered up from the page. They had different eyes, different noses, different lips. The only similarity was their clothing. Each wore a Knight's uniform: a black jacket with gold epaulets, a single bar on the left shoulder—the mark of a squire.

"Which one?" Edna asked.

Clem pushed the journal closer to her. "They're all the same. Can't you tell?"

She certainly could not tell. They were all different.

Kiernan stabbed at his eggs.

Benjamin examined the pictures. "Yeah—yeah, you're right. Wow. *Wow.* I can't believe you figured that out from *photographs.* Good job, kid."

"I'm not a kid," Clem said, but she pinkened at the praise. Her plate shuffled toward her, but she shoved it away again.

Edna pored over the photographs, mystified by whatever the two young people saw in them. "They all look different to me."

"That's because they are different." Clem traced one of the photographs with a finger, still pink. "It's a spell. If you look close, you can see signs of it around the eyes."

"It's the same woman," Benjamin said, "but she's disguised herself with magic."

Kiernan's jaw clenched.

Edna returned to her eggs, stumped. "I'll take your word for it. Why are we interested in them? Her?"

Clem turned another page. Dates and names covered this one.

"I figured from pretty early on it had to do with the Knights, whatever Redway's doing. So I've been keeping tabs on them, too. And I noticed a woman enlists at each base before an attack and defects right after, only it's always a different woman. But it was too coincidental, you know? So I looked into them and noticed the evidence of spellwork."

"So your plan is to find this woman," Kiernan said skeptically, "and ask her nicely, and she'll tell you what Redway is up to?"

"No. My plan is to find this woman and tell her there will be consequences if she doesn't tell me what Redway is up to."

Her voice was ice. Edna was glad she was on their side.

Or at least she wasn't against them.

Kiernan attacked what was left of his eggs. Clem folded her map back into a square tiny enough to fit into the overflowing journal. Her plate pouted at the other end of the table.

"How do you know it'll be any easier to find this woman than Redway?" Benjamin asked. "Good job with this research, seriously, but—"

"Dominion's huge. I don't know where we'd even start looking for him."

"Yeah, but this woman could be literally anywhere."

Clem slipped the map back into her journal. "We have no way of knowing where in Dominion Redway is based. This is a narrower search."

She reached into a different pocket of her backpack and pulled out her phone. She poked at the screen, read something, pinkened again, swiped it away, and set the phone on the table so the others could see.

Onscreen was another photograph like those in the journal: an unsmiling woman in the black jacket of a Knight, with a gold bar on her shoulder. She had olive skin and shining black hair in a severe bun, thin shoulders, and dark eyes blank in a government-issued-ID way.

"She enlisted yesterday," Clem said. "Monica Evans. Santa Alvara. If she's the one, we can expect an attack on the city within a few days. A week if we're lucky."

Kiernan scared them with a violent coughing fit; he'd swallowed some egg the wrong way. His fork clattered to the floor.

Benjamin pounded on his back until the fit passed. "Are you all right?"

Kiernan held up a hand. "I'm fine."

Benjamin glanced him over with an air of professional authority, his sheepishness of the night before forgotten in the face of a potential medical emergency.

Kiernan coughed again, briefly. "Really."

"Hmm," Benjamin said, but he retrieved Kiernan's fork without comment.

Edna reached for her knitting.

"Thank you," she said to her plate. It dipped into a dishware version of a bow and flew off to the sink. Clem's plate joined it sulkily. "Santa Alvara, isn't that where Sir Carmichael was from?"

Sir Carmichael Barstow, the first and only Knight known to have killed a mountain dragon single-handedly, back in 1871, armed only with a snuff box and a mostly empty book of matches. Everyone assumed some serious magic had been involved, but most stories involved Sir Carmichael using his wits to fashion a MacGyver-like dragon-killing machine out of the contents of his pockets.

Clem nodded. "The first chivalric school he built is still in use, but you can tour it and stuff. Marisol always wanted to go."

"A week doesn't give us much time," Edna said.

Clem scowled. "That's why we need to get going. As soon as our carpet is done."

CHAPTER SIXTEEN

Red awoke with magic crashing at his insides. The nightmare was back, worse than it had been in years. He'd plummeted over a cliff into a ravine gaping with fanged mouths and the bloodied swords of Knights.

Sweat trickled down his forehead. He fought his magic under control, waiting for the mouths and swords to fade into the darkness.

He touched Shira's shoulder. She stirred but didn't wake. Red curled around her athletic form, burying his face in her curls.

The others didn't understand his need to have someone in bed with him. No matter how he denied it, they were certain he and Shira were sleeping together in a sense that involved suggestive eyebrow movements and stifled giggles. They ribbed him about it every chance they got.

Never in front of Shira, though. She didn't take kindly to teasing.

He did actually like her, but sex wasn't what he wanted from a bedmate and never had been. He wanted her solidity. She was wiry and muscular and real, serious and no-nonsense—everything the nightmare was not.

She'd never once comforted him when he'd awoken sweating and shaking, never patted his back or told him it was just a dream. Most nights, she didn't wake.

He didn't know why she'd agreed to be his bedmate, when he'd awkwardly approached her a year after her arrival, but he wasn't about to look a flying horse in the pinfeathers. She was something to hold onto when the night teetered around him.

He slipped out of bed, groped around in the dark for a t-shirt, and stepped out into the hallway.

The keep was silent. Red put a hand on the wall. He didn't need it to find his way; he'd carved out most of the mountainside himself. He felt the whole place in his bones, in his magic. But the rock was cool and rough. Solid. His breathing steadied as he focused on it.

He went up to the kitchen, a small chamber with shelves and counters carved into the stone walls by magic. Braids of garlic and strings of dried vegetables hung from the ceiling. Preserves lined the shelves in mason jars of varying sizes. In the corner, firewood stood in splintered stacks beside the ancient woodstove they'd salvaged on a supply run years ago.

A fire crackled in the woodstove. In the room's center, Old Joe sat at the table, a rough-hewn thing Red had built himself when he was young and even angrier. Joe had given him the project herself. Red had made it by hand; he hadn't yet begun to harness his magic. He hadn't known how to use the paltry tools they had, either, and the table had been splintery and uneven. Now, after almost three decades of breakfasts and coffees and late-night conversations, it was worn smooth.

Potatoes piled high on the table. Joe sat beside them with a knife, peering at a half-peeled potato through her ancient reading glasses like she'd found a message there.

Red pulled up a chair. "You're up late."

"I'm up early. Couldn't sleep?"

He shrugged and grabbed a potato, which peeled itself in midair.

Joe grunted. "Show-off."

Red grinned and set another potato peeling. Joe had learned magic alongside him, to a point, but it had never come as easily to her as it had to him. At last, she'd declared, "You can't teach an old wizard new spells," which wasn't actually true, and given up. Household tasks weren't beyond her reach, but she preferred doing them by hand.

They peeled potatoes in silence. Then Joe said, "I don't like it," and Red knew she wasn't talking about his use of magic.

His next potato peeled itself faster than necessary. "We've been through this."

"Too much can go wrong." Joe scratched her ear with the handle of her knife. "There'll be so many Knights in town."

Red gritted his teeth, willing the potatoes to peel themselves more slowly. It didn't work. Sweat dripped down his forehead.

"That's the point. The more Knights there are in one place, the more we can get rid of in one go."

Joe shook her head. They'd had the same argument every day since Lena left for Santa Alvara.

"I don't like it," Joe repeated. "They're not stupid. That many Knights in one place, if they're armed—"

"They won't be armed. It's a conference."

"—there's the school right there. Think how many more Knights, how much more weaponry—"

"Enough!"

Half a dozen potatoes shot from the pile and smashed into the wall, exploding in a smattering of pale, starchy flesh.

Red blinked sweat from his eyes. He was on his feet, somehow.

Joe regarded him over her glasses as if he were a naughty child, but her voice trembled. "Shoddy. I'm right here. You'd think one might have hit me."

His hands clenched and unclenched at his sides.

"We leave in five days," he said, "whether you like it or not."

He kicked his chair aside and stormed off. Magic stabbed at his insides, sparking in his eyes and fingertips, lighting the keep with red flashes. Pressure built in his head. He kept going, faster and faster until he was sprinting. He burst through the front door into the warm, humid air of a Dominion dawn.

With a yell, he released the magic, hurled a bolt of fire onto the rocks below. They cracked and scorched.

Red ran a hand over his face, gulping down air. It hadn't been this bad in weeks.

The sun rose swiftly over Dominion, drenching the mountain in color. Wisps of cloud chased each other into the sunrise. Light spread over the jungle below. Steam wafted through the foliage, a sign of river dragons surfacing beneath the canopy. Red calmed, lost in Dominion's beauty.

Rocks clattered nearby. Copernicus, his favorite dragon, slipped on scree lower down the mountain.

Red snorted. Copernicus glared at him out of snakelike orange eyes.

"Just fly up, you idiot."

Copernicus made a noise halfway between a roar and a hiss.

Red shrugged. "Fine. Stay there."

Copernicus made the noise again, lifting into the sky with a flap of his wings that ruffled Red's hair. The ground trembled as Copernicus landed and padded over to Red, curling on the ground with his massive head in Red's lap. Normally, when he did this, Red told him off, but he didn't mind just now.

Not that it made a difference anyway. Once a dragon decides to do something, you have to wait for it to decide it's done.

"Joe said I'd find you out here."

Red glanced around so quickly he cricked his neck. Shira slipped out the front door and sat beside him. Her tawny curls blew around her face in the morning breeze. Red loved her hair.

"I didn't mean to scare her," he said. "I just—"

"Got angry. I thought you were working on that."

She tied her hair back. She had high cheekbones, bronze skin, and dark, unsmiling eyes. She was beautiful. And showered. And fully dressed. And he was in a sweat-soaked t-shirt and his boxers.

"I *am* working on it," he said shortly. Copernicus huffed at him. Red cuffed the side of the dragon's head. "I—"

A headache was coming on again. Red sparks leapt from his fingers.

He held his breath. The sparks abated.

"I'm so angry," he said, "all the time."

Shira gazed at the jungle. "We all have things to be angry about."

She was so calm, so damnably calm, and it reminded him of Joe, and her doubts, and their fight, and his anger. The sparks returned, biting his legs as they leapt from his fingers. The headache intensified over his left eye. Copernicus shifted in his lap but didn't get up.

He wanted Shira to lecture him, to pick a fight. He wanted her to give him a reason to get angry so he wouldn't have to sit here, holding it back, shoving it down.

Instead she sat in silence, her chin resting on her knees. Her eyes followed the steam billowing up from the river.

Red's headache spread. Copernicus's massive head weighed down on him.

He smacked the dragon away, leaping to his feet. Copernicus shook his head with a growl. Shira ignored them.

In the middle of the night, Red loved her for never reacting to anything. Right now, he hated her for it.

"Shira."

Rage simmered in his voice, but she didn't turn her head. She was so calm she sounded bored.

"Yes?"

Lightning crackled in his eyes, anger crashed at his insides like a tide, and the pain in his head was building, blinding—

Then he was on Copernicus, and they were winging northward through the sky, with the wind rushing so loud in Red's ears that it drowned the sound of her shouting after him.

CHAPTER SEVENTEEN

Amir spent two days in his workshop from sun-up to sundown, and they were the longest two days of Edna's life. She longed to get some fresh air and explore the market properly, but Benjamin worried someone would recognize Clem from her carpet theft. With Kiernan there, they couldn't train with the sword, either. He might be suspicious if Clem, the supposed Chosen One, taught Edna to use a sword that only the Chosen One could use.

Cooped up in the apartment and impatient to get going, Clem fidgeted endlessly. She clacked her teeth. She stalked through the apartment, from fireplace to fridge and back. She picked fights with Benjamin about whether it was acceptable to magically translate Amir's books–most on carpet-enchanting, the rest volumes of poetry, and almost all in Arabic or Urdu–into English so they could read them.

"You could translate them back afterwards," Edna said, in an attempt to keep the peace, but Benjamin snorted.

"Yeah, right. They'll probably get stuck that way if she's the one enchanting them."

Clem swore at him. Edna sighed. Benjamin didn't retort only because he caught a glimpse of amusement in Kiernan's eyes and shut up, embarrassed.

The only reprieve came at day's end, when Amir traipsed upstairs with dust in his beard and the young people called an unspoken truce. Clem rummaged through the cabinets, trying to remember how her mom made pollo guisado. Benjamin and Kiernan set the table. After dinner, while Benjamin and Kiernan did the dishes, Amir settled in his armchair and read Urdu poetry aloud to Clem. Edna brought the carpet-enchanter a strong cup of coffee, worrying over his exhaustion and recalling wistfully the days when Percival and his father were both alive.

The third afternoon, they sat in the living room with sunlight pouring in on them. Edna was working on her scarf again. Benjamin paged through a book on carpet-enchanting, this one in English, while Kiernan read over his shoulder. Clem contemplated the barren fireplace, scowling at nothing in particular.

When Amir appeared on the stairs, smiling, they looked up.

Clem scrambled to her feet. "Is it done?"

"Let him breathe a minute!" Edna said, but she laid her knitting aside.

Amir laughed. "Come and see."

Clem raced downstairs with Benjamin and Kiernan close behind her. Amir and Edna hobbled down together. The carpet-enchanter gripped the handrail until his knuckles turned white.

"Are you all right?" Edna asked.

"Oh, you know." His breath rattled. "Enchanting is not as easy as it once was. I usually give my clients a timeline of several weeks. The pace is easier. But–"

"You should have told me," Edna said at once. "We could've waited. You shouldn't have–"

The corners of his beard lifted.

"Mrs. Fisher," he said, "it could not wait."

"I wish you'd call me Edna."

Clem appeared at the bottom of the stairs. "Are you guys coming?"

"Give us a minute." Edna steadied Amir as he stumbled on the last step. He didn't tense at her hand on his elbow, and it worried her. "Some of us aren't as young as we used to be."

The carpet lay on the workshop's table. The table's usual detritus littered the floor. Edna tripped over a spare jar. Benjamin caught her.

No one noticed when Kiernan slipped out the front door.

"Aren't there any chairs in here?" Benjamin asked Amir. "You look like you're about to keel over."

Amir tottered close to the table. His frame caved like he'd gone too long without a meal, though he'd eaten only this morning.

"I'm fine." He ran a hand over the carpet. "One more spell must be done."

Benjamin eyed him. "Do you have the energy for one more spell?"

Amir bent with a groan to retrieve a jar of silvery liquid. He clawed at the lid.

"I do not need the energy. Mrs. Fisher must do the spell."

Clem took the jar from him and popped the lid.

"Oh—no," Edna said, certain she'd heard wrong. "I don't know any spells. I don't know even the most basic techniques—"

Amir dipped his finger in the jar, coating his fingertip with the silvery substance inside. "I'm sure you'll do perfectly. The naming ceremony does not require any knowledge of magic."

"Naming ceremony?"

"Mmm, yes." He traced silvery geometric patterns on the carpet. "The owner of the carpet must always name it."

"But you can buy pre-fab carpets," Clem said.

Amir peered over his glasses at her. "Yes, I am aware of mass-produced carpets."

The girl blushed. "There's no naming ceremony when you buy pre-fab."

He continued tracing things on the carpet. The silvery substance glowed on its surface before sinking into the weave.

"Naming a carpet gives it its purpose. The carpet is bonded to its master such that it will do whatever one bids, within its abilities. Without the naming ceremony, a carpet is only a carpet. It will fly where and when one tells it, and how high, carrying what weight it can. But a carpet that has been named anticipates one's needs."

He finished with the silvery substance and set the jar back on the floor. The carpet glowed like an evening sky.

Benjamin's concerned expression diminished in the glow.

"Wow," he said softly. "So naming a carpet, like...brings it to life?"

"In a manner of speaking." Amir smiled at Edna. "This carpet, once named, will be a great help to you. It will continue the journey without instruction if you must rest, it will come at your call, it will rescue you from danger—which I think you may need, given the nature of your journey."

A flying carpet had been exciting enough without the extra thought he'd put into it, but naming it sounded like important magic. Edna couldn't even do normal magic. "Oh—well—what kinds of names do carpets usually have?"

"A good name gives the carpet its purpose," Amir said. "Most people name them for their intended journey or for their speed. The Star of the East, Silver Comet, names of that sort."

They sounded like trains to Edna, and far too grand for her. She supposed her carpet's name ought to have something to do with dragons or Dominion or destiny, but she'd always been dreadful at names. She'd once adopted a stray cat and named it Kitty.

"Can I have a minute to think about it?"

Their faces shone blue in the glow of the carpet. Benjamin's eyes were wide and luminous, his fingers twitching like he longed to poke and prod the carpet to discover exactly what the magic was doing to it.

"Of course," Amir said. "The spellwork is ready. Take as long as you like."

The minutes stretched out. Clem crossed her arms, clacking her teeth. Benjamin elbowed her. She glowered at him and didn't stop.

Edna felt stupid with their eyes on her, so she said the first name that popped into her head.

"Beatrice."

Clem stifled a giggle. Benjamin sighed; this was just what he'd expect from Edna.

"Beatrice?" Amir said in a delicate voice.

"Yes." Now that the name had popped out, Edna knew it was the right one. "It was my mother's name."

Amir hesitated. "Very well."

He traced a final symbol on the edge of the carpet. A silver stream of light followed the path of his finger until it formed a circle with a complicated star inside. Benjamin leaned in for a better look. Even Clem eyed it curiously.

"Put your hand here," Amir said.

Edna pressed her palm to the circle.

Light exploded from the carpet. Benjamin and Clem jerked back, covering their eyes. Edna pressed her hand harder to the circle, squinting. A wind blew from beneath her hand, threatening to push them all back, a strong, warm wind smelling like grass and water and spring flowers.

"Name your carpet," Amir said.

His calm, quiet voice was somehow audible over the wind, but Edna couldn't help shouting, "Beatrice!"

The burst of light and wind died away.

Edna unsquinted. Benjamin and Clem uncovered their eyes. The workshop seemed strange, the juxtaposition of the clutter with the lingering scent of spring perplexing.

"Is everyone all right?" Amir asked calmly.

The carpet felt velvety soft beneath Edna's fingers.

"Fine," Benjamin said.

"Did it work?" Clem asked.

Silver curlicues glimmering on the carpet's surface faded. The carpet glowed a little brighter before returning to normal.

"There is one way to find out," Amir said. "Mrs. Fisher?"

Edna gasped; his kind brown eyes had gone milky white.

He smiled gently. It was the same smile, even with his pupils—still black—ringed with that unsettling white. "It's quite all right. A side effect of the enchantments, nothing more."

"Are you sure?" Edna asked. "Are you sure it doesn't...there aren't any...long-term effects?"

"It's fine." Clem hugged herself, sounding shaky. "The same thing used to happen to Abuela with certain spells."

"My magical theory professor, too." Benjamin toyed with the hem of his t-shirt. "She'd do demonstrations sometimes. If someone who's not a witch or wizard does a really powerful spell..."

Amir inclined his head. "You flatter me. I am not accustomed to thinking of my trade as powerful magic. Go ahead, Mrs. Fisher."

She felt sillier than ever and discomfited by the change to his eyes. "Beatrice?"

The carpet shook itself like a wet dog and drifted into the air. Silvery light dripped from it like water.

"My goodness," Edna said softly. The carpet—Beatrice—twisted around and sidled up to her, nosed at her, arched and rubbed against her like a cat. She laughed. "Well, hello to you too!"

Amir swayed, smiling. "Is it to your liking?"

"Oh, yes. Very much so." Affection for the carpet-enchanter overwhelmed her. "Thank you—thank you. I—"

Her gratitude gave way to a shriek as Amir, still smiling, collapsed.

Kiernan strode around the block with his phone pressed to his ear. He didn't worry about anyone seeing him. The dilapidated brick buildings near Amir's shop were mostly abandoned, or at least unused, and on a weekday afternoon, Eastern Market was quiet. Distant traffic rumbled, but only the occasional vehicle—magical or otherwise—passed by on this block.

The call rang out. Kiernan jabbed the call icon.

"C'mon, Red, pick up."

He'd been trying to call for days with no luck, the irony of which was not lost on him. Phone reception was shoddy in Dominion. Sometimes he thought they ought to invest in magic mirrors, but magical communication was even less reliable in Dominion than cell service. Too much interference from the dragons.

He wouldn't have worried except for two things: Red didn't know about the Chosen One's change of plans, and it wasn't a connection issue.

It was a Red-not-picking-up issue.

Voicemail.

Kiernan swore at the robotic voice, hung up, and redialed. Voicemail again.

He dialed twice more before trying Shira's number instead. She answered on the fourth ring.

"Where is he?" Kiernan said without preamble.

If a shrug made a sound, it was Shira's voice. "Where is who?"

"Who the hell do you think?" Kiernan snapped. "Red. Where is he? He won't pick up his phone."

Her hesitation scared him, because Shira so rarely hesitated. Kiernan's stomach clenched. He ducked into a doorway, ignoring the NO TRESPASSING signs plastered on the door and the surrounding windows.

"I don't know," Shira said at last. "He flew off in a rage yesterday morning."

"What happened? No—" Kiernan interrupted himself. "Okay. Okay. How much longer until you leave for Santa Alvara?"

"Four days."

Kiernan ground his teeth.

"I can hear you doing that," Shira said.

Kiernan ignored her. For years, whenever Red's rage got the best of him, he'd head out on a dragon. Going somewhere, anywhere, nowhere in particular. He'd fly until he felt he'd gone far enough and set fire to whatever he found there. A town. A base. An empty field. It didn't matter. It took the fight out of him for a while, and he'd come home.

But unexpected dragons setting fire to random cities drew attention. And it didn't do any good. And those back at the keep never knew how far Red had flown or how long it would be until he returned or *if* he'd return. Sometimes he was back the same day, after attacking an outpost on the edge of Dominion. Other times he'd fly thousands of miles and vanish for days.

Once, he'd been gone more than a week. So long that the others started wondering if he was dead, what they'd do if he was. He finally reappeared, drenched in sea spray. He never told them where he'd gone, but on a supply run a few days later, Kiernan had heard that a mountain dragon had been spotted in Europe for the first time in over two hundred years.

He'd thought those days were gone.

Apparently not.

"If he's not back by then," Kiernan said now, "you guys can't go to Santa Alvara."

"We have to. There's a conference starting the day we fly in. Knights from around the country will be there for it. It's the perfect time to attack."

"We'll have to find a different perfect time. The Chosen One knows we're going."

A long pause. "How do you know?"

"She told me. She knows about Lena."

Shira swore. A stagecoach rattled by overhead, turning onto a busier street. Thin clouds gathered on the horizon, promising another night of rain despite the clear day.

"They've got the name and ID and everything," Kiernan said. "Let him know. If he gets back before you're supposed to leave, tell him. If he's not back—"

"I know," Shira said, and she hung up.

Kiernan sucked in a breath. Someone knew now. They wouldn't fly in clueless. If Red didn't get back to Dominion soon, they wouldn't fly in at all. Shira had a good head on her shoulders, a lot of common sense, and less unquestioning loyalty to Red than the others. She and Kiernan had that in common: if Red seemed in danger of screwing up his own plans through sheer stupidity, neither of them was above disobeying him to make sure he succeeded.

Kiernan felt better as he headed back to the carpet shop. Shira would care for everyone until Red got back, and maybe Kiernan could remove the danger. He just had to get the girl alone.

He slipped his phone into his back pocket, opened the door, and found the shop in an uproar.

CHAPTER EIGHTEEN

Benjamin took charge the moment Amir collapsed. He had Clem call 713, examined Amir's head for bruises, bumps, and glass from the surrounding jars, and spoke in a firm voice that calmed Edna enough to stop her shrieking.

The shop's bell tinkled; when Benjamin saw Kiernan, he said, "Good, you can take Edna upstairs."

She protested, but he stood his ground.

"What happened?" Kiernan asked, escorting her to the apartment.

"I don't know." She wrung her hands. "He rushed the enchanting for us, I guess, and—"

She suppressed a sob. He put a hand on her shoulder without thinking about it.

As the gathering clouds outside cast shadows across the living room, Edna sat in an armchair with her hands clasped together. She would've sat there in the dark if Kiernan hadn't lit the lamps.

If only she were the Chosen One, he thought, now would be his chance. Instead, he sat in the other armchair with his hands in his pockets.

After a good long while had passed and she hadn't moved, he asked, "Are you all right?"

Edna rummaged through her handbag, but her hands shook too badly to knit. "What?"

The paramedics came and went. Benjamin and Clem appeared at the top of the stairs.

Edna pushed up from her chair so quickly that she staggered. "How is he?"

"On his way to the hospital. We can go if you—"

"Then let's go."

She sat by Amir's bedside until long after nightfall. The hospital staff stopped trying to convince her visiting hours were over. Making the assumption she was his wife, they thought it best to let her stay. She didn't correct them.

Once medical professionals with magical malady experience had taken over the situation, Benjamin admitted he was worried.

"I don't know what to expect," he said. "My healthcare work has always been in a strictly nonmagical field, so I don't know what might..."

"Nothing will happen," Edna told him, more stoutly than she felt. "He'll be fine."

He looked relieved, like the fifty years she had on him meant something. As if her say-so guaranteed the carpet-enchanter would be all right.

She didn't often wish she were young again. Age had its compensations; she'd said so at every age she'd been so far. Being too old to care what anyone thought had a certain freedom to it. But she wished she could look at someone older the way Benjamin had looked at her and know that everything would be all right simply because they said so.

Alas, the older you got, the fewer people you could look at that way.

Edna was afraid the carpet-enchanter might slip away while no one was with him. She sent the others to the lobby so she could be afraid in peace.

The machines around the bed blipped softly. Otherwise, the room was silent.

Amir turned over in bed, mumbling. Edna pulled out her knitting. The scarf was coming along nicely. She didn't care much about working on it right now, but she couldn't stand sitting here, doing nothing.

In the lobby, the others whispered together about their next course of action.

"We need to leave." Clem paced back and forth. "Monica Evans has been in the Knights for days. We still need to get to Santa Alvara, we still need to find her, and who knows how long that'll take?"

Benjamin rubbed his forehead. "Edna won't go, not while he's like this."

"He'll be fine," Clem said, but she stopped pacing. "Magical exhaustion, right? That's what they said. Like when I crashed the van. He overdid it trying to get the enchantments done so fast."

"Because of us."

Clem fiddled with her necklace. "He just needs some rest. I bounced back in five minutes."

"Yeah, you're like sixty years younger and didn't spend three days straight doing powerful magic. It's going to take him more than rest to recover."

He didn't say *"if* he recovers," but he didn't have to. They were all thinking it, and Clem more than the others. She'd been the one to lash out because three days was too long a delay. And now, having taken three full days, Amir was unconscious in a hospital bed. Still, Clem felt impatient. The carpet was finished, named, ready to go, yet they were stuck at the hospital. And she couldn't run off this time, because the Sword of Destiny, still in ring form, was in Edna's handbag.

She resumed pacing. Something suspiciously like guilt gnawed at her for even thinking that. Amir had been so kind to her, reading to her each evening when his work was done, as if he'd forgotten she'd yelled at him and destroyed half his shop.

Guilt was stupid and pointless, however, and Clem had good reasons for being impatient, so she scowled the guilt away.

"Be right back," she muttered, and she headed off to find a vending machine.

Kiernan leaned toward Benjamin. "Why don't I go on ahead with her?"

Benjamin's face warmed at his proximity. He was so *attractive.* It was unfair. "Who, Edna?"

"What?" Kiernan said in confusion, but he went on before either of them could work out Benjamin's blunder. "No, Clem. There's no need for all of us to stay here. If you're worried about her traveling alone—"

"Oh—"

Panic whirled in Benjamin's head. He tried to remember everything he knew about past Chosen Ones.

"She's not ready." His voice slid to a higher pitch. He fought to keep it at its normal register. It would look suspicious if he went high-pitched now, not to mention he'd prefer Kiernan never hear his voice do that. "She still needs, you know, her...mentor. We can't send her on without Edna."

Kiernan's eyebrows contracted. "What exactly is Edna teaching her?"

"Magic," Benjamin said, or rather that was the first word that popped out of his mouth. Well, that lie was going to crumble the minute Kiernan decided to ask Edna for help with literally any spell.

Kiernan sat back in his chair. "I didn't realize she knew magic."

"Uh," Benjamin said, "it's, uh, it's not so much the actual, you know, magic, as like, well, you haven't really seen how bad Clem is at keeping a lid on it, have you?"

He was spared further explanation by Clem's reappearance with a bag of chips and two candy bars. She threw the candy bars at them. One of them hit Benjamin in the face.

Back in Amir's room, a raspy snore greeted Edna's next row of stitches. Amir turned over again, onto his back this time, and lay there with his mouth wide open. A second snore rattled out of him, giving way to more.

Edna released a breath she hadn't realized she'd been holding. He'd barely woken in the past several hours, always shivery and feverish and bleary when he did. But snoring had to be a good sign. It cracked the awful silence.

The snores broke into coughing. Amir hacked and choked, his face red, spittle flying from his mouth. Edna's knitting fell from her hands.

"Oh—" She leapt to her feet, but her cane slipped and crashed to the floor. "Nurse!"

Edna reached for her cane, her knees and hip in agony from jumping up. Amir's skeletal fingers gripped the quilt like a lifeline. His back arched, his face turned purple, he was choking, and she couldn't bend far enough to grab her cane.

She screamed at the top of her lungs. *"Nurse! Benjamin! Someone!"*

The machinery around the bed lit up bright green and blipped faster, ringing in Edna's ears until her hearing aid screeched. People in scrubs jogged into the room, throwing commands back and forth in sharp, clinical voices. They shunted Edna to the side. She pressed against the wall, shaking. Amir disappeared in a wall of scrubs and elbows jostling for space.

The machinery calmed. The wall of scrubs dispersed, leaving Edna alone with Amir and a turbaned doctor. The doctor took the carpet-enchanter's pulse, wrote something on the clipboard hanging at the end of the bed, and strode from the room, running a hand down his beard and muttering to himself.

Someone had righted Edna's cane and set her knitting on the arm of her chair. Edna sat, shaking all over.

Amir's eyes were open now and fever-bright. Blue sparks danced in his beard and hair. They bounced along his torso and vanished into his blanket, zipped around his eyes like crazed fireflies, sank into his pupils and disappeared.

Edna clasped her hands together.

"Amir," she said, "can you say anything?"

The corners of his beard lifted. His voice was so quiet and hoarse she had to lean in to hear him.

"I am fine, Mrs. Fisher, I assure you."

Tears slipped out before she could stop them.

"Why, Edna," Amir said in surprise. "What is this?"

She laughed and hiccupped at the same time, wiping her eyes. "I thought you were dying, you silly old man! You look like death warmed over, which is entirely my fault—"

He hesitated, then took her hand gingerly. His eyes had lost some of their glassiness.

"This is my life's work. I am never happier than when I am enchanting, although—I admit this is not the first time I have perhaps overexerted myself." He smiled. "But I'm seventy-nine years old. I must accept that I may not have much time left on this earth."

Edna hiccupped again, reprovingly, which only made Amir chuckle. His hand relaxed on hers.

"Why, seventy-nine is just a baby," she said. "I hope you have another twenty years at least."

The power went out.

Nurses shouted orders in the hallway. Orbs of light flickered into being along the ceiling, bathing the room in a soft, white glow. The machines surrounding Amir's bed came back to life.

"What was that?" Edna asked.

A harried nurse, in the dark green scrubs of a staff witch, poked her head in. "Is everyone all right? Everything's working again?"

"Yes, but—"

"Good," the nurse grunted, and she withdrew. "I'll be back."

"Wait," Edna said, "please, tell us what—"

The nurse had moved on.

Edna craned her neck. "What do you suppose—?"

The building shook. People screamed. Dim orange light flickered through the window.

The shouting in the hallway grew louder, more panicked. Edna went to the door for a look, but Clem appeared in the doorway.

"What's going on?" Edna asked.

Clem shoved her way into the room. "Dragon."

"Ya Allah," Amir said in bewildered tones. "It can't be. Michigan hasn't seen a dragon in more than fifty years."

Clem's eyes glittered in her pale face. She rifled through Edna's handbag. "Where's the sword?"

"Clem—"

"There you are!" Benjamin charged into the room with Kiernan close behind him. "You can't keep running off like that."

"What are you, my babysitter?"

"We need to stick together."

Edna looked at Kiernan, who stood in the doorway. He thrust his hands into his pockets.

"There isn't really a dragon?" Edna whispered. He nodded.

Clem found the bejeweled silver ring and dropped Edna's handbag on the chair. She muttered something. The ring transformed back into a sword.

The gears in Kiernan's brain jammed up. She did have the sword.

Clem hefted it, testing its weight, and headed for the door.

Edna blocked her path. "Where do you think you're going?"

Clem scowled. "I'm not going to sit here and do nothing. Not when I've got the sword."

"You can't use it," Edna said pointedly, with a glance at Kiernan.

He didn't hear her. He had a feeling he knew where the dragon had come from. This was not part of the plan.

"Doesn't matter," Clem said. "It's not Redway."

"How do you know?"

"It can't be. It's a single dragon."

Kiernan knew better.

"Move," Clem said, but Edna remained in the doorway. "Come on, Grandma, this is serious."

"So am I. You're not going anywhere."

"Get the fuck out of the way."

"Clem–"

The girl thrust out her hand with a snarl. Edna doubled over, clutching her stomach. Clem slipped past and was gone.

"Are you okay?" Benjamin asked.

"I'm fine," Edna gasped. "Clementine–"

"On it," Kiernan said. He sprinted from the room with no intention of searching for Clem. He had someone more important to worry about.

An alarm blared. The flickering orange light danced in the windows. A robotic voice droned over the PA system.

"The hospital is going into lockdown. Remain calm. Repeat. The hospital is going into lockdown. Remain calm. Repeat. The hospital..."

Lockdown! Edna looked at Amir. Clem wouldn't be able to get back to safety if the hospital locked down with her on the wrong side of the doors.

"Go on," Amir said. "I did not make you a carpet so you could sit in a hospital with me."

Edna wanted to cry.

"Stay safe," she told him. "Benjamin–"

He was hyperventilating, wide-eyed, his hands shaking. He looked at her like he was floundering in the water and she was a life ring.

"It'll be all right," she said, and she scuttled out the door to find Clem.

CHAPTER NINETEEN

The halls seethed with activity. Hospital staff jogged back and forth. Families in waiting areas shrieked for their patients. Patients tottered around, half-dressed or in gowns, some with medical equipment still attached to their bodies.

Edna kept one hand on the wall and the other on her cane. As she neared the door, people outside screamed. The dragon roared, somewhere too close for comfort. Over it all, the PA system droned on and on, "The hospital is going into lockdown. Remain calm. Repeat. The hospital is going into..."

Custodians stood in the doorway, stemming the tide of panicked people.

"We're locking the doors," one of them said. "I'm sorry, you can't leave right now. You'll be safer inside–"

He stood aside as a herd of staff witches jogged toward the door. Edna plunged into their midst and let them carry her past the custodians.

Outside, chaos. Alarms blared. Emergency vehicles rumbled through the streets. Flying vehicles evacuated people from high-rise apartments, appearing and disappearing, ghostlike, through the smoke and flame devouring the cloudy night. Children and flying horses screamed.

Edna caught her first sight of the dragon. Her first sight, in person, of any dragon in decades.

She'd either forgotten or never realized how massive they could be. From snout to tail, the dragon was the length of a city bus. Coal black, with leathery wings that cut through the smoke blotting out the stars. It stretched out its neck and vomited fire on Eastern Market.

Edna's heart stuttered.

"Clementine!" she shouted, but she could barely hear her own voice over the shouts and screams and shrieks, the alarms and sirens, the roar of the flames, the roar of the dragon, the overwhelming cacophony. "Clem!"

A small figure stood frozen on the edge of the parking lot, watching the dragon fly closer.

Edna hurried toward her. "Clementine!"

The girl's eyes were fixed on the dragon, but her hand slackened on the sword.

The dragon wavered like a mirage in the heat. It winged closer and closer until its orange, snakelike eyes gleamed through the haze.

Edna grabbed Clem's shoulder.

"Come on, dear," she said. "Come on, let's get inside—"

Clem shrank into her.

"Not again," she whispered.

"Clementine, come on—"

"I can't—"

The staff witches encircled the hospital. The dragon belched fire, but they shouted a word as one and the flames dispersed. Heat whooshed past and dissipated. Sweat dripped down Edna's back and bosom and armpits. The dragon circled.

The sword slipped in Clem's fingers. The dragon dove, neck outstretched. Was that a shadow between its wings, or the miniscule figure of a rider?

Edna pulled Clem toward the hospital. The sword clanged to the ground. Clem clung to Edna, hiding her face in Edna's chest with a sob. The dragon roared—the witches shouted—

Edna snatched up the sword and hauled Clem toward the hospital. A custodian barring the door made to block their way, noticed that one of them was a frantic old woman, and let them in.

"Thank you," Edna gasped, dragging Clem down the hall. She didn't stop until they were back in Amir's room.

By the time they got there, Clem's fear had smoldered into anger.

"Do you think they'll be able to kill it?" Edna asked Amir in a low voice.

Clem kicked the wall. "We should've killed it. We have the sword."

"Yes, and I saw your face when that dragon flew at us. You didn't look ready to kill it."

Clem flushed. "I'm not scared."

"I am," Amir said, peering over his glasses at her.

Benjamin moaned.

"I didn't say you were," Edna said. "But there's nothing wrong with being scared."

She had a sneaking suspicion, however, that Clem was right: they ought to do something. She was the Chosen One. There wouldn't be any alarms to sound when she faced Redway.

Not for the first time, she thought Clem would have made a better Chosen One. Maybe the girl had frozen up, but she'd been willing to throw herself headlong into danger. To do *something*.

Edna gripped the sword tight.

"Stay here," she said to Clem.

Clem scowled, but Edna prodded Benjamin toward the door, hoping a job would keep him grounded.

"Make sure she stays in this room," she told him.

"Where are you going?"

"Never mind that. Don't let Clem out of your sight."

"I don't need a babysitter!" Clem raged. "I'm sixteen."

"So you keep saying, dear," Edna said, and she was out the door.

Benjamin closed it behind her and stood sentry. Unable to shove him aside, Clem shouted curses through the door. Edna was sorry to leave them with Amir, but they had to stay somewhere she knew they were safe. Somewhere she could find them when she came back.

If she came back.

She wasn't coming back with that attitude, she thought crossly. It was only one dragon. If she couldn't handle one lousy dragon, she didn't have a prayer of handling Redway and his whole flight of them. Tonight, she wouldn't have to deal with him. Just a single, riderless dragon.

At least, she thought it was riderless. That shadow atop the dragon might've been a person.

Surely it had been her imagination.

The front doors were now bolted shut. Edna traipsed back down the hall in search of an unlocked door.

Scared doctors calmed families as best they could while medical staff herded patients back into their rooms. Custodians, gift shop clerks, and cafeteria workers went around locking the other exits.

Edna tried door after door until, at the end of a quiet, dimly lit hallway, she found an out-of-the-way emergency exit.

She tested the handle. It gave. If the alarm went off, it was muffled by the other alarms and the PA system reminding her, as if she needed reminding at this point, that the hospital was going into lockdown.

Outside, the staff witches linked hands. They chanted in one, long, breathless drone that reverberated in Edna's teeth. The dragon had abandoned the hospital in favor of chasing winged horses through the city.

Edna swallowed, gripping the sword tight.

"Beatrice?" she said experimentally, but her voice was lost in the flames and sirens and screams and the witches' chanting and the alarms still blaring. How on earth was a carpet sitting in a stack of carpet shelving in the parking lot supposed to hear her?

"Beatrice!" she shouted, as loud as she could.

Carpets didn't have ears anyway.

"Beatrice!"

In the distance, the carpet shelving rattled. Beatrice burst free and hurtled toward her.

Edna clambered aboard. They zipped into the air, past the skylanes, over the rooftops, out of the smoke. Wind rushed in Edna's face, cold and damp with unfallen rain.

Far below, through the smoke and flame, Kiernan caught a glimpse of them. He blinked sweat from his eyes. He couldn't make out its rider, but the sword glinted in the firelight. The girl. He'd been so focused on getting to the dragon that he'd raced right past her on his way out of the hospital.

Copernicus coiled around the Fisher Building. It reminded Kiernan of a movie he'd once seen. He pictured planes dive-bombing the dragon, remembering how the whole thing had ended for the movie monster.

He whipped his bow off his shoulder and aimed at the receding carpet. Fired. Missed wildly because the carpet was out of range.

His chest heaved. He had to get to Red. He sprinted toward the building, throwing his bow back over his shoulder.

High above him, the cool, damp air cleared Edna's head, but the dizzying height and the burning city below muddled it again. The church fire flashed through her mind. The flames raining from the ceiling. The groaning of the choir loft as it collapsed.

Her grip tightened on the Sword of Destiny. The sword felt powerfully, savagely joyful. It shivered, glowing gold as the dragon roared.

Edna's fear evaporated. She felt it, too: the lust to kill the dragon. To find the soft spot in its breast, to drive the sword into it. She would kill the dragon and save the city.

"Let's go, Beatrice."

The carpet flipped a corner at her inquiringly.

"Of course I'm sure. Why on earth do you think I called you in the middle of a dragon attack?"

Beatrice figured an escape was a good reason to call a flying carpet in the middle of a dragon attack, but Edna wouldn't have listened even if the carpet could have spoken.

They shuttled into the heat. Smoke gusted into Edna's face. She didn't feel so savage now, with the dragon growing bigger and smoke clawing into her nose and lungs and throat.

The sword glowed brighter. Edna stifled a coughing fit and held it in front of her.

She could kill a dragon, she told herself, trying to forget she was an inexperienced old lady brandishing an overlarge sword. She could kill a dragon.

People shouted below as Beatrice flew closer. At least one said, "What the hell is that?" and Kiernan, in their midst, looked up so fast he cricked his neck. Far above, a tiny figure zipped about on a tiny carpet.

The Chosen One, Kiernan thought, that's what. His jaw clenched, but he couldn't shoot, not from this distance. Not at the carpet and the girl aboard it.

But the armed guards—

Bulletfire crackled. Beatrice loop-de-looped to avoid the hailstorm. Edna did her best to keep a grip on both the carpet and her dinner.

"Hold!" someone shouted.

The dragon roared, so loud and close that it made Edna's hearing aids squeal. Purplish-black blood rained from the beast's left hind leg. Fire jetted from its jaws.

The sword's jeweled hilt dug into Edna's hand as Beatrice hurtled towards the dragon.

"I can kill a dragon," she said. "I can. I can kill a dragon."

The dragon was fifteen yards away—ten—five—its scales gleamed in the firelight—it bared its teeth—

Edna squeezed her eyes shut.

"I can't kill a *dragon!"* she shouted, and she stabbed at it with the sword.

The blade bounced off its scales.

Edna opened her eyes, her heart sinking. A normal sword wouldn't do much good against a dragon unless you caught its belly or, better but riskier, its eyes, but she'd thought the Sword of Destiny—

She stabbed at the dragon again, not sure what else to do. The blade caught in the chink of a loose scale, jarring her arm. Her shoulder ached, but she dug into the crack beneath the dragon's scale. She wasn't sure it would do anything, but—

The scale flipped back with an ugly crack. Edna fell forward as the sword plunged into the dragon's side.

The dragon screeched. The sword sank deeper as Edna tugged at it, her heart pounding. Fire whooshed by, so close that her house dress fluttered in the warm gust, but the dragon couldn't quite angle its head the right way to set her aflame.

Screams from below. A magically amplified voice. "On my signal!"

That didn't sound good.

Edna yanked at the sword. It slipped half an inch out of the dragon. Blood oozed around it. The dragon spewed fire at Edna again and again but missed. It twisted one way and another, trying to get rid of this thing in its side.

Edna pushed her glasses up her nose, slick with sweat, and glanced upwards. Her heart skipped a beat.

Someone was aboard the dragon.

No doubt about it this time. He was shadowy in the haze, but he was there. His head turned in her direction, his neck craning. She hoped he couldn't see her.

She yanked the sword harder. Another inch of blade rewarded her. Blood spurted onto her glasses. The dragon's wings unfurled, hiding its rider.

Beatrice flinched, jerking Edna away from the sword.

"No—closer, Beatrice, I'm sorry, dear, but you'll have to get closer or—"

The dragon's wings beat. Slowly at first, then faster. The Sword of Destiny swung away from Edna's outstretched hand.

Her throat constricted. They couldn't lose the sword.

Below, the magically amplified voice shouted, "Aim for the wings!"

"Beatrice!"

The carpet darted toward the dragon. The beast peeled away from the building and rose into the sky, its gunshot leg dangling. It bellowed, belching fire at the armed masses below. Water from a fire engine met the flames with a hiss. White steam engulfed everything.

Edna couldn't see the dragon now, let alone the sword. Her ears strained for the flapping of wings. Beatrice followed the sound.

"Get ready!" the amplified voice said. "Once the steam clears—"

Beatrice bumped into the dragon's long, sleek tail. Edna swallowed, but the dragon couldn't see them in the steam. Beatrice slipped around the dragon's left. The steam cleared as they flew higher, breaking off into little white wisps—

"There it is!"

The dragon's flight had dislodged the sword. It dangled more than halfway out of the beast's side, which oozed blood.

More screams. The amplified voice shouted, "Open fire!"

"Snickerdoodles!" Edna cried, lunging for the sword.

A hail of bullets peppered the air. White-hot pain grazed her arm. She yanked the sword from the dragon's side.

Above her, a voice rumbled like a thunderclap. The bullets froze in midair, glinting in the firelight. Then they hurtled back to earth. The guards yelled, ducking for cover.

The dragon pulled away from the Fisher Building and winged across the city, breathing fire as it went. Beatrice zipped toward the ground.

Kiernan collected the spent arrows from the three guards he'd shot, liberated a motorcycle from the remains of a nearby parking lot, and streaked after the dragon.

Edna clutched the sword and let Beatrice fly her back to the hospital, her stomach turning like she might throw up.

CHAPTER TWENTY

Kiernan tore through the burning city on the stolen motorcycle. "Red!"

Copernicus zigzagged for five miles, belching fire at shabby houses, abandoned factories, theaters, colleges. Firetrucks and ambulances screeched down main roads. Flames shattered the windows of the DIA.

Kiernan barreled past without seeing any of it.

"Red!"

Kiernan's chest tightened. He hated it, hated Red for doing it to him. The motorcycle skidded to a halt. Kiernan fired an arrow as close as he could to Copernicus's head without hitting him.

The dragon winged north, away from the inferno, without setting anything else aflame. Kiernan's chest heaved. Red had seen the arrow.

Copernicus landed on the roof of an abandoned hospital on the outskirts of Highland Park. Rain fell on the burning city. Kiernan braked the stolen motorcycle.

Red magicked himself to the ground. He looked like he'd just rolled out of bed—no flight mask, no jacket, no boots, in his boxers and a sweat-drenched t-shirt that clung to him like a second skin.

"Kiernan?" His voice was hoarse with smoke. Sparks leapt from his fingers, his eyes, running along his body. "What the hell are you doing here?"

"What the fuck are you doing here?" Kiernan countered.

"Kiernan," Red warned darkly, but Kiernan was too scared and pissed off to care.

"I'm here chasing after your stupid Chosen One! She's got a flying carpet—I saw her. She came after you with the Sword of Destiny. I don't know what act of providence saved your ass, but—"

Red lifted his head like a chimera scenting its prey. "So she is here."

"I don't know where she is right now—"

"If I took her now—"

"You're not listening to me—"

Red stuck his fingers in his mouth and whistled. Copernicus growled but lifted himself off the roof. Purplish-black blood oozed from his leg and side. Red swung himself onto the dragon's back, but Kiernan examined the injuries. A bullet in the leg. A stab wound in the side, where—yes—Copernicus had had a loose scale for months.

"Red!"

Behind them, sirens and flashing lights whirred up Woodward Avenue.

"I'll find her."

"You fucking won't, you idiot!" Kiernan screamed. "Pern's injured."

Red leapt off the dragon. Fresh sparks crackled in his eyes.

"Red," Kiernan said. "Red—Red, listen."

"I'll get her for this," Red said quietly.

Kiernan wanted to scream. Again. Wordlessly.

"Listen to me, would you? You have to know—she knows about Lena. She knows about Santa Alvara. She's heading there—she's not planning to go to Dominion."

The sirens and flashing lights grew louder, brighter.

"What?" Red said.

"She knows about Lena; she's going to Santa Alvara—"

"She's going to Santa Alvara?"

"Yeah, so—"

The sparks died away. Kiernan stepped back, not sure what that meant.

Red smiled grimly. "Perfect. I want you to keep eyes on her until we get there. Stop her from finding Lena, if you can manage it. Keep her from warning the Knights. We'll intercept her and bring her back with us."

Kiernan fell silent. Not a bad plan. Easier than keeping up the draconologist charade the whole way home. Safer than trying to nab her now.

"That...might actually work."

"I do have good ideas on occasion," Red said drily.

Copernicus whined. Red touched the dragon's side. His hand came away sticky with blood.

Red muttered something to stop the bleeding. Not a full healing; just a patch to keep Copernicus safe until they got home.

"Get out of here," Kiernan said. The sirens wailed. "Red—"

Red patted the dragon's neck and swung aboard.

"You can't do this again," Kiernan said. "I mean it. You have to keep a lid on it."

"Who are you?" Red asked. "My mother?"

Copernicus launched into the sky, leaving Kiernan on the ground with the rain, the dying flames, the stolen motorcycle, and the emergency vehicles pulling up outside the abandoned hospital.

Several miles away, a dome of greenish light hazed around the hospital to which they'd brought Amir. It was translucent but impregnable, the work of the staff witches. Edna couldn't get inside.

She whimpered. Rain soaked her hair and dress and Beatrice. The carpet shuddered, dappled with purplish-black dragon's blood.

Edna wanted to cry. Using the carpet had taken less time to wreck it than enchanting it had taken to wreck Amir's health, although Beatrice would've disagreed with her definition of "wrecked," if she'd asked.

Edna pounded on the dome. The sword hung heavy in her hand, glowing faintly.

A voice niggled at her, deep, serious, mistrustful. Theobald Smith. *Breaks through protective spells, things like that.*

Edna hefted the sword, staggering. She heaved it to the dome and sliced through. The greenish haze parted.

An alarm sounded inside the hospital, but Edna stumbled through the opening, crying with relief. Beatrice fluttered after her. Within, the dome was free of smoke and flame. The grass shone damp in the hospital floodlights. The building was whole and clean, undamaged.

A staff witch slipped out the hospital doors warily. Edna might have been an old lady, but she was an old lady holding a sword and covered in dragon's blood.

"Can I help you?" the witch asked.

"Please." Edna hated how small her voice sounded. "Please, my—grandchildren are in there."

The witch eyed her. "What's with the sword?"

Edna wiped her eyes on her arm.

"I'm the Chosen One," she said, too miserable to lie. Dragon's blood stiffened her dress.

"Ah." The witch poked her head back inside, calling, "It's all right!"

She jogged over and ran her hands across the opening. The greenish haze repaired itself. "I'd heard it was an old woman."

The sword was so heavy. "We had been hoping to keep it quiet."

"They had to announce they'd named someone."

Taking her hand gently, the witch laid the sword on the carpet. Dragon's blood smeared the blade, drying to a sickly lilac color.

"I need to clean it," Edna said, but she made no move to pick it up. Her fingers ached.

"Plenty of time for that later."

The witch ran her hands over the air around Edna, reminding her of Benjamin when he was in nurse-mode.

"People were screaming about Redway," the witch said. "The Knights have been trying to track him, but they're having a hard time of it since it's their bases he's attacking. They're too preoccupied with cleaning up after him to figure out where he'll strike next."

Blood flecked Edna's glasses. Perhaps she had another handkerchief in her handbag, or lens wipes. She didn't check.

"Public outcry against the Council of Wizards has been pretty bad," the witch continued. "The Knights don't have much truck with magic, beyond magically imbuing bullets with extra power—their philosophy has always been, if we're fighting magical creatures, we ought to do it using as little magic as possible. They want to distance themselves from the enemy, I guess, and magic doesn't do much against dragons anyway, unless you really know your stuff and have a lot of power. At any rate, everyone's looking to the Council of Wizards instead. They didn't like to say who they'd picked, but they had to let it out they'd named *someone.* They were none too happy about it, let me tell you."

She finished her examination of the air around Edna and studied her hands and arms instead.

"I gather they wanted to give you more of a head start," she said. "They didn't give any details, but the Grand Coven works pretty closely with that—what's his name? M...something. Marconius, maybe? I don't think that's right, but anyway—"

"Methodius?"

"That's the one," the witch said. "He's a ray of sunshine, all right, but he's almost the only one of them who thinks witches ought to be allowed on the Council, so he meets with the Coven a lot. There was a meeting a couple days ago. Anyway, it's all hearsay, but witches' rumors tend to be more accurate than non-witches' rumors, no offense—"

"None taken," Edna mumbled.

"—I don't know precisely how it came up, but after that meeting, we started hearing they'd chosen an old woman. It's exciting, isn't it?"

"Too exciting," Edna mumbled. She was exhausted.

The witch laid her hands on Edna's ears, then her eyes. "I don't mean to say it won't be difficult. But they've always chosen teenagers before. You're really breaking new ground here."

"I suppose," Edna mumbled.

The witch removed her hands from Edna's person. "All right, not too much damage. Mostly exhaustion, smoke inhalation, and muscle strain, I think. Nothing a little rest and some painkillers won't take care of. It looks like a bullet grazed your upper arm. You're lucky it didn't hit you outright, but there's a small burn I could remove, if you're not allergic to magic?"

"Not to my knowledge."

"Better not risk it," the witch said. "Not until I've had someone else look you over, at any rate. We can clean and bandage it in the meantime. Your aura's a little dingy, too, not exactly unexpected after the excitement you've had. I could clean it for you, but I like to leave auras to themselves unless there's something really wrong with them."

"That's all right," Edna said.

Her cane sank into the muddy grass. She staggered. The witch looped an arm through hers and led her toward the building.

Outside the dome, fire smoldered in the rain. Smoke rolled in the sky and dissipated. Fire trucks scattered through the city, hosing down burning buildings while firefighters searched the rubble for people. An acrid smell stung Edna's nose: some of the streets had melted from the heat.

They stopped outside the hospital doors.

"I can do something about that sword for you," the witch said, "if you'd still like to keep it quiet that you're the Chosen One."

"It was a ring," Edna said. "We had it disguised as a ring."

The witch nodded, took the sword from Beatrice, and turned it back into a jeweled, silver ring. It fit perfectly.

The witch rapped on the doors until one of her colleagues let them in. She helped Edna down the hall. Edna had forgotten which room was

Amir's, but a familiar angry voice shouting in one of them left no doubt they'd found the right place.

Maybe she should pretend this was the wrong room. She wanted to lie down somewhere quiet.

The witch left, saying she'd be down again shortly to treat the burn on Edna's arm. Edna knocked on the door, once. Twice. The shouting subsided. The door opened.

Benjamin threw his arms around her.

"Oh my god, you're all right, you were gone forever, I thought—is that blood?"

"Not mine," Edna said.

"Where's Kiernan?"

Edna's heart sank. She glanced over her shoulder like he might have caught up with her.

"I don't know." If she hadn't asked him to come with them, he would've been safely out of Detroit by now. "I never did see him after he went after Clem. He must've run right past her."

Someone launched herself at Benjamin like a small torpedo, flinging him aside.

"What the fuck do you think you were doing?"

Edna had never been fixed with such a glare as Clem wore now. The girl's face was pale and strained, her lower lip ragged and chapped like she'd been biting it, her eyes so wide that they seemed to swallow up her whole face.

"What the hell happened?" she demanded.

Edna grabbed her handbag from Beatrice and dug around for a handkerchief, a Kleenex, anything to clean the blood off her lenses. She wanted a shower and someplace quiet to rest. A good wash for Beatrice and clean clothes for herself. She scrubbed her lenses with a crumpled cotton handkerchief.

"If you were worried about me," she said, "you can just say so."

Clem flushed. "I wasn't worried."

"That's a relief."

Edna put her glasses back on. She felt a little better no longer seeing the world through a smear of purplish-black.

"I was," Benjamin said.

His eyes were red. Edna squeezed his arm.

"I'm fine," she assured him. "And we'll find Kiernan."

Amir was unconscious. Edna's heart palpitated. She thought he'd been improving earlier, but she must have been mistaken: his eyes were dark bruises in his face, his cheeks sunken. He looked so old it scared her.

"What happened?" she asked in a strangled whisper. "Is he all right?"

Benjamin fidgeted with his t-shirt. "I don't know. We were fighting and he told us to knock it off and then this siren started going off and the staff witches were shouting, I guess something was wrong with the protective spell they were putting up? Or they were having trouble with it or something, I don't know, and–"

"He collapsed again," Clem said. "I think he was trying to give them some extra magic. But he'd already exhausted himself, so he didn't have much magic to spare."

If Edna let herself sink into the bedside chair now, she'd never get up again.

She didn't want to leave him.

"How long until Redway's in Santa Alvara?" she asked.

"A few days, if we're lucky," Clem said. "Why?"

Edna rubbed her forehead.

"Because," she said, "I think I just saw him."

CHAPTER TWENTY-ONE

Kiernan jogged through the ruined streets. Making a clean getaway had meant leaving the motorcycle behind, and he'd had to use some luck to get this far. Whenever he was unsure of his path back to the hospital, he'd let his luck steer him in the right direction.

The streets in Highland Park, several miles from Red's destruction, were intact and abnormally quiet, but the carnage worsened as Kiernan neared the Fisher Building. He paid it little attention until he came upon the guards he'd killed.

They'd meant nothing to him. Red had been in danger; Copernicus had been in danger. Kiernan had killed the guards without thought, as he'd been trained to kill in the Knights fifteen years ago. As he'd been doing for Red ever since.

Whenever they attacked a city, Kiernan was on a dragon, high in the air. The people he killed looked like small cutouts of people. And they were Knights. And he was killing them for his people.

Red liked to say, for others like them, for others who had gone through what they'd gone through, but Kiernan was under no illusions about that. Squires were in those cities. Squires who suffered like they'd suffered.

But squires became Knights, and for his people Kiernan would kill them all. When he thought about it, he had an uneasy feeling his grandfather wouldn't approve. So he didn't think about it.

But these people weren't Knights; Detroit didn't have any. Kiernan doubted if more than a couple hundred Knights were stationed in the whole of the Midwest, outside of the AKG's headquarters in Coldwater. Dragons simply didn't come here anymore. The people spread-eagled on the ground before him wore no Knights' regalia nor even proper armor. They were volunteers, like volunteer firefighters, volunteers who had been given special training so that, on the off chance a dragon ever attacked, someone could kill it.

One of them stirred. Kiernan reached for his bow. He knew he ought to shoot again, to kill them in case they could identify him.

The person coughed, a horrible wet cough that grated on Kiernan's nerves. Against his better judgment, he left his bow on his back and trudged over. He turned the person onto their back.

It was a boy so young that Kiernan was outraged he'd been allowed to volunteer as a dragon-fighter—until he remembered he, not the dragon, was responsible for the boy's death. Rain spattered his pale face. He had thick, sooty eyelashes that reminded Kiernan uncomfortably of a cousin back in Ethiopia. Kiernan crouched beside him.

"Water," the boy whispered.

"I don't have any," Kiernan said. "I'm sorry."

"Please."

But Kiernan didn't have any water, or a bottle or a cup or a canteen, and he didn't know any spells to produce some from thin air. He hated the way the boy gazed at him so patiently, thinking he was a friend.

"It's your own fault," Kiernan said hoarsely. "Becoming a dragon-fighter?"

The boy's breath rattled.

"Dragons don't deserve this any more than you do." Kiernan blinked raindrops from his eyes. "I know. We tell stories. They taught us to speak."

He wasn't sure why he'd said it. Wasn't sure why he was sharing Andenya legends with a dying human in the first place, why that legend in particular. His grandfather had taught him that, that dragons once spoke, but Kiernan had always been skeptical. His people lived for thousands of years, but no one living remembered a time when this was true.

The boy's eyes fluttered closed. Rain glistened on his lashes and washed trails through the ash on his face.

"Highland savanna dragons," Kiernan clarified. He hadn't seen a mountain dragon until he'd left for the Knights; Ethiopia didn't have any. "You've never seen anything like them. They're these spindly, gazelle-like creatures with green-gold scales. They're beautiful."

The boy coughed again. Blood spurted from his lips, mixing with the ash on his wet face. Kiernan held the boy's head in his lap.

Then, because he was sorry, because he'd killed this boy but couldn't take it back, because he had nothing else to give, Kiernan told stories. He told the boy every story he knew about dragons, embellishing in places where his memory was worn threadbare, singing in Andenya half-remembered songs about the things dragons had taught his people in the days of their ancestors.

The rain stopped; the fire died. Stars ventured into the smoking sky when Kiernan finally ran out of songs and stories. He brushed damp hair back from the boy's pale forehead, his own throat dry and sore, and listened to the astonishing quiet of the dark city. Tears dried on his face. The songs and stories had dredged up memories he'd spent the last decade largely suppressing. He missed his grandfather. His mother and uncle, his siblings and cousins. Bahir Dar. Lake Tana with its islands. His people.

The boy was dead. Kiernan kept holding him, idiotically.

He was still sitting on the pavement, the body cradled in his lap, when the others found him. He didn't hear Benjamin call his name from somewhere overhead, didn't see Clem's scowl or Edna's wan expression, didn't notice that the dress the old woman wore was not the same one she'd worn several hours ago.

"Kiernan!" Clem shouted as they neared. "Get up! We need to go."

Benjamin frowned at her. He'd calmed down considerably once he'd found the city dragon-free, but he was uneasy leaving Amir at the hospital. It was stupid. He knew Amir was better off there than on a flying carpet above a smoldering city, with exactly one medical professional who had an anxiety disorder and no experience with magical maladies.

"Kiernan!" Clem shouted again, but Benjamin caught sight of the body huddled in Kiernan's arms.

"I'll get him."

She turned her scowl on him. "Make it quick."

Edna twisted the jeweled ring that was the Sword of Destiny around her finger. Beatrice swooped lower. Benjamin dismounted, ignoring Clem's sigh behind him.

"Kiernan?"

He didn't recognize the young man in the elf's arms—boy, really. He couldn't have been more than twenty. Kiernan was holding him like a brother, bent over him protectively. The elf's expression was stoic as ever, but tear tracks had dried in streaky trials through the wet ash on his face.

Benjamin's brow furrowed. He wouldn't have expected Kiernan to be so distraught over the death of a stranger. If it was a stranger. "Hey."

He touched Kiernan's shoulder. Kiernan turned his head, his gaze traveling from Benjamin's hand up the attached arm and shoulder as if trying to figure out where the hand had come from.

"Hey," Benjamin repeated, giving him a smile more like a grimace. "Who's this?"

"He's dead," Kiernan said.

Benjamin sat on the ground beside him. "Are you okay?"

"I'm fine." Kiernan laid the boy on the pavement so gently it broke Benjamin's heart. "Let's go."

He stood.

Benjamin scrambled to his feet. "Whoa, hang on a minute."

"I said I was fine."

"Yeah, I know what you said, but I'm not an idiot."

"You're doing a good impression of one."

Benjamin fidgeted with his t-shirt. He'd heard worse at the nursing home, from people who hadn't been cradling a dead body the moment before.

"Who's the boy?" he asked again, softly.

A muscle twitched in Kiernan's face. He shrugged.

"I don't know. No one. It doesn't matter."

"You don't look like it doesn't matter."

"I don't care what it looks like."

"Kiernan–"

"Shut up."

Benjamin pushed his glasses up the bridge of his nose. He wasn't the best with grief; he didn't know how to navigate it. Sometimes he wished he were more like Edna, who never hesitated to comfort someone with a touch, even if she had nothing to say.

But at least he could shut up when someone told him to.

Kiernan avoided his eyes. "Let's just go, okay?"

Benjamin put a hand on Kiernan's shoulder, squeezed once, and let go. The weight of his hand was comforting, and Kiernan wished it was still there before he could think not to.

Edna greeted him with an approximation of a smile as they boarded the carpet. "Are you all right, dear?"

She wouldn't care, if she knew why he was there. Benjamin wouldn't care, wouldn't have tried to comfort him, if he knew the boy had died because Kiernan had killed him.

"It was dangerous to stick around," Kiernan said.

Her smile didn't widen, exactly, but it became more a smile and less an approximation of one. "We wouldn't have left you."

Kiernan hesitated. "Thanks."

Night hung over the dark, silent city. Beatrice rose above the street, above the buildings, above the skylanes, until their faces stung with cold and the stars seemed close enough to touch. Benjamin wrapped his arms around himself. Edna patted his knee.

Kiernan had the uncomfortable feeling he owed Benjamin something. He wasn't used to people taking care of him, even if it was his own fault for acting like he didn't need it. Like he just had, calling Benjamin an idiot when Benjamin had just wanted to comfort him.

"Are you all right?" Kiernan asked.

Benjamin gripped the edges of the carpet. "I don't like heights."

He swallowed, catching a glimpse of the ground below.

Kiernan grabbed his t-shirt and pulled him further back. "You were fine on the ride to the hospital."

"We were in the skylanes. I don't know if you noticed, but this is, like, a little bit higher than that."

Kiernan let go of his shirt. "They're safer than airplanes."

Benjamin squeezed his eyes shut. "If you say so."

Kiernan let out a huff of laughter before he could stop himself. The carpet headed deeper into the cold night.

CHAPTER TWENTY-TWO

With the young people accounted for, Edna had nothing to distract her from her first encounter as Chosen One. Getting the sword had been busywork, something Methodius or any wizard could have surely done rather than wasting her time when a dracophilic sorcerer was on the loose. She glared at the ring twinkling innocently on her finger.

It had felt powerful. And hungry. She hadn't liked it, how it had felt hot and ready for blood and vengeance. What good, exactly, had it done her anyway?

None, that's what.

The sword had bounced—*bounced*—off the dragon's side. If she hadn't found a loose scale, she wouldn't have done any damage at all. Why a sword? Why not a magically imbued machine gun of destiny?

Probably because a sword was traditional, or something similarly silly.

Not that a gun would've done her any better. The city's dragon-fighters had carried guns, yet at least three of them had died. The rest hadn't killed the dragon or even seriously injured it; Redway had seen to that. That shadowy figure had sent their bullets hurtling back to earth with a spell. Magically imbued bullets were the only real weapon anyone had against dragons, if there weren't a powerful enchanter around to help out. If Redway could magick them harmless, what on earth was one little old lady supposed to do about him and his dragons?

Dragons. He had *dragons.* This had been one dragon, *one,* with one horrid sorcerer riding it, attacking Detroit because—well, she wasn't sure why, since he was supposed to be targeting Knights.

For fun, she supposed. Burning a city for fun. She shuddered.

The point was, one dragon ridden by one sorcerer had burnt up half the city, melted streets, crumbled buildings, left the acrid smell of smoke lingering in the sky.

Edna picked at her dress. She'd changed at the staff witch's suggestion but swore she could see the sickly lilac of dried dragon's blood on the clean dress. She picked harder, wishing she had a washcloth, or a washing machine, though the witch had told her a washing machine would lose the fight against dragon's blood.

Dragon's blood crusted Beatrice's weave, too. Edna couldn't do anything about that, either.

"What are you doing?" Clem said.

Edna picked at the imaginary stains with a thumbnail.

"Stop that," Clem said.

Edna stopped. A moment later, she started again, picking at the blood dried into the carpet. Beatrice shuddered.

Clem scowled. "Stop it, I said."

Edna did not stop it.

"Cut it out."

Kiernan glanced over his shoulder. He sat at the back of the carpet with his legs dangling over the edge. Benjamin slumped against him, asleep, snoring softly. Kiernan caught Edna's eye and turned back to the brightening horizon.

Beatrice bristled as Edna picked at the dragon's blood. Clem slapped her hands away. Edna folded her hands in her lap.

"Okay," Clem said, "what the hell's wrong with you?"

Edna stared at her shoes, the black, rubber-soled loafers that Golden Years preferred residents to wear so as to avoid falls. "What?"

"I said, what's wrong?"

The dragon's blood had come off the shoes, but the toes were scuffed. The sole of the right shoe peeled away from the rest of it.

Clem scooted closer. "Seriously. Are you okay?"

Edna's eyes welled up. She blinked, but tears sloshed down her face. Clem patted her shoulder, once, twice, and let her hand fall back to her side.

A sob slipped out before Edna could stop it.

"Oh, dear," she choked. "Oh—what good did it do?"

"What?" Clem said helplessly.

Edna shuddered and cried and tried to stop crying, thinking about Amir and Beatrice and the burnt city and her son and Clem's sister and—

"I haven't even finished my scarf!" she burst out, and she sobbed so hard she couldn't speak.

Clem's hesitation vanished. She held Edna fiercely. If tears were a person, they would have taken one look at her and run the other way.

Edna sobbed until she wore herself out, then sat hiccupping in Clem's arms. Kiernan stayed firmly turned around, for which she was profoundly grateful.

She couldn't know how puzzled he was. He mulled over her tears, wondering why she seemed so much more upset about what had happened than the Chosen One did.

Edna had already forgotten him.

"I should have stayed at the nursing home." She felt a hundred years old and briefly hoped she wouldn't live that long. "It didn't do anything. It didn't do any good."

Clem set her handbag in her lap. Edna produced an obscenely bright yellow silk handkerchief. She sniffled, dabbing at her eyes and blowing her nose with a honk. Salt spotted her lenses.

"You're too young." Edna crushed the handkerchief in her fingers. "You think killing Redway will bring your sister back—don't you?"

Clem picked at her fingernails and said nothing.

"I know you do," Edna said. "You've spent so much time trying to figure out how to get at him, but it won't do any good. She's dead."

The minute the words escaped, she wanted to take them back.

Clem's jaw tightened.

"Fuck you," she whispered.

"I'm sorry," Edna said. "I'm so sorry. I—"

"Shut up."

Edna shut up.

Clem drew her legs up to her chest and buried her face in her knees. Edna resisted the urge to pat her back.

Clem sniffled.

Edna twisted her handkerchief into a ball. "Clem—"

"Don't." Clem looked up, pushing her hair out of her face. "It's not like I haven't heard it before, okay?"

She dashed tears from her cheeks.

"Freshman year, I had a panic attack in class, and Mr. Nichols sent me to the counselor," she said, "and the counselor didn't know what to do with me. When she found out it had been two years, she told me to suck it up, Marisol was dead and there was nothing anyone could do about it, and crying wasn't going to help anything."

"A *counselor* said that?"

Clem tied her hair back. "I stopped crying in class after that."

She wiped her nose on her arm. Edna handed her a fresh handkerchief, this one edged in crochet.

"Thanks."

Edna hesitated. "I shouldn't have said it."

"Probably not."

"I didn't mean it."

"Did so." Clem scrubbed her face with the handkerchief. "I know it won't bring her back. But I can stop him from hurting other people."

"I hope so," Edna said fervently. "Oh, I hope so."

Clem folded the handkerchief into a tiny square. "Can I hang onto this?"

"Of course, dear."

Clem stuffed the handkerchief in her pocket. Edna dabbed at her nostrils. They sat in silence, watching the stars fade.

"What was your son like?" Clem asked.

Edna rummaged around in her handbag. "Would you like to see a picture?"

She produced a faded photograph in a tarnished silver frame: Percival, eighteen, lanky and proud and a little awkward in his new squire's uniform, with an arm around a smiling Edna who was younger but already gray and plump.

Clem raised an eyebrow. "You look old enough to be his grandmother."

Edna chuckled. "I am, at that. I was nearly forty by the time he was born. Never meant to have children, but, well, Walter and I couldn't keep our hands off each other."

Clem made a face. Edna laughed harder, spraying them both with snot. Kiernan shifted at the other end of the carpet.

"Oh, dear," Edna said, chortling wetly. "Sorry. Walter proposed the minute we found out I was pregnant, but I told him, look here, just because I'm having a baby when I didn't mean to doesn't mean I have to up and get married when I didn't mean to. I think I hurt his feelings, but he never said another word about it, just helped raise the baby until he died...heart attack," she added. "Percival was fifteen."

Clem studied the picture. At eighteen, Percival had grown too tall for his frame. His face was round and boyish, ablaze with excitement at the prospect of adventure.

"He looks nothing like you."

"No, he's the spitting image of his father."

Edna tucked the photo away with a sigh.

"There were closer bases." She gazed at the wilted handkerchief in her hand. "But he'd never left home, and the Knights had proper funding for the first time in decades, with the Cold War ending... All the young people were clamoring to join up. He wanted to be right on the front lines."

Clem nodded. "Marisol, too."

They sat in silence. At last Clem asked, "Was it an attack on his base?"

Edna shook her head. "In Dominion."

Clem rested her chin on her knees with a frown. "What was he doing there?"

"That's the million-dollar question, isn't it? He wasn't supposed to be there. I understand some of his friends got an assignment, and he snuck off with their unit. Couldn't wait to get in on the action, I suppose."

The corner of Clem's mouth twitched. "Like his mom."

"I suppose," Edna said. "But I wish he hadn't."

Their silence, this time, was more lasting. Embarrassed by her outburst of tears, Edna buried herself in her knitting.

She wasn't given to prolonged bouts of depression, no matter the circumstances, and she'd always had to be strong for people, back to her earliest days. Her mother. Her younger sister. Walter and Percival. By the time Percival died, she was so used to putting on a brave face that she took more care of the relatives who came to the memorial service than they did of her. Bob—her oldest nephew, the one who'd put her things in storage when she left the home—was the only one who saw her break down all week, and only once.

After the relatives had left and the house was horribly, silently empty again, she'd thrown herself into work, returning to her job as a railway attendant. She'd always been all right as long as she could keep moving.

So, the journey helped, as journeys always had. The skylanes here, over farmland and plains, were higher and emptier. America stretched below, a patchwork of blues and greens and grays and golds.

Edna worked on her scarf, watching the world go by below. Kiernan had magicked an invisible barrier around them so the wind wouldn't sting their faces as they zipped through the sky. Benjamin asked him question after question about the spell's minutest details, many of which Kiernan couldn't answer.

"I don't know," he said, more than once.

"But was it more of a wrist motion or—?"

Kiernan looked at his hand in bewilderment. He'd never *thought* so much about his magic before. You didn't think about magic; you just did it, unless apparently you were Benjamin and spent all your time thinking about it and none of your time doing it, for whatever reason.

"I don't know. I just—"

Kiernan tried to repeat the motion he'd made while doing the spell, only to find he couldn't do it while thinking about it.

Clem ignored them all, wearing earbuds that weren't plugged into anything. Midway on their second day out from Detroit, she twitched them out of her ears and interrupted Benjamin in the midst of a long, rambling question about luck magic that bewildered Kiernan even more than the questions about his spell. Luck magic was an Andenya secret that few humans and virtually no Westerners knew a thing about.

"So do you have to actually, like, use it," Benjamin was saying, "like say anything or, or, or, I don't know, activate it somehow? Or does it do things on its own when you—?"

Kiernan scratched his hairline with a thumb, too bemused by this line of questioning to even begin to answer. "I still don't understand how you know about it. Even other elvish nations don't know about it."

Benjamin waved a hand.

"My favorite professor in grad school studied in Bahir Dar—her advisor was Andenya. I don't know. It came up a couple times when I went to her office hours, I don't know." He leaned in, his face ablaze with excitement. "But okay, seriously, is it passive or active magic? She couldn't even tell me that much, she just kinda knew it was a thing—"

Clem sighed loudly. "You know I can hear you through these things, right?"

Benjamin broke off mid-question. "So? I wasn't talking to you."

"Yeah, but I can *hear* you. And it's annoying."

Benjamin flinched, glancing sideways at Kiernan. He *had* been asking a lot of questions.

"It's not annoying to me," Kiernan said, though he was still utterly bewildered.

Clem scowled at him, but she hardly could've scowled at anyone else on earth with less effect.

Benjamin relaxed; he hadn't asked for reassurance, yet Kiernan had said he wasn't annoying. Emboldened, he said to Clem, "What else am I supposed to do? It's a long flight."

Clem twiddled with her earbuds. "Will you shut up if we play a game or something?"

"We don't have any games, genius."

"We will in a minute."

Clem ran her hands over her earbuds. They glowed and turned into headphones.

"Fuck." She tried again.

This time, the earbuds transfigured into a battered game of Monopoly. Edna wasn't sure whether it was so battered because Clem wasn't the best at magic or because it was a copy of her own game at home. Come to that, Edna wasn't sure if it was a pair of earbuds masquerading as a Monopoly board or a Monopoly board that had been masquerading as a pair of earbuds.

The young people spent the rest of the trip playing board games. Rather, Clem spent the rest of the trip decimating Benjamin and Kiernan, who spent the rest of the trip ganging up on her in a futile attempt to win. Clem would do anything to beat them, sometimes within questionable bounds of the rules. Benjamin followed the rules religiously, was convinced she was cheating, and couldn't catch her at it to save his life. Kiernan cheated outright but was never caught by either, although it didn't do him any good. Clem was more familiar with the rules, and Kiernan was too busy trying to help Benjamin win to try to win himself.

He wasn't sure why. He'd had an idea of beating Clem when they'd started playing. Just to prove he could. But he didn't understand the point of Monopoly. And Benjamin was cute when he was badly losing a board game to a teenager.

Benjamin was cute in general, with those big, brown eyes and broad shoulders. If things were different, Kiernan might've pursued a hookup.

He didn't often. Never at the keep. No matter what the others got up to, it seemed like a bad idea to hook up with someone living in the same space. Most of the time, he could take or leave sex anyway. His rare hookups happened on supply runs, when his mutual attraction with a stranger aligned with his occasional feelings of desire.

Considering why he was here, pursuing something was a bad idea. But it didn't stop Kiernan from sitting next to Benjamin as they played, or from watching the play of light on his brown skin and the way his brow scrunched whenever he thought Clem was cheating.

As long as his flying horse was hitched to their stagecoach, Kiernan might as well enjoy himself.

Edna worked on her scarf, enjoying their gameplay. It reminded her of Walter and Percival and the extended family playing games together at the holidays.

As the journey wore on, however, she couldn't help her bouts of uncertainty. Up here on a carpet, she had plenty of time to think about what an inadequate Chosen One she was, how grand a destiny this was for someone who wasn't grand and never had been. She couldn't stop thinking: it was only one dragon. And the journey to Santa Alvara ate into their time to find Monica Evans before Redway attacked again.

It plagued her more and more the further they flew. When she felt most doubtful, she threw herself into the young people's games. Benjamin eyed her, but she didn't dare tell him what was wrong with Kiernan aboard.

Their first sight of Santa Alvara did nothing to improve her mood. By the time they lowered into the city's skylanes, fog hung thick along the California coast. It made the morning darker and grayer than it should've been.

"It's the change in time zones," Clem said. "It's messing with your head."

"Whatever it is," Edna said, "it's not my idea of California at all."

She'd hoped for a glimpse of Santa Alvara's skyline. It was famous for the statue of a dragon that rose above the buildings, built in honor of Sir Carmichael Barstow on the hundredth anniversary of his death. She doubted she'd see it in the fog.

Quiet residential roads gave way to a traffic-clogged downtown that could have been the center of any major city in the country. Skyscrapers and office buildings jostled for space. The streets were a confusion of six-lane roads and tight, cobbled, one-way side streets. Carpets, broomsticks, and flying horses choked the skylanes. Where was the famous statue? Where was the Santa Alvara Museum of Knighthood? Or the Barstow School of Gallantry?

They turned a corner. A green lawn stretched before them, surrounded by snow-white Greek-revival school buildings. In the center of the lawn, larger than life, there it was: a scrap-metal dragon launching itself into the sky, its wings half open, its neck stretching toward the clouds, its tail trailing behind it.

Half a dozen squires threw a Frisbee back and forth in the dragon's shadow, but they scrambled to attention as a squadron of Knights marched past.

A tour bus rumbled by. A crisp, feminine voice blared through its speakers.

"...first formal chivalric school in the United States. Founded by Sir Carmichael Barstow in 1879, the school has run continuously for over a hundred and forty years..."

The sun burned away the morning fog, glinting on the dragon's coppery snout and the snowy school buildings. Edna's spirits rose with the mist. For the first time since she'd left the nursing home, she felt like she was on a grand adventure.

CHAPTER TWENTY-THREE

The Royal Crown Hotel was a Victorian mansion past its prime. It had more stained glass and spires than were strictly necessary and a sagging wrap-around porch with wicker sets and porch swings everywhere. Moss and lichen colored the roof gray-green. The hotel was at least four different colors, all of them faded, except on the left half of the porch, where someone had freshened up the railing's white paint. Colorful blooms exploded from the flowerbeds. Palm trees stood sentinel on either side of the front steps.

Edna loved it.

Benjamin eyed the hotel like he might've eyed a manticore. "At least the garden looks nice."

"It's wonderful," Edna said.

Star jasmine wrapped around the porch columns like it was holding them up. Kiernan bent to smell it. "Some fae lives here."

"Half-fae," Clem mumbled.

She shrugged her backpack up her shoulders and mounted the porch steps. They groaned underfoot.

The front door was propped open to let in the morning air. Through the screen, polished hardwood floors gleamed. A man hunched over the reception desk, reading a newspaper. Without looking up, he called out, "Y'all can come on in. I don't bite."

Clem led the others inside. Beatrice remained on the porch, slung over a railing.

They'd stepped into an overgrown garden. Creepers snaked up the walls like stripy wallpaper. Honeysuckle perfumed the air. Fuchsia hung from the ceiling like a chandelier; its flowers glowed, casting dancing pink light on the ceiling and floor. Forget-me-nots draped the sides of the reception desk, which looked like it wanted to be left alone for a nap, thank you, and ivy clung to its sides.

Even the man hunched over the desk had a peony tucked behind his ear. His mouth lifted into a tired smile. Except that he was human, he might have grown from the desk: his skin was the same color, equally worn but less polished. He couldn't have been older than forty, but the furrows in his brow rivaled Edna's.

"You folks got a reservation?" he asked, in the carefully polite voice of someone who already knows the answer.

Clem twitched towards her necklace, but she stopped herself before she touched it. "Rodriguez?"

The man's smile widened. He leaned over the desk for a closer look at her, creaking like an aged tree.

"You must be Clementine."

"Clem," Clem said in a small voice.

"Jada will be pleased as poppies. Let me call her."

He pressed a button behind the desk. Tiny lights like fireflies lit up on the wall and raced throughout the hotel, over the creepers, up the wide, moss-carpeted stairway to the left. They blinked twice, all together, and went out.

"Here she come," the man said.

A girl bounded down the stairs, a petite girl with dark brown skin and a crown of black hair pulled back with a flowered headband made of real flowers. She threw her arms around Clem with a laugh.

Clem blushed. She returned the hug, her arms angled out as if she were afraid of crushing the girl, but the girl pulled back and grabbed her hands.

"Oh my gosh, you're even prettier in person!" she squealed.

Clem's blush deepened. The girl let her go, smiling. She had a gap between her teeth and the same nose and eyes as her father at the reception desk. Sweet alyssum blossomed in her hair like tiny stars.

Clem caught Edna's eye. "Right, sorry. This is Jada Wyatt. We're pen pals."

"Oh!" Edna said. "I had no idea people still did that. How do you do?"

"You're, uh, you have to come over here," Clem said. "You're on her deaf side."

Jada introduced them to her father, Demarco, with a flourish that brought a smile to his lips. It faded a moment later. His face tightened; he slouched against the desk.

"Bed," Jada said immediately.

"I'm fine."

"Pops." She was at his side before he could object further, slipping his arm around her shoulder. "I can watch the lobby. You need a break."

He slumped against her. "Maybe for a little bit. If you run into trouble..."

"I know."

She led him through a door behind the desk and returned alone, with frown lines scoring her young forehead. Clem wanted to do something, maybe touch her shoulder, but she couldn't quite work up the courage.

"How's he been doing?" she asked in a low voice.

"Better," Jada said, but not like she meant it. "The doctor said she's optimistic, but he's so tired. Like, all the time. She says it's a normal side effect, but..."

"Can't they do something about that? With magic?"

Jada shook her head, clicking around on the computer. "He coded the moment it hit his blood stream."

Clem's palms were sweaty. She rubbed them on her jeans, reached across the desk, and squeezed Jada's hand.

Jada gave a wobbly smile. "Thanks."

The screen door opened behind them. The newcomer was a man in his mid-thirties, with black hair graying at the temples, wearing a Knight's uniform and carrying a duffel bag. He dropped his duffel bag on the floor by the desk.

"Reservation name of Miller."

Jada's smile hardened.

Clem scowled. "Excuse you, we were here first."

He glanced at her and turned back to Jada—only for a moment. His head whipped back around like he'd seen a ghost.

"Clem?" he said. "Clem Rodriguez?"

To everyone's astonishment, Clem laughed. The man wrapped her in a bear hug, both of them speaking at once.

"—doing here?"

"What am I—what are you!"

"—how long, four years?"

"—can't believe you—"

At last, their chatter died down. They grinned at each other. The man looked much younger for it.

"God, you look just like your sister."

Clem rubbed her arm. "Yeah. I get that a lot."

Their grins faded. Clem avoided the man's gaze.

Benjamin nudged her. "Are you going to introduce us, or what?"

"Yeah, sorry." She fussed with her necklace. "Dan, this is Benjamin, er, Benjamin—"

She realized she didn't know his last name and covered by saying authoritatively, "This is Benjamin," and moved on before he could ask who, exactly, Benjamin was. "Kiernan Abbott. And Edna Fisher."

"I'm a friend of her grandmother's," Edna offered.

"Yeah," Clem said. "Sorry. It's just, I wasn't expecting—"

"It's been a long time," the man said.

"Yeah. Guys, this is Dan Miller. He was in Marisol's cohort of squires. He taught me some swordplay when I visited her."

His mouth twisted into a smile. "Our squad leader made me clean the bathrooms with a toothbrush when he found out. Said he had enough for me to do without wasting my time teaching a little girl to handle a sword. He always had it in for me anyway. I was so much older than the other squires."

"How many rooms did you need?" Jada asked Edna pointedly.

"Oh," Dan said in surprise. "Sorry, I didn't realize you were—"

"Well," Clem said, in tones nearer apologetic than Edna had ever heard her, "we were."

With a small frown, she turned to Jada. "Rooms? I thought we were crashing on your couch or something."

Jada's eyes crinkled into a smile. "Right, like we're gonna let you stay in Santa Alvara and *not* see the Crown. Pops offered to let you stay while you're in town. One for each of you, or—?"

"Heavens, no," Edna said. "Two will be fine, if you've got them."

Benjamin looked at Kiernan with panic in his eyes. "Two?"

No one heard him. Kiernan was gazing around the floriferous lobby and hadn't considered the implications of the four of them sharing only two rooms.

Clem wasn't sure how to answer Jada's questions about what kind of rooms they wanted. She'd never booked a hotel room before and felt like they were taking advantage of her hospitality, no matter what Jada's dad said. Edna took over the room situation instead.

Clem used the intervening minutes to catch up with Dan. He was stationed in southern Florida now, he said.

"What are you doing here?" Clem asked.

"There's a conference in two days. Half the brass in the country must be in town. This isn't the closest hotel, but it was cheap, and it was the only place with rooms available this late."

Jada's eyes were fixed on the computer screen, but her lips thinned.

"It's beautiful," Clem said, a little uncertainly, "don't you think? With the flowers and everything?"

Jada caught her eye and smiled almost imperceptibly.

Dan gave the lobby a once-over.

"The flowers, sure." He sounded like he didn't much care about the flowers, or the hotel. "What are you here for? Not the conference, I'm guessing."

Clem drummed her fingers on the desk. "Hamilton's playing in San Francisco next week, but I've wanted to visit Santa Alvara since Marisol joined the Knights. And Edna wanted to see her granddaughter—Monica Evans. You wouldn't know her, I guess. She's a squire here."

Edna smiled in an appropriately grandmotherly way. She had already pretended to be Benjamin's grandmother and Clem's grandmother, and she supposed it was only a matter of time until she pretended to be Kiernan's grandmother. Adding Monica Evans to the mix was no big deal.

The other half of the lie meant nothing to her. The only Hamilton she could think of was a historical figure who had something to do with banking. Banking, a duel, and maybe a lake monster.

Perhaps Clem had dropped Monica Evans's name too quickly, however, or perhaps her face went a little too mask-like as the lies slipped out. Whatever it was, Dan's jaw tensed, so fleetingly that Edna wondered if she had imagined it.

"Maybe we can do some sightseeing together," he said.

Jada came around the desk. Clem blushed at her proximity.

"Your rooms are ready." Jada gave Dan a mechanical smile. "I'll have yours in a minute."

"Sure thing. Catch you later, Clem."

"Bye," Clem mumbled. Jada led them down the hall to their rooms.

Someone might have stuck a hotel suite in the middle of a forest. Heath pearlwort carpeted the ground, thick and springy and emerald green, dotted with little white flowers. The ceiling was sky blue, as were the walls, though they were hidden behind vines, leaves, moss, lichen, and bark. Saplings grew out of the floor and twisted into the frames of two four-poster beds, draped with hangings of Spanish moss.

It would be like camping, without the mosquitoes and pollen. Jada's plants were far too well-bred to release pollen with guests around.

"It's this one and the one across the hall," she said. Benjamin choked on air. Jada touched her flowery headband as she spoke to Clem. "I didn't realize you were gonna be out so much. I thought we could spend some time together or something. I mean—"

Her words tumbled out in a rush.

"—if you want to sightsee, it's fine, obviously, like of course you should see the city, you don't have to stick around here all day, but I thought—"

Clem flushed. "No—I mean, yeah, sightseeing's not the only—I mean—"

Edna disguised her chuckle as a cough. Benjamin was still panicking about sharing a room with Kiernan. Kiernan didn't think anything of it, since he'd already decided a hookup was a bad idea; he went across the hall to make himself comfortable.

"I *mean,*" Clem said, fiddling with her hair, "I'd love to spend some time with you. Like. I don't know. Maybe we could do makeovers or something tomorrow."

The flowers in Jada's hair grew a little bigger. "Yeah! That'd be great. So, uh, come to reception after breakfast?"

"It's a date." Clem blushed again. "No. I mean. Not a date. I mean. It's—"

Edna choked back laughter.

"I'll make sure she finds you after breakfast," she said to Jada.

Jada smiled and all but danced from the room.

Benjamin edged across the hall to stare into the bedroom he'd share with Kiernan. Two separate beds. He relaxed marginally. Not that two beds did away with the implication of sharing a hotel room with someone ridiculously attractive who put up with his many questions about magic. But at least it prevented any zany romantic-comedy-esque arguments about who should take the floor until whoever took the bed insisted the other join them, purely for the sake of politeness and comfort, of course.

In the other room, Edna sat with a groan. Clem flopped beside her, buried her face in a pillow, and screamed into it.

"It wasn't that bad," Edna said.

Clem emerged from her pillow. "Not that bad? It was a disaster. *I'm* a disaster."

"You're not a disaster."

"This whole stupid thing is a disaster," Clem said. "What the fuck was I thinking?"

"I'm not sure what you were thinking, backpedaling like that." Edna removed her shoes. "'Not a date.' Really, Clementine. I'm not pretending I'm an expert, but it seemed to me like you'd like a date with her."

Clem sat up, picking at the quilt. "Yeah. Eventually. I guess."

"Then what's the problem?"

Clem blushed, mumbling something.

"What?"

"I said"—Clem's blush deepened—"if we go on a date, she might think...she might expect...What if she wants me to kiss her?"

"I'd consider myself a lucky girl, wouldn't you?"

Clem hid in her hair. "I've never kissed a girl. I've only kissed boys. Two of them. And I'm not even good at it."

"Says who?"

"Says them."

"Oh, what do boys know?" Edna said.

"And the last one"—Clem spoke faster and faster, as if she had to say this quickly or she wouldn't say it at all—"he broke up with me because I wouldn't—I wouldn't—I didn't want to—"

She hugged her knees.

"I think I know what you mean," Edna said.

"Yeah, that." Clem sounded relieved. "He broke up with me. If Jada wants—that—I don't think—I don't want that. I don't think I want it. I mean, I haven't—you know—but I think, I mean, I'm pretty sure I'm ace."

She had to explain what that meant, because Edna thought blankly of a deck of cards and couldn't understand what it had to do with sex. Clem gave a long, rambling explanation that made Edna's insides prickle. True, she and Walter hadn't been able to keep their hands off each other. But until she'd met him, Edna hadn't been particularly interested in sex—and she hadn't been particularly interested in sex since he'd died, either. It wasn't exactly what Clem was describing, but it was close.

At present, however, Edna was more concerned with Clem than herself, so she filed the thought away for another time. Clem wiped her nose on her arm. Her face was redder than ever, and a little damp, and her mascara was smudged.

Edna tucked the girl's hair behind her ears.

"If you two like each other," she said gently, "you'll work something out."

"Yeah. Maybe."

Edna patted her knee. "You're getting a little ahead of yourself, don't you think? You might want to ask her on a real date before worrying about all that."

"I guess." Clem rested her chin on her knees. Then she threw herself back onto the pillows with a vehement, "Fuck!"

"What on earth is it now?"

Clem sat up, hugging a pillow to her chest. "I can't spend the day here! We need to find Monica Evans. Did you hear what Dan said? There's a conference in two days. I bet that's what she's here for. He said Knights were coming from all over! What if—?"

"That's enough of that," Edna said. "You stay here with Jada and don't worry about it. We'll find Monica Evans."

Clem snorted.

"Need I remind you," Edna said primly, "no matter what we're telling people, I'm the Chosen One."

Clem flopped back onto the pillows with a loud sigh.

"You must be feeling better," Edna said.

Clem stuck her tongue out. Edna laughed.

"So," she said, "what about this Dan fellow? Should we tell him what we're really up to?"

Clem frowned. "Why?"

"If he wants to sightsee with us, we're going to have to make excuses. And he is a friend of yours, isn't he? I don't see any reason to lie to someone unless we ought to."

"We ought to lie to everyone," Clem said. "Chosen Ones always run into trouble when word gets out about who they are."

"I don't know if you've noticed," Edna said, "but I've already run into trouble."

Clem shrugged. "He's a Knight. I don't know how he'd feel if he knew we were looking for another Knight."

"But she's not really a Knight."

"I don't exactly have proof."

"Oh. Well, I don't suppose he'd be much help finding her, anyway, since he's not stationed here." Edna wiggled her feet and pulled her shoes back on. It was going to be a long day. "With any luck, we won't see too much of him. Let's get the boys and figure out our next course of action."

Clem rolled off the bed, stretched, and clomped toward the door.

"By the way," Edna said, "it's Cooper."

"What?"

"Benjamin. His last name is Cooper. In case you find yourself needing to introduce him to any more old friends."

CHAPTER TWENTY-FOUR

The Carmichael Center and Museum, the main tourist attraction at the Barstow School of Gallantry, was white and columned and hung with a banner proclaiming the upcoming conference. Its lobby was cool and dim, but the welcome center was more brightly lit and included a gift shop, an information desk, a cafe, bathrooms, and a drinking fountain. The carpet-ride there had been long and hot, the skylanes filled with traffic, and Edna slurped water up gratefully.

She headed for the information desk with Clem close at her side. Benjamin paused by the gift shop, itching to examine the tchotchkes on display, then hurried after them. Kiernan trailed after him, fists clenched in his pockets. He couldn't stop glancing around. He wasn't in any danger here, he knew, but the stark lobby reminded him too much of the base he'd joined at seventeen.

At the information desk, a young man flipped through a magazine.

"Hi there," Edna said. "I'm looking for my granddaughter, she's a squire, and I was wondering if–"

"Can't help you," the young man interrupted in a bored voice.

Clem raised her eyebrows. Edna continued before she could butt in.

"If you could point me in the direction of a directory or—"

"The directory's here," the young man said, "but it won't do you any good. Campus is closed to the public today."

"The public, yes, but my understanding was that family—"

"Unless you're enlisted, no dice. There's a conference in two days and they've got intensive testing and training going on before they're overrun. The museum's the only place you can be until tomorrow." He turned another page. "I'm surprised your granddaughter didn't tell you."

Edna faltered. "Oh, well, you see, she actually doesn't know we're here. It's her birthday this week, so I thought I'd surprise her—"

"You'll have to surprise her tomorrow."

Clem's eyes were snapping. It was a good thing Edna, not Clem, was holding onto the Sword of Destiny.

Benjamin moved closer to Clem than he really wanted to, with that look on her face, and said in a low voice, "It's fine. Edna's got this."

Clem clenched her fists. Sparks leapt from her fingers. Benjamin jerked away. Kiernan didn't notice, glancing around the building, his whole body tensed.

"If you could tell me what dorm she's in," Edna said hastily. "Even if I can't visit until tomorrow, surely—"

The young man snapped his magazine shut. "Look, lady. You can't get in to see her. If I could confirm with her that you're supposed to be here, that'd be one thing. But if I tell you what dorm she's in, and you sneak in to see her when you're not supposed to—"

"I would never," Edna said, ignoring Benjamin's snort behind her.

"—that's on me. I could lose my job, the Knights are insane about security, so—"

"Where is she?" Clem snarled.

"Oh, dear," Edna said.

"I can't tell you," the young man repeated.

Clem slapped her hands on the desk. Sparks raced up her arms. "Bullshit."

"Clementine," Edna said.

"Shut up."

Sparks showered the young man's magazine. It burst into flame.

Benjamin pulled Edna away from the desk with a yelp. They bumped into Kiernan. He snapped to attention, the collision jerking him out of his unpleasant memories of knighthood.

"Where is she?" Clem demanded.

The young man's voice quivered. "If you call her and ask her to confirm with me—"

"Thank you anyway," Edna said quickly, and she dragged Clem away from the information, or rather informationless, desk. Sparks bit into her skin, threatening to set her dress aflame, but she didn't stop until she had dragged Clem halfway down the front steps. Benjamin followed, fluttering his hands uselessly.

Clem wrenched herself from Edna's grasp.

"What are you doing? He can tell us what dorm she's in."

"You heard him. He's not going to."

"Not with that attitude."

"I'm not letting you torture him for information, or whatever it is you were planning on doing," Edna said, turning away from her. "Where's Kiernan?"

Benjamin looked around. "What—? He was right behind me a second ago."

"At least it's a plan," Clem snapped, "which is more than you have. Why are you such a fucking failure?"

"Hey," Benjamin said weakly, but the sparks alarmed him too much for him to argue.

Edna was considerably less alarmed. She hitched her handbag higher up her arm.

"What exactly do you want me to do, Clementine? We asked a question; we didn't get an answer. And if the welcome center desk clerk isn't going to give us an answer to a simple question, what do you think the Knights are going to do? Escort us to her room?"

"I want you to act like you care what happens to the Knights!" Clem's hands balled into fists. "I want you to act like you realize Redway could attack any day and destroy the whole stupid city!"

"I do realize that, but—"

"If I were the Chosen One—"

"Clementine—"

"I'd do whatever it took." The sparks had thickened, leaping from Clem's fists, running up and down her arms. Benjamin shied away from her. *"Whatever* it took."

Clem's pain was so fresh and raw, so young and angry. Edna wanted to say she understood, but her loss had been nearly thirty years ago. Long before Clem or her sister were even thought of, maybe even before her parents had met. A lifetime. And she knew it wasn't why the wizards had chosen her.

Edna wanted to say that she, too, would do whatever it took to save the Knights.

But she wouldn't.

"There are some things," she said in a low voice, "there are some things I just can't do."

The sparks burst into a whirlwind, a swirl of magic around Clem's body. Benjamin dragged Edna further away, stumbling on the stairs.

Kiernan, coming out of the building, paused on the top step. The tornado of magic around the girl reminded him of something—of Red. Red when his magic spilled out of him, rage-red, ready to destroy anything in its path.

But this was a sixteen-year-old girl. Athletic, sure, and handy with a sword by all accounts—though he had yet to see her use it, except as a smudge of black against the Detroit sky—but terrible at magic and barely five feet tall. He understood now what Benjamin had meant about Edna teaching her to keep a lid on it.

So far, she didn't seem successful.

Kiernan approached Clem carefully. Sudden movements around someone bursting with enraged magic got people hurt—them, if you managed to sneak away or put up a defensive spell; you if you didn't. Touching them was an even worse idea. If it had been Red, with powerful magic and three decades of rage in him, Kiernan might not have done anything. But Clem was a kid.

"There's no need for that," he said. "She's in Reeves Hall."

Clem turned to him slowly. He shivered despite himself.

"He talked?" she asked.

He shrugged. "We'll have a time getting there without being caught, but..."

The sparks swirled slower and slower, thinner and thinner, until they winked out.

Clem swayed. Kiernan steadied her without thinking. She had bags under her eyes that hadn't been there before, but she met his gaze in a way he could almost admire. He'd been like that as a teenager. Not as angry, but wiry and scrappy and ready to fight. Ready to do whatever it took.

"Reeves Hall?" she said. "He told you?"

"Room 203."

Her eyes glittered, but she slumped against him, fatigued from the anger and magic. It happened to Red, sometimes, and he'd been angry and out of control for decades.

Kiernan stood statue-still, not sure what to do with this teenager leaning into him for comfort. He wasn't supposed to be comforting her. He was supposed to be killing her, if he could, or at least kidnapping her.

Edna put an arm around the girl's shoulder. Benjamin approached more cautiously.

"Are you all right?" Edna asked gently.

"M'all right." Clem sounded exhausted.

Edna hugged her, speaking to Kiernan over her shoulder. "How on earth did you get him to tell you where she is?"

"Sympathy."

"He didn't seem sympathetic," Benjamin said.

Kiernan offered a rare smile.

"Played up our lie. I told him her old grandma had some difficult news to give her. By the way," he said to Edna, "if he asks, you're dying, and it's your dying wish to spend one last birthday with your only granddaughter."

Actually, the bit about dying had been more of a threat, directed more immediately at the desk clerk. The clerk hadn't given in—pointing shakily at a security camera—until Kiernan informed him he'd cast a charm to disable the camera the moment they'd walked through the door. It wasn't entirely true, but by the time he yanked the clerk over the desk by his collar, the camera was indeed charmed into not recording anything out of the ordinary.

Edna let out a breath. "Thank you. I thought...well..." Her eyes flickered to Clem. "Thank you."

Kiernan felt wrong-footed without knowing why. "No problem."

Benjamin clapped him on the shoulder. "We should have you help with this stuff more often. I was worried there for a second."

Kiernan didn't know what to say, so he said nothing.

They struck out for the dorms, but the clerk had told the truth: campus was closed to the public. Kiernan suggested splitting up, certain that, alone, he could worm his way further into campus to find Lena. No dice. Even he couldn't sneak past the guards, fences, and security checkpoints. All he accomplished was getting away from the others for a bit. Time to himself, to clear his head.

He drew his luck up enough to feel it there, warm and golden, and let it go. He wouldn't use it. If he couldn't get to the dorms with pure skill, he was confident the others couldn't, either.

They met up back by the Carmichael Center, their endeavors fruitless. Clem fidgeted with her necklace.

"It's all right," Edna said. "We'll come back tomorrow, first thing. We know where she is now. I'm sure—"

A voice called across the lawn. "Little Rodriguez!"

Clem glowered at this mode of address, but she waved. The voice belonged to a Knight with the epaulets of a high-ranking officer. He was blond, with the kind of pale skin that never tans, only burns. His sunburn had formed an uneasy truce with his face.

He smiled. Edna returned the smile, but he paid her no attention. He jerked Clem's ponytail. She twitched it over her shoulder.

"Dan said you were here," he said. "I haven't seen you since you were yea high." He held his hand at a height no shorter than Clem's height now.

"I was twelve, not a baby," Clem muttered, but he didn't hear her.

"Who are your friends?"

She introduced them, in a voice that said plainly she'd rather not. The Knight's name was Agravain Sullivan.

"Ag," he corrected, shaking hands all around—almost all around. Kiernan's arms were folded, and he didn't care to unfold them to shake hands with a Knight. "Look at you, Rodriguez! All grown up. You look just like your sister."

"I always thought she favored my side of the family," Kiernan said.

He didn't know why he said it, but the look on the Knight's face was worth it. Kiernan put an arm around Clem's shoulder like he might a niece, trying to act like he'd done it before. She scowled. Benjamin bit back a smile. Edna disguised her laughter as a fit of coughing.

After a moment of confusion, Ag laughed. "Traveling with family, huh? Did you enjoy the museum?"

Clem extricated herself from Kiernan's grip.

"We haven't looked around much yet," Edna said. "Actually, I'm here to see my granddaughter—Monica Evans?"

Ag shrugged. "Not familiar."

"She's a new recruit," Edna said. "I know where she is, but I've been trying to get in to see her for half an hour now and—"

"Sorry," Ag said. "Can't give you access to campus today. Come back tomorrow."

"Yes, I'd heard campus was closed, but I'm sure if *you* said it was all right—"

"I can't give you that kind of clearance."

"C'mon, Ag." Clem smiled, looking like she hadn't had much practice fake-smiling at people. "We won't stay long. Just so my friend can see her granddaughter?"

He laughed. "I admire persistence, but it's a no-go, kid. There are friends, and then there are regulations. Come back tomorrow."

Her smile, such as it was, slipped back into a scowl.

Ag chuckled. "Now you look more like Mari than ever. Come back tomorrow."

Clem stalked off.

"Clementine," Edna called, but she didn't respond. "Sorry about that. Talking about her sister, uh..."

"I understand," Ag said. "It was hard on all of us. Nice meeting you."

He started the opposite direction, but Edna had a thought. She sent Benjamin and Kiernan after Clem and scuttled after the Knight.

"Wait!" she called. "Excuse me!"

Ag turned back with polite quizzicality on his sunburnt face. Edna was unsure how to word her warning, so she said it as bluntly as possible.

"Look," she said, with such unexpected urgency that his polite quizzicality took on more interest. "Redway's going to attack Santa Alvara."

He raised his eyebrows and waited. For what, she wasn't sure.

"Soon," she said, because she felt like she should say something more. "Soon" didn't sound half urgent enough. *"Very* soon."

She listened to the echo of her own words. "Maybe even tomorrow."

His brow furrowed.

"Meaning no disrespect," he said, sounding like that wasn't precisely true, "but how did you come by this information?"

Edna hesitated. "I can't say."

"Then why should I believe it?"

She fidgeted with her handbag. She hadn't decided yet whether or not to tell him the truth when he said, "Santa Alvara is built for dragon attacks."

"Santa Alvara is built for *single* dragon attacks," Edna pointed out.

"If he does attack, he'll find us more than ready."

Ag said this with such grim finality that Edna almost believed him.

But she remembered the news stories. The fires. The sky black with dragons. The attack on Detroit, a single dragon under Redway's command destroying so much. Her inability to stop it.

Santa Alvara had withstood dragon attacks before, but nothing like what Redway was capable of.

Ag turned away.

Edna grabbed the back of his jacket. "Please, you have to believe me—"

He wrenched himself from her grasp, eyeing her warily. Then he realized he looked ridiculous, backing away from a short, plump old woman with a cane and one hell of a sunburn. He straightened, smoothing his hair.

"If you can't tell me how you know," he said, "there's nothing I can do."

He strode off, but Edna shouted after him.

"I know because I'm the Chosen One!"

He stopped. She clutched her cane, her heart hammering.

For one beautiful, glorious moment, she thought he would come back. Perhaps he'd escort her to his superiors so she could pass the message on herself.

Then he looked her up and down. She knew exactly what he saw: a shriveled woman so old and wrinkled that she ought never to have been allowed out of the nursing home. Unarmed and incapable of magic. Useless. Not someone the Council of Wizards would ever entrust with something so important.

Ag's lip curled.

But she was Mari's kid sister's friend, or whatever, so he smiled instead. That smile made Edna's heart drop down to her toes and curl up there, hidden.

Ag walked away. Edna had never felt so small in her life.

CHAPTER TWENTY-FIVE

Unable to search for Monica Evans, they stopped at a post office so Edna could return Methodius's ring, then spent the rest of the day sightseeing.

None of them were pleased about this. Benjamin had had enough adventure for one day and would've been happier reading a journal on the wicker set back at the hotel. Clem couldn't care less about sightseeing when they'd come so close to Monica Evans, only to be turned away because campus was closed to the public. Kiernan was starting to think that spending more time with the others was a bad idea, but he needed to keep an eye on them.

And Edna, thinking about the curl of Ag's lip when she'd said she was the Chosen One, was spared from anyone noticing her lack of cheer only by the abject misery of her companions.

When they returned to the Royal Crown Hotel, it was drizzling. Edna had wanted to watch the sunset from the mouth of the Carmichael Memorial Statue—the giant scrap-metal dragon—but by the time the long and disappointingly dull lecture on the dragon's making was over, clouds had gathered. The sun winked through redly, dimmer and dimmer until it winked right out.

Rain pattered on the walkway as Beatrice pulled up to the porch. Dan sat in a wicker armchair, leafing through a book on the use of magical weaponry in World War II.

"Hey." He closed his book. "Where've you guys been all day?"

"Out," Clem muttered.

Edna elbowed her. "Sightseeing."

"Hope you didn't see everything. I was hoping we could do some stuff together tomorrow. The conference isn't for another day and I'm tired of sitting around the hotel."

Clem made for the door, but Edna grabbed the back of her shirt. She wasn't going to stand here lying to Dan by herself. "We're actually going to see my granddaughter tomorrow."

"All of you?"

"That's the plan," Edna said breezily.

"Why don't I come with you? I'd love to see the school."

"Oh," Edna said, less breezily. "Well—well, I wouldn't mind, except—"

She almost told him she wanted to see her granddaughter alone, but she'd just said they were all going.

"I won't be a bother," he said, "and afterward maybe you can show me the sights, if you've already been—"

Clem sighed loudly. "Edna doesn't have a granddaughter."

Benjamin made a noise like a mouse being trodden upon. Edna elbowed him.

Dan stared. "I don't—"

"Monica Evans. She's not Edna's granddaughter."

"Then—"

"She works for Redway. I'm the Chosen One."

Benjamin looked like he needed a paper bag. Kiernan put a hand on his shoulder instinctively, his head cocked with birdlike interest.

Edna patted rainwater from her face. She hadn't expected this. But if Clem thought it safe to tell Dan the—well, not the truth, exactly, but the same lie they'd told Kiernan, it must be all right.

Clem crossed her arms. "You can't come with us. Get it?"

"So, you're not here about Mari?"

Kiernan's gaze shifted from Clem to Dan, but Clem merely scowled.

"I mean, she's kind of the point."

Dan's face relaxed into a smile.

"You look like her more than ever when you do that." He set his book aside. "So. Chosen One. That's a pretty big deal."

"A humongous deal," Clem agreed in a bored voice. "We're not sightseeing tomorrow, and you can't come with us, capisce?"

"Capisce," Dan said, very seriously, then laughed. "Chosen One. Wow. *Wow.* Should I wish you luck, or...? I don't really know what to say—"

Clem's arms uncrossed. Benjamin was hyperventilating and trying to act like he wasn't. Kiernan squeezed his shoulder, then realized what he was doing and let go.

"Me neither," Clem said. "Look, it's not like I don't want to hang out with you—"

"No, I get it. You've got a job to do. Some other time, maybe."

"Maybe."

They went inside. Jada was hunched over the reception desk with her chin propped on a fist.

"Are you okay?" Clem asked.

Jada's face slackened. She and Dan were quite a pair, Edna thought; she'd never seen two young people so old before their time.

It had been a long day. Jada's father had been bedridden with fatigue and pain. She'd been alone at the reception desk for hours.

The flowers in her hair drooped. "I thought we could hang out tomorrow. If you guys aren't going out again."

She said it like she'd be perfectly fine if they wanted to do more sightseeing instead, deceiving none of them. Clem blurted that she'd love to stay. She blushed.

The flowers in Jada's hair perked up. "Great."

Halfway down the hall, out of sight and earshot, Clem moaned in a high-pitched voice, "It is *not* great! Oh my god, what is *wrong* with me?"

"What's the problem?" Edna asked. "Stay here. We don't all need to go. I'm sure the poor girl could use the company."

Kiernan frowned. "Shouldn't the Chosen One—?"

Edna fumbled with the door to her room. Benjamin let out something like a small scream and disappeared into the room across the hall.

"We have to find Monica Evans first, don't we?" Edna said. "Clem doesn't need to waste her time with that when she could be, well, you know, practicing her magic and whatnot."

Kiernan's frown deepened. Edna strode into the room, hoping she gave off an air of authoritative knowledge.

"Anyway," she said, "it's not as if the girls will be here having fun all day. I'm sure Jada has to watch the lobby for a while. Clem could come out with us in the morning and head back in the afternoon if we haven't found Monica Evans. We'll head out first thing, all right? Tell Benjamin for me."

Kiernan's frown hadn't left, but he did, and he took it with him.

CHAPTER TWENTY-SIX

Clem's cell phone woke Edna before sunrise, playing a song from a musical.

The song cut off. Edna lay in the dark, wincing. Her sunburn felt hot and tight, ready to peel.

The phone went off again. Edna listened to the chorus of brass and drums, waiting for Clem to answer. In the darkness, Edna couldn't make out anything but the shadowy outline of the Spanish moss hangings of Clem's bed.

The song started a third time. Edna groped around, but the phone rang out.

It started up again. She fumbled to answer it. "Clem's phone."

Silence.

"Clementine's all right," she added. "She's asleep."

The person on the other end said something, but Edna didn't have her hearing aids in yet.

The bathroom door opened, slicing the room with light. Clem slouched out of the bathroom with her arms around her stomach. Edna put a hand over the phone, not exactly sure where the mouthpiece was, if you could call it a mouthpiece when phones were slim, black things with no clearly differentiated parts.

"Clem, dear, you have a phone call."

Clem dove for the phone. She twisted her hair with a hand as whoever was on the other end yelled at her. Edna felt around for her hearing aids.

"¡Ahora *no*, mamá! I'm sorry about Abuela but—Mom, would you just—" Clem grimaced, holding the phone farther from her ear. At last she snapped into it, "I gotta go," hung up, and turned to Edna. "Don't answer my calls."

"I wouldn't if you did. It rang four times."

Clem threw the phone down and clicked the bedside lamp on with violence. "Okay, well, I was a little preoccupied with—"

She wrapped her arms around her stomach again with a groan. Edna dug around in her handbag for ibuprofen and tossed the bottle to Clem.

"What's the plan this morning?"

Clem swallowed two pills without water. "Aloe vera, that's for sure. You should've worn sunscreen yesterday. That's why you have so many wrinkles."

Edna threw a pillow at her.

"I have so many wrinkles," she said, "because I'm eighty-three."

Clem supplied Edna with a doctored version of their quarry's ID photo, more school-picture than government-issue, to support their story that Edna was Monica Evans's grandmother. Clem had planned to head out with them while Jada spent the morning at reception, but Jada's eyes were red when they passed by. Clem stayed in to cheer her up. The other three returned to the school.

It was sweltering again, but Edna was well-equipped with sunscreen, and gaining access to campus was easier.

A different clerk was on duty at the welcome center today. She signed them in and almost called Monica Evans to let her know her grandmother was here, until Edna insisted on surprising her.

They ran into momentary trouble. Edna had nothing to prove she was a relation except the photo, which, the desk clerk pointed out—correctly, though she didn't know it—anyone could procure or doctor. Edna was at a loss. She was about to let the desk clerk call Monica Evans after all when Ag walked in.

Edna wasn't prone to blushing, but the sight of him put his sneer fresh in her mind.

"Hey all." His smile turned down as he looked at them. "Where's Little Rodriguez?"

"Staying in," Edna said. "Too much sun yesterday."

His lip curled at the sight of her own sunburn.

"I'm here to see my granddaughter," she said, though he clearly didn't care what they were there for if Clem wasn't with them. "But they won't let me in. Something about not having the proper identification, or I-don't-know-what."

Ag waved a hand at the clerk. "They're fine. I know them."

The clerk bit her lip. "Sir—"

Ag's face clouded. "I said I know them."

"Yes, sir." The clerk handed them visitor's badges without looking at them.

"Do you know where you're going?" Ag asked.

"Actually—" Edna started, but he cut her off.

"Great."

He pulled a phone from his pocket and headed farther into the building.

Benjamin gawked. Kiernan shrugged.

"Shall we split up?" he asked.

"No," Edna said, "I think we'd better stick together. I don't want any of us getting lost alone on campus."

Kiernan ground his teeth.

The Barstow School of Gallantry may have been a tourist attraction, but it was first and foremost a chivalric school and base. Sidewalks cut its lawns into grids; in each one, squadrons of squires and first-year

Knights exercised, trained, or practiced with weapons. Sergeants yelled at them. Officers strode back and forth, on their way to important meetings.

A tour guide led a group in matching t-shirts past the scrap-metal dragon. Various Knights—out-of-towners come in for tomorrow's conference—wandered about in pairs.

There wasn't a campus map in sight. Edna, Benjamin, and Kiernan finally found one of the dormitories around late morning, but it was the wrong one.

A passing recruit informed them the dormitories were on each corner of campus; Reeves Hall was on the northwest corner. But the dormitories were empty. The recruits were out training, except those heading to the first lunch hour in the mess hall.

"How are we supposed to find her in all this?" Benjamin asked.

Edna didn't have a clue. She was hot and sweaty. Her feet hurt, her knees hurt, her hip hurt, her back, everything. And she realized all over again that she was absolutely useless at planning, investigating, and thinking things through. The only plan they'd had was finding Monica Evans on campus. But even knowing her dorm and room number, they couldn't find her.

It hadn't even been Edna's plan. It had been Clem's plan. If she and Benjamin hadn't met Clem, there wouldn't *be* a plan.

Reeves Hall loomed over them, a utilitarian brick building.

"Maybe we could wait in her room," Edna said helplessly. "Sit inside until she gets back from...wherever she is."

"Maybe," Benjamin said. "What if they won't let us wait?"

"I don't see the Knights letting us hang around a dormitory while the recruits are out," Kiernan agreed. "Not unless Clem's friend happens by again."

"We won't know unless we ask." Edna stumped inside, but she was out again in less than a minute. The building was just as utilitarian inside as out, without any sort of seating or common area inside. "Well, never mind that. We can't wait in her room and there's nowhere else to wait in there."

Benjamin scratched his head. "Now what?"

"We'll figure something out. Benjamin, dear, I don't mean to be a bother, but I'm terribly thirsty. If you wouldn't mind—"

He pulled a water bottle from his messenger bag, found it empty, and hopped up the steps to see about some water.

Edna sagged. "I haven't the faintest clue what now. I haven't had the faintest clue this whole time."

Kiernan worried his forehead with a thumb. Damn her. Damn all of them. He shouldn't want to *comfort* them. He was only *pretending* to give a shit.

"It's not your destiny," he said at last. "It's not like you have to know."

Edna gripped her cane tighter. "I suppose."

She sighed. She was deeply red, though she'd reapplied sunscreen twice already.

"Everything'll be fine," Kiernan said.

She smiled at him. He felt guilty for reasons he didn't care to examine.

"I'm sure you're right, dear."

He hesitated. "We could split up."

She agreed, somewhat glumly. He was off before Benjamin returned with his refilled water bottle—just as well. Benjamin made him want to do things like offer comfort, too. Kiernan shook the thought away, turning his focus to Lena.

She went underground on every mission, speaking only to Red and providing no specific information about her whereabouts. Kiernan hadn't spoken to her since the day they'd both left the keep, he to find the Chosen One, she to join the recruits in Santa Alvara. She'd had no idea which dorm she'd be in, and Kiernan hadn't thought to ask. It had never occurred to him that he might follow her here.

His prospects weren't great. Knights drilled all over campus, under sergeants as apoplectic as they'd been fifteen years ago at a base much farther south. Red-faced and shouting, with veins throbbing in their necks. Memories Kiernan wouldn't have known still bothered him—if not for his sudden tenseness in the Carmichael Center yesterday—flashed through his head, but he headed into the chaos.

Edna had no such memories; she'd never been on a base before. She hadn't had the money to fly down and visit Percival when he'd been a Knight. All she'd had were weekly phone calls, which had thinned out to biweekly and then monthly before finally stopping.

But she had her own memories of shoutings and beltings, things she hadn't thought about in a long time. Decades. More. Edna swallowed the memories back; she had to focus on finding Monica Evans.

She and Beatrice flew around at random. Maybe another squire would know where Monica Evans was, but the squires were training and their sergeants bristled at any interruption. Used to tourists they may have been, but tourists typically left their trainees alone. Edna's heart pounded in her throat as each officer she approached turned on her, veins popping in their foreheads, spittle flying from their mouths.

The bell rang for the next lunch hour.

"Now maybe we'll get somewhere," Edna said, more stoutly than she felt. Her heart hadn't stopped pounding.

She headed for the nearest recruits. Sweat drenched their uniforms. Two of them bent double, retching into the grass.

"I did not dismiss you!" their drill sergeant roared.

The troops straightened, their chests heaving. Beatrice set Edna down as if to say that if Edna wanted to walk up to an angry drill sergeant, that was her business. Edna clutched her chest, waiting.

At long last, the sergeant dismissed the troops. They staggered toward the mess hall. Beatrice nudged her.

"Yes, yes, I'm going. Thank you so much for the support."

Edna called after the two recruits who had retched. They turned around, so shaky and sweaty it made her want to tuck them into bed and feed them chicken soup. She asked if they knew Monica Evans.

"Sure," the slightly-less-sick-looking-one said. "She's not in our squadron, though. We see her at lunch sometimes."

That was all they knew, so Edna and Beatrice headed for the mess hall. The public wasn't allowed inside, however; tourists were encouraged to purchase food at the pricey museum restaurant.

Unsure what else to do, Edna and Beatrice went back to Reeves Hall. After a morning of flying around and getting on and off the carpet, Edna's hip ached worse than usual. The sun beat down; her throat was parched. The water Benjamin had given her seemed forever ago.

But on their way, passing one of the school buildings, Edna spotted her quarry.

Monica Evans crept along the building as if going quietly enough might make her invisible. Edna forgot her hip, her parched throat. She followed at a distance, feeling like a spy.

Monica Evans glanced over her shoulder. Beatrice whooshed upwards, hovering over the roof of the building. Monica Evans disappeared into a service drive.

Beatrice edged forward so Edna could see over the side of the building. The service drive was deserted.

They drifted back to earth. Edna slipped off the carpet, sure Monica Evans had turned down here. Yet the drive was empty, with nowhere to hide and only a single, small, locked door.

Edna peered around. "Hello?"

The air shivered. Edna mopped her face with a flowered handkerchief.

The air stilled.

Monica Evans stood before them with a sword in her hand.

"Why are you following me?"

Edna had no idea how old she was or looked when she wasn't magically disguised, but Monica Evans had a young face made older by the tension in her jaw and cheeks.

Her dark eyes glimmered. "Who are you?"

Edna's mind had gone blank. It could've been the heat. Or the sword pointed at her. Or how Monica Evans looked ready to flee, as if Edna were the one who posed the danger.

"I just want to talk," Edna said.

Monica Evans drew farther into the service drive as a unit of Knights jogged past. She rubbed her neck as if she'd strained a muscle.

"Are you all right?" Edna asked.

She knew nothing about this woman except that she worked for Redway—or probably worked for Redway. Or Clem thought she probably worked for Redway.

But Edna was constitutionally incapable of not asking after someone's welfare.

A blank stare greeted her question.

Edna blinked sweat from her eyes. "I was only asking."

"What do you want with me?"

"You might start by telling me why you were sneaking off when it seems you're supposed to be somewhere else."

Monica Evans rubbed her neck again. Bruises peeped out beneath her sleeve as it slipped up her forearm.

Edna's mouth went dry. Those shouty sergeants, she thought, dredging up ancient memories, making her jumpy.

But she couldn't help asking.

"What are those?"

Monica Evans tugged the sleeve into place. "Nothing."

She might've said something about how drilling was rough and bruises were routine, but she didn't. She shrank into the shadows as another unit jogged past.

"If something's wrong—" Edna didn't know why she said it. Monica Evans didn't want her, didn't need her, and probably didn't deserve the offer. "If someone's been—"

"Been what?" Monica Evans's voice dared her to finish the sentence.

Edna took a step closer, and another, right past the sword. Monica Evans's eyes widened, but otherwise she didn't react. Edna grabbed the young woman's sleeve and pushed it up to her elbow.

Her arm was covered in bruises. Dozens. Purplish-green, pus yellow, some almost black.

Edna sucked in a breath. Monica Evans jerked away, rolling her sleeve down.

"Who did this to you?" Edna asked in a low voice. "Was it Redway?"

Monica Evans gave a hollow laugh that choked off as more Knights jogged past. Edna's heart pounded in her throat, threatening to suffocate her.

"The other squires? The instructors? Did they do this to you?"

If Monica Evans answered, she didn't hear. Her blood beat in her ears, hot and loud and angry. She floundered with the flowered handkerchief. She hadn't felt like this in a long, long time, and it frightened her. Monica Evans wasn't her responsibility. Beatrice nudged her ankles.

"We have to tell someone."

Monica Evans pointed the sword at her. "No way."

Edna's voice shook. "They can't—this won't—I won't stand for it."

She thought of her mother. It had been so difficult for her mother to run away with her, with another on the way. It had been so much worse afterward, when they were found.

She swallowed.

"That's enough," Monica Evans said, something low and dangerous simmering in her voice.

Edna stepped back, coming to her senses. This woman worked for Redway. She had been at every site Redway had attacked so far, enlisting out of nowhere and melting away again in the inferno. She was good at magic. She had known Edna was following her.

Edna reached for her knitting needles, the closest thing to a weapon she had; the sword was in her handbag, but she didn't know how to change it from ring to blade. Beatrice lowered to the ground, ready for a quick getaway.

Monica Evans rubbed her arm.

"Are they for sympathy?" Edna asked. "The bruises? Did you think your disguise needed a disguise?"

"I'm a good illusionist," Monica Evans said, "but I didn't need to invent those."

Edna's grip tightened on her knitting needles, but she couldn't stop picturing the bruises. Those two recruits throwing up as their sergeant released them for lunch, how pale they'd been. And Monica Evans flinched at every passing Knight, like she knew she'd catch it if they found her somewhere she wasn't supposed to be.

Edna let the knitting needles slip from her fingers, back into the recesses of her handbag.

"I meant what I said." She clutched her cane tight. "If something's going on...if the instructors, the other squires, anyone—"

Monica Evans stopped rubbing her arm.

"This was a mistake," she said. "I'm sorry."

"Sorry—?"

She flung out a hand. Beatrice darted in front of Edna but something blew through her like wind, turning her bones to ice. The last thing she saw, as she crumpled to the pavement, was the blurry form of Monica Evans bending over her.

CHAPTER TWENTY-SEVEN

"Where'd you find her?"

"Nowhere that made sense."

"It was a service drive?"

"Yeah."

The voices came from far away, tinny and echoing.

"Heat exhaustion, you think?"

"Must be. She's burning up."

What were they talking about? She was frozen.

"We shouldn't have split up," the first voice said. "I shouldn't have let her go alone, I—"

"Benjamin?" Edna croaked, and she opened her eyes.

She had a blurry view of the Spanish-moss hangings of her bed in the Royal Crown Hotel. Benjamin's face blocked out everything else.

"Oh my god, are you all right? I'm so sorry, I shouldn't have sent you off by yourself. You were so sunburnt, probably dehydrated—"

"Did you find Monica Evans?"

Clem lounged against the wall with her arms folded.

Benjamin rounded on her. "Who cares about Monica Evans? Edna could've *died,* and you'd better thank Kiernan for finding her, because if he hadn't—"

Clem scowled. "The whole point was to find Monica Evans. Did any of you find her?"

Benjamin swallowed a retort as the door opened. Jada poked her head in.

"Pops sent me to see if you guys need—oh, hey, you're up." She smiled at Edna. "How are you feeling?"

"Oh, just dandy."

Edna cracked a smile, but smiling stung; her sunburn was blistery and raw.

But her bones were ice.

Jada slipped into the room and touched the wall beside the bed. An aloe plant sprouted from it, unzipping one of its leaves.

"Thank you," Edna said, but her arms were too heavy and stiff to help herself to it.

Jada perched beside her, dotting her face with aloe. Clem reddened and fiddled with her necklace.

Jada glanced at their sober faces. Heat exhaustion hit a lot of tourists, but it hit the oldest and youngest tourists hardest. Too much sightseeing without enough sunscreen, water, or time indoors.

She patted Edna's arm, which was almost as red and warm as the old woman's face. "Call if y'all need anything."

The talk turned back to Monica Evans. Edna told them what she remembered. Whether from the heat or the spell, she didn't know, but her memory was hazy. She remembered the bruises but left them out. Monica Evans's voice echoed in her head.

This was a mistake. I'm sorry.

A lot of good it did, being sorry right before you cast a spell on someone and knocked them out, but Edna heard her saying it over and over.

She left that out, too.

The ice in her bones kept her shivering all afternoon. She ached worse than usual. Her skin was stretched so tight that she felt it would snap. Benjamin piled blankets on her and checked on her so frequently that she pretended to be asleep so he'd leave her in peace.

At some point, she really did sleep. The room was dark when she awoke. She pulled the quilt around her shoulders and wandered out to the lobby, her teeth chattering.

The fuchsia chandelier glowed pinkly. Fireflies drifted along the handrails of the staircase and over the reception desk.

Clem sat alone behind the desk in a t-shirt and sleep shorts. "You're up."

"Where's Jada?"

"In back. We were watching a movie, but her dad needed to lie down. She went to check on him."

"Is he all right?"

"I don't know." Clem buried her hands in the forget-me-nots draped over the desk. "I'm sorry about earlier."

"I know."

Edna headed for the porch. Fireflies floated around the wicker set, where Benjamin and Kiernan were sitting. Jada returned to the front desk, smiling thinly. Clem hesitated.

"Go on," Jada said. "I don't mind."

Clem followed Edna outside.

The night was velvety, warm, thick with stars. Frogs and crickets sang across the hotel grounds. Edna joined Benjamin on the wicker sofa.

"How are you feeling?" he asked.

"Well, I'm up."

Kiernan was sitting in an armchair with his boots on the coffee table. Clem curled in the armchair at the table's other end.

Benjamin scrutinized Edna. She fluffed up the quilt so he wouldn't see her shivering.

"Nice night," she remarked, determined to keep the conversation on anything other than what had happened earlier.

"We were just talking about Monica Evans," Benjamin said. "Whether or not there's any point renewing the search in the morning."

"She's probably long gone by now," Kiernan said.

Edna twisted her hands together in her lap. She hoped he was right.

"What's with you?" Clem asked.

Edna wanted very badly to knit, but she'd left her handbag in the room.

"It's just," she mumbled, "you see, she had these bruises..."

She told them everything she hadn't told them before, except for Monica Evans's parting words. She couldn't make heads or tails of them, but they felt private. Something for her alone.

"That was stupid," Clem said. "She got you to feel sorry for her, and then she attacked you. You shouldn't have let your guard down."

"It was dangerous," Benjamin agreed, wringing his hands.

Kiernan said nothing.

Edna's fingers curled into the quilt. "I think she was really in trouble."

"Yeah, she's trouble," Clem said. "She's working for Redway."

"That's not what I mean."

"You shouldn't have offered to help."

They didn't understand. But in eighty-three years, she'd never told anyone about her father. Not even Walter or Percival. "I had to."

Clem snorted. Benjamin sighed. Edna laughed despite herself. He hadn't sighed like that in days. It must have been a record. At the home, she'd earned herself a good sigh every other day.

A lot of the fun had worn off the adventure since the home.

"These people are killing Knights," Clem said. "I thought you wanted to stop them."

"I do," Edna said. "That doesn't mean I can't feel sorry for them if the occasion calls for it."

"It kinda does."

Edna pulled the quilt closer. "You don't know what it's like. That kind of abuse."

"They could leave."

Edna didn't feel like getting into workings of abuse, or the reasons someone might stay in an abusive situation, year in and year out. She certainly didn't feel like explaining how she knew any of that.

She hadn't decided what to say, whether she should say anything, when Kiernan answered instead.

"It's not that easy. You're under contract for two years. You can't leave."

"Monica Evans—"

"Monica Evans takes advantage of the chaos in the aftermath of the attacks to leave. They'll chalk her up as MIA, presumed dead. If she disappeared under normal circumstances, they'd call her a deserter and court-martial her." Kiernan put his hands on his knees. "And it's not as if it's instant abuse the second you join up. It's not like it's constant. It's part of the experience. Like hazing. Makes you a real Knight. I don't know why she's got bruises already, but—"

The others stared at him. Lightning flashed in Clem's eyes.

"Kiernan, dear," Edna said hesitantly. "I don't mean to pry, but were you—"

"A Knight?" His fingers dug into his knees. "It was a long time ago."

"I didn't know that."

"I don't talk about it."

Edna scrunched the quilt in her fingers.

"I didn't know that," she repeated, and she fell silent.

Kiernan met Clem's glare evenly.

"So you see," he said, "I know what I'm talking about."

"Do not," Clem snapped. "My sister was a Knight, you can't—"

"Then your sister went through it, too."

"She didn't. She would've told me."

"If she was in it long enough, she probably joined in."

"Shut up!"

Fire erupted from Clem's fingertips. Benjamin yelped. Edna tried to shield him, but Clem was already on her feet, sparks in her eyes, flames at her fingertips—

Kiernan waved a hand, and the flames went out. He'd been ready as soon as he'd seen the lightning in her eyes.

She stood over him with her fists balled.

"Don't you dare," she said. "Don't you *dare* talk about my sister."

She kicked her chair aside and stormed into the hotel, slamming the screen door behind her.

Edna struggled to get up, but Benjamin grabbed her hand. His voice shook. "I think maybe you better let her go."

Edna nodded sadly and sat there holding his hand. She understood, or thought she understood, how Clem felt. She didn't know how far back the abuse stretched, whether it was a recent phenomenon or a time-honored tradition.

She'd always thought the Knights were necessary. They'd formed swiftly after the Revolution left the fledgling United States without the protection of the British military's dragon-fighting branch. When they'd been so underfunded in the 1970s, dragons had encroached once more, terrorizing cities as far north as Portland and as far east as Pittsburgh. Edna had wanted to go back to work after staying home with Percival for several years, missing the trains, but she and Walter had decided it was too dangerous.

The Knights' work was important. She'd always thought so. But she didn't like this. Percival had wanted to be a Knight his whole life. He'd looked up to them—they both had. She'd been so proud of him.

Maybe he'd gone through this, too.

She didn't like thinking that.

"Was that why you left?" she asked Kiernan.

He shifted in his seat. "Among other things."

Benjamin's grip tightened on Edna's hand. She patted his arm absently.

"I'm a little surprised you joined," Benjamin said. "I've read about their conflicts with your king—what's his name?"

Negusu, but Kiernan didn't tell him that. The unexpected mention of his grandfather was like a punch in the gut.

"I didn't know all that," he lied. "I was a stupid kid."

A firefly alit on his arm, blinked once, and took off. He rubbed the blue triangle inked on his inner wrist, thinking of his grandfather. His people.

"Even if you disagree with what Redway's doing," he said, before he could decide not to, "you can't pretend fewer Knights is a bad thing. I'm not saying I agree with killing them"—he added, as if he hadn't personally attended several of the attacks—"but you don't know what it's like for my people. A few Knights less would help us."

He wasn't sure why he'd said it. He wasn't going to convince them it was necessary; he wasn't sure why he wanted to. He rubbed his tattoo, his heart thrumming in his chest.

Benjamin toyed with the hem of his t-shirt. "This isn't helping your people."

"What would you know about it?"

Benjamin twisted his hands together.

Kiernan's pulse raced. "The Knights-General have been trying to gain a foothold in Bahir Dar since before I was born. They don't care that my people live or die by our dragons—that they're already hunted for their scales and claws, and Westerners don't leave them alive as we do. It's the same shit they pull in Brazil. The government lets them do whatever they want in Dominion no matter how much the tribes protest."

Edna wore an expression Kiernan couldn't read and didn't care to.

"My grandfather partnered with Amhara leaders decades ago to stop the Knights from entering Ethiopia, but—" The night closed in around him, hot and dark, sizzling with the blinking of fireflies. "If there are fewer Knights, I'm glad."

He felt like he'd run a marathon.

"Kiernan," Benjamin said.

"What?" Kiernan snapped.

Benjamin flinched like he'd been struck. "It's, I mean, there aren't fewer Knights. Even if you account for the Knights who've been killed, there are more Knights now than when Redway started attacking them."

The fireflies made him dizzy. "What?"

"Yeah." Benjamin ran a hand through his hair. "Recruitment's the highest it's been in, like, thirty years. They use the attacks in their commercials and everything. People love it."

That couldn't be right. Knights had been *dying.* There couldn't be more of them.

"And...there's this." Benjamin handed his phone to Kiernan. "It broke last week."

It was a story from MNN, the Magical News Network.

KNIGHTS GET GO-AHEAD FOR BASE IN BAHIR DAR, AKG ANNOUNCES.

The screen blurred in front of Kiernan's eyes.

Benjamin took his phone back. "I don't know how they managed it, but I'm sure they used the attacks somehow."

"No," Kiernan said hoarsely.

"It doesn't sound like it's going to be a big base at first, just twenty or thirty Knights to start, but they already have a site."

"It can't be."

His grandfather would never allow it. Their people, their human neighbors, no one had wanted Knights in Ethiopia.

"Kiernan?"

A base in Ethiopia. More Knights than ever. The Knights they'd killed, the bases they'd destroyed, the cities they'd burned, and there were more Knights than ever.

He stood. "I need some air."

"Kiernan–"

He was down the steps, across the lawn, and up the street before they realized what was happening. Benjamin bit his lip.

"Should we go after him?" Edna asked.

"I got it. Go back to bed."

She considered it, as Benjamin jogged off into the night. But sleep eluded her. Monica Evans was still on her mind. Monica Evans and her bruises and her *I'm sorry.*

"It's not as if it changes anything," Edna murmured to herself. "She's still one of them."

She went inside. The lobby was empty, the front desk unmanned. Edna sat at the desk, figuring someone ought to until Jada or her father got back, and it might as well be her.

She was up again a moment later, with the quilt tight around her shoulders, shuffling around the lobby aimlessly. The floor creaked underfoot.

"You all right there?"

It was Demarco, leaning on a cane, fully dressed. His gentle smile reminded her of Amir.

"May I use your phone?" she asked.

She needed a phonebook, too, but he didn't have one, so he found the number online. She didn't know if Amir was still in the hospital, nor how Detroit was handling the aftermath of the dragon, nor what time it was there. Earlier? Later? She didn't know what time it was *here.*

Someone answered the phone. They wouldn't wake Amir; it was three in the morning. They assured her he was recovering, would be discharged in a day or two, and had somewhere to go: Akida would take him to her in-laws' home in Dearborn. They didn't know if his shop was still standing.

Edna hung up with a sigh. She considered calling the nursing home, too, but dismissed the idea. If it was three in the morning in Detroit, it was three in the morning there. No one would wake Marguerite so Edna could talk to her. Likely Marguerite wouldn't know who she was on the phone with anyway.

"You should get some shut-eye," Demarco said.

Edna smiled with an effort. "Yes, I think I will."

She couldn't bear the thought of lying awake in bed. She shuffled back and forth down the hall, until the tapping of her cane and the creak of floorboards brought Clem out of their room.

Clem gave off the distinct impression of having been seething in bed since leaving the porch.

"Are you coming to bed or what?"

"I can't sleep."

Clem rubbed her eyes. "Okay. Come on."

A short while later, Edna sat on her bed, holding a glass of green sludge. Clem ordered her to drink it, dimmed the lights, and set about lighting candles.

Edna did not want to drink the sludge. "What are the candles for?"

Clem's match fizzled out. She lit another.

"They make me feel witchy."

"They..."

She lit a candle and moved onto the next. "I feel like a real witch when there are candles. They make me feel like I know what I'm doing."

Edna tried not to worry about it. The sludge sat in its glass judgmentally.

"Seriously." Clem glanced at Edna. "You need to drink that."

Edna gazed into the depths of the sludge. A bubble popped on its surface. She pinched her nose and downed it. It tasted like kale had run away with sweaty gym socks. She didn't ask for the ingredients.

She clutched the glass, trying not to throw up. She wasn't sure she wanted to fall asleep this badly.

"Are you sure that was safe?"

"I told you it would suck." Clem lit a final candle. "Okay, we're ready. The sooner we get to sleep, the sooner we can wake up and track down Monica Evans."

The sludge sloshed in Edna's stomach.

Clem frowned at her. "You do want to find her again."

"I suppose," Edna said.

Clem's frown deepened. "What do you mean, you suppose?"

"I'm sure she's gone by now."

"What do you mean, you suppose?"

"You didn't see her."

Clem scowled. "Yeah, that was a mistake. I should've gone."

"What would you have done if you had?"

The sludge burned. Edna wished she hadn't drunk it.

"I would've gotten answers out of her. And then—"

Edna shivered at the ice in her voice. "And then what? It's not an easy thing to kill a person, whatever they've done."

"What would you know about it?" Clem retorted. "I have the Sword of Destiny."

The candlelight flickered on her face, making her look older, grimmer. The sword, in ring form, glinted on the bedside table.

"It won't do you any good," Edna said, with more conviction than she felt. "You're not the Chosen One, Clem. It won't work for you."

"At least I know how to use it."

"Clementine—"

Someone knocked on the door.

"Come in," Edna called at the same moment Clem snapped, "Go away."

A pause. The door creaked open.

Jada stood in the doorway wearing lime-green pajamas, a darker green robe, and a purple hair wrap. Her bare toes curled against the floorboards. Alyssum sprouted around her heels, perfuming the air.

"What do you want?" Clem asked, more aggressively than was strictly called for.

Jada's lips parted in surprise. "Nothing. I got up to check on Pops and he thought he heard—"

"We're fine."

"Are you sure? It sounded like—"

Clem leaned against the wall without looking at her, folding her arms. "I said we're fine."

"Okay, I just—"

Edna had hoped Jada's appearance might soften Clem, but it only seemed to have angered her.

"We're busy," Clem snapped. "You don't have to cling to me every single second."

"Clementine," Edna said sharply.

The alyssum wilted. Its perfume turned to the smell of decay.

Jada tugged her lime-green sleeves over her hands. "Okay. Never mind."

"Thank you for checking in on us, dear," Edna said. "Good night."

Jada gave a small smile in return, but her brow furrowed as she closed the door.

Edna peered down her nose at Clem.

"That was uncalled for. The poor girl didn't do anything."

Clem flushed but didn't relinquish her scowl. "She's a distraction."

Edna gaped at her. "A distraction! You didn't seem to mind when she invited you to stay in today. You can insult me all you want, I don't care, but you will not speak to Jada that way."

"Whatever."

"You'll apologize to her first thing in the morning."

Clem flicked her wrist. All the candles went out at once, plunging the room into darkness. Sheets rustled as she got into bed.

"Good luck falling asleep," she said.

The sludge burned at the back of Edna's throat.

CHAPTER TWENTY-EIGHT

Kiernan strode through an abandoned parking lot, under burnt-out streetlights, and past a factory plastered with yellow KEEP OUT signs as battered as the factory itself. He turned down an alleyway, hopped a chain-link fence. The buildings opened onto a beach. The Pacific Ocean stretched before him, glimmering in the moonlight. He trudged through the sand.

Sirens called out from beneath a rotted dock as he passed. Clumps of seaweed, garbage, and the occasional dead fish littered the beach. Behind him, high-rise hotels glittered with light.

Kiernan stopped at the far end of the beach as if he'd had this spot in mind when he'd left the Crown. His clothing felt heavy, restrictive. He kicked off his boots, peeled off his socks, tore off his jacket, rolled up his jeans.

He waded into the water until he was hip-deep and glared at the horizon as if he could see Bahir Dar from here if he tried hard enough. Waves crashed around him, drenching him in sea spray.

It couldn't be true. Couldn't be. His grandfather would never allow Knights in Ethiopia. So what if recruitment was up? It wouldn't matter once they'd destroyed all the bases, killed *all* the Knights.

It couldn't be true. Red would know. And if Red knew, he would tell Kiernan.

Shouts from the dock. The sirens had accosted someone who didn't want to be accosted, someone with a familiar, panicky voice.

Kiernan waded out of the water, his shirt plastered to him like a second skin, and headed for the dock. Sure enough, Benjamin was curled in the sand. A siren crouched over him, singing.

Kiernan pulled Benjamin to his feet. The siren turned her song and her sharp-toothed smile on him instead, but her smile vanished when he bared his teeth at her. The other sirens laughed; she turned on them angrily, and Kiernan headed back down the beach.

Benjamin followed. "Thanks."

He took in Kiernan's feet, coated with sand, the water glistening on his bare calves, the shirt sticking wetly to his stomach and back. He opened his mouth to ask where the rest of Kiernan's clothing was but changed his mind. The sirens resumed singing.

Kiernan didn't want company, but anything was better than this distance, this emptiness. His world caving in.

Together they stared at the stars, the moonlight glimmering on the ocean. At last Benjamin said, "I'm sorry."

Kiernan didn't say anything. None of this was Benjamin's fault.

Benjamin tried again. "It didn't occur to me you wouldn't know."

Kiernan's eyes burned. He should've known.

"How long have you been studying in Dominion, anyway?"

His grandfather didn't even know he was alive.

"Too damn long."

Benjamin gave a small laugh, like he wasn't sure whether or not he was supposed to. Kiernan hadn't exactly been joking, but Benjamin's laugh started piecing the world back together.

"If it helps," Benjamin said, "there's a lot of pushback against it."

Kiernan laughed hollowly. "Yes, I'm sure my people are pushing back very hard."

Benjamin's fingers flexed at his sides.

"That's not what I meant. Wait, no. I mean. No. Obviously you guys are fighting. I didn't mean—" Everything he said made him sound like an idiot. He would've liked for Kiernan not to think he was an idiot. "Look, there are people here fighting for you, too. I just meant, you know, you're not alone."

Kiernan's fingers curled into fists. "People here grew up hero-worshipping the Knights."

Benjamin hesitated. "I didn't."

Kiernan snorted.

"No, I—" Benjamin felt as if he were admitting to treason. "I mean, yeah, my uncle's a Knight, the way my dad goes on about him, you'd think he shits gold or something, but—"

His palms were clammy, his fingers cold and stiff. His ears and the back of his neck burned. Silly to get so anxious admitting this, especially to someone he knew didn't like the Knights.

But he was used to the nursing home: eight years of senior citizens going on about how wonderful the Knights were, acting like anyone anywhere who said anything against them was un-American. Criticizing the Knights went over as well as saying you didn't think Communism was that bad.

Then there was Edna.

"When I was younger, he told us all these stories about life on the base, and it, I don't know, it sounded—it sounded bad, you know? He always laughed it off and said it was no big deal, that it happened to everyone, it made the recruits tougher—"

Kiernan's fists tightened, but he didn't interrupt.

"—and then when I got older, I learned about, like, the poaching, and the flouted environmental regulations, and, like, they're really careless about other cultures? I mean—" Benjamin ground to a halt. "I mean, you, uh, you obviously already know that."

Kiernan said nothing.

"I still, you know, I don't think it's right," Benjamin said, "what Redway's doing. And we do need to do *something* about dragons. Like I know grasslands dragons aren't the same, but mountain dragons? They're—"

He broke off, because Kiernan specialized in studying mountain dragons and definitely knew more about them than he did.

"Well, they've been a problem here," Benjamin finished, feeling stupid. They hadn't been a problem in *his* lifetime, not until Redway's attacks had started. His parents had been children the last time dragons overran the land.

Kiernan still hadn't said anything.

Benjamin's hands shook. "That wasn't my point. It was the..."

What had his point been again?

Kiernan roused himself to say, "People pushing back."

"...yeah, that."

They fell silent.

"Don't tell Edna," Benjamin mumbled.

Kiernan frowned. "Don't tell her what?"

"That I don't think the Knights are that great."

The frown deepened, and so did the heat in Benjamin's face.

"Are you not allowed to have an opinion?"

"It's—" Benjamin's stomach churned. "Her son was a Knight. A long time ago. I take her to the cemetery every year on his birthday."

Waves crashed on the sand. Up the beach, the sirens sang. Kiernan wondered if his grandfather and mother did anything on his birthday. If they had a totem for him, acacia wood carved with both the same triangle he wore inked into his wrist and his name. Not Kiernan Abbott, but his real name. The name he'd left halfway across the world when he'd joined the Knights.

"I won't tell her."

"Thanks."

Benjamin wanted to say something more, but he'd already made things worse. He ought to have let Kiernan go and apologized later.

They were sharing a hotel room, though. That might've made things even more awkward.

Benjamin shivered, his teeth chattering. Anxiety always burned his face and neck, froze his body until he trembled all over. His lungs constricted until he couldn't get enough air no matter how deeply he tried to breathe. He hated it. Though calm in the face of medical emergencies, he came over cold and shaky at the smallest worry or inconvenience—or sometimes for no reason at all.

Kiernan picked up his jacket, brushed sand off it, and held it out. "Here. You look cold."

Benjamin didn't take it. "Oh—no, I, uh, it's, uh, anxiety."

"An anxiety disorder?"

Benjamin wouldn't meet his gaze. Maybe Kiernan tolerated his many, many questions about magic. But even the most supportive boyfriends Benjamin had ever had—the ones who found his questions endearing instead of annoying—were miffed by his anxiety, his need for reassurance that his very existence wasn't an irritation.

"An anxiety disorder," he finally responded. "Yeah."

Kiernan half expected him to bound away like a jackalope. He shrugged and dropped his jacket back in the sand, irked without knowing why that Benjamin hadn't taken it.

"There are spells to treat that sort of thing."

Benjamin picked at his t-shirt. "I don't actually know any spells."

"You know more about different kinds of magic than anyone I've ever met."

"Theoretical magic."

"I can't believe you of all people don't know any spells."

Benjamin scratched the back of his neck. Magic was dangerous. It had been hammered into him time and again, *magic is dangerous, don't mess with magic,* until magical theory was all he was brave enough to handle, no matter how much practical magic fascinated him.

"If you met my dad," he said, "you'd understand."

Kiernan hesitated. He shouldn't do this. He shouldn't want to. But Benjamin had come after him, again, just to make sure he was okay, even though he'd given Benjamin no reason to do so.

"Give me your hands."

"What?" Benjamin said, but he had already held them out.

Kiernan gripped his hands, casting around for a spell. Something simple. Something nice.

He settled on one from Andenya weddings. Usually, all the wedding guests performed it together, not because it was difficult but for the effect.

He focused on his magic. It reached for the magic that was in Benjamin though he'd never tried using it. Which wasn't to say he *hadn't* used it. Humans rarely realize the things they chalk up to luck or quirk or coincidence are evidence of untapped magic at work. Kiernan suspected Edna's endless procurement of handkerchiefs was just that.

Their linked hands glowed. Benjamin inhaled sharply.

Kiernan opened his mouth but hesitated. He should've picked a less embarrassing spell. Oh, well.

He sang in Andenya, almost under his breath. It was an elvish wedding song they'd sing, his people, as the newlyweds performed a ceremonial dance. His voice was nice enough, but he didn't often use it. He'd never liked singing outside the anonymity of a crowd.

Bright gold petals erupted above their clasped hands. The stream of petals thickened the longer he sang. It glowed, shining faintly on the sand and the water and reflecting in Benjamin's eyes, swirling over their heads and between them and around them.

Kiernan stopped singing. The petals drifted, casting soft shadows across Benjamin's eyelashes and lips. The golden glow shone on his nose and forehead. He had a dimple in one cheek, Kiernan noticed for the first time.

Something pulled at Kiernan's stomach like a tide.

The petals fell to the sand, rustling. Benjamin laughed.

"Lost my concentration," Kiernan said.

Benjamin picked petals out of his locs. He brushed them from Kiernan's shoulders, letting his hands linger there.

There was another pull at Kiernan's stomach. A pull at his shoulders, Benjamin's fingers tightening, their faces drawing closer together. Their foreheads touching.

He could see every one of Benjamin's eyelashes. The moonlight reflecting in Benjamin's glasses. A tiny scar he hadn't realized Benjamin had on his cheek.

"Benjamin?" he said hoarsely.

Benjamin's lips were on his. His hands tangled in Kiernan's locs. The tide crashed in Kiernan's stomach, and something in that kiss held up the sky and made the world feel less empty. The kiss went on and on, and beside them the ocean crashed on the shore, and behind them the sirens sang their songs.

And even though Kiernan knew it was a bad idea, he kissed Benjamin back.

CHAPTER TWENTY-NINE

For the second time, Clem's cell phone woke Edna. Edna had been having a dream in which a dragon in a top hat and monocle tap-danced closer and closer to her.

Exhaustion settled deep in her bones. She let the phone ring out.

Getting out of bed seemed a Herculean task. She wasn't sure if Benjamin and Kiernan had ever returned, but she couldn't bring herself to check. Strange that getting out of bed should be so hard when hours ago she'd found it so hard to sleep.

Whoever was calling wasn't giving up. Clem's mother again, Edna thought. Anger flared in her stomach.

She fumbled for her hearing aids, put them in, and reached for the phone. "Clem's phone. Edna Fisher speaking."

If Clem woke up and caught her, so be it.

The voice on the other end had been speaking Spanish to someone in the background but now switched to English.

"You're Edna Fisher?"

"Yes, that's—"

"Will you please talk some sense into my daughter and tell her to come home?"

Edna sat up with difficulty. "I would if I thought I could. She can be, well...stubborn," she said at the same moment Clem's mother said, "Hard-headed."

Clem's mom laughed wetly.

"Please," she said, "please just tell me where you are. She won't tell me. I'm sure my mother knows, but she won't say anything either."

Clem's four-poster loomed in the darkness. She must have—Edna hoped she had—a reason for not telling her parents where she'd gone. She'd probably be furious if Edna told them.

"Santa Alvara," Edna said. "We're in Santa Alvara."

Clem's mother let out a long breath. "Thank you. Thank you so much. I just wanted to know she was safe."

"Of course you did."

"It's been so hard not knowing—"

"I understand."

The bedside lamp clicked on. Edna's heart stuttered.

Clem ripped back the bed hangings and glowered down at her, her eyes ringed in dark circles. Sparks leapt from her fingers.

"Give me the phone."

"Oh, dear," Edna said.

Clem wrenched the phone from her hand, snapped something into it in Spanish, said, "I'll call you later. *Yes,* I promise," and hung up. She rounded on Edna, showering her with sparks.

"What did I tell you about answering my phone?"

"What did I tell *you* about answering your phone?" Edna said in a chilly voice. "Especially when it's your mother calling."

Clem's eyes widened. "You didn't tell her where we are?"

"Someone had to, seeing as how you wouldn't."

Edna reached for her handbag, which was sitting on the bedside table with Clem's necklace and the Sword of Destiny, but Clem grabbed her wrist. A jolt of electricity shot through Edna's arm.

"Did it occur to you there was a reason for that?"

"Yes, I'm sure it would be terribly inconvenient if she turned up to drag you home."

"It's so she wouldn't worry about me."

Edna shook her off, snatching her handbag off the table. Her wrist and arm smarted.

"Did it occur to *you,"* she said, pulling out her knitting, "that it might worry her more not knowing where you were? Good heavens. If you were my daughter, I'd be out of my mind."

"Yeah, until you found out where I was just to turn on the news and see dragons attacking the same place."

Edna stabbed herself in the thumb with a knitting needle. "I didn't think—"

"No," Clem snapped. "You didn't think. I *told* you not to answer my calls. Why'd you have to—?"

Edna threw her knitting aside, red-faced. "Because I'm a mother, Clementine Rodriguez. Because I know how it feels not to know where your child is. If you expect me to lie for you to your own mother, I have news for you: I won't."

Sparks showered from Clem's hands. "Oh my god, my mom's going to *freak*—"

"I'm sure she 'freaked' enough when you left. What did you do, run off without telling anyone where or why you were going? I never should have brought you with me. I should have sent you home the moment I met you."

Clem swung the hangings closed and stormed off. Edna stuffed her knitting back in her handbag, sucking on her thumb. She hadn't broken the skin, but it hurt.

The door slammed. Edna peered through the Spanish-moss hangings. Clem was nowhere to be seen. Her necklace had vanished from the bedside table.

So had the Sword of Destiny.

"Snickerdoodles!" Edna said violently, and then she decided to stock up on some really good swear words later, because sometimes "snickerdoodles" just doesn't cut it.

Her joints cracked and her arm tingled, but she stumped across the hall and hammered on Kiernan and Benjamin's door.

The door swung open. Kiernan raised his eyebrows at the sight of her in her nightshirt. He was one to raise his eyebrows that way, she thought, answering the door in nothing but his boxers. But she barged into the room, already forgetting his relative state of undress. Benjamin was burrowed in rumpled bedclothes but reached for a t-shirt when Edna entered.

"Clem's gone." Panic flooded in to replace her anger. "She's gone after Monica Evans, I know it—"

Kiernan guided her to his bed, so well-made you could bounce a quarter off it.

Edna clung to him. "You have to go after her, please, Kiernan—"

"Let go of me and I will."

"She'll get herself killed—"

He extricated himself and was dressed and out the door in another moment. Benjamin calmed Edna down enough to find out what had happened but not enough to convince her not to go after Clem herself.

"Kiernan will get her; you don't have to—"

"Yes, I do!"

"Your hip—"

"Bully for my hip. We'll take Beatrice."

He drew the line at letting her run out in her nightshirt, however. It was several minutes before they finally set out, past a bewildered Jada, off the front porch, toward the Barstow School of Gallantry.

CHAPTER THIRTY

If Edna had sent Kiernan after Clem a few days ago, he would've thought it the perfect opportunity.

Now he wasn't sure.

Until Edna had knocked on the door, he'd been curled into Benjamin's side, with a hand on Benjamin's stomach, listening to him breathe as he slept onward. Even asleep, Benjamin was a comforting presence; Kiernan had liked the gentle rise and fall of his belly. He was solid and steady and kind–things Kiernan was not. Things Kiernan maybe wanted to be, or at least things he wanted from someone else. It made him wonder if he'd always wanted those things but hadn't noticed because he'd been too busy making sure Red's plans succeeded, even when Red was too busy being stupid to make sure of it himself. With Benjamin beside him, Kiernan had fallen asleep calmer and more content than he could remember ever being.

Then Edna had hammered on their door, and he'd remembered his reason for coming here. To betray them. Benjamin didn't know his real name or who he really was or anything about him except what Kiernan had bared to him last night.

Kiernan wasn't sure whatever fragile thing they had would survive when Benjamin learned the truth.

But he was positive there'd be no recovering it if he did what he'd come to do.

He caught sight of Clem downtown, shouldering through the crowds as best she could. It was a beautiful day, a weekend, and people poured into the city for sightseeing and the conference. It'd be hard work to catch up. She had to be heading for the school, so Kiernan googled a faster route.

Lena didn't worry him. She was long gone. He'd sent her away when he found her standing over Edna, sobbing and panicked and looking like herself instead of Monica Evans. Something had upset her so much it had shattered her illusion.

She wasn't the calmest person in the best of times, but she was a great illusionist and had been in the Knights more recently than the others. She could easily disguise herself, fit in long enough to figure out whether or not it was a good time to attack. To find Knights who might want to join Red.

Kiernan hadn't asked what happened, though the sight of Edna lying in the service drive had made him deeply uneasy. He hadn't been able to stop thinking of her flying around Detroit to find him after the dragon attack. Asking him if he was all right. Admitting her uncertainty to him, when she never liked to appear anything less than perfectly cheerful.

He was more relieved than he cared to admit when he realized Lena had done nothing more than knock her out.

Now, he made his way through side streets and public buildings until the shadow of the scrap-metal dragon fell over him. He stood on a nearby bench to see over the crowds.

Today was the day. His fingers curled into fists.

Red would attack today, because of the conference.

Kiernan caught sight of Clem. His jaw clenched.

Her face was set and pale as he hopped off the bench. She shouldered past him, but he strode alongside her.

"I don't need a babysitter."

"I'm not babysitting."

Clem scowled. "Don't bullshit me."

A silver ring set with large stones, too big for her, glittered on her middle finger. The Sword of Destiny.

"Edna's worried about you."

"Edna's always worried," Clem said, which didn't seem like an accurate assessment. If anyone was always worried, it was Benjamin.

Kiernan tried not to think of Benjamin. His scar. His single dimple. His body curving in toward Kiernan's.

Clem's voice broke through his thoughts. "You're not going to stop me."

Kiernan glanced at her.

"I'm going to find her," Clem said viciously. "I'm going to stop him. He's never going to hurt anyone else ever again."

He didn't answer.

She eyed him, her face strained. "Aren't you going to try and stop me? Tell me it's too dangerous?"

Kiernan had been barely older than she was when his grandfather sent him to infiltrate the Knights. "You have to do what you think is right."

Clem's brows knit together. "That's a dumb thing to tell a teenager."

The corner of his mouth turned up, but he caught himself. He was already far too soft with these people.

"I can tell you how dangerous it is, if you like."

She put her hair into a ponytail and tightened it. "Shut up."

"Little Rodriguez!" a voice called across the lawn.

Clem sighed but slowed up as Ag and Dan approached. Ag jerked Clem's ponytail. She scowled. Dan bit back a smile at her expression.

"What do you want?" she asked.

Annoyance cut through Ag's customary grin. "Someone woke up on the wrong side of the bed. We just came to say hi."

Clem gave an exaggerated wave.

"Hi. Look, I don't mean to be rude"—sounding as rude as she'd ever sounded—"but I'm busy, so—"

"All right, all right. We are too." Ag jerked his thumb at the Carmichael Center. "We're on our way to the conference. First lecture'll be starting any minute. C'mon, Dan."

The Knights drilling on the lawn kept drilling, but civilians, officers, and out-of-towners headed toward the building. Dan said goodbye to Clem, but her eyes fixed on the crowds streaming up the steps.

A conference, she thought. Knights coming from around the country.

"Oh, no," she whispered.

Kiernan worried his hairline with a thumb. "Clem?"

In the distance, a siren blared—a slow, reluctant warble swelling to a steady, grating wail. A clutch of nearby tourists turned in the direction of the sound.

"What's that?"

"Fire?"

"Tornado."

"It's not a tornado. We're on the ocean."

"This is California, you idiots, it's an earthquake—"

The bells ringing for the start of the conference gave way to alarms. Sergeants roared at their trainees to stop drilling, to get to the armory, to get in formation. The laughter and chatter turned to panicked questions, until someone shouted, "Dragon!"

Not just a dragon. The shadows of giant wings slid over the grass. Clem clenched her fists. A black swarm of them, like the day Marisol died. Dragon*s*. So many that they almost blotted out the sun.

They descended upon the school, belching fire.

Flames roared to life all around. In Clem's head they roared higher still, around the dorms, around the gymnasium and the tree she'd tried to climb and the broken window where Marisol's friend had said she could see them training.

Get me an orange, chamaca?

Her eyes locked on the familiar man beside her. She tried to remember who he was.

"Are you all right?" he asked.

Her breathing was ragged, shallow. "Kiernan?"

Her voice clutched at him as if he were leading her through a dark room and had the only light. He thought of Red, the nightmares. Shira said he still had them.

"Yeah," he said, more gently than he'd intended.

Clem swallowed. "You weren't there."

Kiernan flinched. "No," he lied. "I wasn't there. You're in Santa Alvara."

"Santa Alvara." Clem squeezed her eyes shut, took a deep breath, opened her eyes. "Okay."

She wrenched the ring off her finger, and it transformed into a sword. She darted down the lawn, where the first dragons were already landing.

"Clem!" Kiernan shouted again, an unfamiliar sense of panic rising inside him. He wasn't sure if he meant to stop her, nab her, or help her escape.

For the first time since he'd left Dominion, he wasn't sure what to do.

CHAPTER THIRTY-ONE

Shadows dimmed the streets as Beatrice zoomed toward the School of Gallantry, over the skylanes, heedless of any police officers who might be watching. Benjamin said, "It's dragons," over and over, until the words gave way to hysterical giggles. Edna twisted the straps of her handbag, her eyes peeled for Clem and Kiernan.

Fire engines tore up the campus lawn. The scrap-metal dragon looked alive, wavering in the heat. Knights poured from every direction, armed with magically fortified guns and swords. Edna's stomach clenched. The squires were so young, so pale. They'd likely never seen action. They clenched their weapons, their horrified gazes following the dragons.

The dragons' riders dismounted, and Knights rushed them. Steel clanged on steel. The Knights outnumbered the riders, but their dragons provided a distinct advantage.

Benjamin's face was pure panic, but his giggles dissolved into hiccups. "There she is!"

Clem sprinted into the midst of the dragons. The Sword of Destiny glinted in the firelight. Edna's heart was in her throat. She urged Beatrice faster.

Benjamin's hiccups cut off. He gagged. "Up, Beatrice."

The carpet arced over the field and the dragons and the Knights battling the dragons' riders.

"What are you doing?" Edna cried. "We need to get to Clem!"

"We're not flying right into a SHITLOAD OF DRAGONS, EDNA."

She was so shocked she didn't argue.

Smoke billowed from the Carmichael Center. The building was in flames, the white columns smudged gray. The screams of those trapped inside and the stink of burning flesh assaulted Edna as they flew past. Sirens rang in her ears.

"Clementine!" she shrieked.

Clem emerged from the smoke. A gash on her forehead bled freely. Her face was pale but set, her eyes glittering. It was like she'd never frozen at the sight of the fire and the distant dragon in Detroit; she was so swallowed up with rage her fear couldn't touch her. Magic crackled on her skin as she swung at anyone not in uniform—or anyone maybe not in uniform. The smoke and ash turned everyone the same grimy black. It was harder and harder to tell who was on what side.

Edna knew Clem was good with a sword, but knowing it was one thing; seeing her in action was another. When a figure ran at her, Clem flung out a hand, shouting a word. Nothing happened, and the figure was on her. Clem struck; they dropped.

Edna's breath caught in her throat. She didn't know if the figure was dead or alive, but at least Clem had gotten them before they'd gotten her.

"Clementine!" Edna screamed again.

Beatrice barreled toward the girl. Edna clung to the carpet's edge, shouting Clem's name. Benjamin gripped her shoulders.

Another figure emerged from the flames. This time, Clem didn't bother with magic. She struck with the sword, but the figure dodged. Unlike the last, they matched Clem easily. With another blow, they knocked the Sword of Destiny from her grasp.

Beatrice raced for the ground. Wind tore at Edna's sunburnt skin, and she gritted her teeth. Benjamin clung to her.

Clem dove for the sword. She grabbed it, too late. The figure closed in on her and—

Ag launched himself across their path, beating the figure back. Dan sprinted after him and yanked Clem off the ground. He was sweaty and heaving, his uniform scorched.

"Get out of here!" he shouted.

Clem scrambled to her feet with the sword in her hands.

Dan shoved her. "Go!"

She had no choice, because Beatrice dipped down and tripped her. She fell onto the carpet with a yelp. Benjamin wrestled her into something like an angry bear hug.

"Let me go!"

"No way."

Clem twisted in his grasp. "Let *go!* They're—"

"They're giving us a chance to escape," Edna said.

"I have to find Redway!"

"How, Clem?" Benjamin said shrilly. "All these people look the same."

The battle raging on the lawn was a confusion of dragons, blackened figures, and weaponry. The fire cast a reddish glow over the campus—over the whole city. Clem paled as flames spread beyond downtown.

"Jada," she breathed. "Beatrice—"

The carpet raced toward the hotel. Downtown was chaos. Those in the streets abandoned their deadlocked vehicles; those in the skylanes descended to escape the dragons still airborne. Beatrice zipped around crumbling buildings. Heat singed the carpet's edges; the three humans dripped with sweat. The flames lessened as they escaped the center of town, but dragons circled over the whole city.

The hotel huddled in its gardens, like the dragons might not notice it if it shrank down small enough. The air shimmered with heat.

Clem leapt off before they had stopped, sprinting to the door. Beatrice pulled up at the porch, ready for a quick getaway.

Jada appeared, gripping the doorframe. Her eyes widened at the blood on Clem's face.

"Clem?" Her voice was thin and frail. "What's going on?"

"Redway's attacking the city."

Jada gripped the doorframe tighter. "You're bleeding."

"I'm okay." Clem wiped her forehead with her wrist but smeared the blood over her cheek. "Where's your dad?"

Jada's gaze fixed on the dragons circling the city. "He..."

Clem dropped the sword with a thunk and grabbed Jada's shoulders. "Jada. Hey."

Jada's eyes flickered back toward her. "He's asleep in back."

"Okay." Clem's voice was low and urgent. "Wake him up, get him somewhere safe—"

"Where—?"

A dragon's roar shook the hotel. Jada flinched, but Clem squeezed her shoulders.

"Anywhere. Out of town. Don't stop until you're far away, okay? And don't come back, not for anything. Not until I tell you it's safe."

Jada's eyes welled up. "The hotel—"

"Forget the hotel."

"It's all we have."

Clem bit her lip. "I know. But it's your hotel, or you and your dad and your hotel."

Tears splashed down Jada's cheeks.

"Okay." She wiped her eyes. "Okay. Clem?"

"Yeah?"

Jada pressed a kiss to Clem's cheek. "Don't do anything stupid."

Clem flashed a crooked smile. "Never."

Jada vanished into the depths of the hotel, screaming for her father. Clem squeezed her eyes shut and took up the sword.

The hotel shook with another roar, louder than the last.

A deep green, whip-like dragon tail descended from the smoke, followed by the dragon's legs and wings, its neck and toothy maw. Its landing was an earthquake. It glared at them, its eyes blazing yellow.

Edna swallowed. Benjamin yelled in her ear, but everything had gone silent. Her eyes were stuck on the dragon's, sucked into the yellow depths that looked so much like the fires blazing in every corner of the city.

Benjamin shook her. The sound came rushing back. Him shouting in her ear, the roar of flames, the hot wind and the creaking and groaning of the porch and a crash as something collapsed inside.

Clem screamed. The dragon's rider grabbed her, throwing her onto the beast's back as if she were no heavier than a sack of flour. Clem swung at her, but the rider dodged her, snatched the sword, and called to the dragon.

"Clementine!"

Beatrice rushed the dragon, but a single beat of its massive wings hurled them into the hotel wall. The fire spread to the porch roof. Burning trim smashed on the floor. Ash stung Edna's eyes.

"Clementine," she croaked.

The dragon lifted off the ground. Edna had already lost sight of the girl and her captor behind its wings. Far overhead, Clem screamed for her, fainter and fainter as the dragon shrank into the fiery sky.

CHAPTER THIRTY-TWO

Kiernan reached the hotel as she took off. Shira, recognizable by her dragon, a small, emerald-green beast with chartreuse belly scales. The girl was screaming. Something like regret plucked at Kiernan's insides, but he couldn't do anything about it now. Nothing left to do but head home and find out how much Red had known.

Or maybe he'd liberate another motorbike from this flaming hellhole and take a trip. Get some time away from dragons and Knights and idiot best mates and sweet, cute guys with single dimples and old ladies who cared too much for people who didn't deserve it.

But the hotel held his gaze. The star jasmine growing up the porch columns curled into blackness. The fae girl's work. She and her father hadn't done anything to deserve this.

Kiernan couldn't turn away from the burning building. He didn't know where they were. Edna. Benjamin.

Beatrice whipped by, aflame, and flopped about on the sidewalk in a frantic attempt to douse the flames.

On the porch, trim crumbled and fell in a shower of sparks. Beyond it, a withered voice called the girl's name. Kiernan's insides twisted.

The carpet, now flame-free, if a bit crispy around the edges, weaved back and forth like an unhappy dog. If carpets had voices, it would have been howling.

Kiernan approached the hotel. How often had Edna fretted over him, though he'd been there to steal away her almost-granddaughter? He thought of Benjamin's laugh on the beach, the golden glow flickering over him, in his eyes.

Kiernan tested a creaking step and leapt onto the porch.

He heaved Edna into his arms. She gazed at him blearily. He whistled for the carpet, set her down on it, and turned back into the flames for Benjamin.

Half the porch ceiling fell in. Choking on smoke, Kiernan covered his nose with a sleeve and squinted through the haze.

The top of Benjamin's head poked through the ashes. Rubble pinned the rest of him.

Kiernan picked through charred wood and threw smoldering rubble aside. The porch groaned. Shingles melted, fusing things together. With a sucking sound and a roar and a crash, the floor gave way beneath Kiernan's left foot.

Kiernan sank six inches before he caught a board covered in hot tar to steady himself. He wrenched himself out of the floor, cleared the rest of the rubble, and hoisted Benjamin into a fireman's lift.

The porch steps gave way. Kiernan stumbled, collapsing in the grass with his head on Benjamin's stomach. He coughed wheezily.

"Benjamin?"

Benjamin didn't answer. Kiernan scrabbled up and knelt at his side. Shook his shoulders, felt for his pulse. Couldn't find it.

"Benjamin. *Benjamin."*

"Is he all right?" a quivering old voice asked behind him.

Kiernan didn't hear her. He touched Benjamin's eyelids, his temples, his wrists. Maybe he couldn't find Benjamin's pulse because his own raced so thunderously; maybe he couldn't find it because there was no pulse to find.

He didn't know what to do. He didn't know a single spell, a single charm or word that might help, so he squeezed his eyes shut and chanted the names of his ancestors.

"Will it help?" the old voice quavered. "The spell?"

"It's not a spell."

"Then what?"

The words caught in his throat. "A prayer."

The voice did not interrupt again.

Kiernan hadn't prayed in years, but he chanted the names over and over and over and *over*, until Benjamin jerked upright, coughing. Ash spewed from his nose and mouth. Kiernan put a hand on his back, swallowing his own panic. Behind him, Edna panicked openly, clutching her singed handbag until her knuckles whitened.

Benjamin slumped back on his elbows, breathing hard.

Kiernan touched his cheek. "You're all right," he said hoarsely.

Benjamin groaned, coughed up something slimy and gray. "In my professional opinion, you're wrong."

Kiernan laughed and pressed his forehead to Benjamin's, thanking his ancestors.

Benjamin's fingers found his face. Thoughts of the night before flooded through him, Benjamin's fingers like this on his face, on his chest and stomach.

Kiernan sat back. He'd let them take Clem.

Brass and drums chorused from Clem's phone where it lay nearby in the grass. Kiernan stared at the phone dully, but Edna snatched it up. She jammed the phone to her ear.

It was the one person who could make her feel worse right now.

"Clementine?" Clem's mother cried. "Mija, thank god! I've been so worried. They're saying on the news—"

Edna took a deep breath. "Mrs. Rodriguez?"

The speech broke off.

Edna closed her eyes. There would be a moment where Clem's mother would not accept that it wasn't Clem on the phone. She would be certain she had misheard—until that moment passed. Maybe she would scream, or cry, or faint, or maybe she would do nothing, turn gray and silent and old in an instant and go about her work because she couldn't do anything else.

The only comfort Edna could give her was that Clem was not, as far as she knew, dead.

"Where's my daughter?" Clem's mother asked. "I want to speak to her. Put her on."

"Mrs. Rodriguez—"

"*Put my daughter on the phone*!"

Another voice in the background, incoherent. A struggle. Clem's mother was crying, but she shouted at the other voice in quickfire Spanish, her voice suddenly faraway.

An older voice spoke into the phone. "Lo siento. Mi hija no es misma en momento ¿Quién es? ¿Senora Fisher?"

Edna didn't know what the voice was saying. "Is this—is this Clem's grandmother?"

The voice brightened at the mention of Clem's name. "Clem, si. ¿Dónde está? ¿Está bien?"

"I'm going to find her," Edna said. "I'm going to get her back. I'm so sorry."

In the background, Clem's mother was still yelling in Spanish. Another struggle, and she was back on the phone.

"¡Ni siquiera hablan inglés, mamá!" she hissed in the background, before returning to Edna. "Please, just tell me she's all right."

Edna hesitated. "She's alive."

"Thank god." Her voice broke. "Thank god. Oh my god, why did she go off like that? I knew something would happen, I knew it."

"It's all right," Edna said, though it was not remotely all right. "I'm going to get her back, I promise."

"Get her back? What do you—?"

The call cut off.

"Mrs. Rodriguez?" The words CALL DROPPED flashed across the screen. Edna shouted into the phone. "Mrs. Rodriguez! Are you there? Hello?"

No one answered. The screen went black.

Edna thrust the phone at Kiernan. "Call them back!"

The elf gazed at her like he couldn't conceive of such a thing as a phone call. She shoved the phone into his hand.

"I can't." He handed it back to her. "There aren't any bars."

Edna had no clue what he meant. "Make it work. They're worried about her."

"I can't make it work. That's what I'm telling you."

Edna threw the phone into her handbag in a rage and immediately pulled it out again to make sure she hadn't damaged it. She yanked a handkerchief from her handbag, a handkerchief so dirty and torn it might have been outside her bag instead of in it. She burst out sobbing at the sight of it.

"Oh!" She pressed the handkerchief to her mouth. "Kiernan, I said such awful things to her."

His chest tightened.

"I don't understand." Edna's voice cracked. "Why would they take her? She's only a girl."

Kiernan sagged into the dying grass beside a quiet Benjamin. "She's the Chosen One. They were going to target her eventually."

Edna wrung her handkerchief. "But she's not the Chosen One."

Kiernan jolted upright. "What?"

"She's not the Chosen One." Edna mopped her eyes. "I am."

Something jammed in Kiernan's brain. "But—you said—"

"I know what I said," Edna said miserably. "I lied. It's me. I'm the Chosen One." She threw the handkerchief on the ground. "And a bang-up job I'm doing of it."

She nattered on, but her words buzzed around him like flies. She couldn't be the Chosen One. She had to be at least eighty. The wizards would never...

It clicked, suddenly. So many fleeting things had bothered him throughout their time together, things he'd never bothered investigating because he'd been so certain Clem was the Chosen One. The Sword of Destiny always in Edna's possession. Edna's insistence that the girl didn't need to come to campus with them. Benjamin's response in Detroit when Kiernan had offered to go on ahead with Clem.

Edna had asked him something.

"What?"

"Please—please—can you take us?"

"Of course," he said, without having any idea what he'd agreed to.

"Kiernan?" Benjamin's voice came from a distance. Benjamin, still lying on the grass at his side. Kiernan's stomach clenched. "Hey, are you all right?"

"Fine," Kiernan said tersely. "Let's go."

CHAPTER THIRTY-THREE

Wind whipped Clem's hair as the dragon winged south. The other dragons followed close behind. Clem squeezed her eyes shut and buried her face in her kidnapper's shoulders, remembered it was her kidnapper, and sat back so quickly that she nearly tumbled off the dragon.

Without turning around, her kidnapper shot out a hand and pulled her forward. All Clem had seen of her so far, aside from her mass of tawny curls whipping in the wind, was her flight jacket and lightning-fast hands.

Southern California was a mass of beige beneath them. The ocean flashed in the sunlight. They were so high up.

Think, she told herself. But thinking was hard when you were thousands of feet up, the air was thin, and you had been kidnapped by a woman on a dragon.

Normally, when things were bad, she thought of Abuela. No good in this case. Her grandmother, in her day, had been a powerful witch. And Clem was, well, not. Whatever Abuela would do if she were in this situation, Clem probably couldn't.

She breathed deep, thinking of Edna instead. Clem's heart clenched as she remembered their fight. How she'd shouted at Edna and run off, right into danger, without thinking. As usual.

Tears slipped from her eyes, freezing on her cheeks in the frigid wind.

Edna didn't know magic. She didn't know how to handle a sword. But she would do...something. Clem wasn't sure what, but she was positive Edna wouldn't put up with being whisked away to Dominion.

Inventory, Clem thought, because it seemed like a resourceful person would take inventory. She didn't feel resourceful, though. And taking inventory is probably useless when your inventory looks like hers did. Herself (basically useless). Rope (around wrists). The Sword of Destiny (technically not her destiny and out of reach anyway, pressed against her kidnapper's leg).

That was all Clem had. Her stupid, useless self; rope around her wrists, too short to be of use; and a sword she couldn't get at.

The land below turned greener as they flew, the trees like broccoli far below. Clem hated broccoli.

She turned the list over in her mind, stuck on her pitiful inventory and how terribly, terribly high up they were and how worried Edna would be. How worried her parents would be. She'd meant to protect them by not telling them where she was going or why. No one had known except Abuela.

Edna's voice echoed in her head, stern and accusing.

I know how it feels not to know where your child is.

Clem's heart clenched again. She squeezed her eyes shut, focusing on what she could hear. The wind rushing through her hair. The occasional whoosh of the dragon's wings. The creaking of the woman's jacket as she shifted positions. Her own breath going in and out.

Clem sat like that for a long, long time. Her heart thudded away, faster than normal but not as frightened-rabbit as when she'd nearly fallen off the dragon.

She'd nearly fallen off the dragon.

She peered down, swallowing. The silvery thread of a river glinted in the sun.

It was a terrible idea. Really the worst. Her mom would kill her, if the fall didn't. Or whatever beasts lurked in the trees below. Or Redway, if she ever made it to him.

Clem straightened slowly. Her kidnapper half-turned but said nothing.

First step: get herself out of this rope.

Clem tried to work her hands loose, wishing she'd studied nonverbal spells harder. She could undo the rope magically, but her kidnapper would hear.

Plus she'd probably end up setting her hands on fire or something.

The sun sank lower. The temperature dropped. Clem worked at the rope, wiggling her wrists back and forth. She mostly succeeded at chafing her wrists. But the rope felt looser. She eyed the sword, pressed against her kidnapper's leg maybe six inches away.

The rope loosened further as Clem worked at it. Her breath crystallized in front of her. The silvery river below glinted more and more dimly.

Her hands slipped free.

She bit back a triumphant shout. Phase one, complete, she thought, trying to sound like a badass television character. Or maybe "phase one, complete" was more of a villain thing to say. Whatever. Her hands were free.

Her kidnapper wasn't paying any attention. She probably didn't think Clem could slip the ropes. She definitely didn't think Clem could escape with the ground so far below.

Clem bit her lip. This was really going to suck. Her heart was pounding again, so hard she felt like she might throw up. Maybe it was the thin air.

She could stay up here, she thought. She'd wanted to find Redway. But she'd wanted to confront him on her own terms. Not like this.

Her kidnapper shifted. Her leg was no longer touching the sword, but it didn't make a huge difference; she'd notice if it started moving. But maybe not as soon. A few seconds could make all the difference.

Clem reached—and came up a finger-length short.

Holding her breath, she stretched and leaned and reached a little farther. Her fingers brushed the hilt and wrapped around it.

Her kidnapper's head snapped around. "What do you think you're doing?"

Clem yanked the sword backward, scrambling to her feet.

"Escaping," she said.

She took a deep breath, closed her eyes, and jumped.

It would've been really, really cool, if the woman hadn't snagged the back of her shirt.

A moment later, she was tied up again, this time with hastily muttered enchantments on the ropes so they couldn't be undone without magic. An extra rope bound Clem to her kidnapper. The Sword of Destiny was secured further up the dragon, well out of reach. Clem's kidnapper double-checked her new security measures and turned back to the horizon.

Clem leaned into her and cried.

CHAPTER THIRTY-FOUR

Edna's eyes fixed on the dragons, unable to tell which one carried Clem. Benjamin kept rolling over to retch over the side of the carpet. Kiernan steadied him with a hand on his shoulder, but his own head hung in his other hand like a lead weight.

They raced along far below the dragons. They needed a plan. Surely the dragons were heading for Redway's Mountain of Doom, or whatever name was fashionable for evil lairs these days, and surely Edna couldn't waltz right in after them.

She couldn't even be sure of finding their landing place; Beatrice fell farther behind the longer they flew.

Edna urged the carpet faster, to no avail. The edges were blackened and burned, frayed and warped. Amir had worked so hard, worn himself out, made himself sick, and already his enchantments were wearing thin. They could have withstood ordinary fire, but dragonfire is one of the few things to reliably destroy magical objects and undo enchantments.

Edna wished she'd been able to speak to Amir that night on the phone.

She whispered into Beatrice's weave. "Please, Beatrice, dear. Please try."

The carpet fluttered and strained. The dragons pulled farther ahead, silhouetted blackly against the sky.

Miles away, the dragons touched down.

Storm clouds rolled in. Clem's kidnapper dragged her off the back of the dragon. Clem got a good look at her for the first time as she removed her flight mask. Dark, serious eyes, high cheekbones, that curly hair whipping around her. Short and wiry, no taller than Clem but more muscular.

She nudged Clem's shoulders, pushing her forward.

They had landed on a wide, flat ledge before a finger of rock that stabbed into the sky. Below was a jungle so green it hurt her eyes. Humidity weighed on the air. The clouds thickened and darkened. Thunder rumbled. The other dragons touched down one at a time to let their riders dismount before taking off again.

Clem stumbled toward the rock finger. Her kidnapper placed her palm flat against the stone.

A door appeared. At another touch, it scraped inward.

Fingers prodded at Clem's back. She stumbled into darkness and met no resistance. It felt like she'd been thrust into space, or the desert. Somewhere wide and empty.

Think, she told herself. *Think.* But her brain felt fuzzy. This wasn't how she'd planned to meet Redway, dragged through his halls as a prisoner. She'd planned to walk in with her head held high and point the sword at his heart.

"Hello," she would've said. "My name is Clementine Rodriguez. You killed my sister. Prepare to die."

And she'd run him through.

She halted. Marisol quoted each line of the movie with increasing volume, until finally she said, *Prepare to die*, and attacked Clem with tickling fingers.

"Hey." Fingers prodded her again—not tickling, not Marisol's. "Keep moving."

Marisol's voice echoed in her head.

Her kidnapper's fingers returned, hard and insistent. "Get going."

Clem stumbled onward. Her kidnapper flicked a hand, and white orbs materialized overhead, revealing a cavernous room filled with tables. Clem pressed close to the wall, grateful for something solid at her side.

Behind her, the voices of the other dragon-riders echoed through the room, murmurs and whispers and the occasional laugh. Clem swallowed. She wasn't sure what she had expected, but it wasn't to be outnumbered so badly. Redway had dragons in spades, but she had given little thought to the people riding them beyond the fact of their existence.

But here they were. Thirty or forty of them—though, with their voices echoing around her, it sounded more like a hundred. Different genders, different ages, from a blond kid barely older than she was to a woman maybe fifteen years younger than Edna.

Clem's hands shook. She focused on Edna. Edna leading Clem through a fiery church. Edna searching for Clem in the rain. Edna flying through the middle of a battle even though Clem had shouted at her and lost control of her magic and hurt her, even though Edna had been right about everything.

Edna would rescue her. Until then, Clem would make her proud. She sucked in a breath, following the white orbs with her head held high.

CHAPTER THIRTY-FIVE

They had almost, *almost* reached the mountain when Beatrice faltered like a stalling car.

"Oh no," Benjamin said. "Oh no, oh no, oh no—"

A coughing fit choked out the rest. Edna gripped his shoulder, trying not to look down. She didn't want to see the rocks that would break their bodies when they were two yards away from the safety of a ledge.

Kiernan launched himself off Beatrice.

Edna yelped, but he landed like a cat. He stretched as far as he could, grabbed the edge of the carpet in both hands, and yanked it toward him. Beatrice crashed into him. Edna and Benjamin went flying.

Edna's shoulder caught rock, and she tumbled to a halt.

"Is everyone all right?" Kiernan asked.

Beatrice flopped an apology on the ground.

Benjamin groaned. "Yeah. Edna?"

She crawled over to him. Kiernan surveyed the finger of rock jutting before them.

Edna's shoulder throbbed, but she hardly felt it. She still heard Clem screaming for her as the dragon shrank into the sky, almost as loud and real as the thunder rumbling overhead. The mountain shook.

Benjamin examined her shoulder.

"You'll have a nasty bruise." His voice was still hoarse with smoke. "But I think you're okay."

She struggled to her feet. "Let's go."

The clouds hung dark overhead. Monkeys hooted in the jungle below.

"Go where?"

The dragons were gone—not far, Edna feared, but gone—and so were their riders. Where was a mystery. It had to be this rock finger, jutting higher than any peak in the area. If this wasn't Redway's evil lair, Edna didn't know what was.

But there was no way inside. No door, no cave. She hurried toward the nearest fracture in the rock, her mouth set in a grim line, but found only an ordinary fissure.

"There must be something. They didn't vanish into thin air."

Benjamin sagged against the rock. "Maybe it's hidden. Like, with magic."

Edna's fingers dug into the fissure. "We have to get inside somehow."

Kiernan watched them prod at the rock wall. His eyes flickered to the door, invisible but there. It would open if he touched it.

He ran a hand through his locs. "Maybe we shouldn't do this."

"I'm not leaving her here."

"You don't know they went in there. And if you do get in, there's no guarantee you'll get out again. With your hip and Benjamin being—"

Edna flew in Kiernan's face like an elderly fury. "Bully for my hip! And bully for Redway! And bully for Knights and dragons and useless wizards and I-don't-care-what! I'm not leaving without Clementine."

Kiernan's stomach clenched. "Of course not."

Benjamin gaped at her. She dug a faded rose-colored handkerchief out of her handbag, clutching it like a security blanket.

"I'm sorry," she said to Kiernan. "You needn't come with us, you know. It's not your quest. I shouldn't have asked you to come along. Maybe you ought to stay here. Benjamin too."

"No way," Benjamin said.

"You inhaled a lot of smoke—"

"So did you. I didn't come this far to let you go on alone now. We're getting her back. Together."

"If anything happened to you—"

"Nothing's going to happen to me," Benjamin said, his voice pitching upward. "I'm coming with you, end of story."

A muscle ticked in Kiernan's neck. "I'm coming too."

They resumed their examination of the rock. Edna scrabbled at every crevice, sure each one would let them inside. Even Beatrice tried to help, flopping along the ground to nose at the rock wall.

Kiernan laid his hand on the mountain.

The door materialized.

"Here."

His hand was glued to the rock.

Edna bustled over. "Oh, well done!"

"How'd you do that?" Benjamin asked. "What spell did you use?"

"Spell?" Kiernan said quietly, but they were already pushing the door open, too worried about Clem to give it further thought.

"Wait here, Beatrice," Edna said, and she disappeared inside. Benjamin gave a wobbly smile and headed after her.

Kiernan's heart contracted at his dimple. He caught hold of Benjamin's wrist. "Wait."

Benjamin's eyes followed Edna inside. "What is it? Is everything okay?"

Kiernan's hands slid up his arms. He gazed at Benjamin, memorizing the dimple, the scar, the laughter lines at the corners of his eyes and the worry lines in his forehead.

Benjamin touched his cheek. "What is it?"

His eyes were deep and flecked with stars.

Kiernan wished they were back in their room at the Royal Crown Hotel, with its moss-furred walls and flowers springing from the floor.

Benjamin didn't even know his real name.

His hands dropped to his sides.

The clouds broke open, drenching them.

"Nothing," he said, and they followed Edna inside.

CHAPTER THIRTY-SIX

Deep in her bones, Edna knew she could find Clem inside the mountain. Something like a line tethering them to each other would show her the way. Magic, love, call it what you would; it would lead her to Clem. With that certainty burning inside her, she stumped through the keep like she owned the place.

Five minutes later, she wasn't so sure. There was a fork in the path.

She waited for something inside to tell her which way to go, but the seconds slipped away into minutes, and nothing was inside except a rising panic. Sibilant voices echoed around them, but she couldn't tell which fork they came from.

"Which way?" Benjamin whispered. Despite his insistence on coming with her, he sounded terrified of going in either direction.

Edna listened hard, trying to pin down the voices.

"I don't know." Tears stung her eyes, but she blinked them back. "I don't know."

She dug through her handbag. She didn't need anything, but she dug through the bag anyway, past the photograph of Percival and the other of Walter, past crumpled tissues, past forgotten keys to unremembered doors, past a pill bottle and face wipes and a half-used tube of lipstick and the handful of tampons she still carried in case someone needed one. Tears slipped down her face.

"Edna—"

Benjamin touched her shoulder, but she didn't want comfort. She wanted Clem.

"I'm fine, dear."

Kiernan looked at the fork in the hallway, then at her shoulders shaking and the tears dripping into her handbag.

He nodded off to the left. "It's that way."

Edna laughed wetly. "If only I could feel so certain."

"Guessing's the best we can do," Benjamin said. "There's a fifty-fifty chance he's right."

"No, I—" Kiernan's fingers clenched and unclenched at his sides. "I'm not guessing. I know where they've taken her. It's that way."

Benjamin craned his neck to see down the left fork. "How d'you know? Your luck magic, or—"

Edna laughed again, sounding more like her old self. "Good heavens, who cares? Let's go!"

She stumped down the left-hand fork faster than she'd moved in years, bursting with certainty now that a choice had been made. Clem was somewhere down this echoing stone hallway. That was her only thought. Kiernan was an elf, undoubtedly with access to magic that Edna could only dream of. How he knew it was the right way didn't matter.

Behind her, he said in a strangled voice, "Don't go that way."

"You just said it was this way," Edna said without stopping.

"It is. Listen—" He jogged after her and grabbed her arm. "The dormitories are downstairs. I can hide you there until he's done with her—I'll get her away somehow and bring her to you, I'll get the three of you out of here, and then—"

Ice flooded Edna's veins. She wheeled around.

"What are you talking about?"

He let go of her. "I don't know what he'll do if he sees you. He thinks he's got the Chosen One, he told me to bring her to him, but he has no use for you as far as he knows—"

Edna's thoughts slipped and skidded.

"—if he finds out you're the Chosen One, I don't know, if he thinks he doesn't need her—"

Edna's lips were numb. "What are you saying? How do you know all this?"

He jammed his hands in his pockets because he didn't know what else to do with them.

"I know because I'm one of them."

Benjamin's lips moved soundlessly for a moment. "What?"

"I'm not a draconologist. He sent me to find the Chosen One. Red." Kiernan wiped his palms on his jeans. "Redway."

Thunder shook the keep.

"What are you talking about?" Benjamin asked.

Edna couldn't believe it, so she didn't.

"Nonsense," she snapped, and when Kiernan opened his mouth confusedly, she only said it louder. "Nonsense! We don't have time for this foolishness."

"It's true."

"It is not!"

"The door—I didn't use a spell to find it. I knew where it was. It recognized me."

"If this is a joke," Edna said, "it's in very poor taste. I'm the Chosen One, so if you were sent to find—"

"We didn't know it was you," Kiernan said miserably. "I thought it was the girl."

Benjamin's voice shook. "Her name is Clem."

Kiernan closed his eyes briefly. "Clem. I know. I'm sorry."

He was serious.

The ice inside Edna splintered into rage. A moment later, her rage was swallowed up by horror: anything he had done was her fault. She'd told him Clem was the Chosen One. She'd asked him to lead them through Dominion. She'd insisted he come with them, though Clem had said they didn't need him. For protection, Edna had said. She'd thought he'd be good to have around if they ran into trouble.

Now Clem was Redway's prisoner. And it was Edna's fault.

"Please." Kiernan met Edna's eyes, but she looked away. "I can get you out of here safely, but—"

Edna's fingers curled into fists.

Benjamin was shaking. "We're not going anywhere with you."

He'd liked Kiernan—thought Kiernan had liked him. Of course Kiernan didn't really like him. Benjamin was anxious and annoying and overly interested in all things magical, just like his father had said, just like everyone he'd ever dated had said. Everything that had made it seem like Kiernan liked him—his indulgence of Benjamin's questions, his reassurance that Benjamin wasn't annoying, their kiss on the beach and everything after it—all of it had been an act.

He'd used Benjamin to get close to the group. And Benjamin had fallen for it.

"I trusted you," he said bitterly.

Kiernan flinched. "I thought I was helping my people. I didn't know—"

"You should have."

Kiernan knew that better than anyone.

"I'm begging you," he said to Edna, because he couldn't face Benjamin. "Look, you don't have to trust me, but please listen to me."

She turned away, her insides roiling with guilt and fear and anger. Benjamin wiped his face on his arm. Edna squeezed his shoulder and headed down the hall. He followed close behind her.

"Please, you have to listen—"

"Leave us alone." Edna spoke without turning. "You've done enough."

"You don't know what he's like—"

Edna whirled around, white-faced. Her eyes glittered.

"I don't care what he's like! This is what I'm here for, isn't it? I'm the Chosen One. I have to face him at some point. He'll answer to my knitting needles if he's harmed one hair on Clem's head. If you think for one second I'm leaving her—"

"I'm not asking you to leave her," Kiernan said desperately. "I'm asking you to let me help."

Edna barked with laughter. "Help? And how fast would you have spirited her away if you'd had the chance?"

He stepped back like she'd slapped him. He opened his mouth several times but said nothing, looking like a stunned fish. In his expression, Edna glimpsed a flash of the truth. She almost asked, but the idea was too monstrous.

She continued down the rocky hallway with Benjamin at her side. Kiernan made no move to follow them.

Benjamin sucked in a large, shaky breath and doubled over, coughing. The sound echoed off the stone walls.

Edna's heart hammered. She didn't know who might hear them, and it sounded so *bad,* his coughing, like he might choke on his own breath. She clung to him, whispering repeatedly, "It's all right, you're all right," because she didn't know what else to do.

Kiernan's fingers twitched until he could stand it no longer. He jogged to catch up to them, but even in the midst of his coughing fit, Benjamin pulled away. The look in his eyes stopped Kiernan in his tracks.

Benjamin's breathing eased. He leaned on Edna.

"I'm fine," he rasped.

"Benjamin," Kiernan started, but they limped away from him together. Benjamin's eyes were red.

The hallway rounded a corner, leaving Kiernan behind. Edna slipped her hand into Benjamin's. They went down the hall in silence, hand in hand, listening to the tap of Edna's cane and the shuffling of their feet echo off the walls.

Back around the corner, Kiernan sat against the wall with his head in his hands and regretted every decision he'd ever made.

CHAPTER THIRTY-SEVEN

Prodded onward by her kidnapper, followed by the dragon-riders, Clem entered a small stone chamber at the back of the keep. Deep cracks ran through the ceiling. Rough wooden chairs clustered in rows. At the far end, a threadbare red armchair held council like a throne. Behind it hung a large map, much like her own, marking the sites of their attacks.

Examining the map, his head tilted to the side, was Redway.

From the back, he wasn't like Clem's idea of him. She remembered him, always, in the leather flight jacket and mask he'd worn that day. Remembered him towering over her.

Now he wore jeans and a plaid cotton shirt and battered work boots—something her dad might have worn. Average height, with the build of an ex-athlete several kids past his career. His reddish hair, shot through with silver, was pulled into a short ponytail.

No sword to grasp and point at him. Her kidnapper clenched it in her fist.

"Red." She tore her eyes from Clem's face. "She's here."

He turned around.

Clem stepped back before she could stop herself.

After four years of learning and searching and hacking and hunting, here he was. Those eyes. Those blue, blue eyes. A little older, a little sadder and more thoughtful than she remembered them. Trying to get her sympathy.

Clem's hands balled into fists.

He smiled slightly. His smile seemed familiar, too. But she hadn't seen the rest of his face that day, and he certainly hadn't smiled at her.

"My name is Clementine Rodriguez." Her voice cracked. Her legs shook. She didn't sound fearless and determined like she had every time she'd envisioned this.

She meant to go on, but Redway said, "I remember you," and she faltered.

"You—you do?"

He dropped into the worn red armchair as if they were in his living room and she'd come for a visit.

"That girl," he said. "It was your sister, wasn't it? You look just like her."

Her breath came in bursts. Some of the people crowding around wore sympathetic expressions or shifted like they'd stopped themselves from moving to comfort her. She hated them for it.

"Her name," she said through clenched teeth, "was Marisol."

He nodded to himself. Clem wanted to run at him, sword or no sword, punch him in the face, claw him until blood ran down his neck and soaked through his stupid plaid shirt.

"Marisol. I think about her sometimes. This was, what, how many years ago?"

Clem's nails dug into her palms. "Four."

The corners of his mouth turned up. "I'm sorry. It must have been terrible for you."

She ran at him. Someone grabbed her before she reached him, gripping her arms so tight it hurt.

"Don't—don't say—don't you *dare*—" Clem choked back an angry sob. "You killed her."

He waved a hand. "It's all right. Let her go."

The hands lingered.

"I said, let her go," Redway repeated, with annoyance. She dropped to her knees, shaking with suppressed sobs. "Look at me, Clementine Rodriguez."

She didn't want to. She wouldn't.

She did anyway.

He crouched before her. "I didn't kill her."

Her laugh was half a sob.

"It's the truth." His voice lowered until no one else could hear him. "The moment I saw her, I knew what had happened. I was checking on her, that's all. She was dead when I reached her."

Clem let out another laugh, less sob and more bitter. "You destroyed the city."

He returned to his chair, drumming his fingers on its arms. Sparks danced at his fingertips, along the arms of the chair, down to the floor, and back up to sink into his skin. She watched them, mesmerized.

"I was angry."

It simmered in his voice, his anger. Fresh and raw like it had happened yesterday. And those words. Clem had said them herself, to Edna, about the church. She shivered.

"They'd been patrolling our borders for weeks," Redway said, "slaughtered a dragon that had gone too far outside Dominion, and one of our friends, too, when she followed them back and confronted them."

The sparks danced faster from his fingertips, down and up the chair, back into his skin. In the corner of the room, the blond kid drew back, pressing against the wall. Clem's kidnapper didn't move, but her jaw tensed.

Redway closed his eyes, breathing deeply. Clem was struck again by how familiar he seemed. She was still figuring it out when he opened his eyes.

"If she'd lived," he said, "if I'd found a pulse, the faintest breath—any sign she was alive—I would have brought her here. We would have cared for her as one of our own."

Clem tore her gaze away. "She never would have joined you. She was a Knight."

He laughed. "So was I. So were we all, at one point or another. The Knights killed your sister."

"Liar," Clem snarled.

He got to his feet with a lithe, animal quickness. Sparks leapt from his fingers, biting into her arms. They stung, but she didn't cry out. She wouldn't give him the satisfaction.

"Believe me or don't." Anger simmered in his voice again, darker and heavier now. She flinched. "I thought, if I told you—if you knew what the Knights were capable of—"

He swallowed his anger back.

Clem realized why she recognized him.

She remembered where she'd seen him. Why she knew his face, his smile, though he'd worn a mask that day. The room blurred, dizzy and tight, too warm. Her chest constricted.

"I should have known it would come to this," he said. "You are the Chosen One."

Hot tears dripped down her face and fell to the floor. She didn't care what it came to.

She'd been hoping Edna would come for her.

Now, she hoped Edna would stay away.

CHAPTER THIRTY-EIGHT

The cold, stone hallway ended in a door. Edna let go of Benjamin's hand, her fingers aching where he'd crushed them in his own. Neither of them had wanted to let go once they were out of sight of Kiernan.

It struck them how alone they were, walking into the unknown. Perhaps they should've kept Kiernan with them after all, Edna thought.

She had to replay his words in her head over and over to sustain any anger at him. Otherwise, she thought of other things. Kiernan doing the dishes in Amir's apartment. Kiernan playing Monopoly with them. Kiernan holding the body of a volunteer dragon-fighter. Kiernan carrying Edna and Benjamin out of the fire.

She grabbed a knitting needle. Less impressive than the Sword of Destiny, but better than nothing. Marginally.

"Stay here," she advised Benjamin, but he shook his head.

"Not a chance."

Her mouth twitched into a smile. She touched his cheek. "I love you."

He leaned into her briefly. "I love you too."

He pushed the door open.

She slipped into the room as a voice said, "You are the Chosen One."

"Actually," Edna cried, "that would be me."

She elbowed her way through the nearest people. They didn't stop her, thrown by the sight of a little old lady wandering into their midst like she'd gotten horribly, horribly lost on vacation. Benjamin followed, hunching his shoulders like he could shrink down to invisibility. The room smelled leathery from the flight jackets flung over arms or shoulders or hanging from hands.

The sword was nowhere to be seen, but Clem was kneeling on the floor. Alive. In one piece. Edna elbowed past more people until she'd reached Clem. She touched the girl's shoulder, her eyes prickling with relieved tears.

Nothing would happen to Clem now. Edna wouldn't let it.

When she looked at the man standing before them, she dropped her knitting needle. It clattered on the floor and rolled away.

Edna's heart pounded. He was barely three feet from her.

He'd filled out, fit his own body, no longer the gangly beanpole she remembered. His hair had lengthened and—heaven forbid—grayed at the temples, with long streaks turning silver throughout. Grim lines she'd never expected to see there lined his eyes and mouth.

But it was him. Forty-eight now. She'd counted, every year on his birthday. She knew how old he was as if she'd celebrated with him each year instead of visiting the cemetery.

"Mom?" he said hoarsely.

Somehow Edna was in his arms, weeping. Crying his name over and over and over again because she could. Because he was *there.*

Clem cried silently into her hair. Edna didn't notice.

Percival pulled away, resting his hands on her shoulders. She beamed at him through her tears. His face was pale and strained, but he half-laughed.

"Mom," he said, "what are you doing here?"

She laughed. "Why, I'm here for you, of course!"

She forgot about dragons and Redway and the sword and the Chosen One. She had come to find her son. She had come to bring him home.

Behind her, Benjamin said quietly, "Edna?"

His voice broke through. Everything flooded back: the news reports and the wizards and the church fire and her fight with Clem, the attack on Santa Alvara, Clem stolen away, Kiernan's confession, everything.

"Percival," she said, "we have to get out of here. Now. There's a man here, a sorcerer, and he—"

His hands fell to his sides.

"Edna," Benjamin repeated, but she only spoke faster.

"—he attacked Santa Alvara with a flight of dragons, and—"

"Edna." Benjamin touched Edna's back. "Edna, it's him."

"What's him?"

"Redway." His voice dropped so low she barely heard him. "It's him. He's Redway."

He wasn't making any sense. She glanced at Percival, who wouldn't meet her eyes, and then around the room. Everyone suddenly found the floor very interesting. Clem buried her face in her knees.

"No," Edna said, looking back at Percival. "No—you're not—"

His face was still strained, but he inclined his head. Her throat constricted. The wizards wouldn't—wouldn't—they couldn't have known—they never would have named her Chosen One if—

Percival wobbled before her eyes, shifting and blurring, fuzzing at the edges.

"No—" It came out as a gasp. Her lungs seized. "No—"

"Mom," Percival said. "Look—"

She fainted before he could say any more.

CHAPTER THIRTY-NINE

Kiernan abandoned his spot in the hallway. He had to get to the others, be ready to sneak them out at the first opportunity.

Maybe they wouldn't want his help, but he'd never listened to anything Red had wanted him to do or not do. Why start listening to people now?

He was nearly to the war room, as they called it dryly, when the door swung open and people surged out. Benjamin and Clem stumbled along, pushed past too quickly for him to meet their eyes.

Old Joe and Shira and Henry emerged after everyone else, bearing Edna aloft with a spell.

Kiernan's mouth went dry. "She's dead?"

Shira shook her head and said, in an odd, flat voice, "She's his mother."

He didn't understand. Not until Red trudged past a minute later, pale and drawn, his shoulders bowed.

Some of the others sometimes mentioned parents or siblings or cousins or friends, but Red never spoke of his life before the Knights.

Anyone he might have had or been before Dominion might as well have not existed.

Kiernan followed him down the hall. "Red?"

"Go away."

Red traipsed down the stairs to the bedrooms and dormitories. They'd taken Edna to his room. Kiernan made a mental note for later.

"Is she all right?"

Red's voice cracked. "I don't know."

"Red—"

"Not now."

Joe, Shira, and Henry emerged from the room, whispering together until they saw Red. He stormed toward them.

Kiernan followed. "Red, come on."

Red rounded on him, sparks leaping from his eyes. "I said not now."

He slammed the door in Kiernan's face.

Shira shrugged. Joe harrumphed, and Kiernan knew why: as the oldest in the keep, she was the mother of the group, no matter how much she groused, insisting that she wasn't. They disappeared down the hall.

Kiernan pressed his ear to the door. Nothing.

He considered likely prisons. Benjamin and Clem must have been locked up somewhere, but the keep was their home, not a Gothic castle or a sketchy corporate headquarters. They didn't have a dungeon or anything. They'd never had anyone to lock up before.

Preoccupied, he quite literally ran into Lena on his way back upstairs.

"Sorry," he said automatically, and then: "Are you all right?"

Dark circles ringed her eyes. Her shoulders slumped, her arms purple with bruises. The hazing usually began after weeks, sometimes months. But the recruits at Santa Alvara had started in on Lena early, like they'd known she was there to betray them.

"I can't keep doing this," she said. "I can't."

Hers was the hardest job. Enlisting at each site in advance, scoping it out to determine if the time was ripe for an attack, poking around to see if any of the real recruits wanted out. It was risky, exhausting, and put her back in the path of abuse, although she insisted it wasn't that bad.

Someone had to do it, and she was the only illusionist among them. She could change her appearance at will and, more importantly, was good at maintaining the illusion over time.

Just now, she looked like herself. Olive-skinned like her Monica Evans character but with warmer undertones. Taller, with dark eyes and a messy, sun-bleached bun.

Kiernan eyed the bruises. The recruits at his base had steered clear of him. He'd only been seventeen, but he'd been an elf and a foreigner and they were a little mystified and a little afraid. Even the recruits who'd had the worst of the hazing, the recruits he'd defended, had avoided him.

"Have you seen Roman about those?"

Lena shook her head. "They're just bruises."

Maybe not the bruises, but something was bothering her. She avoided Kiernan's gaze.

"It's this," she said. "With the Knights."

He raised an eyebrow.

"I can't keep doing this." She sounded like she was confessing to a crime. "Telling him when it's time to attack. Telling him they're ready. If you hadn't shown up in Santa Alvara—"

She broke off, hugging herself. Kiernan waited.

She lowered her voice. "I wanted to tell him not to come. Then that woman came and—"

Kiernan had never seen her panic like she had standing over Edna in that service drive.

Lena's voice cracked. "Joe said they had the Chosen One, and when I saw her—"

"It's okay."

She bit her lip. "You don't understand. I know her."

And Kiernan didn't understand, because he was thinking of Edna.

"Do you know where they've taken them?"

She didn't ask what he meant. "No, but I can find out."

She vanished.

Kiernan let out a breath. Lena was one of the newer recruits, part of the keep for a few years now, older only than the squires and first-year Knights she recruited herself. He hadn't realized she was so unhappy.

Now he was glad of it. It meant one person might help him get Edna, Benjamin, and Clem out of here.

CHAPTER FORTY

Benjamin and Clem were locked at the bottom of a long, narrow staircase. The space was dimly lit, close, and chilly, but at least there weren't any chains or shackles. There wasn't much of anything: just a wooden crate, a bucket, and an ancient broom, the latter of which seemed odd, because who exactly was sweeping a glorified cave?

Benjamin hurled himself at the door. Edna was somewhere above, unconscious, in the hands of—well, okay, her son. Who, admittedly, had panicked when she collapsed at his feet.

Benjamin wasn't impressed. It tore him apart that Redway was the first to get to her when she fainted, to crouch beside her, to check her pulse and give orders to have her taken to his room.

He didn't have the right. Benjamin was the one who'd spent the last six years caring for her. The one who'd taken her to get her hair permed for visitor's day, though she so rarely had visitors because her extended family was so far-flung. The one who'd sat in on her doctor's appointments and made sure she took her pills on time.

The one who'd gone with her to the cemetery twice a year—once on the anniversary of Walter's death, and once on Percival's birthday because she hadn't known precisely when he'd died.

Except he hadn't died. He'd let her think he was dead for three decades. Now he was allowed to be a son again as if nothing had ever happened?

Benjamin knew *his* mom would never stand for it. She'd feed him too much and tell him she'd kill him herself if he ever pulled a stunt like that again.

His dad would probably say something like, "So you're alive, are you? Still chasing after men? Got a degree that isn't useless yet? No?" and return to his newspaper.

Benjamin collapsed on the floor, sweaty and shaking. Clem knelt beside him, dabbing his forehead with a wrinkled, crochet-edged handkerchief. She'd had it in her pocket since Edna had given it to her.

Her silent ministrations scared him. He wanted her to rage, to swear, to kick the door even if it accomplished nothing.

"Clementine," he said, hoping to provoke her.

She merely guided him to the corner, like she thought he'd hurt himself in his fight against the door, and sat beside him without speaking.

Benjamin couldn't stand it. He wanted to yell at her, to piss her off so she'd return to normal. Since they'd met, she'd been like the annoying little sister he'd never had and hadn't wanted. Annoying him. Picking fights with him over nothing. Telling him he was stupid. He wanted that Clem back.

Fat tears rolled down her cheeks. Benjamin put an arm around her. She buried her face in his side.

"Clem," he said helplessly. Clem wasn't supposed to give up. She was supposed to make bad decision after bad decision, keep making bad decisions as long running headfirst into a fight might accomplish something, because making stupid moves was better than making no move at all. "Hey, no. It'll be all right."

Her voice was muffled against him. "He's her son."

Benjamin tucked her hair behind her ear.

"It doesn't matter." He pushed away the image of Edna running to Redway and enfolding him in her arms. "She'll find us. She'll get us out of here."

It would be hell on her hip and knees, and Benjamin would fret and scold. But he had no doubt Edna would come for them, if she had to trudge down a thousand stairs to do it.

Clem shook her head. "She won't choose us. I wouldn't choose us."

He tried to keep his tone light. "Good thing she's not you, huh?"

She didn't answer.

"Sorry. It was a crappy joke."

"Yeah, it was."

He cracked a smile. "There you are."

Her mouth twitched. He pushed her gently.

"Come on," he said, "swear at me and tell me I'm an idiot."

"Jerk."

"Close enough."

Clem slumped against the wall. The next moment, she leaped to her feet as a young woman materialized in front of them.

The newcomer was several inches taller than Clem, maybe five or six years older, olive-skinned with warm undertones and sun-bleached hair escaping a slapdash bun. Benjamin scrabbled away from her with a yelp, his heart hammering at the sudden appearance.

"Hey, Clemmy," the young woman said softly. "It's been a long time."

Clem said nothing.

"Don't you remember me?" The young woman tucked an errant curl behind her ear. "I showed you the tree by the gym so you could watch us train."

Clem's hands balled into fists. "What the fuck are you doing here?"

Benjamin thought the real question was how she'd gotten there, since she hadn't used the door, but he was relieved to see Clem back to her old self. Even if her old self was a little hostile.

He stood, putting his hands on her shoulders. "Who is she?"

"Lena Vasquez," Clem spat. "Her name is Lena Vasquez and she was Marisol's best friend, so the next thing out of her mouth better be a good fucking reason why she's here with *him.*"

Her fingernails dug into her palms.

"Clemmy–"

"Why are you here? You kill Knights for him now, is that it?"

Lena blanched. "No! No, I could never–"

"Then what?"

"It's easier to show you."

Benjamin's hands tightened on Clem's shoulders.

Lena shivered into a woman with a cooler skin tone and a severe black bun. Monica Evans.

Clem stepped back, right onto Benjamin's foot. He jerked aside. Clem lunged past him, snatched up the broom, and held it like a quarterstaff.

Lena shivered back into herself, raising her hands. "Please, I just want to talk."

"You didn't want to talk when you attacked Edna," Clem snarled.

"I didn't know she was with you."

"What difference would that have made?" Clem swung the broom at her, but Benjamin yanked it out of reach. She grappled with him for it, her voice getting louder and louder. "You're here. You've been helping him. Knights have died because of you!"

"Clemmy–"

"You were her best friend!"

"I know."

"How can you help him? He killed her!"

Lena hugged herself. "He didn't."

Clem let out a scream of laughter. "How do you know? Because he told you?"

"Shhh–"

"Don't shush me!" Clem shouted.

Someone rapped on the door.

Lena shrank against the wall.

"I was there," she whispered.

Another rap at the door. "What's going on in there?"

"Then who?" Clem asked through gritted teeth. Her fists clenched until her nails dug into her palms.

Lena hugged herself tighter.

"Agravain," she said softly.

A third rap on the door. A key in the lock.

Lena froze, her head cocked, and vanished. Clem dove toward her, but she was gone.

The door opened, and a stern face poked in.

"What's going on in here?"

The broom slipped in Benjamin's sweaty palms; a splinter caught in the webbing of his thumb. The face glared at the broom above his head. He lowered it.

"Nothing," he said, hoping the face would believe him. Clem's chest heaved. "She's, uh, you know, a little upset about being locked up."

The face withdrew. The door slammed shut, the key turned, and they were alone.

"Clem?" Benjamin set the broom aside cautiously. "Are you okay?"

"She's lying. She has to be." Clem's voice shook. "She's lying, right?"

He didn't even know what *she* had been saying. He didn't understand what had just happened.

"I don't know."

"I was *there.*" Sparks nipped at Clem's hands. "I saw him. He was standing right over her."

Benjamin bit his lip. He didn't know how to calm her down, but he knew her well enough by now to know she'd *want* to calm down, if she were thinking. She didn't like losing control, didn't like her magic bursting free and hurting people.

"He wouldn't," she said. "I don't like Ag, but he wouldn't. They were friends."

The broom burst into flames. Benjamin beat them out, fighting to keep calm despite the danger. Clem was hyperventilating now, which was a really good way to inhale the smoke sizzling off the broom, he thought wildly.

Her eyes glowed, silver and distant. Benjamin swallowed, resisting the urge to step back.

"He saved me." Clem's fists clenched. "In Santa Alvara. He saved me. He wouldn't have done that if—"

The sparks swirled around her, higher and higher, faster and faster.

"He wouldn't," she repeated in a whisper. "They were friends."

Benjamin's chest tightened with panic, but he touched her shoulder. She shuddered.

"Hey." His voice threatened to slide up an octave, but he fought it. He had to stay calm for her. "Hey, it'll be all right. We'll figure this out, okay?"

Her glowing eyes turned onto him. "Benjamin?"

He took a deep breath. She recognized him. That was something.

"Yeah. I'm here."

The spiral of sparks around her body slowed, the glow fading from her eyes.

The sparks swirled slower and slower and went out.

"You all right?" Benjamin asked softly.

She rubbed her forehead. "Yeah. I think so."

She sat on the crate, and Benjamin pulled her into a hug. She snuggled into him. He rested his chin on top of her head.

"Okay," she said. "Okay. How are we getting out of here?"

CHAPTER FORTY-ONE

Edna awoke in semidarkness. She'd been having a nightmare, but it had already faded. Though the details escaped, the sensation of horror remained. She clutched her comforter to reassure herself that she was in the real world, not the dissolving nightmare.

It was rougher than she remembered, the comforter. The ceiling was the wrong color, too. Edna was certain the home had white walls and ceilings, but hers was the grayish brown of stone.

Someone shifted on upholstery nearby—her roommate? Somehow, Edna didn't think so, yet she wasn't sure who else it could be. The space felt all wrong, the shifting closer than it normally was, like her room had shrunk while she slept.

White orbs drifted along the ceiling, too dim to chase the shadows from the corners. Edna found her glasses on a little wooden table beside her and put them on. The room leapt sharply into focus.

He was asleep in an armchair in the corner. Percival. Looking so much like Walter now that he was grown. A little heavy through the middle. The same nose, the same chin, the same hair but longer. Walter would have told him to cut it, but she liked it.

The nightmare flooded back—only it wasn't a nightmare. It was real. Dragons and swords and dying Knights. Her son, responsible.

Edna's breath hitched. "Percival?"

He slept on. She wanted to wake him so she could see his face alive with emotion, hear his voice again. Hear him say *mom.* She hadn't realized how much she'd missed it until he said it.

But she was afraid of what else he might say.

She drank in his sleeping face like she might never see him again. She already knew how that felt.

He jerked awake. Breathing hard, his eyes darting around the room, but he calmed as his gaze settled on her.

"You're all right," he said. "God, Mom—"

He sat on the bed and hugged her for a long time. She buried her face in his chest, stroking his back as he sobbed into her thin hair. It felt like it had after Walter had died, when he'd been a wiry fifteen-year-old crying into his mother's arms.

At last he sat back, wiping his eyes. She patted his knee, but she couldn't avoid asking.

"Percival," she said. "Is it true? Are you Redway?"

He ran a hand through his hair. "Joe started calling me Red when she found me in the jungle. The media did the rest."

"You know that's not what I mean."

He covered her hand with his. Tears stung her eyes, but she blinked them away.

"Why?" she asked. "You always wanted to be a Knight. Always, ever since you were a little boy. It's all you talked about."

His expression hardened. "I was wrong."

"Percival—" She didn't want to ask, but she had to. "Clem's sister—"

"I didn't kill her."

She wanted to believe him. "But—"

"It wasn't me."

She flinched at the anger in his voice. But if his mother didn't believe him, who would?

"Of course not," she said, hoping more than believing it was true.

He calmed again. "I wanted to help her. She was already dead."

Her fingers tightened on his knee. This was all wrong. She'd imagined this so many times, the impossible. It had always been a joyful occasion. There had been no difficult conversations. Just happiness, no questions asked, because you don't question happiness.

"But," she said, hating herself, "all the cities..."

"Stop it." Magic sparked from his fingers. "Why do you have to do this?"

"Percival—"

"I thought you were happy to see me."

"I am," Edna said, "but—"

"When I saw you, I couldn't believe it. Why can't you leave it alone?"

Tears spilled down her face. "Because you're hurting people."

His jaw tightened.

"I'm hurting Knights."

It felt like he'd doused her with cold water. "Percival—"

He stood, pacing the room like a tiger in a too-small cage. She watched him in bewilderment. He'd never been so tense. Angry. Animal-like.

"What did they do to you?" she whispered.

He stopped pacing and asked, more calmly than she'd expected, "What did they tell you? When I didn't come back?"

She pressed her palms to her eyes, one at a time.

"There was a letter," she said. "They sent a letter. It said you'd gone missing."

He clenched and unclenched his fists. "You didn't question it?"

She sat up straighter. "Of course I did! I made phone calls, I sent emails—I demanded answers—what had happened, if there'd been an attack on your base or an assignment or—"

Her voice broke. Even with him here, alive, it hurt. The shock of it, the lack of answers. The sky had fallen down around her.

"At last they sent a sergeant. He was very kind. He said a unit of Knights had been sent to Dominion on assignment, and after you went missing, one of your friends came forward and said you'd snuck off with them. And when the unit came back, they came back without you. He said they'd been sent back out to look for you, but—" She sniffled. He'd brought it for her, bloody, torn, neatly folded. "All they found was your jacket."

Percival was stone-faced. "I didn't join the unit."

"Then what were you doing here?"

"I wasn't. Some of the other troops beat me so bad it almost killed me, and they panicked. So they hid me here and left me to die."

Sparks shot from his fingers again, more erratic now. They crackled and flashed around him like lightning.

"You don't understand," he said. "The things they do to squires—hazing, they call it, like it's some stupid frat boy ritual. A part of the experience. If you complain, they tell you to suck it up and deal with it, and they treat you worse."

She hesitated. "What—?"

He pulled his collar down to show her a faded, jagged D branded into his shoulder. "This, for starters."

He returned to pacing, like he had to keep moving or the walls would close in on him.

"They beat you? The other Knights?"

"I could handle the beatings," he said, "most of them," and her blood ran cold.

She scrunched the comforter in her hands. Walter had been nothing like her father, but she'd never left a room if he was angry with Percival about anything, no matter how trivial. Just in case.

After all her watchfulness and care, it had happened anyway. Her heart hammered in her ears.

"The instructors would tell you to get patched up and you'd better be back drilling the next day. And everyone knew what had happened, but no one said anything, and if *you* did, no one would talk to you and things would get worse. That was bad enough, but—"

He stopped again, his chest heaving.

"That base, they have this thing they do. They had a dragon out in the jungle. It was a small little beast, smaller than I thought a dragon could be. Emaciated, in chains, with scars and burns and holes in its wings. The minute I saw it, every thought I ever had about killing dragons went right out the window."

Edna's knuckles were white. "What happened to it?"

"I tried to escape with it," he said. "Suffice it to say I failed."

He resumed pacing, more restless than ever. Magic crackled up and down the length of his body, a small storm surrounding him. The white orbs on the ceiling flickered.

"Why didn't you tell me?" Edna asked. "You could have come home. We could have—"

"What, Mom? No one would've believed me."

An orb exploded into darkness. Edna flinched.

"Better you had a son who was dead than a son who was a dragon-lover." His voice was consumed with bitterness. "I thought you'd be ashamed. Every time I called, you sounded so proud of me."

"Percival—"

"When I got here, I realized I wasn't the only one." Another orb exploded, casting long shadows across the room. Magic flickered around him. "It happened to the others, too. Every last one of them. Every last Knight at that base. We're just the ones who left."

She didn't know if he meant the abuse or the dragon or being beaten almost to death. She didn't ask.

Flickering shadows masked his face. His voice boiled over with anger.

"Most of them won't go. If you do what you're told and don't complain, you'll get by. It stops eventually, and by then you're doing it yourself, to the next cohort, because it's what's done. Because you went through it, so why shouldn't they? And meanwhile the outside world sings the Knights' praises and won't hear a word against them."

If only he'd look at her. Maybe this frightful magic storm would die down. Maybe he'd quiet and stop pacing, relight the orbs so his face wasn't twisted with shadow.

"I'm so sorry," she said. "If I'd had any idea—"

"There's nothing you could've done. There's nothing anyone can do." Lightning flared around him, flashing cold and white. "The Knights are too powerful. No one will speak against them, no one can do anything—except me. Because I'm willing to do what it takes."

The hatred in his voice chilled her.

"Percival," she said, but he kept talking, and his words scared her more and more, because he sounded so eager, because he sounded like he expected her to be pleased and proud.

"This will never happen to anyone ever again. Never. One more attack will have them scrambling to regroup—"

"Percival, please—"

"—and I'll take the fight right to the source. Cut off the head, and the body will fall. This will never happen again."

Frightened tears slipped down her cheeks.

"Percival," she whispered.

He calmed suddenly, like he'd just remembered her. His magic quieted into gentler bursts, like fireflies blinking around him. He waved his hand, relighting the orbs he'd shattered. Edna pressed into the headboard as he approached.

"Everything's going to be all right," he said gently. "You're here now."

He hesitated and then kissed her forehead. She squeezed her eyes shut and tried to stop crying.

"Get some rest," he said, and he was out the door before she could call after him.

CHAPTER FORTY-TWO

Something inside Red had come alive when he saw his mother's face, but whatever spark had blazed inside him went out as he left her. He emerged from the room with heat and magic and something akin to grief bubbling inside him. The grief surged high and washed through him, leaving him raw and rudderless and unsure who he was, a son with a mother and a name from a lifetime ago.

He sank to his haunches, grabbing his head in his hands like he wanted to crush it.

"Red?"

Kiernan stood in the dormitory doorway up the hall. Red curled in on himself. Like Clem, the day she'd spoken of her sister's death.

Kiernan's heart clenched at the thought of her, but Red spoke.

"She's my mother." He sounded close to tears, or maybe laughter. "She's my mother, Kiernan."

Kiernan had never seen him this way. "I know."

Red ran a hand over his face.

"When I saw her—" His voice was hoarse. "When she passed out, Shira said, Red, what do you want us to do, and for a moment I didn't realize she was talking to me. For a moment, I forgot my own name." He laughed wetly. "You can't imagine how it felt."

Kiernan twinged with jealousy.

"I was myself again," Red said, "like I'd never been a Knight. Like I'd never been Redway. And then, I don't know, I realized they were waiting for me to give orders, and it all came rushing back. I didn't know what to do. I still don't know what to do."

He ran his hands through his hair. Kiernan said nothing. Seething jealousy permeated his concern for Benjamin and Clem, for Edna, for his plan to get them to safety, confusing and conflicting with the concern he felt for Red because they'd been friends for fifteen years. He couldn't ignore that, despite everything else he was feeling.

Red's gaze snapped to him. "Did you know?"

Kiernan looked at him blankly.

"That she was my mother."

"I would've told you if I'd known."

Red rose in one fluid motion. "You didn't tell me she was the Chosen One."

"I didn't know," Kiernan said. "Not until Shira had already grabbed—"

Red snorted. "You didn't know? How much time did you spend with them, and you expect me to believe you didn't know?"

He shouldered past.

Kiernan almost let him get away with it, because he was right. Kiernan should've known. Maybe he would have, if the idea of an elderly Chosen One weren't so ludicrous. There had been so many signs. If he hadn't been so sure it was Clem, if the truth weren't so outlandish—if he hadn't gotten so distracted by the three of them—maybe he would've realized it was Edna.

But he hadn't. And despite everything they'd been through together, Red didn't believe that.

"Did you know recruitment was up?" Kiernan asked quietly.

Red kept walking.

Kiernan felt cold. "Red?"

"Not now."

"Yes, now," Kiernan said angrily. "Did you know?"

Red didn't answer. Kiernan put a hand to the wall; the hallway teetered around him.

"Oh my god, you did."

"It doesn't matter. However many Knights there are, we'll kill them. Recruitment is up for now, but once we succeed—"

"What if we don't?"

"We will."

They headed upstairs, turned left, and gained the kitchen. The better part of the keep's residents gathered around the woodstove and the rough-hewn wooden table, murmuring together about the Chosen One, Red's mother. They fell silent at the sight of him.

Kiernan blocked Red's path. "Did you know about the base?"

Red stared up at him defiantly. "What base?"

"The base," Kiernan said through gritted teeth, "in Bahir Dar."

Red said nothing.

Kiernan loomed over him. *"Did you know?"*

Red drew himself up to his full height, which didn't do much because he was four inches the shorter.

"Yeah," he said. "I knew."

Kiernan lunged, pinning him to the wall.

"You knew? You knew and you didn't tell me?" His forearm crushed Red's chest. "This whole time, I thought—we've done some awful things, the two of us, but I always thought it was worth it if—"

Behind him, Shira left her spot at the table.

"Kiernan," she called, but blood rushed in his ears and his heart hammered and his chest tightened with rage and regret, and he barely heard her.

"We've destroyed whole cities, and I didn't like it, but I put up with it because I figured you knew best, and what were those cities compared to my people? And I've held my tongue about the squires who have died, every time you've talked about saving them—"

Red's face whitened. Sparks raced up his arms.

"Kiernan, let him go," Shira said sharply, closer now, but Kiernan hadn't noticed his audience. He thought of the base, the increased recruitment, everything he'd kept quiet about for the last fifteen years and longer, everything he'd seen and done in the Knights, everything he should have told his grandfather but never had because he'd been trying to live up to what he thought his grandfather thought he was.

"I've never said a word, because I thought I was helping my people. But I'm not. Fifteen years ago, a base would've been impossible. This is making things worse, and you *knew.*"

Red threw him off, showering the kitchen with an explosion of sparks. Kiernan hit the ground hard; his shoulder smacked stone with a crack. The woodstove roared, vomiting fire.

The kitchen flinched collectively. Shira froze a few feet away, still and silent as a stag watching a hunter.

The fire died down, popping and flickering in the wood stove.

Red's arms were awash with sparks, brighter than the fire in the stove or the white orbs overhead. Kiernan clutched his shoulder but stayed down, breathing hard.

Someone whimpered at the table. Red's blast of magic had knocked Joe off her feet and into the side of the stove. She lay crumpled on the floor, blood trickling from her hairline, but no one dared move to check on her.

In the firelight, with shadows flickering over him and sparks blazing in his eyes, on his skin, Red loomed like a giant, filling the doorway. For the first time in fifteen years, Kiernan was afraid of him.

"So what if I knew?" Red breathed steam, like a dragon, white and thick. It swirled around the room, dimming the fire. "I know what I'm doing, Kiernan. If you don't want to help me, fine. Just stay out of my way."

He turned to the crowd behind them. "Anyone else?"

The kitchen shrank in on itself. No one answered.

"We're heading out," he spat, "get ready," and he vanished into the thickening steam.

Shira moved first, striding across the room to check on Joe. She looked around at the others.

"Well?" she said brusquely. "You heard him. Get moving. Roman, take Joe to the infirmary."

Chairs scraped. Everyone headed down to the armory in silence. They avoided Kiernan as they passed.

All except Lena.

How long she'd been there with the others, he didn't know. As she filed past, she whispered, "They're in the basement. But they're under guard."

She hurried away.

Kiernan's shoulder ached; he thought he'd dislocated it. Ignoring the pain, he slunk out of the kitchen and headed to the dorm for his bow.

CHAPTER FORTY-THREE

Edna dumped her handbag out on the comforter and clawed through her things until she found the photograph. Percival, the day he left for the Knights. He beamed out of the tarnished silver frame, unrecognizable as the man who had prowled before her.

Tears slid down her nose and dripped onto the photograph, blurring his face.

She wished she were back at the nursing home.

She wanted to watch "I Love Lucy" reruns with Marguerite. She wanted to get her hair permed for visitors' day. She wanted to prank the new hires while Benjamin sighed and scolded her. She would rather have played bingo in that stark, white cafeteria, with Jeanine giving her that sugary smile every day for the rest of her life, than be here, now.

Edna shoved the photograph into the depths of her handbag and crammed everything else in after it.

A slim black thing remained in the folds of the comforter. Clem's phone.

Edna turned it over. She had no clue how to use the silly thing. Somehow, Clem had made it work as a magic mirror, but Edna couldn't even make it work as a phone.

"Hello?" she said experimentally.

Nothing happened. The black screen reflected her dimly.

"Please." Her voice shook. "Just tell me why you chose me."

No wizard's voice sounded from the phone's depths to comfort her. She shook it a little, like one of those eight balls some of the cheaper fortune-tellers use.

"I can't do anything," she told it. "I'm completely useless. All I know how to do is knit. A lot of good it's done me."

The screen didn't change. Her reflection stared back at her, wrinkled and white and faded in the streaky surface.

"Fine," she said loudly. "Don't tell me. You—you absolute—"

She couldn't come up with a name bad enough for the phone, or the wizards, or whoever she was trying to insult. She threw the phone back into her handbag.

No use sitting here feeling sorry for herself.

Her cane leaned against the wall by the door. Edna pushed the comforter away and stood, but she plopped right back down again. Her legs wobbled; her hip and knees ached worse than ever. She'd gone too long without her NSAIDs. Her metformin, too. Benjamin would have a fit.

She had to find him. Both of them. Clem would hate her now, but she had to find them. She gritted her teeth and heaved herself up again, swaying for a moment. Then she collected her handbag and her cane and shuffled outside.

The corridor was deserted, but it was dim and long and Edna had no idea in which direction to begin her search.

"Eeny meeny miny moe," she whispered to herself. Left-hand side. "All right, old girl. This way."

She didn't get far. Footsteps approached when she was halfway down the hall. Edna scuttled through the nearest door, pulling it closed behind her.

The footsteps echoed, loud and purposeful, and now voices joined them.

"—so soon?"

"I don't know. I'm telling you what he said."

"I don't like it."

"Then stay here."

"No, I'll go—"

The voices and footsteps died away.

Edna pressed her ear to the door. Nothing.

"Edna?" a voice said behind her.

Kiernan.

"Snickerdoodles," she said, and she turned to face him.

She was in a dormitory. Separated by curtains, cots lined the walls, each with a small set of drawers beside it.

Kiernan stood by a cot in the corner with his bow in his hands, but he joined her by the door. "You're not supposed to be in here."

Edna straightened. "Are you going to turn me in?"

"You need to get back to your room," Kiernan said. "It'll be easier if I get the others and bring them to you."

She forgot to stand straight. "Benjamin and Clem? You know where they are?"

"Yeah. Listen." He avoided her eyes. "I know I can't change what I did, but I want you to know. I mean. If I'd known what I know now, I would've done it differently. But. I didn't know. Uh." His fingers tightened on the belly of his bow. "I'm sorry. I wanted you to know. That's all."

Something caved inside her.

"Kiernan," she said softly, but he continued on in a rush.

"I just want to get you all out of here. We'll get you back to your room and—"

She took his hand. It surprised him so much he shut up.

"You don't need to apologize," she said. "Not to me."

"But—" He broke off, feeling like she was incorrect but also like it might benefit him not to argue the point.

Edna let him go, sinking onto the nearest cot.

"It's my fault, Kiernan. Everything. It's all my fault." She buried her face in her hands. "I'm the one who asked you to come with us. I insisted, even after Clem said we didn't need you. I'm the one who told you she was the Chosen One."

She couldn't remember why she'd done so.

"And my son—" She laughed, but it came out like a sob. "It's my son who's responsible for all this."

Kiernan rubbed the triangle carved into his bow. "His being your son doesn't make it your fault."

Edna didn't hear him, too busy thinking she'd gone wrong somewhere. She must have done something wrong for Percival—Redway—to think this was all right. To think he couldn't have come home to her, all those years ago, and told her what was going on.

"You were fighting for your people. Maybe you bungled it, but you were fighting for them." She wrung her hands. "What can he be fighting for?"

Kiernan didn't answer, but she didn't expect him to.

"Come on," he said. "We need to get you back."

She shook her head. "I can't, Kiernan, I can't sit in that room by myself."

"You're not coming with me. I'll get the others and come back for you."

"I am so coming with you."

"It'll be faster if I go alone."

"Kiernan, please."

He started, surprised she was pleading instead of demanding, given the circumstances. Not that he remotely expected her to stay obediently behind if he refused.

"Okay," he said. "But you'd better keep up."

CHAPTER FORTY-FOUR

"Is something wrong with your shoulder?" Edna asked.

She hadn't noticed when she'd burst in on him, but Kiernan was favoring his right shoulder: limping along, hissing every time his right side bumped against the wall or Edna, no matter how gently. Despite his talk of keeping up, he went down the hallway so slowly that she kept pace with him easily.

"Hurts," Kiernan grunted.

"What on earth did you do to it?"

He didn't answer. Edna didn't ask again.

The hallway ended in a small chamber.

"Through here."

Weapons racks, chests, and cabinets filled the chamber. Whetstones sat on a table in the corner. Pegs lined the wall by the door. Flight jackets hung from three of them, but the rest were empty, as were many of the weapons racks. A staircase in the back-left corner led back upstairs; another, across the room, dove deep into the bowels of the mountain.

"Where are we?" Edna asked.

"The armory."

"Where are all the weapons?"

Kiernan examined a rack still filled with swords. "It must be here somewhere."

Footsteps clattered on the stairs.

Kiernan grabbed Edna and shoved her into a cabinet. "Keep quiet."

Edna pressed her ear to the cabinet door. She froze.

Percival's voice echoed coldly through the chamber. "What are you doing here?"

"I live here," Kiernan said.

Edna choked back something that might've been nervous laughter.

"Don't start with me, Kiernan."

His anger was palpable through the cabinet. A sword snicked as if drawn from one of the weapons racks.

"That's the Sword of Destiny," Kiernan said.

Edna's heart seized.

"That's your bow," Percival said nonchalantly.

Leather creaked.

"You can't use it."

"I'm not leaving it here for her."

More footsteps. A scuffle. Edna squeezed her eyes shut.

"Get out of my way," Percival snarled.

"No."

More scuffling.

"Red–give me–the–"

A wordless snarl, more animal than human. Something slammed into the wall.

The mountain trembled. Edna stuffed a fist in her mouth to keep from crying out.

Percival spoke, low and gutted. "I wish you'd disobeyed my orders."

A pause.

"What, and killed her?"

"You wouldn't have killed her," Percival snapped. "You would've killed the girl. Maybe she never would have come here."

Edna bit down on her fist.

"She loves that girl," Kiernan said.

Another scuffle. The thud of a body slamming against the wall. Wood clattering against stone, footsteps striding away, Kiernan gasping—

Edna cracked the cabinet door. Percival disappeared upstairs, the Sword of Destiny at his hip. She didn't know what was worse: him having it, or her being expected to use it against him.

She gulped down a deep breath and pushed out of the cabinet.

Kiernan was bent double, breathing hard.

"Are you all right?" she whispered. "What did he do to you?"

He reached for his bow with a groan. "Threw me off. I'm fine."

"He dislocated your shoulder, didn't he?"

He said nothing. Edna already knew the answer.

"What now?" she asked.

"He's probably headed to Redding." He glanced toward the stairs, making sure Percival was really gone. "City in northern California. It has the second largest base in the country. We were meant to hit it maybe a week after Santa Alvara. Enough time to regroup and recover and head out again, not enough time for the Knights to prepare for another attack. Then we were going to move on, straight to Coldwater. That was supposed to be our last major strike."

She didn't have to ask what Coldwater was: the headquarters of the Assembly of Knights-General. Like Clem had said at breakfast, back in Amir's apartment. It felt like forever ago.

"Now he's headed to Redding ahead of schedule?" Edna asked.

Kiernan led her toward the downward stairs. "That was the plan. That has to be where he's going, if he's taking everyone—I heard him. He told them they were going. If it was like Detroit, he'd go alone."

Edna sagged. "So he was there. I knew it. I knew I saw someone."

"Yeah." Kiernan let out a long breath. "He used to do that kind of thing all the time. Fly off in a rage like that."

"He wasn't always so angry."

"He's got plenty to be angry about."

They staggered down the stairs in silence. By this point, Edna thought she might have been the more in-shape of the two. Every step jolted Kiernan's shoulder. He hunched his way down the stairs.

At the bottom was a door. Muffled voices whispered on the other side.

Edna's spirits lifted for the first time since Santa Alvara. Voices were good. Voices meant not dead.

Kiernan slipped a thin dagger out of his boot.

"What's that for?" Edna asked nervously.

"The lock. With everyone heading out, Red probably forgot about them. Whoever was guarding them must have gone with the others. Which is great for us, except it means I have no clue where the key is."

Before he could do anything, the lock clicked.

A triumphant shout followed. Benjamin.

"You've done it!"

"Shut up! Someone will hear you."

The door swung open, and Benjamin found himself face-to-face with quite possibly the last person he wanted to see right now.

Kiernan dropped the dagger.

Benjamin's triumph drained away. "What the hell are you doing here?"

Kiernan stepped aside. Benjamin's eyes followed him with confusion. Then he saw Edna and gave a strangled cry.

"Edna! Oh my god, I've been so worried. What are you doing down here? There are like a million stairs. Your hip—"

She cut him off with a bone-crunching hug. Kiernan shepherded them inside. Clem stood beside the door, a hand wrapped around the broom. She eyed Kiernan warily as he stood sentry, but the sight of Edna reassured her. Her grip loosened on the broom.

Edna sank onto the wooden crate, glad to sit even though getting up again was going to be a doozy. She snuggled into Benjamin as he bombarded her with questions. Clem sat on her other side, leaning against her. Edna's eyes prickled with tears, but she burrowed deeper into Benjamin and ignored them.

He set her handbag on the floor. "Edna?"

"I'm all right," she mumbled into his shirt.

"No, you're not."

"Really."

"Edna. Seriously. You don't have to be all right all the time."

She hiccupped once and laughed. She couldn't explain that she did indeed have to be all right all the time, because she was the oldest and because she was cheerful and because people expected it of her.

She twisted toward Clem. The girl had draped over her, a confusion of arms and long, dark curls. A small sliver of face and one tired eye peered through.

"Clementine—" Edna started, but she didn't know what to say. No apology was good enough for what her son had taken from this girl.

Clem buried her face in Edna's shoulder. Suddenly she was sobbing, loud and raw like a child feeling pain for the first time and thinking it was the worst pain in the world because she didn't know there was so much worse to come.

Edna wrapped her arms around her.

"I'm sorry," she whispered. "I'm so sorry."

Clem's sobs quieted. "He didn't do it."

Edna squeezed her eyes shut. "You don't have to say that."

"I mean it." Clem sat up, pushing her hair behind her ears. "I mean..."

She wiped her nose on her arm. A strand of hair fell in her face; Edna tucked it back again.

"I don't know. She said he didn't do it." Clem wrapped her arms around her knees. "I'm sorry I yelled at you. And ran away. And took the Sword of Destiny."

Edna hugged her tight. "I shouldn't have yelled at you, either."

"No. You were right." Clem's arms tightened. "After Marisol died, Dad wasn't really around, he was at work all the time, and Mom was so busy taking care of Ellie and Javi that I thought..."

She ran a hand through her hair. Edna's heart swelled with affection for her.

"I thought they didn't care," Clem mumbled. "I thought...I don't know. I thought they had other kids and that was good enough. I've been so angry with them."

Edna rubbed her back in big circles. "In my experience, you seem somewhat angry with the whole world."

Clem gave a snotty laugh. Edna thought she was crying again, but now the occasional, slightly hysterical giggle slipped out. Clem was here with her, safe. And Benjamin, too, at her other side with an arm around her.

She met Kiernan's eyes and smiled. He worried his hairline with a thumb, but he smiled back. At least she thought he did. It looked more like a grimace.

"Benjamin," she said, "can you do anything for a dislocated shoulder?"

He pulled away instantly, eyeing her. Her smile broadened until her face hurt.

"Not me," she said. "Kiernan."

Benjamin shot a look at him. "I'm not doing anything for him."

Kiernan's chest tightened. Edna gaped; Benjamin had never refused someone medical care before.

"Haven't you taken an oath about doing no harm or whatever it—"

"I'm an orderly, not a doctor. And he's lucky I don't do him harm after what he did."

"Benjamin—"

"He lied to us. He pretended to help us, when all this time—He's the reason we're here."

Kiernan's gaze was fixed on the floor, absorbing it like he was glad someone had finally said it.

Edna wrapped an arm around Benjamin's waist.

"I'm the reason he had the chance," she said. "Who do you think found out where you were and brought me down here? Like it or not, he's helping us now. And I don't see how we have much of a chance without him. Please, dear. Do what you can for his shoulder?"

Benjamin turned to Clem. "Can you believe this?"

Clem put her hair up.

"If he was planning to lock Edna down here with us, he would've left by now. He's still here. I'm pretty sure he didn't come down here just to tell us how sorry he is." She picked at her t-shirt. "At least he better not have. I don't need to listen to some eyerollingly horrible apology from someone who's not even going to help us."

"Not you too!"

She shrugged. "I thought it was stupid to trust him in the first place. But if he's here to bust us out, I'm all for it."

Benjamin scowled. He hated how standing so close to Kiernan made his cheeks warm. How prodding Kiernan's shoulder with his fingers reminded him of their hands exploring each other on the beach, under the moonlight, and back in the hotel room afterwards. How the quirk at the corner of Kiernan's mouth still made Benjamin want to kiss him, because one shitty moment—no matter how mindblowingly shitty it was—wasn't enough to drown out the moments that had made Benjamin like him in the first place.

Kiernan met his eyes. Benjamin scowled with as much ferocity as he could muster.

"I'm sorry," Kiernan said, so softly only Benjamin heard him.

"For what?" Benjamin said through gritted teeth. "Pretending you were on our side or pretending you liked me?"

Kiernan's eyes flickered over him. "I wasn't pretending to like you."

Something buzzed in Benjamin's chest, but anger swallowed it up. He snapped Kiernan's shoulder back into its socket. It wasn't as satisfying as he'd hoped.

Kiernan's face tautened. He breathed hard through his nose. Benjamin let go of him.

"Thanks," Kiernan said.

He'd brought them back together. He'd admitted the truth to them, instead of doing what he'd come to do and letting them find out that way. Maybe, *if* he could be believed, he hadn't been using Benjamin the whole time.

It didn't mean Benjamin had to forgive him.

Benjamin wasn't sure he believed him, anyway.

He ignored the thanks. "Now what?"

Clem toyed with the hem of her t-shirt but said nothing. Edna held her closer.

Benjamin waited for someone to say something. The silence stretched out.

His anger fizzled. "Should we try to find the sword?"

Edna shook her head. She remembered it gleaming vengefully when she fought the dragon, how she had felt holding it, so ready to destroy something.

"I don't want it."

"Edna," Benjamin began, but she snapped at him.

"Do you think I'm going to run my own son through?" She hadn't even let him say whatever he was going to say. In a mumble, she added, "We can't get it anyway."

"Why not?"

"He took it with him." Kiernan's eyes flickered toward Benjamin. "We ran into him on our way down here. Red. Redway. Percival."

His name hung over them like a cloud. Edna stood, biting back a groan. Clem rose alongside her as if attached to her by strings.

"One thing's certain," Edna said. "We're not sitting here doing nothing while he destroys another city. Let's get off this rock."

CHAPTER FORTY-FIVE

They stopped in the armory for swords. Clem strapped hers to her hip. Benjamin handled his like he thought it might bite him. Edna didn't take one.

She didn't know what to do about Percival, but she couldn't do *that.*

"So we're going to Redding?" Clem asked.

Kiernan shook his head. "There's no way we'll catch up before he gets there. The city's lost."

Another city lost, though it had not yet been attacked. No way to stop him before he got there. No way to send word along to warn them. No cell reception, even if they knew who to call. Too much interference from the dragons to work any long-distance spells.

"What are we supposed to do?" Benjamin's voice crept upward. "If we can't stop him from going to Redding and we can't warn them—"

"We'll head straight to Coldwater and warn the Knights-General he's on his way there next."

But Ag had refused to heed Edna's warning in Santa Alvara. He hadn't believed she was the Chosen One. And before that—it felt so long ago—the priest in Marine City had refused to give her the Sword of Destiny because she had no proof it was meant for her.

"What if they won't listen to us?" she said.

"You're the Chosen One. They'll listen to you."

"You overestimate the success I've had with this Chosen One fiddle-faddle."

"They have to listen to you," Kiernan said, "or he'll destroy the city and the entire assembly."

Their footsteps echoed through the halls of the keep. Edna gripped her cane tight. When she'd left the home, she'd thought she'd known what she was in for. An evil sorcerer living in a remote mountain castle, all black stone and spindly towers. An army of dragons ready and waiting. And by the time she met him, she'd surely have learned how to use the Sword of Destiny.

Instead there was her son, his anger, his friends, a kitchen with a worn wooden table. And she hadn't learned how to use the sword. And she didn't *have* the sword.

And if she did, she could never, ever use it.

Clem's whisper echoed down the hall. "Didn't he leave anyone behind to stand guard?"

Benjamin glanced around like he expected someone to race out and attack them.

"He doesn't think when he gets like this," Kiernan said.

Benjamin touched Edna's shoulder, but she avoided his gaze. Eventually, she knew, they'd have to talk about the fact that Redway was her son. She wanted to put that conversation off as long as possible.

They gained the rock ledge outside. The world was greenly wet and humid, dripping. Sparse clouds scudded across the sky.

With a whoosh, a tattered, burnt, soaked carpet shot out from the crevice in which it had been hidden, landing in front of them with a squelch.

"Beatrice!" Edna cried. "Oh, dear, I am glad you're all right."

The carpet's corner flipped up as if to say this wasn't exactly all right, thank you.

"All right it may be," Kiernan said, "but it's not getting us to Coldwater in that condition."

"Then how do you propose we get there?"

"Dragonback."

Benjamin swallowed. "Dragonback?"

Kiernan led them downhill toward a cave. He slid on scree and flung out a hand to catch himself, hissing painfully. He was still favoring his right shoulder.

Edna caught Benjamin's eye, but he shook his head.

"It's back in the socket, but it's still going to hurt like hell. If we had the time and supplies, he'd be in a sling and physical therapy with heaps of painkillers."

Painkillers sounded good to Edna, but her medications had burned up inside Benjamin's messenger bag back at the hotel. So had Clem's backpack.

Snores rattled the mouth of the cave. Steam curled from the entrance and dissipated. Edna followed Kiernan inside, but the others hung back.

The cave spilled over with massive tropical flowers. A dragon so deeply blue it was almost black slept on a thick pile of petals and foliage, crushing them.

"I thought dragons hoarded gold," Edna commented.

"They hoard whatever the hell they want," Kiernan said. "Basil likes flowers. Come on, you two."

Clem squeezed Benjamin's hand. They slipped closer.

A woman with dark eyes and sun-bleached hair materialized in front of them. Benjamin yelped.

Clem crushed his fingers in her grip. "Stop doing that."

Kiernan had his bow up in a heartbeat but couldn't raise it high enough to aim. He grimaced, then saw who it was and slung the bow back over his shoulder.

"Who is she?" Edna asked.

"You'd, uh." Kiernan kicked at a flower. "You'd know her as Monica Evans."

Lena's eyes locked on Clem's face. "Don't go."

Clem squeezed Benjamin's hand so hard he was afraid she'd break bones.

"You could stay here," Lena said. "You don't have to go running into battle. You could stay with us. He'd keep you safe."

"I'm not staying here with him."

"But he didn't—"

"It doesn't matter," Clem snapped. "He's killed hundreds of Knights just like her. And you helped him."

Lena flinched; Edna sagged. Kiernan said nothing. He stroked the snoring dragon until it opened a sleepy yellow eye.

Clem stomped into the cave, dragging Benjamin with her. "Come on."

Lena caught her arm as she passed.

"Please. You don't understand. I was there. I saw Ag push her, I saw her—" Her face tautened. "I saw her fall and hit her head, and I didn't do anything. I didn't tell anyone."

Clem jerked away, but Lena's grip tightened.

"Don't go, Clemmy, please. Stay here. I couldn't save her, but—"

Clem wrenched her arm free. "If you care so much, fight Redway with us."

"I can't."

"Why the hell not?" Clem snarled. The dragon twitched, glaring in her direction. "Why are you helping him? You hate the Knights all of a sudden?"

"No."

"Then what?"

Lena hugged herself. "You don't understand."

"Then maybe you should fucking explain."

"I owe him my life," Lena said miserably. "We swore not to tell anyone what happened that day, but a few months later I just, I couldn't handle it anymore. I was going to report it, but something I said must've put Ag on guard, and he—"

"So come with us. After we stop this, you can tell the Knights-General—"

Lena backed away. "Ag tried to kill me once. I won't give him another chance."

Clem's face hardened. She dragged an unwilling Benjamin over to the dragon.

"Clem—"

"Get out."

"Please—"

Lena turned to Edna, but Edna didn't know what to say. Beatrice draped across the dragon's back, steaming faintly. Clem scrambled up the beast's side with Kiernan's help, her face pale and strained, her eyes glittering. Kiernan gave Lena a small, apologetic shrug with his good shoulder.

"Be careful," Lena said softly.

Clem didn't answer.

Lena turned and trudged back up the mountainside.

Kiernan hoisted Edna onto the dragon's back with a grunt, but it took several minutes to convince Benjamin to touch the beast at all. At last Edna said, "Benjamin, I love you, but if you don't get on this dragon this minute, we're leaving you behind."

He sucked in a breath and climbed aboard before he could change his mind. Kiernan struggled up one-handed, teeth gritted against the pain in his shoulder.

The dragon's yawn shook the cave. It slithered forward, crushing flowers underfoot. Clem clung to Edna, who clung to Benjamin, who clung to Kiernan though he didn't particularly want to.

The dragon spiraled into the sky. The wind rushed in their faces and hair, whipping their sleeves and making their shirts billow. They all clung tighter. Clouds swirled overhead.

Back on the mountain, Lena watched them fly away, thinking about how much Clem looked like her sister.

CHAPTER FORTY-SIX

The flight to Coldwater was long and cold. Kiernan blocked the wind with a spell, but Edna's face numbed anyway. She didn't know how long they'd been in the air, how much longer it was to Coldwater, where they were, if it had been one hour or many. Time stood still, here on the back of a dragon.

Clem spent the flight talking Benjamin through the basics of swordplay. His face twitched, possibly from the flight, possibly from the thought of having to use a sword. Edna watched them, stretching her legs out and rubbing her thighs to ease their stiffness.

She ached to sleep but couldn't. Her body wouldn't let her. Every muscle was tense, ready to spring into action at the first sign of trouble, though trouble was yet hours away.

Kiernan, sitting beside her, felt the same. He stared at the horizon as if he'd never close his eyes again. With the wind silenced, the only sounds were the creaking of the dragon's wings and occasional snatches of Clem and Benjamin's low-pitched voices.

"—feel better if I could actually practice before—"

"Don't swing it around like that. You're going to chop someone's head off—"

Edna pulled out her knitting, spent several minutes trying to untangle it, and gave up. She dug through her handbag.

Kiernan glanced at her. "What are you looking for?"

"Nothing," she said, but she kept digging.

She procured a cream-colored lace handkerchief and dabbed at her eyes. They were streaming, from the cold or the strain. The silence clawed into her head like a living thing. She adjusted her hearing aids, but it didn't matter; there was nothing to hear. Benjamin and Clem had fallen silent, polishing their swords on their t-shirts.

Edna's fingers curled around the straps of her handbag. "Why did you join the Knights?"

Kiernan took so long to answer that she thought he wasn't going to.

"It was my grandfather's idea. He wanted me to learn as much as I could. He thought we could stop them from coming to Bahir Dar if we knew more about them." Kiernan picked at his thumbnail. "I was seventeen. But I was hot-headed and got myself into trouble. Ended up running from some other recruits after I threatened a sergeant. Red found me hiding in the jungle."

His voice was bitter as a potion. "He should've sent someone else."

Edna didn't know whether he meant his grandfather or Percival. She offered him her handkerchief: his eyes were streaming, too. The lace looked silly in his hand.

He cleared his throat. "What are you going to do?"

"I was hoping you had an answer."

Kiernan handed the handkerchief back. "I thought he might listen to you."

She laughed hollowly. "He hasn't seen me in three decades. I don't think I'm likely to get through to him."

She polished her lenses, which were spotted with salt and dust.

"If it makes you feel better," Kiernan said, "he's never listened to me much, either."

She replaced her glasses with a sigh. Clouds rolled across the sky, thick and dark, threaded thinly with silver where the distant sun tried to break through. The dragon stretched its neck, shook its head, and quieted again.

"Why did it have to be a sword?" Edna clenched the handkerchief in her fist. "They must have known, when they chose me—"

"Maybe that's why they chose you. Maybe they thought his mother—"

She shook her head. If the wizards had thought a mother's love could fix this, they wouldn't have sent her after the sword.

Benjamin jerked upright. "Do you see that?"

In the distance, smoke twisted lazily into the sky.

Below, Coldwater burned.

"Shit," Clem said.

Kiernan urged the dragon faster. The smoke thickened as they neared, acrid and stinging. The wind roared with flame. The sky was thick with dragons.

Edna grabbed Kiernan's arm. "I thought you said he was going to Redding."

Kiernan's jaw tensed. "I thought he was."

Their dragon roared, the sound vibrating through their bodies. The air heated and thickened as they dove toward the city.

They landed amidst craftsman-style houses and Greek revival public buildings billowing with flames. Clem slid down, staggering where she hit the ground. Kiernan steadied her and reached for Edna.

He hesitated. "Are you sure about this?"

"No," Edna said, "but I have to do something."

Kiernan lifted her down. The dragon shook itself at a unit of Knights running toward them. Benjamin tumbled past its wings. Kiernan caught him, pushed him at Clem, and had his bow up and ready—not high enough, his shoulder throbbing with pain. His arms trembled. His right arm hardly hurt less than his shoulder, and though he'd killed

Knights before, he wasn't sure he could kill them now. As for Red's crew, if they attacked—

Kiernan swallowed back a rising panic. He couldn't fight Red. His friends. The only family he'd known for the last fifteen years.

But maybe he could protect the other three.

"If you stay close—" he started, but Edna caught sight of Red in the midst of the chaos and hurried away with a cry.

Kiernan wanted to scream as Clem swore and hurried after Edna.

Benjamin shrieked after them, but they had already disappeared. He bit his lip so hard he tasted blood. Kiernan grabbed his wrist.

"Let go," Benjamin whimpered, not sounding like he meant it.

"Don't run off on me." Kiernan wasn't letting Benjamin out of his sight. Benjamin would die in two seconds. "I can't keep you safe if we get separated. We'll find them."

Benjamin squeezed his eyes shut. "This was a mistake. I shouldn't have come. I'm useless. Edna would be better in a fight than me."

Kiernan's grip tightened. He'd keep Benjamin safe. Whatever it took.

"It'll be all right."

He wasn't as certain as he sounded, but he had a plan. He could think of one way to protect them, and it depended on them sticking close together.

He was going to push his luck.

CHAPTER FORTY-SEVEN

Percival moved swiftly between the fiery buildings with the Sword of Destiny in his fist. Whether because of his own magic or some weird transitive property between mother and son, the sword glowed, pulsing with vengeful red light. Edna couldn't take her eyes off it.

A Knight ran at him. He thrust a hand out. The Knight crashed onto the pavement and didn't get up.

Edna's heart pounded. "Percival!"

He moved farther and farther ahead. Fire roared all around. The windows of the nearest building blew out; shattered glass rained onto the street. Edna flinched. Her lungs burned.

Dragons circled overhead. Two touched down on nearby rooftops, roaring and belching fire. A third shook the ground as it landed in the town square.

Edna gripped her knitting needles like knives. Gunfire crackled, swords clanged, fire and dragons roared.

Someone rammed into Edna as they sprinted past, knocking her to the ground. Her knees slammed into the pavement. Pain splintered through her, but she staggered to her feet again. Her hip and knees screamed in protest.

"Percival!"

He had vanished.

She tottered after him. Her lips were white with pain, but she kept going.

She didn't know how to stop him. But somehow, she had to.

Blood pounded in Clem's ears. Edna wasn't supposed to run off. She, Clem, was supposed to run off. Running off was her thing. It was all she knew how to do.

It was different, running after someone. Being scared for someone. And with the flames rising higher, with Knights marching past, shouting orders, calling for weapons, with buildings burning and windows shattering and dragons circling, it felt like she was back at Marisol's base.

Fear threatened to engulf her, but she kept running. *An object in motion stays in motion* flitted through her head, followed by, for no apparent reason, *the mitochondria is the powerhouse of the cell.*

Focus, she told herself, but the longer she ran, the fuzzier her thoughts became. Edna. She had to find Edna. She had to find...

"Clem?"

Her breathing was ragged, harsh, sounded like it belonged to someone else. Fire and dragons roared in tandem. She had a sword clenched in her fist but didn't know why, had to find Marisol but didn't know where Marisol was.

"Clem!"

Someone shook her. She blinked.

Dan.

If Dan was here...

She wanted to throw up. If he was here...

Coldwater, she told herself. She was in Coldwater.

But if Dan was here, it wasn't Coldwater.

If Dan was here, it was another fire. Four years ago. It was a base on the border of Dominion, and she was twelve, and Marisol—she had to find Marisol—

"How did you get here?"

"I'm in Coldwater," she whispered.

"Yeah, but—"

"What are you doing here?" she whispered.

Dan wiped his brow, smudging it with ash. "We were called here, all of us were called here, the AKG wanted to interview any officers who were in Santa Alvara that day."

Clem was scared to turn her head. If she turned her head, she'd see a burnt-out gym with a broken window, a tree she'd climbed, now burning.

She squeezed her eyes shut, forced them open, and looked around.

Everything was on fire—but there was no gymnasium. No tree. They weren't on a base. They were in the middle of a city, its asphalt roads acrid in the heat.

She was in Coldwater.

She let out a long, shaky breath. Dan was saying something.

"What?" Clem asked, but before he could answer, she remembered Edna.

She remembered riding here on a dragon. She remembered standing in a cold storage room and someone saying Redway hadn't killed her sister.

"Did Agravain kill Marisol?" she asked.

A window blew out overhead.

Dan dragged her around a corner. "You have to get out of here. Did you come alone?"

She pulled away from him. "Did Agravain kill Marisol?"

"Where did you hear that?"

"Lena."

His face tautened. "Lena's dead."

"Are you fucking sure? I'm telling you I saw her."

Dan shushed her. "She's not here?"

"She wouldn't come."

He relaxed. "Good."

"She said he tried to kill her, too."

"Don't let Ag hear you say that," Dan said softly.

Clem's breath caught. She shivered. "Dan—"

Two figures ran out of the smoke. Dan shoved her aside, raising his sword, but she grabbed his arm.

"Don't!"

Benjamin skidded to a halt with his hand uncertainly on the hilt of his sword. Kiernan was less cautious.

Clem threw herself in front of Dan. "Don't!"

Mutual if wary recognition all around. Dan shoved Clem toward Benjamin.

"Get her out of here," he said.

He jogged off. His voice sounded in her head, *Lena's dead, don't let Ag hear you,* and so did Lena's, softly, haunted, *Agravain,* clashing with each other like stations too close together on an old dial radio. Under it all was something Clem had forgotten, her reason for running off in the first place. She darted after him, but Benjamin grabbed her.

She twisted in his grip. "Let go!"

"We *just* found you," he said in a high-pitched voice. "Clem, please, we gotta go. We gotta find Edna."

She stopped twisting. "Edna," she echoed.

Benjamin relaxed his grip cautiously. Clem looked around like Edna might happen to amble by.

Kiernan shouldered his bow. Adrenaline had numbed his pain. "You good?"

Clem didn't answer, but she didn't run off, either, so he took it as a yes.

"Let's go."

Phone reception was spotty in the chaos, but Clem managed to pull up a map of the city. The program couldn't figure out where they were; the blue blip glitched on the screen, freezing in one spot long after they'd left it. She and Kiernan examined landmarks and street signs—where street signs were still standing—until they thought they knew where they were.

"Who cares where we *are?*" Benjamin asked. "Where are we *going?* We don't know where Edna is."

They went on anyway, because what else could they do? They headed for Coldwater Creek, which bordered the city to the east and was the target of its evacuation route.

In the middle of a residential area, a unit of Knights spotted them. Kiernan and the others may not have been in flight jackets like Red's crew, but they weren't in Knights' uniforms, either, and the civilians had already evacuated and were unarmed in any case.

Guns fired.

Kiernan whirled in front of Benjamin and Clem. The bullets, no matter where they'd been aimed, fired harmlessly past. Or possibly not harmlessly; they might've hit a bystander. Kiernan didn't care.

The Knights sprinted toward them. Kiernan pulled a dagger from his belt. He'd avoided killing anyone so far, firing at people's legs and arms instead of their heads, throwing guns and spells off course with his luck. But his luck was faltering. He'd used so much of it already.

Two Knights grabbed his shoulders. Pain jolted him, but he threw them off, right into the third.

Something cracked against his head. Blood trickled down the side of his face. He whirled around and rammed his dagger into his attacker. The Knight crumpled.

Another Knight was upon him. Kiernan staggered; his luck strained. Blood blurred his vision. The Knight dodged his dagger—he stumbled, caught himself—knew that, if he fell, he might not get up again—

The Knight collapsed.

Kiernan sucked in a breath, blinking blood from his eyes. Benjamin stood over the Knight with his sword raised. The blade was clean; Benjamin had used it as a club.

"Did I—is he dead?"

Kiernan nudged the Knight with his toe. "Unconscious. That's all."

Benjamin's arms trembled. He lowered the sword, meeting Kiernan's eyes.

Kiernan gave him a small smile. "Thanks."

Benjamin didn't smile back, but he didn't look away. "This doesn't mean I forgive you or anything."

Kiernan felt elated without knowing why. "I know."

Clem had her sword pointed at the remaining Knights; she'd taken their swords after Kiernan dispatched them.

"Are you guys okay?" she called.

"Yeah," Kiernan said.

She nodded and kicked the Knights their swords. They didn't move.

"We're not here to fight you," she said. One of them snorted. Another glanced at their fallen comrades. "Look, you attacked us. That's not our fault. Believe me or don't."

The back of her neck tingled, but she turned away. She forgot the Knights as she saw Benjamin standing over the unconscious Knight.

The corner of her mouth turned up. "You threw all that stuff about using the pointy end out the window, didn't you?"

He wasn't ready to joke about it. Kiernan put a hand on his shoulder and tried not to make a big deal out of it when Benjamin didn't shrug him off.

"He saved me, anyway."

The city was a maze. As dragons took off and landed and stomped around, as buildings fell and flames roared and the phone's map threatened to crash, Clem and Kiernan recalculated their route. Again and again. Sweat rolled down Kiernan's forehead, stinging his eyes. Ash flecked Benjamin's glasses.

Clem's hair stuck to her face and neck. She yanked it away irritably, because irritation was better than fear.

"Look out!" Benjamin yelped.

A figure materialized in their path. Clem struck at them, but the figure stumbled back, just out of reach.

"Clemmy, stop! It's me."

Clem didn't lower her sword. "I thought you weren't coming."

Lena's lips were white and ragged. She was armed, but her sword was strapped to her hip and her arms were tight around her middle. Her eyes flickered toward the others before settling on Clem.

"I just want to get you out of here. Please, Clemmy."

Clem gestured at Kiernan and Benjamin with her sword. Benjamin sucked in a breath. Kiernan nudged the blade away from them.

"We're already getting out of here, in case you hadn't noticed. So thanks for your concern, or whatever, but we don't need you. Come on, guys."

They filed past. Lena hugged herself tighter. Kiernan was about to tell her to come with them when she spoke.

"You're going the wrong way, if you're heading for the river."

"We know where we're going," Clem snapped.

Lena vanished, reappearing right in front of her. Clem shoved her aside.

"I told you to stop doing that!" she snarled. "Holy fuck, I could've run you through."

"I can get you out of here."

"We don't need your help."

Lena snatched her phone.

"Hey–"

Clem reached for the phone, but Lena cupped it in her hands, muttering over it. The phone glowed and darkened again.

"Here."

The map now showed the town as it was this minute, complete with fires, dragons, and little black dots signifying people. The blue dot had stabilized. A gold line led out of town and across Coldwater Creek, shifting and re-emerging as flames spread and blocked the route.

Benjamin and Kiernan crowded around to look.

"Wow," Benjamin said. Despite everything, he had that lilt in his voice, the one that meant he was about to start asking Lena exactly what she'd said and if she'd needed to hold the phone in any particular way when she'd said it.

The corner of Kiernan's mouth turned up at his tone. "Looks good to me."

Something exploded nearby. Benjamin flinched.

Clem scowled. "Fine. Come with us, I guess."

They set off in the direction of the explosion, much to Benjamin's chagrin. The newly enchanted phone seemed to think it was the safest route.

CHAPTER FORTY-EIGHT

Edna's dress was singed. She'd had a choice between squeezing by a burning building or squeezing by a dragon, its rider, several Knights, and a number of weapons. She'd chosen the building, which at least couldn't hurt her on purpose.

She had thermal burns on her right arm and leg, but she didn't notice. Everything was numb. The city was burning down around her, she hadn't seen Percival in ages—hadn't seen the others, either. She'd run off after her son without thinking about it. Now she didn't know where they were, or if they were injured, or maybe dead.

Ash stung her eyes and smudged her glasses. Edna squinted.

A figure in a flight suit wavered before her. It looked shorter than Percival, but maybe—

The figure solidified. Not Percival. Someone with curly hair and a wiry build. Edna's heart jolted.

Clem's kidnapper. Shira, of course, not that Edna knew her name.

Her jacket was slick with blood and ash, her sword bloodied, but surely she'd know where Percival was. Edna lunged toward her, grabbing her arm.

Shira swung around.

Her brow furrowed. "What are you doing here?"

"Please—have you seen my son?"

"What are you doing here?" Shira repeated. "How did you get here?"

"The same way you did, I expect, but—"

"Our dragons don't let anyone ride them but us."

"Please, I need to find him. If you know where he is—"

Shira's nostrils flared. "It was Kiernan, wasn't it?"

"Please—"

Shira wrenched free. A unit of Knights caught sight of her. Edna reached for her again, but Shira stepped away with a whistle.

An emerald-green dragon lumbered toward them, emerging from a side street with its maw fiery and gaping.

The Knights readied their guns. Shira leapt on the dragon and took off.

"Wait!" Edna cried. Too late.

Guns fired. Shira spat out a spell. The bullets hurtled back to earth.

A falling bullet caught Edna's foot, but it barely slowed her as she limped after the dragon.

A Knight sprinted toward her with her sword raised. When she saw it was a little old lady, she sheathed the sword and grabbed Edna's shoulder, shouting something.

"What?" Edna asked dazedly.

"Civilians should have evacuated by now—"

"I can't," Edna said. "I have to find him."

"If you give us your address, fire and rescue can—"

Edna shrugged her off and limped onward.

"Ma'am—"

Edna didn't look back. The Knight, after waffling for a moment, decided it wasn't her business if a little old lady wanted to wander a fiery inferno. She rejoined her unit. A few minutes later, she had forgotten all about Edna.

CHAPTER FORTY-NINE

Kiernan stuck close to Benjamin as they wound through the city with Lena and Clem. Benjamin was in danger of shutting down. He swung his sword half-heartedly at Knights who took them for enemies, squeezing his eyes shut as if hoping providence might guide the blade. Mostly, he shouted for Edna. His voice climbed higher and higher.

Kiernan fended Knights off more deftly, disabling rather than killing them. Attack spells he avoided. His luck was a thread stretched and fraying, ready to snap.

"Stay down," he advised the latest Knight. She wore a scowl to match Clem's and looked like she might get up to sock him despite her injured leg. "Don't make me kill you."

Her scowl melted into confusion.

Kiernan moved on–tried to. Another Knight, younger, in the epaulets of a squire, ran at him with sword raised. Kiernan's bow was up again in a second, but the squire was young and dark-skinned, with cheekbones like Kiernan's mother and oldest sister, and big doe eyes like Benjamin, and thick, sooty lashes like the guard he'd killed in Detroit.

The guard's waxen face glimmered in the smoke, haunting him. Kiernan stood there without shooting. The squire closed in on him.

"Kiernan?" Benjamin whimpered.

Clem raised her sword, but her brow furrowed; the squire was hardly older than she was.

Kiernan lowered his bow. Confused, the squire skidded to a halt.

Kiernan wanted to tell them the squire reminded him of someone. He wanted to tell them he was tired of killing people and that his old mantra–he had to, he was helping his people–didn't work anymore. That it had never really worked anyway, because he'd known the whole time that his grandfather would have disapproved. It didn't matter that these people were Knights. It didn't even matter that they were trying to kill him.

"We're not here to fight you," he said.

The injured Knight probably could have argued this point, given her leg, but she frowned without comment. Benjamin touched Kiernan's back cautiously, confusedly.

Lena grabbed his arm. "Shira!"

It's Kiernan, Kiernan thought, but he wrenched himself out of his thoughts about dead guards who hadn't deserved it and dead Knights who maybe did.

An emerald-green dragon had landed nearby. Shira leapt off its back and strode toward them, sword raised. The squire swallowed, raising his own sword again.

"Don't," Kiernan advised. "She's a better fighter than you, I promise you."

Lena shielded Clem, but Clem shoved her aside, eyes narrowing in recognition.

"She's your friend, though, right?" Benjamin asked, sounding as if he hoped rather than thought this was true.

Lena hugged herself. Kiernan stood between Shira and the others.

Clem tightened her ponytail. Her eyes glittered.

"Just shoot her," she said to Kiernan. "She kidnapped me."

He didn't shoot, but his fingers tightened on his bow. Magic swirled at Shira's hands—not sparks, not erratic, but a purposeful golden glow encasing her hands like gloves, shining on the blade of her sword.

"Knights behind you," Shira said in her usual flat voice, but her eyes glinted strangely. "I know you didn't see them, since they're still alive."

The squire gripped his sword tight. The Knight tried to stand, but Benjamin prevented her. Panic threatened at the sight of this woman with her calm voice and sharp eyes and bloodied sword and glowing hands. Giving someone medical advice, even obvious medical advice like "don't stand with an arrow in your leg," calmed him down slightly. Very slightly.

"Then again," Shira continued, "you don't seem to have noticed the escaped prisoners following you around, either."

She lunged.

Benjamin cried out—Kiernan's bow wasn't raised; his dagger was in his belt—but Clem's sword clanged against Shira's.

Lena moaned. Clem threw off Shira's sword and struck at her, but Kiernan grabbed the girl and shoved her at Lena.

"Get out of here." He drew his dagger. Despite his warning, the squire stood beside him with his sword raised. "Take Benjamin with you."

"I can fight," Clem raged.

"Lena—"

Kiernan didn't have to tell her twice. She grabbed Clem's wrist, kicked Benjamin's shoe.

"Get up," she said shrilly. "Get up, come on—"

Benjamin rose obediently, tugging the injured Knight with him. She turned white as she put weight on her leg. He picked her up.

Lena smacked his shoulder. "Leave her, come on, let's go—"

"I'm a medical professional," he said, like this one fact was all he was clinging to. "I can't leave her here."

"You've got to be kidding me!" Lena moaned, but she didn't argue.

"Go!" Kiernan screamed, and then he had to hope they listened, because Shira was swinging her sword with a fury he'd never seen from her before.

The squire might not have been as good a swordsman and far less experienced to boot, but Kiernan was glad to have someone fighting beside him. The two of them forced her back, slowly. The squire narrowly avoided a sword in his side. Kiernan had already been nicked twice and worried his luck was the only thing saving him from worse injuries.

He slipped past Shira's defenses. His dagger caught her in the side.

She gasped, touching her side. Her fingers came away bloody.

The stoic mask she always wore dropped. She lunged at Kiernan, but the squire caught her in the arm. Her sword clattered to the ground.

The squire leapt at her. Kiernan held him back.

"Don't," he pleaded.

They'd always understood each other, he and Shira. They'd been the only ones unafraid of Red's rages, the only ones willing to work against him when he was being an idiot. The only ones ready to do whatever it took.

"She tried to kill us!"

"You tried to kill me," Kiernan said. "Please. *Please.*"

"Fine," the squire said, but he kicked her sword out of reach, picked it up, and handed it to Kiernan. "You might want one of these."

Kiernan took the sword hesitantly. "Thanks."

They backed away. Shira made no move to follow. She breathed raggedly, hands glowing, eyes glinting.

Kiernan glanced over his shoulder, but the others hadn't gotten far. With the Knight in Benjamin's arms, it was slow going.

When he looked back, one of Shira's hands was outstretched. Not toward him and the squire, but past them, toward the others. Her voice was a thunderclap.

"Shira, don't!" Kiernan cried, but it was too late, so he lunged into the spell's path.

His fraying luck stretched and broke.

The spell hit him.

Flames licked inside him. They burned through his stomach and ribs, scorching his organs. He lay on the pavement with his innards burning and stared into the sky, trying to breathe.

The squire shouted for the others. Shira's eyes widened like she couldn't believe what had just happened, but the squire turned on her. She sprinted away; he ran after her. Their footsteps grew fainter and fainter.

Benjamin's face filled Kiernan's gaze, drawn and frightened. His fingers scrabbled at Kiernan's shirt, yanked it up to assess the damage. Kiernan thought of how Benjamin had peeled his shirt off in their hotel room and wished he had more time for that sort of thing.

"Oh my god," Benjamin said. "Oh no, oh no, oh no—"

"Is he all right?" a voice asked, but Kiernan didn't know whose.

He concentrated on Benjamin. Benjamin's hands on his chest and stomach. The anxious little lines in Benjamin's forehead though he didn't deserve Benjamin's anxiety.

"Of course he's not all right!" another voice said anxiously. "Attack spells are Shira's specialty."

Benjamin was wheezing and gasping and repeating "no—no—no no no no." Kiernan wanted to tell him it wasn't worth it. Instead, he mumbled, "My name."

"What?"

Kiernan's breath was a groan. "My real name. Kokebe Negusu. I want you to know."

If Benjamin heard him, he didn't understand.

"Oh my god." His voice had gone higher. He prodded gently at Kiernan's skin, which turned ashy and gray as the spell slowly spread. "This is bad. This is so, so bad."

Someone knelt at his side. Clem, twisting her ponytail between her fingers. "Why did you do that?"

Sharp breaths stabbed from Kiernan's lungs. He met Benjamin's gaze fuzzily. "Had to get back in your good graces somehow."

Benjamin's face crumpled. He pressed his forehead to Kiernan's, his breath warm on Kiernan's nose and chin and cheeks.

"You're an idiot," Clem told Kiernan.

"I'd do it again."

"This still doesn't mean I forgive you," Benjamin said thickly.

Kiernan wiped Benjamin's tears away with his thumb. "I know."

Benjamin laughed wetly. Then he was kissing him, soft and wet and perfect. His fingers scrunched in Kiernan's shirt, gently, like Kiernan would break if he held him too tightly, because maybe he would.

Kiernan smiled into his mouth. "Worth it."

"Gross," Clem said.

Kiernan laughed, but another groan swallowed his laughter. The fire stabbed at his insides. He reached for his bow; his fingers fell short.

"Please," he said hoarsely. He wasn't dying without his bow. Not without that.

Benjamin placed the bow in the elf's hands. Kiernan's fingers curled around it.

A unit of Knights passed without noticing them. Clem stiffened. She shot to her feet, her sneakers squeaking on the pavement, and drew her sword.

Lena grabbed her arm, but Clem threw her off.

"Clemmy, don't."

"He killed my sister," Clem snarled. "I'm not letting him get away."

"What?" Benjamin asked, his voice creeping up again, but Clem ran off without explaining. Lena sprinted after her, crying for her to stop.

Kiernan's eyes fluttered closed. Benjamin's fingers tightened in his shirt. He didn't want to leave Kiernan. Despite everything. Because of everything.

"Go on," Kiernan said. "She'll get herself killed."

Benjamin smoothed his locs. As if it made a difference now.

"I'll stay with him."

It was the Knight whose leg Kiernan had injured. Benjamin had set her on the pavement when Kiernan collapsed. The arrow was still lodged in her leg.

Benjamin bit his lip. "He shot you."

She eased herself down beside Kiernan, grimacing. "And then he saved my life. Fair's fair."

Benjamin looked after Clem but didn't move.

"I won't kill him," the Knight said. "I'll even keep him alive if I can. I owe you that much. You could've left me here."

"No, I couldn't."

She nodded. "There you go."

Benjamin wiped his eyes on his t-shirt. The Knight's fingers flexed like she was considering patting his shoulder and saying, "there, there."

"Go on," she said instead.

"I'll come back for you. Both of you." Benjamin's voice trembled. "I promise."

CHAPTER FIFTY

At last, Edna saw him.

She had long since lost sight of the dragon, and the heat had been playing tricks on her eyes: slinky black things crawled out of broken windows, disappearing around the corners of buildings. The air quivered.

But this was no mirage, not with the magic crackling around him and the Sword of Destiny clenched in his hand.

His other hand stretched toward a barricade of crumbled building. Beyond the barricade, Knights sheltered together. They couldn't get close enough to use their swords, and bullets were useless against his magic. The few who knew some spells stationed themselves at the front to protect the rest.

"Percival!" Edna shrieked.

He jerked around. A Knight leapt out from behind the barricade, thrusting his hand out with a shout. Percival whipped back around, not fast enough.

The spell hit him. He reeled.

Edna felt like it had hit her, too, like it had punched the breath from her lungs. It hadn't been her intention, but was she perhaps a little glad—?

Percival straightened, panting, but the Knights had already fled.

Edna wanted to cry, to laugh. She didn't know whether she was relieved they'd left him alive or wished they'd taken advantage of the moment.

He turned toward her slowly. She wanted to come closer. She'd meant to, when she shouted, but her feet were seared to the ground. Her injured foot was numb, leaden.

Footsteps behind her. Percival's eyes glittered through his flight mask. The sword was glowing, his hand at the ready. Voices followed.

"Please, he's dangerous—"

"So don't come with me."

Edna's heart leapt. Clem.

"Don't," Edna whispered, as if Percival could hear her whispering from here. "Please."

The footsteps came closer. He raised his fist—

Clem and Lena emerged from between two buildings. Percival frowned as he recognized them. He lowered his fist—

The windows blew out in the building behind the barricade. Smoke billowed. Edna inhaled a lungful and bent double, choking. Her vision fuzzed around the edges; the buildings wavered. The footsteps passed her by in a blur of bodies.

"No—"

Edna hacked something onto the pavement. Her legs shook.

Clem and Lena shimmered in the heat, sprinting away.

Percival was gone.

Edna rubbed her glasses hastily on her dress, smudging them worse with dust and grime.

The girls shrank in the haze. Edna stared at the spot where Percival had been standing, like she could make him reappear if she stared hard enough.

Then she hurried after Clem, wheezing and gasping.

Far ahead, the girls closed in on the unit of Knights with Ag and Dan marching at its rear. Lena snagged Clem's arm, but Clem wrenched away.

"Clemmy, I'm begging you—"

"Leave me alone."

"If you tell him you know—"

Clem's lungs burned, but she sped up. The Knights were close.

Lena huffed, disappeared, and reappeared right in front of Clem. Clem skidded into her and fell.

"Would you stop fucking doing that?"

Ag's head snapped up at her snarl. He turned, expecting to see Clem—and saw Lena.

The color drained from his face. Oblivious, his unit continued on without him, but Dan turned back as Ag fell behind. He, too, froze when he saw the girls.

Lena put a hand on her sword.

"You're dead," Ag said. "You're supposed to be dead."

Lena's voice trembled, but she said, "I'm not."

Clem scrambled to her feet. Dan gestured at her to leave, but she shook her head.

Ag flushed vermilion from his hairline to his neck. A horrible smile unfurled on his face.

He lunged at Lena. His sword clanged against hers, and he struck again. The clang of metal sang out as Lena deflected his blows, her breathing loud and panicked.

Clem's mouth went dry. She hadn't believed it, not really. She hadn't wanted to believe Edna's son had killed her sister, but she'd *seen* him there. But now Ag's eyes shone with hatred, his cool smile barely masking his fury.

"What are you doing?" she cried.

His eyes cut to her. He lowered his sword slightly, his fury abating.

Lena threw him off. She turned a strained face on Clem. "Get out of here!"

Clem's heartbeat pulsed in her ears. Dan stood behind Ag with his sword half-raised, not fighting. Not stopping him. Lena's breath burst out of her.

Ag lunged at her again. He'd been Marisol's friend. He'd tugged on Clem's ponytail like an annoying older brother. Marisol had trusted him.

"What are you doing?" Lena cried to Clem. "Go on!"

Ag slashed at her. "You should've stayed dead."

Their voices rang like distant bells in Clem's ears. The world spun. She stumbled. The hilt of her sword dug into her palm.

Their fight spilled into an alleyway. Fire raged at either end. Clem staggered back, slipping into that other fire, that other battle.

"Clem!" Lena screamed.

Icy darts of thought pierced Clem's hot brain. She hefted her sword and launched herself at Ag.

"What the—"

"Clem, don't—"

"*Move*," Clem snarled at Lena. She shoved past the older girl, hacking at Ag.

He fell back. "Dan!"

Dan joined him, sword raised, but Clem bashed into him so hard she knocked the sword from his grasp. Her blade whirled before her. Ag swore.

He recovered and forced her back. She was smaller, faster, more inventive, but he was stronger, and he came at her with rage.

"I don't—want—to hurt—you—" he grunted, as he struck at her in a way that suggested the opposite. Clem dodged him. "This doesn't concern you."

Clem's heart beat so fast it hurt. "You killed my sister."

She thrust at him. A spatter of blood rewarded her. He put a hand to his side, looking at the blood on his hand with disbelief.

"You little—"

He lunged at her with renewed fury.

Suddenly, fighting him didn't seem like a good idea.

Clem slashed at him, panic rising. Uneven pavement caught her foot, and she tumbled to the ground. She scrambled to get up, but Ag pointed his sword at her chest.

"Ag." Dan put a hand on his shoulder. Ag threw him off. "Come on, man. She's a kid."

Ag ignored him.

Clem's eyes welled up. "You were her friends."

He barked with laughter. "If we were such friends, why'd she threaten to go to our superiors?"

Clem had no idea what he was talking about. She backed away on her elbows. His boots hit the pavement with angry thuds.

"It was my only prospect, the Knights. It's something I'm good at, it's something I could do for the rest of my life. If there had been an investigation—"

He planted his boot on her stomach.

"She made such a big deal out of it." Clem grabbed his boot, trying to unbalance him, but his foot pressed into her. "I wasn't the only one hazing new recruits. You want to be a Knight, that's what you do. But she couldn't understand that."

Clem clawed at his foot, gasping for air.

"Ag," Dan tried again.

"She threatened me." Fury burned in Ag's eyes. "One of the recruits wound up in the hospital for two weeks. Mari wanted to tell our sergeant what really happened to him. It wasn't my fault. She hit her head. It wasn't my fault."

Clem's shoulders scraped against the pavement. After all her talk about protecting Clem, Lena had disappeared. Shouts, clangs, and footsteps echoed out on the street, but Clem didn't have enough air to call for help.

"Lena," she croaked.

Ag laughed again, angrier. "That coward won't help you. She didn't help Mari. She moped around the base until she grew a spine and decided to tell our sergeant what happened. As if she's any better than me. She was there and she didn't do a damn thing. I would've let her go if she'd let it alone. Dan here's never breathed a word about it to anyone, so tell me—who's the real friend?"

Dan turned away.

Ag raised his sword, but Clem's was out of reach, back where she'd fallen. She couldn't breathe.

Metal scraped and clanged as someone appeared out of thin air and snatched her sword up off the ground.

Lena.

Ag pointed his sword at her, his face like curdled milk.

"Let her go." Lena's voice quivered. "She hasn't done anything to you."

Ag struck at her so quick she barely blocked him. Clem shoved his boot off and scrambled to her feet.

He whipped back around to face her, but Lena vanished and reappeared between them.

"Go!" she screamed at Clem.

Ag buried his sword in Lena's gut.

Clem still felt the weight of his boot on her stomach.

Lena crumpled with blood on her lips. Confusion muddled with the panic in her eyes, like she hadn't realized a sword fight could end this way.

Clem's breath caught. Ag turned on her, yanking his sword free of Lena's stomach.

A spell blasted between them, into one of the buildings that shadowed the alleyway. A corner of the building splintered in an explosion of dust and brick. Glass rained into their hair.

Clem lost sight of the two Knights as dust rolled over them. She fell to her knees beside the older girl and held her.

Lena coughed blood. Clem hid her face in Lena's hair. It was matted with sweat.

"I'm sorry," Clem whispered. "I'm sorry."

Lena coughed up more blood. She lay in Clem's arms, her eyes growing more and more panicked until they lost expression. Her blood soaked Clem's jeans and pooled on the pavement. Flames flickered in the ruins of the building beside them.

Clem cried into Lena's hair.

CHAPTER FIFTY-ONE

Dust swirled around Edna. Ahead, Clem emerged from an alleyway. Edna gasped. Clem was white and shaking, with blood on her clothes and arms and a smudge on her left cheek. She sprinted toward two Knights who were coughing in the billowing smoke. Sparks leapt from her hands, running along the blade of her sword.

Edna limped toward her. Her knees flared with pain. "Clementine!"

Clem's sneakers echoed on the pavement. One of the Knights straightened, raising his sword.

"Clementine!" Edna screamed.

The girl lunged at the Knight, sword jabbing and biting. She twirled it around her to block the Knight's blade in a shower of sparks, thrusting at him whenever she had an opening.

Edna recognized the Knight as she limped closer. The tall blond with the perpetually sunburnt face, the one she'd tried to warn about the attack on Santa Alvara. Dan stood behind him, sword half-raised, ducking more than blocking Clem's blows.

Edna dug her fingernails into her palms. Clem was good with a sword, but her movements slowed and her blows weakened, even as Edna watched.

Ag's blade bit into Clem's shoulder. She fell to her knees, her sword clattering to the ground.

Edna screamed. Ag twisted around. Clem's shoulder was bleeding, her face pale, and Edna, without thinking, closed the distance between them and rammed a knitting needle into Ag's back.

To her astonishment, it sank into him—not much, but deep enough to hurt. Deep enough to—blast it—stick.

He yelped, dropping his sword. She twisted the needle, sickened by his cries of pain until she saw Clem in front of him, reaching for her sword and struggling to her feet. Edna yanked the needle out of him and stabbed him again.

"Get her off me!" Ag spat, but Edna pointed her weapon at Dan, and he hung back. Being old had that advantage: no one ever thought you were a threat.

Ag lunged for his sword, but Edna snatched it away from him. The Knights eyed her but didn't attack, not sure what to make of this little old lady and her deadly knitting needles.

"You leave her alone," Edna hissed.

Her voice was tight but didn't shake. Ag's fingers twitched as if he was thinking about grabbing the sword back from her, but she pointed it at his throat.

"Don't you come near us. Leave her alone or I'll run you through." Edna backed up until Clem was at her shoulder. "It's all right, Clementine. Come on."

Walking backwards was difficult. Her cane in one hand, the sword heavy in the other, Clem close beside her leaning on her own sword, which was a less than adequate walking aid. But Edna didn't want to turn her back on the Knights.

Ag spoke to Dan through gritted teeth. "Is your sword for decoration or are you going to use it?"

Dan's sword was still half-raised. "I'm not about to kill an old woman."

Ag snatched the sword from him. Edna grabbed Clem and dragged her along.

"Ag, please–"

"Do you want to be next?" Ag snarled.

He threw Dan aside, swinging his sword. Edna released Clem and blocked him. His blow jarred her arm, her shoulder, her teeth. The clang of steel rang through her head.

Another blow almost knocked the sword from her hand. She redoubled her grip, but she didn't block his next strike fast enough.

His sword glanced off hers and into her hip.

Edna gritted her teeth, stabbing at him. Her hip hurt like the dickens, but it always hurt like the dickens; she'd worry about the blood later. Her strike missed wildly, but it surprised him, made him step back. Edna dragged Clem away as fast as she could.

The street opened into a massive roundabout encircling a lawn. A fountain spurted improbably in the roundabout's center like it hadn't noticed the chaos–though, admittedly, the chaos was less chaotic here. The lawn had withered in the heat, and a smoky haze hung over everything, but flames had not yet spread this far. Columned buildings ringed the roundabout, tall and imperious, like they were far too important to let a little dragonfire burn them down.

Edna pulled Clem across the lawn. Ag strode after them. Clem couldn't lift her sword. Blood flowed from her shoulder. Ag raised his sword–Clem hid her face in Edna's shoulder–

The sword stopped inches above Clem's head.

Edna's fingernails dug into Clem's arm.

"What the hell?" Ag said under his breath, trying to slice through air that had become inexplicably solid.

Clem wiped her nose on Edna's dress. She nudged Edna, nodding behind her.

On the steps of a building on the far side of the roundabout, Percival stood with his hand stretched toward Edna and Clem.

He met Edna's eyes. Her chest heaved.

He turned away and leapt up the stairs.

"Ag—" Dan had seen him, but Ag still had his sword. "Ag, look—"

Ag did not look. He bared his teeth at Edna and Clem. He struck again, but his blade glanced off thin air. Blood leaked from the wound in his side, from Clem, and the one in his back, from Edna.

"Ag, come on, it's him, he's *here*. He's in the council chambers—"

"Come on," Edna whispered into Clem's hair. "We need to get you to a medic."

Clem closed her eyes. "I'm fine."

"Clementine—"

"Look, Grandma." Clem tugged her across the lawn. Ag prowled after them, slashing periodically only to have his sword deflected by nothing. "You're not the Chosen One so you can get me to a medic. You're the Chosen One so you can stop him from killing people."

"But your shoulder—"

"Edna. This is what you're here to do."

Edna stumbled along with her. "I don't know how to stop him."

She couldn't even stop Ag, who'd already been injured, who had a sword but no magic, who was now hurling himself against the barrier before them, heedless of the blood flowing from his wounds. Whom she hadn't stopped even though she'd stabbed him viciously, twice.

"You have to think of something. That's the AKG's chambers he went into."

The fountain sprayed them as they passed by, shockingly cool. Edna wished she could stand under it until everything disappeared: the fire, the dragons, Ag lunging at them, Percival in that building doing she didn't want to know what. She staggered out of the spray. Her burns blistered and stung.

Ag lunged at them again, his sword sinking slowly through the air before them.

"Edna!"

Edna's heart leapt. Beatrice hurtled in their direction with Benjamin aboard. Clem tugged her along faster, stumbling over the curb on the other side of the roundabout.

They dragged themselves up the steps. Edna lost her grip on her sword, but she didn't dare turn back for it. It clanged its way down the stairs.

Her chest tightened. The aches and pains she'd forgotten when she'd seen Clem struck down flooded back with a vengeance, threatening to tear her apart. She concentrated on each stair.

Beatrice landed at the building's door. Benjamin hopped off, grabbing Clem as she reached the top of the steps. He shoved her toward the door and leapt down the stairs two at a time to retrieve Edna.

Dan blocked the bottom of the stairs, snatching up Edna's sword.

"Ag, stop," he said, but Ag did not stop. He was on Dan before Dan could strike, turning his sword on him like he'd forgotten they'd ever been friends. Dan crumpled with blood blooming across his uniform. Edna's sword hit the ground the moment before he did.

Ag raced past the body, up the stairs after Edna. Clem flung out her hand with a shout. Ag hit a wall of air and tumbled back.

Clem slumped on her sword. Tears stained her cheeks. Her shoulder bled freely.

Benjamin dragged Edna up the last two steps. Blood stained Ag's uniform, but the Knight hurled himself against the barrier Clem had cast as if he could shatter the air itself.

Maybe he could. Edna wanted to be inside before he did.

Benjamin wrenched the door open. Edna limped inside with him and Clem at her side and Beatrice zipping in overhead. Benjamin stuck his sword through the handles to bar the door. They still had Clem's sword. Edna's knitting needles, too.

"Where's Kiernan?" Edna whispered.

Benjamin's face crumpled. Edna's breath caught, but she merely squeezed his arm. He leaned into her.

With the door shut and barred, the building was cool and quiet, like the turmoil outside was forbidden to enter. Despite the haze in the air, the black and white tiles of the entrance hall shone.

Clem crumpled against the wall.

"Clementine!"

Benjamin knelt beside her, examining her shoulder. He swore. "We need to patch this up. She's lost a lot of blood."

Edna reached into her handbag for a handkerchief. She produced one larger and thicker than any handkerchief had a right to be. Practically a shawl.

Benjamin gaped. "That'll work in a pinch, I guess."

He wound it around Clem's shoulder as best he could, but it was too loose to stem the tide of blood.

"Is there a spell we can use to make this stay put?" Edna asked.

Clem's breath came in short bursts.

"I can't. I'm too tired." She squeezed her eyes shut. "Ag killed them. He killed all of them."

She let out a sob. Beatrice twisted beside her.

Edna grasped Clem's hand and squeezed. She wasn't sure if she had to focus on giving Clem some of the magic the girl had said was in her, in everyone, or if holding her hand was enough.

Benjamin saw what she was thinking and took Clem's other hand.

"The spell," he said. "You just have to say the words. We'll help. Okay?"

"Okay."

Clem muttered under her breath, gripping their hands. Something sparked inside Edna like a gentle buzz of electricity, a humming in her veins. The massive handkerchief sealed itself to Clem's injury.

"It worked," Benjamin said. He squeezed Clem's hand. "Good job."

Clem let out a long breath. "Thanks."

Footsteps overhead. Distant shouts. Edna whirled around.

"Go," Clem said.

Edna hadn't let go of her hand, and neither had Benjamin. "Not without you."

"I told you, Grandma–"

"I'm not leaving you here."

"I'll stay with her," Benjamin said, but Edna shook her head.

The doors shuddered as Ag rammed into them.

"We all go or none of us do. I need to know you two are safe."

"Clem can't walk."

Clem scowled, looking more like her old self. "Can so."

She pushed herself up on her sword. Her lips whitened.

"You've made your point," Edna said, "now sit back down. We'll take Beatrice."

Beatrice hurtled them upstairs. The shouts and scuffle of footsteps grew louder. Swords clanged. Three bodies lay in the hallway, in the black uniforms and scarlet capes of the Knights-General.

Edna sucked in a breath. The walls compressed around her.

The door at the end of the hallway had been blasted off its hinges. Its remains littered the floor. Swords and bursts of magic flashed in the room beyond.

Inside the room, chairs lay on their sides. Hot wind blew through a shattered floor-to-ceiling window. Papers rustled, tumbling across the floor.

Percival towered in the center of the room, the Sword of Destiny in his hand with its blade glowing red. More bodies surrounded him.

The remaining Knights-General were barely younger than Edna. They escaped through the window, a couple at a time, onto winged horses wheeling outside. The youngest was a fellow with a salt-and-pepper beard who blocked Percival's every blow as the others fled. The horses' screaming rang in Edna's ears. Benjamin shrank against her, his eyes wide.

The bearded Knight seemed to know some protective magic. But every time he blocked one of Percival's spells, Percival slashed in his direction with the sword, scowling, and the Knight's counterspell came undone.

He wouldn't have the sword if not for her, Edna thought. She'd made him even more powerful by giving him something that could so easily undo the magic of his enemies.

"Percival, stop!"

He battled the Knight harder than ever. The last of the others made it out the window; the flying horses winged away with them, still screaming. The bearded Knight backed toward the shattered window, his steps slow, his face sunken, and he was either going to fall to his death or succumb to Percival's sword or his magic.

Edna's fist curled tight around her knitting needle.

Her heart hammered in her ears, so loud it drowned out the distant screaming of the horses, the fire, the dragons' roars, the thunderous echo of buildings collapsing. She raised her fist and—

Percival whirled around and caught her wrist in an iron grip. His eyes flashed. Edna's wrist throbbed.

"Stop," she whispered. "Please."

The bearded Knight escaped on the last flying horse. Percival's eyes flickered toward him.

"Percival, please—"

He released her.

He strode across the room, stuck his fingers between his teeth, and whistled.

Then he leapt out the window.

CHAPTER FIFTY-TWO

Edna clutched her chest, too startled and frightened to scream. Clem slumped against her. Benjamin squeezed her arm.

Out the window, Percival rose on the back of a dragon. He raced toward Coldwater Creek after the Knights-General.

"Quick, Beatrice," Edna croaked.

Beatrice strained after the dragon, buffeting in the slipstream of its beating wings. The city burned below, the creek glinted ahead, and beyond it civilians and Knights and emergency workers crowded into an astonishingly green riverfront park.

"Percival!" The wind whipped Edna's hair and clothes, a wind hot with ash and smoke. "Don't do this. Please—"

Hair escaped his ponytail, blowing across his face and neck. "You don't understand."

Edna urged Beatrice faster. The carpet shuddered. Benjamin yelped, but they stayed airborne. Percival glanced back at them.

"Look at the city!" As if to prove her point, a building below collapsed with a rumble. "Don't you care?"

His jaw tightened. "No."

Edna urged Beatrice past him. She had one idea, and it was, as usual, a bad one.

"Hold on tight," she told the others. Benjamin didn't need to be told twice.

Beatrice halted, colliding with the dragon's snout. Edna reached for Percival. She tumbled onto his dragon, rolling right into him.

"What the—?"

She lunged for the Sword of Destiny. Percival held it away from her.

"Mom, stop—"

They scuffled over the sword. The dragon shook itself with a roar, and they rolled across its back—then right off, into the open sky.

Edna squawked and clung tight to Percival's waist. The dragon flew on, not realizing it had lost its passengers. Beatrice hovered nearby; Benjamin lay on his stomach with his hand outstretched, his eyes wide with panic.

"Keep going!" Edna shrieked, but she didn't look to see if they listened.

The ground rushed toward her. Percival spat out a hasty spell. Sparks raced down his body, biting Edna's arms and shoulders and face, smoldering where they hit her dress, but she clung tighter. Their descent slowed, not enough for comfort.

A hot wind rushed around them. They zipped forward, but their descent continued. Coldwater Creek rushed white below them.

Edna's toes dipped into the rushing water. She clung tighter around Percival's waist. He gritted his teeth and pushed forward—they sank lower but cleared the creek—they tumbled to the ground in the muddy grass along its banks.

Percival lay in the grass, breathing hard. Edna scrambled to her feet and limped toward the bandstand, whacking the smoldering spots on her dress. She wanted nothing more than to lie in the grass, too. Her bones ached, her skin smarted, her muscles throbbed, and her cane was with

Clem and Benjamin and Beatrice. But Percival would recover quickly, and when he did, he would move so much faster than she could.

"Edna!"

Her heart leapt at the sound of Benjamin's voice. He stood by a bandstand, which the Knights-General had crowded into, drawing weapons mostly ceremonial in nature.

Civilians huddled around a nearby playground. An ambulance's tires cut up the grass between willow trees shading picnic tables and grills. Knights guarded a hastily erected medical tent and either end of the bridge spanning the creek. The winged horses circled overhead, screaming.

The bearded Knight stood at the top of the bandstand steps with his cape thrown over his shoulder. Clem stood on the bottom step, leaning heavily on Edna's cane and Benjamin. She spoke to the Knight, pointing at Edna and Percival.

Edna hurried toward them, but the bandstand didn't get any closer. Behind her, Percival got to his feet, ripping off his flight mask. She sped up, her hip and knees in agony. Her dress stuck to the wound in her hip, smeared with blood.

Percival staggered past. Edna grabbed at his jacket, caught it for a second. He half-turned—

"Percival, please."

—he yanked his jacket free. Two squires saw him coming, this man with his strained, white face and bedraggled ponytail and leather jacket and his angry, glowing sword.

The squires raised their swords, each waiting for the other to go first. Percival raised the Sword of Destiny—their scared young faces reflected in its blade—

"*Don't!*" Edna shrieked.

He hesitated. His eyes slid over their reflections.

Edna thought sickly of the bodies in the upper-floor hallway of the assembly building.

Percival turned away from the squires, lowering the sword. Lightning fast, he swiped a hand through the air.

Electricity crackled. The squires were on the ground, gasping.

Edna bit back a scream and staggered toward them—but no, no, they were alive. Frightened, winded, possibly slightly barbecued, but alive.

"I'm so sorry," she said to them, but no time for more. She had to catch him before he reached the Knights-General.

Clem threw Edna's cane to the ground as Percival staggered closer. She raised her sword, thrust out her hand, and shouted a word. A dome arced over the bandstand, hazing greenly like the one the witches had cast over the hospital in Detroit.

Percival sliced at the dome with the Sword of Destiny. It vanished.

Clem's face slackened. Benjamin took her hand as she shouted again. Again, the spell lasted only as long as it took Percival to swing the Sword of Destiny.

The bearded Knight joined them at the bottom of the steps, stood beside them, shouted the word with them, but it didn't matter. The sword broke through their defensive spells again and again.

The final dome broke beneath its blade. Clem's face was pale and drawn, but she raised her sword, and Edna was scared he wouldn't hesitate. He'd race to meet her, with his sword glowing red, and kill her.

"Percival, *stop!"* she shrieked.

He stopped.

He stood at the base of the stairs, grasping a sword that hummed with magic and vengeance. His other hand clenched and unclenched at his side. He glared up at Clem, who glared right back.

"Stand aside."

"No," Clem said.

Surely that would be the end of it. Clem would never back down. Percival wouldn't hurt her—not after he'd protected them from Ag—not when she meant so much to Edna. He would have no choice but to give up.

Sparks flew from his fingers. "Stand aside."

Clem glared harder. "No."

The sparks intensified. Edna couldn't believe he had enough energy left for any magic. He was going to explode; she could see it building up in him.

"I don't want to hurt you."

"I'd like to see you try," Clem snapped.

Edna was torn between the ridiculous urge to laugh and the fear he'd take up the challenge.

He clenched his fist again. She didn't know if he was holding back because of Clem, or because she was coming up behind him, or merely because he had this planned out in his head, because he wanted to do it a certain way, and letting his magic explode out of him and kill them wasn't it.

"I don't understand," he said through gritted teeth. "I told you, I didn't kill your sister."

Clem screeched with laughter. Benjamin flinched. The bearded Knight raised his sword higher.

"You don't get it, do you?" Clem spat. "It doesn't matter if you didn't kill Marisol. You've killed hundreds of others just like her. You've destroyed whole cities. And if she'd been alive when you found her, if she'd been running around with a sword like the rest of them, you *would've* killed her. But I'm supposed to be fine with it because that's not how it went down?"

Percival's blue eyes were electric, blazing in his white face.

"You don't understand. You can't. What they've done—"

Something flared deep in Edna's gut.

"That's enough," she said.

She marched past him, plucked her cane from the grass with a groan, and joined the others on the bottom step of the bandstand. The bearded Knight looked confused, his comrades on the bandstand even more so.

Percival's eyes snapped to her. "Mom—"

She was angry. Angry at him for thinking his pain justified everything he'd done. At the Knights for their abuse. At the wizards for naming her and abandoning her, at herself for being such a poor excuse for a Chosen One.

"I said that's enough."

People crowded the bandstand. Experienced Knights. Fresh-faced squires with eyes haunted by the day's events. EMTs. Civilians. Percival's friends or soldiers or whatever exactly they were to him. Ag, his sword still bloody in his hand.

Edna ignored them all. "Look at the city, Percival. Look at what you've done."

A muscle twitched in his jaw. "You don't understand."

Edna lost it.

"Don't you dare say that to me!" she cried. "I'm eighty-three. I'm not a child. And I'm sick and tired of people telling me I don't understand. Well, rot! What exactly is it you think I don't understand?"

He flushed.

"I've had my share of pain." Her voice quivered, but Benjamin touched her arm, and it helped. "My father was a cruel man. I wish I'd told you. Maybe you would've known that you could've told me what was happening. I'm sorry for what you went through. I wish I'd stopped it. I wish I'd brought you home and gotten you whatever help you'd needed and made you understand I was on your side no matter what. I'm sorry. I'm so sorry. I should've protected you."

Her chin was quivering now, too. She wished she could go back and undo everything: the whole, long, lonely thirty years in which she'd thought him dead, in which he'd been hurt and angry and lashing out at everyone and everything.

She took a deep breath. Her hip ached. Her legs trembled. Benjamin's hand at her arm steadied her.

"I'm so sorry," Edna repeated. "But you can't use your own hurt to keep hurting other people. You can't. At some point you have to decide to do something else with it."

His voice was quiet. "Mom—"

"I'm not finished." Her chest heaved. She didn't want to say these things to him. She wanted to hug him and tell him again and again how sorry she was and that everything would be okay now. "Think about the squires."

His eyes filled with confusion.

"The squires," Edna snapped, her voice steady again. Those crowded around peered at her warily. "The squires here, the squires in every city you've attacked. Squires have died in your attacks."

"What of it?"

Was he really so clueless?

"I thought you wanted to protect them. That's what you told me. You said you wanted to keep this from happening ever again, and instead—"

"Keep what from happening?"

A nearby squire stepped forward. He had brown skin and black hair and big, dark eyes like Benjamin's—eyes, she thought privately, that were unsuited to Knighthood. Her heart contracted at the sight of him. Blood had congealed on the side of his neck. He was, though Edna didn't know it, the squire who had fought alongside Kiernan.

Some of the other Knights gave him dirty looks. Percival turned to him slowly. The squire swallowed but stood his ground.

Percival pulled his collar down to show his brand, red and raw like it had been stamped into him yesterday instead of almost thirty years ago. Edna squeezed the head of her cane.

The civilians and EMTs seemed confused. By the brand, by what it had to do with the Knights. Percival's friends met each other's eyes.

"What is he saying?" one of the Knights-General whispered to another.

The squire's doe eyes darkened. He rolled up the sleeves of his uniform and held out his arms.

"Me too," he said.

CHAPTER FIFTY-THREE

Bruises and scars covered the squire's arms. Another squire stepped forward and rolled up her sleeves. A third squire did the same. Then an older Knight, hesitantly. Then more. Percival's chest heaved.

Knights muttered to each other. The sound buzzed through the crowd like angry wasps. Percival's friends tensed, their hands on their swords. But most of the squires and several older Knights, nearly a third of the Knights around the bandstand, were soon standing there with their sleeves or pant legs rolled up or collars pulled down to reveal bruises and scars and burns.

Clem inhaled sharply. Edna grasped her hand. Benjamin's fingers tightened on her arm.

Percival's grip slackened on the sword. Edna let go of Clem's hand and approached him. The magic threatening to burst out of him had died down.

Edna leaned close. He was shaking.

"Percival," she said, "put down the sword."

He dropped it, staring at the bruises and burns and scars around him. Edna touched his shoulder gently; when he didn't flinch, she gave him a squeeze.

"What is all this?" a doddery old Knight-General asked from the bandstand.

He tottered down the stairs. The doe-eyed squire started to roll his sleeves back down, but the Knight said, "Let me see, son."

The squire stared at the ground as the elderly Knight examined his arms. At last, the Knight patted the squire's shoulder and said, "All right." The squire hid his bruises away again.

"Who did this to you, my boy?"

The squire said nothing.

The bearded Knight-General sheathed his sword. "Your superior officer asked you a question."

The squire looked like he wanted to sink into the ground. "The others, sir."

Percival was statue-still. Edna's fingers tightened on his shoulder.

"What others, boy?"

The squire's voice went quieter. "The other Knights, sir. Some of the sergeants. A lot of my friends. Anyone bigger than me, really. I, uh." He faltered. "Sometimes I join in. When it's someone else. It takes some of the pressure off."

Edna wrung her hands. The bearded Knight frowned. The doddery old Knight-General peered at the others with their cuffs rolled up, all wearing the same wanting-to-sink-in-the-ground expression as the squire. The rest of the Knights-General came forward to examine them.

"This is the same for all of you?" the old Knight said. They each glanced around to make sure they weren't the only one nodding. "This is serious."

"A stain on our noble calling," the bearded Knight agreed. "We may need to investigate."

The squires could hardly believe it, but the civilians were befuddled. The Knights who had been muttering before looked furious.

"Investigate what?" Ag pushed through the crowd. Blood crusted his uniform. "The fact that some of the new recruits can't handle a little hazing?"

The old Knight's brow furrowed. "This is quite beyond hazing, my boy. Back in my day, hazing meant being thrown in the duck pond. I don't know what I'd call this—burns and bruises and I don't know what—but hazing is rather an understatement."

"You're not actually going to investigate because this man"—Ag pointed at Percival, whose eyes were still on the squires—"this man, who flew in on dragons with the intent to destroy the city, says the Knights—"

"This man says?" the bearded Knight repeated. "And what do you make of the state of your fellow Knights?"

The old Knight spoke over them both. "This man will be dealt with. But his crimes do not erase what these recruits say their fellows have done."

Ag's face reddened. "You can't—"

"Can't what, young man?" The doddery old Knight drew himself up to his full height, which was not tall. "We are your superiors. If we decide to launch an investigation, there will be an investigation, and we will expect the full cooperation of everyone involved."

"I won't—"

"Won't?" the bearded Knight snapped. "Have you learned nothing as a Knight but insubordination?"

Ag shut up, but his eyes blazed at the doe-eyed squire. He shoved past the old Knight, knocking him to the ground. The squire drew his sword, too late, as Ag sliced toward him.

For the second time that day, Ag's blade unexpectedly hit solid air.

Percival lowered his hand.

Ag turned to him with a roar, but another sword blocked his next blow.

"You killed my sister," Clem said. "I'm not letting you kill Edna's son."

Ag swung at her. She blocked him again, whitening at the force of his blade against hers. He swung again, and their rage splintered into a duel, their swords awhirl, and no one seemed to know what to do about it. Blood seeped through the handkerchief sealed to Clem's shoulder.

Edna snatched up the Sword of Destiny. It glowed golden in her hands. She slashed at Ag.

This time, she hit him.

Not much—a nick, really. But enough. He swore, his sword slipping from his grasp. He grabbed at it, but another Knight beat him to it and held it out of reach.

"What are you doing?" Ag demanded hoarsely. The Knight didn't respond.

Clem sagged against Edna. The sword was still glowing. Edna pointed it at Ag and said to the crowd at large, "I don't actually know how to use this thing, you know, so if someone wanted to step in, this would be the time."

Everyone was confused, but the bearded Knight stepped forward and spoke firmly. "Stand down, captain."

Ag's chest heaved. With a yell, he threw himself at the bearded Knight, but the doe-eyed squire shoved him off balance from the side. Staggering, Ag turned blazing eyes on him, but the squire leveled his sword at him. An older Knight stepped forward with his sword drawn, too. Several other squires and Knights surrounded Ag with their own swords, and at last, looking like they had no clue what was going on, the Knights-General joined them. Percival's friends slipped out of the crowd cautiously and stood at his side.

The bearded Knight knelt beside the doddery old one, who hadn't managed to get to his feet since Ag had knocked him down.

"Arrest that man," the bearded Knight said angrily. "And that other one, too. And—well—you're going to have a lot of arrests to make."

The whole thing ended in confusion as Knights tried to arrest each other and Percival and Ag and several civilians and two of the EMTs and even Edna, until she beat them off with her handbag, saying crossly, "Do you really think he meant me?"

Percival was hauled to his feet and dragged off to who-knew-where. Edna wanted to say something to him, but she hardly knew what.

He wasn't looking at her anyway. His eyes turned skyward; the dragons were winging away, back to Dominion. She wondered if he wished he were going with them or if he was tired of living that way.

Benjamin broke away from her. "I'll be back."

Edna reached for him, scared to be separated though the danger was past. "Where are you going?"

"I said I'd go back," he said, already out of reach. "I promised him I'd go back for him."

Kiernan. Her stomach tightened. Maybe Benjamin was going back for a corpse. She didn't want him to have to.

"Of course, dear."

His mouth twitched into something that was meant to be a smile. He nodded to the doe-eyed squire. They jogged out of the crowd together, over the bridge to the ruined city on the other side.

Edna tried not to be afraid for them. The fighting had stopped, except where people were trying to convince Knights not to arrest them for various reasons. With the dragons gone, the firefighters would be able to douse the burning city.

Clem was still standing where she'd stood over Percival, her sword stuck in the ground in front of her. Fat tears slid down her face and dripped off her nose.

Edna held her arms out.

"Clementine," she said.

The girl turned and wrapped her arms around her. Edna hugged her and rocked her and felt the same.

CHAPTER FIFTY-FOUR

The Royal Crown Hotel looked far better than it had six months ago, even before the fire. It wasn't quite finished. The insurance money had been slow in coming, with all the claims people had filed after the back-to-back attacks on Coldwater and Santa Alvara. Rebuilding had been equally slow, as Jada drained her powers to regrow so much plant life and her father took frequent breaks.

But one wing was complete, the leaves vibrant and green, the flowers bright and fragrant, the paint fresh. The floor no longer creaked. And for the first time in years, the hotel overflowed with guests.

Tourists filled most of the wing. Some had refused to delay trips to Santa Alvara just because the city was recuperating. Others were helping relatives settle back in after the attack. A few had somehow caught wind of the fact that the Chosen One was here.

Edna sometimes caught them squinting at her, but she'd come here for a break. She'd been touring the country for months, fundraising for the cities her son had terrorized and advocating for Knights who had been abused in the ranks, and she'd been televised multiple times. But reports out of Coldwater had been confused and contradictory, and she looked enough like a stock photo of an old lady to escape questions about her identity.

Worn out and ready for Christmas, she'd returned to Santa Alvara in December and rented a room indefinitely. She wanted to live as far from the nursing home as possible—although she did miss Marguerite whenever "I Love Lucy" came on—and across the country seemed about far enough.

"Mail for y'all," Demarco said, entering the lobby.

He handed envelopes to Amir and Edna. The carpet-enchanter had taken the room beside Edna's; the warm weather agreed with him, especially after his hospital stay. He had cut back on enchanting and was selling decorative carpets out of his room while he negotiated on a small piece of land nearby, where he hoped to build a shop with an apartment in back.

He slit his envelope open carefully, perused its contents, and smiled. "Hassan has a business meeting in San Francisco next month. Akida wants to bring the children for a visit."

"That would be delightful," Edna said, ripping her first envelope open far less carefully. Inside was a card from the Council of Wizards, long overdue and, once she opened it, not worth the wait. The image of a sword shed glitter on the front. Inside, foil letters said, "Congratulations on a job well done." Someone had stamped a signature beneath them, and it would have felt impersonal even if handwritten: it read *Council of Wizards* rather than any particular name. Edna sighed, turning to her other envelope.

To her shock, it was a much more satisfactory letter from Methodius. He'd filled several sheets front and back, praised her exploits, apologized for his earlier attitude, and assured her none of them had had a clue about Redway's true identity. He thanked her for the return of his ring and offered his assistance when she was ready to return to her advocacy work.

She needed it. The Knights-General had been considerably less interested in the issues in their organization since the initial revelation.

She had to fight constantly to keep the abuse in the public eye, let alone getting the Knights to actually do anything about it. Trying to get them to so much as talk about the base in Ethiopia was even harder.

"Anything interesting?" Benjamin asked from the loveseat. Needles dropped onto his jeans from the scraggly, leftover Christmas tree. He brushed them off.

"Not to speak of." She perused Methodius's letter until the others stopped staring at her and went back to what they'd been doing.

Most of the tourists had gone up to Mavericks for the day to watch the surf competition. Without them, the hotel was quieter. Clem's grandmother was crocheting a blanket; her mother was reading a mystery novel. Ellie, her younger sister, was playing peekaboo with Javi, her still younger brother. Her father sat in a chair beside the reception desk. Clem sat on the floor beside Edna's armchair with Jada, behind her, braiding red flowers into her hair.

Demarco returned to the reception desk, turned up the jazz playing on his computer, and argued the merits of various operating systems with Clem's dad. Benjamin whistled along with the music. Edna listened, trying not to think of her card, her letter, or her impending appointment.

Kiernan limped into the lobby, dressed in a colorful tunic and trousers rather than black denim. His locs hung loose around his shoulders. He leaned on a cane not unlike Edna's: magical treatments and physical therapy had brought him a long way in the last six months, but walking was still painful and difficult. His hands trembled frequently. The shoulder he'd dislocated was stiff.

He sank onto the loveseat beside Benjamin, in his habitual spot, closest to the Christmas tree. His hands trembled worse than usual.

Benjamin put an arm around him. That had come a long way in the last six months, too. "Kokebe?"

Kiernan shook his head. He'd asked them to ease him back into his birth name. He tried it on in the mirror and in Benjamin telling him to come to bed. In Edna reminding him of his PT appointments. In Clem asking him if he wanted company, when she awoke from a nightmare at two a.m. and found him in the lobby with the tree lit up, awake from pain.

Most days, it didn't fit.

Benjamin rubbed his back. "You all right, K?"

Kiernan laid his head on Benjamin's shoulder. Edna gave him a small smile, set her mail aside, and returned to her knitting. Her scarf was long since finished; she was making socks for Amir.

Clem's grandmother, Claudia, leaned in for a look. She and Edna had been trying to teach each other their respective yarncrafts, despite the fact that they didn't speak the same language. Edna had started learning Spanish when Clem called to say her family was coming up for the holidays, but so far, she only knew numbers, colors, days of the week, food, some pronouns, and various forms of the verb "to be," the last of which she mixed up constantly. Not exactly the stuff of scintillating conversation.

"Se ve bonito," Claudia said, nodding. "Good."

Edna cleared her throat. She knew so little Spanish yet, and she was certain she was butchering the pronunciation. But she tried. "Gracias. And, er, bien what, er, what usted...are doing there with that blanket."

Clem's mom sighed at them, turning a page in her book. Clem leaned into Jada. Jada kissed the top of her head.

Kiernan grabbed his cane and headed outside.

"K?" Benjamin called.

The screen door slammed behind him.

Edna completed a few more stitches. Undid them, dissatisfied. She stuffed her knitting in her handbag, wrapped a cardigan around herself, and followed Kiernan onto the porch.

He surveyed the January gardens, his cane propped on the porch railing.

Edna leaned beside him. The flowers in bloom were different than those blooming there back in July, but the gardens overflowed with midwinter plants. It was chillier now, especially in the mornings and evenings, but she'd take it over Pennsylvania snow any day.

"I feel like a stranger," Kiernan said. "Like I'm trying to infiltrate my old life." He picked at a loose thread in his tunic. "It's been fifteen years."

He put his face in his hands. Edna rubbed his back.

"I don't know if I can face him." His voice shook. "I knew, the whole time. I knew what we were doing."

Edna hesitated. "Kiernan–"

"Don't try to defend me to myself."

She fell silent.

He worried his hairline with a thumb and said bitterly, "The only reason I didn't get arrested with the rest of them is my luck."

"I think it might've been your diplomatic immunity. Or the fact that you were half-dead when the rest of them got arrested."

He let out a huff of air.

"Sorry. Look, Kiernan, I don't know your grandfather. But if it were me–" Edna picked at the railing. "Well, I'd be glad to see you alive. No matter how complicated it got afterwards."

They fell silent.

He looked at her. "When are you leaving?"

She smiled faintly. "I'll wait until your grandfather's here."

"Thanks."

Laughter and scolding filled the room when they went back in. Benjamin had abdicated his seat and was now in the clutches of Clem's siblings. They delighted in sitting on him; he pretended they were too strong for him to push off and lay on the floor, begging them for mercy. Clem's grandmother chortled over her crochet.

Kiernan and Edna sat together on the loveseat and waited. Kiernan almost managed a smile as Clem's siblings got the better of Benjamin yet again.

Clem glanced up from the floor, where she was now lying with her head in Jada's lap. "Someone's here."

A muscle twitched in Kiernan's jaw. Edna patted his knee.

The door opened. Kiernan was on his feet without knowing how he'd gotten there.

The elf in the doorway wore a tunic like Kiernan's and a cloak; he had Kiernan's brown eyes and high cheekbones. His white locs were done up in an elaborate hairdo like a crown. He didn't notice how silence fell at his entrance.

He didn't notice anything, in fact, except Kiernan.

Kiernan's hands twitched at his sides.

The old elf strode across the room, pressed his forehead to his grandson's, took his face in his hands, and cried. Kiernan cried, too, saying over and over again, "Āyati." His grandfather said, "Kokebe, lijē," and cried harder, and the rest of the room thanked their lucky stars that the tourists had gone out for the day.

Once things calmed down, Edna ceded her seat to Kiernan's grandfather. He sat with an arm around his grandson as if Kiernan were a little boy, patting Kiernan's arm again and again to reassure himself of his grandson's presence.

Now everyone bombarded him with questions. When he spoke, he most often addressed Amir, whom he had met once nearly thirty years ago; he'd arrived on the carpet Amir had made for him. His carpet was pristine despite its age; he'd clearly taken care of it. Beatrice, perhaps a little jealous, rebuffed its advances out on the porch.

Edna returned to her knitting, but she had one eye on the clock. Now that Kiernan's grandfather was here, patting his arm that way, she was even more aware of her own appointment.

Amir reached for her hand across the armrest of his chair. He often spent his evenings like this, working on a carpet while she worked on her knitting. They didn't say much, but they didn't have to.

"Are you all right, jaanu?"

Her smile was stiff, but she squeezed his fingers. "Oh, I'm fine."

He peered over his glasses at her.

She chuckled despite herself. "I'll be back in a while."

He nodded, patting her hand.

She gathered her things and slipped out in the midst of Benjamin's long and rambling question about the exact workings of luck magic, which neither Kiernan nor his grandfather seemed to know how to answer, even if they were so disposed. Beatrice flipped up a corner as she stepped onto the porch.

"Oh, no, dear, I'll walk. It's not far."

Beatrice curled up into a shape like an eyebrow.

"Maybe you're right," Edna said. "My hip does ache something awful."

"Hey, Edna?"

Clem slipped through the screen door, wrapping her arms around her stomach.

Edna stopped at the top of the steps. "Is everything all right, dear?"

"Yeah. Um." Clem picked at her t-shirt. "I thought maybe you'd want someone to go with you."

Edna opened her arms. Clem hugged her hard.

Edna brushed her hair back. "Are you doing all right today?"

"I guess," Clem mumbled against her. "I couldn't sleep again last night."

"Have you called your therapist?"

"I don't want to bother her. Do you want me to come with you?"

"I'll be all right." Edna planted a kiss on top of her head. "Go call your therapist. I won't be long."

Clem watched Beatrice zip her down the porch steps and went back inside.

They found the site easily; it was where the construction was happening. A good chunk of the city had been rebuilt in six months, but there was more work to do. Edna caught sight of Percival several yards away, in work boots and jeans and a standard-issue t-shirt. He magicked some scaffolding to where it needed to be.

"Hey, this is a construction site, you can't be—oh, Mrs. Fisher."

Edna smiled with difficulty at the woman in charge of the site.

"Sorry," the woman said. "I forgot you were coming today."

Edna gazed at Percival and asked softly, "How's he doing?"

The woman shrugged. "We've made a lot of progress on this site."

Edna hadn't really been asking about the site, but the woman said nothing more. Edna stepped off Beatrice and headed toward her son.

He turned and smiled slightly, wiping his brow. "They said you were coming to visit."

He looked like he was debating whether to hug her. She was debating the same thing.

"How are you doing?" she asked.

He held out his hands. An amethyst ring encircled each wrist. "They're helping me control my magic. Think they were worried I'd get mad on the job and blow something up."

He spoke lightly, like he was trying to make a joke, but she couldn't laugh.

"They assigned me a counselor," he said. "To, uh. To work on my anger issues."

Edna patted his arm, and he brightened, and it broke her heart a little. "That's good, dear."

His expression sobered.

"Mom," he said. "I'm so sorry."

She almost said, "It's all right," but caught herself, because it wasn't.

"I was so angry," he said. "I spent so long thinking about what they'd done to me."

He squinted at the scaffolding. It glinted in the winter sunlight.

"Now I'm mostly angry at myself." He bit his lip. "Hey, thanks for—it means a lot that you came to see me."

Edna nodded and tried not to cry. She didn't want him to be angry at himself, either. She wanted him to be okay.

"They've shut down a couple bases on the border," she said, because she wanted to say something to make him happy. "A few Knights are facing court-martials."

A few was likely all it would be, based on the way things were going, but he didn't need to know that. Not for now. She'd keep fighting anyhow.

A glimmer of anger passed over his face, so much less than it used to be. "Good."

They stood in silence.

Percival gave a reluctant smile. "Back to work, I guess."

With a sigh, Edna watched him turn away. It was better than nothing. Better than dead. Better than enraged and cold and setting fire to cities.

"Percival?" she called softly.

He turned back, the look in his eyes so hopeful it hurt. She opened her arms again, uncertainly, not sure he'd want it. But the next moment, he was in them, hugging her as hard as Clem had on the porch of the hotel.

Her eyes prickled. She held him tight. He was sweaty and dirty, solid and alive, hugging her so tight that his arms were like bands around her.

A strand of hair had fallen out of his ponytail. She tucked it behind his ear.

They pulled apart. He shoved his hands in his pockets awkwardly. Edna clung to her handbag, wishing she had pockets to shove her own hands into.

"So," she said.

"Yeah," he said.

He scuffed his boots on the ground.

"Back to work?" Edna asked, trying to smile.

He huffed a laugh. "Yeah. Back to work. Really."

She resisted the urge to call after him again as he walked away. She imagined he stood straighter now, walked with a little spring in his step.

Beatrice drifted gently against her ankles. She clambered aboard in silence.

Her cell phone rang. Benjamin had tried and failed to convince her to get one after their adventure was over. He'd finally bought her one himself, for Christmas, more a present for him than her.

"Edna?" he said. "Hey, I don't mean to cut your visit short, but K's granddad is hungry and we were thinking we could all go for dinner together."

Edna smiled at the sound of his voice. "That sounds delightful. I'll be there soon."

"Cool," Benjamin said, "see you soon," and they hung up.

Edna tucked her phone back into her handbag, wiped her eyes, and headed back home to her family.

THE END

ACKNOWLEDGMENTS

First, thank you to author Carrie DiRisio, who runs the Twitter account @broodingYAhero and wrote the tweet that started it all.

> *It's amazing how many prophecies involve teens. You'd think they'd pick more emotionally stable people, with more free time. Like grandmas.*
>
> @broodingYAhero, 2015

A screenshot of this tweet sat in my Writing Inspo folder until I needed an idea for a new novel and it leapt out and grabbed me. With the tweet as inspiration, I drafted *Remarkable Retirement* over the course of a year and a half as part of Last Man Standing (Round III) on Young Writers Society. Eternal thanks to Carrie and the creator of LMS. This book wouldn't exist without you.

Thank you to the team at Hansen House: to Cate Pearce for seeing the potential in a manuscript that had had a rough time in the trenches; to Elizabeth Jeannel for making me feel so immediately on our call that Hansen House was a great fit for this manuscript; and to Shawna Barnett for her thoughtful editorial notes and incredible understanding of what I was trying to do with this book. Thanks to Cal and Jennifer for their copy edits and proofreading. Additional thanks to Elizabeth for her enthusiasm for my many, many ideas about cover design, book merch, wild marketing schemes, and more, as well as answering my many, many, *many* questions throughout the publishing process.

I have so many amazing friends and beta readers that if I thanked you all by name, the acknowledgements would be as long as the book. I appreciate each and every one of you more than I can say. But there are a few people I want to mention in particular.

First, thank you to Arianna Emery, my oldest writing friend and irl bestie. I appreciate all the feedback and support you've given me over the years. I also love our walks and zoo trips. I can't thank you enough for saying, “You’re ready. Go forth and query.” Without you, no doubt I’d still be fiddling with this manuscript and my other projects wouldn’t exist.

Thank you to Milo, aka Keeper of the Benjamin Lore, aka one of *Remarkable Retirement’s* first number one fans, and Benjamin Cooper’s number one fan forever. Your comments and especially memes are my favorite things.

Thank you to Rinnah for being one of the story’s earliest readers and drawing my first fan art. I have all your drawings and comics saved. After all this time, I’m still awed by how well you captured these characters (and I still laugh every time I look back at the dragon-Edna Snickers-commercial cartoon). Thank you also to soundofmind for creating the first character art I ever commissioned, which I still share absolutely everywhere for every reason and also for no reason at all. You captured Edna, Benjamin, and Clem perfectly.

Thank you to SJ Whitby, Kamilah Cole, Abbey Francis-Williams, Ashley Varela, and Victoria Castonguay, my personal cheer squad who I’m pretty sure all yelled and cried when they found out Edna was getting published. Extra shoutout to Abbey, the first reader whose love of Amir rivals my own; Ashley, who’s always down for random poetry or Savannah Bananas videos being yeeted into their DMs; and Victoria, the only person who dealt with my shameless whining about querying on a regular basis. Extra thanks to Victoria for ~~avoiding her own revisions by~~ helping with my post-offer revisions and for being the self-appointed head of my marketing team.

Thank you to Arcticus, Hatt, and other YWSers for helping me with Amir’s character in an early draft, and to Lib for your later feedback on and excitement for his character.

Thanks to Shoshana Grauer for your pitch wizardry and for sharing your amazing stories with me, especially Sophie’s, which I will scream about forever. I can’t wait to see her in print.

Thanks to Chelsea Abdullah for being a wealth of publishing knowledge and a spot of positivity in the Twitterverse, as well as for championing this story whenever you can.

Thanks to Katelynn Telles and Elyse Schroeder, who aren't writers but are *always* ready to hype my work.

Thanks to the Cool Kids™ Table, the larger Twitter writing community, and the Young Writers Society community, especially the YWSers who helped me brainstorm titles when I went begging for ideas, and the YWSer who ultimately named the book. Thank you also to my fellow LMS Round III participants and my co-winner, Rachel Visick.

Thanks to Matt, who believes in me and supports me in so many ways. Thanks to my mom, who has been a one-woman guerilla-marketing team for this book since before I had a publisher, and my dad, who got a surprise coming-out while I was busy with book things and reacted like "thanks for trusting me with this, but I already vibed your queerness from your book." Thanks to my sisters for being among my earliest fans, and thanks to my brother-in-law for being among my latest editors.

(Elijah and Nate, you are too small to have done any work on this book. Or to read. But now your names are in a book forever. You're welcome. Love, Tia Beth.)

Extra thanks to Lucy for posting about the book on Tumblr, which proved to bring it far more visibility than I think either of us were expecting! I can't overstate how many more people heard about Edna thanks to this one Tumblr post.

On that note, thank you to the many, many Tumblr users who interacted with that post in any way, asked questions about preorders and international availability, and left messages of enthusiasm and support. The sheer number of notifications overwhelmed me there for a bit, but I'm so grateful to you all. It's thanks to your interest that my publisher decided to pursue an audiobook.

Thank you to my grandparents, especially my grandfather, Robert Trautman. You were my earliest and greatest writing support, and I could write a novel's worth of acknowledgements just for you. I wish I could share this with you.

Finally, thank you, thank you, thank you to my readers. I'm so grateful for the opportunity to share this book with you: this has been my dream since I was twelve years old. If you love Edna, if you see yourself somewhere in these pages, if you share this book with friends or followers, if you produce fan art or fanfic, if you drop me a DM just to say you liked the story—*thank you.*

About the Author

E.M. Anderson (she/they) is a queer, neurodivergent writer and the author of *The Remarkable Retirement of Edna Fisher*. Their work has appeared in *Wizards in Space Magazine,* SJ Whitby's *Awakenings: A Cute Mutants Anthology*, and *Dark Horses: The Magazine of Weird Fiction*, with more forthcoming from *Windmill: The Hofstra Journal,* GutSlut Press, and Wyldblood Press. She has two master's degrees and a feral passion for trees, birds, and Uncle Iroh. Despite all her book smarts, it is her doom to one day vanish into the depths of a mysterious forest, never to be seen again, after ignoring the warnings of the locals because she wanted to befriend the trees, or maybe find a cool rock.

Until that fateful day, you can find her on Twitter, Instagram, Facebook, or Tumblr at @elizmanderson.

Printed in the USA
CPSIA information can be obtained
at www.ICGtesting.com
LVHW051605241123
764798LV00003BA/158

9 781956 037210